Falling
from
Horses

Falling

from

Horses

❖
❖ ❖
❖

Molly Gloss

HOUGHTON MIFFLIN HARCOURT
Boston   New York
2014

For information about permission to reproduce selections from this book,
write to Permissions, Houghton Mifflin Harcourt Publishing Company,
215 Park Avenue South, New York, New York 10003.

www.hmhco.com

Library of Congress Cataloging-in-Publication Data
Gloss, Molly.
Falling from horses / Molly Gloss.
pages cm
ISBN 978-0-544-27929-2 (hardcover)
1. Trick riding—Fiction. 2. Stunt performers—Fiction. 3. Motion picture industry—
California—Los Angeles—Fiction. 4. Horsemanship—Fiction. I. Title.
PS3557.L65F36 2014
813'.54—dc23
2014016712

Book design by Greta Sibley

Printed in the United States of America
DOC 10 9 8 7 6 5 4 3 2 1

PROLOGUE

WHEN I WAS NINETEEN YEARS OLD, I took off from home, went to Hollywood, and worked in the movies for a year or so. This was back before the war, 1938, 1939. Jobs were still hard to come by in those days, but they were making cheap cowboy pictures as fast as they could churn them out, and I met a bronc rider at the Burns Roundup who told me you could get work down there if you could fall off a horse without breaking any bones. Or, if you broke one, at least not cry about it. He'd been working in the movies himself, but he went back to rodeo because bronc riding was duck soup compared to stunt riding, he claimed, and he wasn't looking to get killed or crippled.

Well, I was foolheaded in those days, looking for ways to get myself into trouble—carrying too much sail, as we used to say—and all I'd been doing for the past year and a half was picking up ranch work when I could and riding rodeo without ever making much money at it. I figured I might as well get paid for what I was good at, which was bailing off.

When I was a kid I'd had the idea that the cowboys made those two-gun westerns more or less the way we played games, one of us saying, "Okay, you get shot this time." I had some notion that they'd put me on a silver-trimmed saddle and a flashy pinto and I'd be riding hell-for-leather alongside Ken Maynard or some other cowboy star.

I was still only a half-baked kid, so I guess you could say I didn't know any better, but when I got down to Hollywood I ran into plenty of men thirty and forty years old who'd come into town with that same idea, fellows hanging around Gower Gulch in their pawnshop cowboy clothes looking to get hired to be the next Tim McCoy. Well, I wound up in a picture with Tim McCoy. I rode in a Ken Maynard movie, met Harry Carey, Hoot Gibson, all those actors, which doesn't mean much anymore—kids these days wouldn't know who the heck I was talking about. But back then every kid was cowboy-proud, cowboy-crazy, even the ones like me who'd grown up riding horses and working cattle and should have known better.

I was late coming to understand that the cowboy pictures didn't show much about real ranching. You never saw a movie cowboy hauling salt up to the high pastures or building fence around a haystack or helping a heifer figure out what to do with her first calf. Those movies were full of bank robberies and stage holdups, feuds, galloping posses, murderous Indians, and claim jumpers—nothing I ever saw growing up. But in the movies it all made sense. A bad guy was to blame for whatever had gone wrong, and at the end everything turned out right. If death came for anybody in the picture, it was always clean, unlingering, unsuffering. If somebody you cared about was dying, they had the strength and breath for last words, and that seemed to make it almost okay. I don't remember actually thinking my life in Hollywood would be like the movies, but some of that must have come into my mind.

The plain truth is, some of those cowboy stars I admired turned out to be sons of bitches, or fakes who couldn't ride worth applesauce, and what I did for the movies was mostly act like I was shot and fall off horses that were a long way from flashy. There were more than a few days I wondered if it was worth it. I saw men get busted up, I saw horses killed, and I discovered there wasn't a bit of glory in making those damn movies.

All that picture business was finished for me a long time ago. For that matter, you could say Hollywood is finished with the cowboy. I used to have to cross the street to keep away from whatever hay-burner was playing in town, used to turn off the television to keep from seeing all those horse operas every night of the week—I just knew too much about how they got made. But now I can't recall the last time I saw a horse on the screen. Seems to me the movie cowboy has gone downtown and into outer space: now it's all squealing tires and things blowing up, every picture trying to make a bigger fireball than the last one.

I might be tempted to think the whole country is done with cowboys, except every so often I open up the newspaper to see some Yale or Harvard lawyer who's gone into politics, posing in his new white Stetson and ironed Levis, sitting on a tall horse and squinting into the camera like he's spent his whole life in the West Texas sun, and I think, *Well, there it is again.*

I will say right here that this isn't the whole story of my life; somebody else will have to take that up after I'm dead. The time I studied with Benton, the work I did for the Autry Center, the frescoes in Santa Fe and Carson City and the Truman Library, the book art for Jack Schaefer—none of it would have happened if I hadn't grown up the way I did and spent that year riding horses in the movies. When I was starting out as an artist, I thought I would just paint what I knew of life in the rural West, a life where people did real work, significant work, and the risk and the suffering were real. But I floundered for a long time, feeling I didn't have the language to say anything new. It was Lily Shaw, arguing with me in letters that went back and forth between us for thirty years, who helped me see where my Hollywood year fit into things, the intersection where the West I knew growing up cuts across our great mythmaking machine, which is Hollywood. And the way those two things have always bent and shaped each other, have always been so tightly bound together they can't be untangled. I grew up with Tom Mix as the model for how to be a cowboy, so I know I was tangled in it myself.

What I want to write about is what I saw and did down there in Hollywood and what it meant—what it means—in my life and work.

I am writing this for Lily. And also for my sister, and in some way for my parents, which I guess will become clear elsewhere in these pages.

ONE

1

MY FOLKS WERE STILL LIVING UP IN OREGON in 1938, but they had lost the Echol Creek ranch a few months after my sister died and were back to hiring themselves out, taking work wherever they could get it, like they'd done before I was born. So I guess I shouldn't say I took off from home, because in '38 they were running a small outfit for an absentee owner in Klamath County, over around Bly, and I never did think of Klamath County or any of those hired-help places as home. Home, to my way of thinking, was the ranch on Echol Creek, where I had lived all my growing-up years. After we left there I headed out on my own, picking up work for the big spreads around Harney County and following the rodeo some, so I'd been sleeping in barns and bunkhouses and bus stations for the past couple of summers, spending just a few weeks in the off-season bunking with my folks at whatever ranch they were working at. None of that was "home."

Then what happened is that I won second-place prize money off roping a calf at the Chiloquin Roundup and I made up my mind to buy a bus ticket to Hollywood.

That was toward the end of September. I hadn't seen my parents since sometime in March, and here I was, not more than fifty miles from where they were living, but instead of hitching a ride to Bly to spend a few months helping them feed cows, I caught a ride to Klamath Falls. I had a well-used roping saddle with me, a handmade Hamley that old Arlo Gantz had given me after I saved his dog from drowning in a mud sink. I sold the saddle to the fellow who gave me the ride, and then I just got on a bus and went south. I figured if I took the bus straight through, sitting up to sleep, and if I scraped by on candy bars and coffee, I'd have enough money left over to see me through the first couple of days in Hollywood until I landed work— this is what I thought.

I caught a short-line bus in K Falls right after daybreak and rode it down to Weed. There's some nice cattle country along the first part of that road, and when you see it early in the morning, the cows casting long shadows across the grass, the sun flashing off the windows of the ranch houses, you can talk yourself into thinking ranching is what you ought to be doing with your life even if you damn well know better. The air was clear as a bell that day: you could see all the way to the Trinity Mountains, their ridges white with early snow but stained orangey red by the sunrise.

That's not the main thing I remember from the ride to Weed, though. I hadn't ever crossed the Oregon state line and had only seen Shasta as a little knob against the distant sky. The biggest mountain I'd seen up close was Steens, which is nothing but a big fault-block slab. But when the bus got to the top of the pass around Mount Hebron, suddenly there was Shasta, as big as you please, a white ice cream cone of a mountain, like the ones kids draw even if they've never seen such a thing. When we topped out a second time up above Grass Lake, those massive shoulders seemed to rise straight up from the valley floor. From the bus stop in Weed it looked like I could reach out and touch the big knurl on the side of that mountain. I wished I had paper and pencil to try to sketch it—that's what I re-member.

And then, on the interstate bus, I met Lily Shaw. She wrote about

8

that bus ride in her Hollywood memoir, so maybe you will find these next few pages familiar ground. But she and I had some different memories of that trip, so maybe not.

Even then Lily was just about fearless and too smart by half, and she had a blunt, outspoken manner that all her life people took for arrogance, but she wasn't much more than a kid, twenty-one or maybe twenty-two, leaving home for the first time, so everything you may know about her—the marriages and the lovers, the films, all that business at the McCarthy hearings, everything she wrote about in her Hollywood tell-all, everything written up in her obituary—was still to come, waiting out there like weather over the horizon. She had graduated college without ever having lived away from home: the University of Washington was a half-hour streetcar ride from her parents' house on Queen Anne Hill. So the two nights she spent on the Greyhound bus traveling from Seattle to Los Angeles were the first nights in her life she had not slept in her own bedroom.

She'd been on the bus for the better part of a day and a night when I got on in Weed. Her dress was wrinkled, her eyeglasses all smudged up with fingerprints, her hair greasy-looking and askew. Well, there weren't many empty seats, and she and I were the only people older than twelve and younger than forty on that bus, so I guess that's why I sat down next to her. She looked over and said, "Hi," and I said, "Hey," and for a while that was it.

When you head south out of Weed you've got Shasta right there on your left shoulder for the next ten or fifteen miles, and I just couldn't get enough of looking at it, staring past Lily in the window seat. Those ice cream cone mountains are a dime a dozen around Seattle, so she wasn't as taken with the view as I was. Mostly she occupied herself with what was in her lap, a couple of cardboard folders stuffed full of typed pages. She turned the pages over slowly, reading and sometimes scribbling a few words in pencil in the margins. Once in a while she looked up and stared into the middle distance. She jiggled the pencil or tapped it when she was trying to think of a word, and she kept jiggling her feet and twirling a lock of her bangs

9

or playing with the collar of her dress, pleating it and then smoothing it out and pleating it again.

I didn't have a lot of experience with girls, but it crossed my mind that she might think I was sneaking looks at her under the cover of looking at the mountain; I thought she might be wondering whether I found her pretty. She wasn't pretty, at least by my standards back then. She had thick, dark eyebrows that just about met over her nose—she hadn't yet begun to pluck them—and she was so skinny there was nothing to fill out the front of her wrinkled dress. Plus the dress was bright green with an orange collar, which might have looked all right on the right girl, but it threw an orange pallor onto her face. I didn't have any interest in her, not in that way, and I figured I had better be clear about it. So I said, "I wonder if you'd mind switching seats. I like looking out at the country going by."

It took her half a minute to lift her attention from that pile of pages and figure out what I had just said. She looked over at Shasta as if she had not realized it was there and then cut her eyes briefly to me. "Well, all right, but I might want to switch again later." After we changed seats, she immediately went back to her reading, and I realized she wasn't interested in me—that none of this had been on her mind at all and she just had a lot of twitchiness in her.

We stopped at Dunsmuir for lunch. The big mountain was behind us now, and I was beginning to feel that the steep woods around there were too much like the wooded ridges I had known back home on Echol Creek, so when we climbed back on the bus I asked if she wanted to take back the window seat. She shook her head and said, "No, that's all right. This twisty road is making me queasy," and I nodded and said, "It'll do that," as if being road-sick was something that only happened to girls.

After Dunsmuir the road went from bad to worse. These days the interstate highway has taken out a lot of the kinks, but the road used to closely follow the Sacramento River, with a lot of zigzags through the canyon, plus a steep grade to boot. And they were doing a lot of rerouting just then, cuts and fills and gravel detours, because they had started building the Shasta Dam, which when it was finished would put parts of the old road underwater. They hadn't yet built or rebuilt the masonry guardrails on some of the sheer dropoffs, and the north-bound cars, feeling crowded on the curves by our big bus taking up the whole lane, would sometimes lay on the horn as they scraped past us with inches to spare. From the window seat I had a nice bird's-eye view of every close call and the edge of the road where it fell two or three hundred feet down a steep rock face to the river. Given where I was in my life then, I began hoping the bus would go up on two wheels on one of those curves, and I leaned my weight against the window to help it along.

Lily stuck with her reading for a while, and anyway, being Lily, she wouldn't have admitted to nerves, but we were taking the curves pretty fast, and when she closed the folder of pages and asked me where I was from and where I was headed, I figured it was to take her mind off the curvy road and the likelihood of our bus plunging into the gorge. I don't know if that's right—she has written otherwise—but it's what I thought at the time.

I told her I was going down to Hollywood to work in the cowboy movies, which caused her to perk up slightly. She said she was headed there too, to get into the business of writing for the movies.

She asked if I was an actor, and I told her I was just expecting to ride in posses and such, which wasn't really acting. Then I told her what I'd heard—that the work was mostly riding fast and pretending you'd been shot off your horse. She had never been on a horse in her life, but she'd seen enough cowboy movies to know what I meant. "You might have to jump onto a runaway buckboard to save the girl," she said, "and maybe shoot the gun out of the bad guy's hand." She said all this with a straight face—she had a dry sense of humor and never liked to give away that she was joking. It wasn't exactly a test, but if I'd taken her for serious I imagine she might have decided I was too dumb to bother with. My dad had always made fun of the bloodless fistfights, though, and how the hero's fancy horse was bul-letproof even when other horses were falling dead all around him, so

I figured Lily was mocking those movies in the same way. I said, serious as church, "Lucky my six-shooter never runs out of bullets." She smiled slightly and gave me a sidelong look, and I believe that was when she made up her mind I might be worth talking to.

Lily Shaw was the most straightforward, unconcealed person I've ever known, and she had a bold streak in her already, like she was heading to Hollywood to burn down the town. It's one of the reasons I took to her. But I should tell you right now: when we met, I was the one who was more reckless. I had been nursing a dangerous streak for a couple of years, which she took for boldness, and I imagine this is one of the reasons she took to me.

I didn't tell her where I was from—nothing at all about Echol Creek. I told her about picking up ranch work, traveling around to rodeos, working as a cook's helper on a dude ranch. She didn't tell me a whole lot about her life either. She said she had been writing for the women's pages of the *Seattle Times,* but she had a letter from a friend of her dad's, promising to put her to work in his Hollywood talent agency. His clients were mostly actors and actresses, but he had a few writer clients and he needed a secretary to read the stories they sent in and maybe go at them with a red pencil, which she figured would be more fun than her work for the *Times,* writing about casseroles and table etiquette. What she really wanted to do was become a screenwriter herself; the pages in her lap were a couple of screenplays she had written.

Some screenwriters, when you ask what they're working on, will flinch and clam up, but a lot of them are dying to tell you not just their bright idea but every damn camera angle and the casting of the bit parts. That was Lily. She held up the thick folder she was still fiddling with and said it was a war movie, *Death Rides the Sky,* about a college boy who's hit by a taxi on his way to enlist in the Air Corps. His limp keeps him out of the service, but he ends up as an aviation mechanic for the Belgians, then flies a plane to rescue a beautiful French girl caught behind the lines spying for the Allies. Lily didn't need to say this was the first Great War; there hadn't been a second one yet. Or we hadn't completely figured out that the fighting in Spain and the Japanese invasion of China were already the kickoff to the second one.

"And this one," she said, tapping the other folder, "is a New York City crime story." She hadn't ever stepped foot in that city, but a New York story was cheap to make, she said, "because they can use stock footage for the traffic and the skyscrapers and whatnot."

I knew "stock footage" didn't have to do with livestock, but I didn't know what it meant and I wasn't about to ask. Then she went ahead and told me: "See, they've got all these bits they call 'short ends' that they've clipped from old movies, just about anything that doesn't have the actors in it, and they use those over in the new movies because it saves a lot of time and money." She was matter-of-fact about it. "I've seen the same taxis go by on Central Park West in about a dozen pictures, but people hardly ever notice."

This started me thinking about all the cattle stampedes I'd seen in the movies and whether I'd failed to notice the same cows bawling past the camera over and over. I wouldn't say I was pissed off about it, but this felt like being tricked. And it was maybe the beginning of my education about Hollywood moviemaking.

2

WE CHANGED BUSES IN REDDING at the head of a long valley. While the luggage was being moved over, I went into the station and used the bathroom. The sink in the men's room was rust-spotted and had a tin bucket under it to catch the leaks. In the big waiting room a bald guy manned the ticket booth and a Mexican man was behind the doughnut counter. The floor was sticky with grime and scattered with cigarette butts. An old man lay sleeping on one of the scarred benches, defending himself from the overhead lights with a newspaper spread open across his face. I had slept in bus stations more or less like this one half a dozen times in the last year.

I bought a doughnut from the Mexican and went back outside. Lily had gone in too, and when she came out I caught her glancing at the sugar on my fingers. Back then I tended to treat certain kinds of girls like they were my little sister, which was something I was almost aware of. Lily had a few years on me, but she was a tiny thing with skinny legs; she was so short I could look down at the white line of the part in her hair. I didn't know her yet, and at this point in our acquaintance I guess I thought she was one of those girls—a girl who needed looking after. I broke off part of the doughnut and offered it to her. "Thanks," she said and put the whole piece in her mouth, then sucked the sugar off her fingers.

After Redding we left all the curves behind. The ground began to be taken up with strawberries and corn and sugar beets, rows of walnut and plum trees just yellowing toward leaf-drop, and dairy cows grazing on oak-studded pastures. We passed a lot of fruit stands by the side of the road, and I was wishing the bus would stop so we could buy something that had come right off those trees, but we went barreling along, only stopping at filling stations or roadside cafes with restrooms. We went through a lot of little towns, every one of which I could see coming from a long way off: a church steeple and a water tower rising above a grove of trees. The road crossed and recrossed the river. I remember there were hundreds of redwing blackbirds in the cattails and willows along the riverbanks and beside the road, and when the bus drove past they flew up like blown leaves. Every so often we drove through an avenue of big trees overhanging the pavement, trees that must have been sycamores or eucalyptus, though I didn't know their names back then. And by the time we got to Corning I was seeing other things I'd never seen growing before: olives and palms and wine grapes. I couldn't get enough of looking out at that valley, the wide river lined with oaks, the neat rows of orchard trees. I just about had my forehead plastered to the window, looking at it all.

Down around Willows we began to see sloughs and wetlands and some rice fields still holding a bit of water. The rice must have been harvested at least a month before, but I'd never seen rice growing, so those diked paddies were a mystery to me: I thought maybe there was too much water in that part of the world and the dikes were meant to keep it out of the fields. All that water, shimmering in the low sun, was alive with thousands and thousands of birds jostling together, passing through from their breeding grounds to their wintering grounds. I figured these were the same birds I'd seen the day before, when I was hitching from Chiloquin to Klamath Falls. The big flocks congregate on the string of lakes and marshes through the middle of Klamath County, the same flocks that used to come through Echol Creek. We were hopscotching our way south, those birds and me, is what I happened to think.

Even with the bus windows shut I could hear the gabble of geese over the whine of tires on the pavement, and I remembered how my mother used to throw the window open in the early morning to hear the birds better and to see the shifting skeins in the gray dawn sky, how she liked to watch them sailing down to the sloughs and ponds below the house, how she especially looked for the white pelicans and the sandhill cranes. My sister and my mother shared an interest in science and nature—they used to pore over the colored plates in *The Book of Knowledge* to learn the names of the birds that nested on the parkland below our house and the wildflowers that popped up on the banks of the slough in the spring. I couldn't have said why, not in so many words, but watching birds rising up from the rice fields singly and in flocks, veering across the evening sky, I got to thinking about our family before everything fell apart, and about my mother especially, and I began wishing I'd phoned her up before I climbed on the bus.

Just at the edge of night, a great flock of pintails flew up in unison against the darkening sky, turning so the light undersides of their wings caught the seam of sun at the horizon, the reflection flashing as if somebody had tossed a bunch of silver coins in the air. Lily had gone back to her reading, but she looked out and caught her breath and said, "Oh, that's so pretty, did you see those birds?"

I had been thinking about Echol Creek, which must be why I said, "Back home, we had some wet meadows and sloughs on the ranch, and those birds used to come through twice a year, thousands of them."

If she'd asked me where "home" was, I don't know what I would've said. I didn't want to tell her anything about the ranch. What she said was, "Bud, are you and your folks farmers?" She was leaning across me to peer out the window, following the birds as they made off toward the west.

I was holding in my hands the good flat-crown hat my folks had given me for my fourteenth birthday and wearing the good stack-heel boots I'd won in a calf-roping contest at the Labor Day Fair in Burns the summer before Mary Claudine went missing. My hands were callused from rope burns, and I thought anybody looking at me would know I'd been riding horses and rounding up cattle since before I could walk. It didn't occur to me that the difference between a rancher and a farmer might not be as crystal clear to everybody else as it was to me.

The only farmers I knew were the ones living in the scrub hills around Echol Creek when I was a kid. They had come into the countryside in swarms in the 1910s and '20s, but by the '30s, after a string of dry years, most of them couldn't grow enough to feed their own children, and their little hardscrabble places began emptying out. "Book farmers," my dad called them, on account of most of them didn't know a damn thing about farming except what they'd read in pamphlets. But he had sympathy for their situation—he blamed the railroads and the government for selling them a bad idea. I was already in a bit of a touchy mood, though, and it put me somewhat crossways to be taken for one of them.

I said, "Nothing against farming, but I wouldn't do it for love or money." I imagine I was working on my imitation of William S. Hart, that scowl when he's standing outside a cabin checking his guns, preparing to go in and shoot it out with seven bad guys holding a woman tied to a chair.

Lily's eyebrows pinched down over the bridge of her nose. "I don't know why you're taking offense at that question."

I couldn't have said why myself. I'd never heard of the ancient contempt of herders for tillers of the soil. "I'd just rather be roping steers than pushing a plow," I told her, which was not any kind of answer, and the truth was, I had been plowing up ground for hay fields since I was six or seven. I should have smiled and said as much and made a joke out of it; I'd been brought up with right manners, taught from an early age not to go around shooting off your mouth.

But when you're nineteen years old, sometimes words pop through the gate before you can herd them off, and then you're too stubborn or stupid to call them back.

She relaxed her brows and said, with a complete falling away of interest, "That's no reason," and she drew the folder of pages into her lap and took up reading again.

We rolled on for quite a while in silence. Finally I said, "Those were pintails."

She looked up.

"Those birds. They were mostly pintails. Might have been a few wigeons too."

"What kind of bird is a wigeon?"

"They're ducks. Good to eat if you don't mind that they're small and usually full of shotgun pellets." I waggled my eyebrows like Groucho so she'd know I was kidding.

"Well, you just spit those out through your teeth," she said, and you'd never have known she was kidding—this was Lily. But I smiled and flourished my eyebrows again so she'd know I got the joke, and maybe that won me back a point or two.

I imagine if Lily had any interest in me back then, it was from her belief that I was the one needing looking after. At Williams, when we stopped for supper, I bought a candy bar and a soda pop and sat on a bench in front of the cafe trying not to bolt it down. After a few minutes she came out and said, "I can't eat this whole thing, do you want it?" and handed me half a tuna fish sandwich. I was six feet tall by then, still growing toward six-two; I'd had a boiled egg at six o'clock that morning while I waited for the bus in Klamath Falls, and since then nothing but a ginger ale for lunch in Dunsmuir and that doughnut when we changed buses in Redding. Tuna fish was never my favorite, but I wolfed down Lily's sandwich and was glad to get it, which shamed me at the time and now just makes me think well of Lily.

3

WE CHANGED BUSES AGAIN AT SACRAMENTO, and then Lily turned off the overhead light and we tried to sleep. Those seats reclined a bit, and we must have dozed off and on, but you can't get much sleep on an interstate bus. People went on talking, for one thing, and all night long the bus stopped every forty minutes or so to pick up or drop off passengers in that string of towns running down the lower valley—Stockton, Modesto, Merced, Madera, Fresno, Tulare. And if we weren't stopping for passengers we were stopping at filling stations or all-night cafes so people could use the restrooms. Lily's head would tip sideways, but when the bus geared down she'd jerk awake. Once, when her hands went slack with sleep, the glasses she was holding in her lap slipped off onto the floor. I bent down and fished them up and tucked them into the pocket of the seatback in front of her. Then I folded up my jacket and pushed it against her head so she wouldn't always be tipping onto my shoulder.

At one stop I climbed out just to stretch my legs and get a breath of air, and I stood off alone at the edge of the road, looking around at the dark farm fields, smelling eucalyptus, I think it was, on the cool air. Everything about it felt strange, not my country, and an uneasiness came over me all at once, a strong qualm about what I was doing. I thought about not getting back on the bus. It was one of those times you think of afterward, a hinge point in your life. But my duffle bag was still on the bus, and then the people who had gotten off to use the restroom began to make their way back, and the driver, standing by the door smoking a cigarette, looked over at me. I guess that was all it took, because I just walked back and climbed on. When I sat down next to Lily, she was more or less awake. She peered at me nearsighted without her glasses, but we didn't speak.

Years afterward, I told her about how I almost didn't get back on the bus, and she said she remembered it. She said she had seen something in my face when I sat back down. Maybe she did. But she was damn near blind without her glasses, so maybe not. She always liked to think she knew me better than I knew myself.

Then in the small hours, somewhere between Tulare and Bakersfield, with the highway straight as a string and hardly any traffic to speak of, the bus ran off the road and wrecked. What happened is that a guy in a Chevrolet coupe headed north—the only car in ten minutes—fell asleep, I guess, and drifted into our lane. He would have run straight into us if the bus driver, who'd come on at Fresno, hadn't been on the ball and wide awake. He jerked the wheel hard to the left, and the Chevrolet just clipped the corner of the bus. We went veering across the highway, squealing and weaving, and then off the pavement and bumping down a grassy embankment into a dry ditch, where the bus tipped onto two wheels and hung there a few seconds, making up its mind, before rocking back onto four.

This all seemed to happen slowly. Or not slowly but as if each fraction of a second had its own point of interest, its own separate weight, a feeling you can get when you think you might be about to die. I've had it happen a few times in my life, and this was not the first. It was dark—the dim lights in the bus went out completely as soon as the engine quit—and for a couple of seconds nobody said anything. Then a baby started shrieking and children started crying and people were yelling and a woman toward the front of the bus started reciting the Lord's Prayer in a loud, churchy way, as if she expected all of us to join in.

Lily had fallen over halfway into my lap. I hoisted her up—she was as light as a child—and then I grabbed hold of a seatback to stand up and bumped my head on the overhead luggage caddy. I hadn't ever been in a wreck, but now that it was over I didn't think this was very much of one. When I'd leaned my weight against the window on that curvy mountain road earlier, I'd had a different sort of picture in my mind. My head smarted from bumping it on the luggage rack, but otherwise I didn't have a damn thing wrong with me. I didn't think Lily was hurt either, but I said, "Did you get hurt?"

"What happened?" she said, which I thought was a pretty stupid question, but she had been asleep when it happened.

"We had a wreck."

She said, "Oh," as if this was mildly interesting information, and I took this to mean she was all in one piece. She turned her head. "I can't find my glasses. I hope they didn't break." I felt along the seatback until I found where I'd put her glasses and held them out to her. Then I happened to think of my hat, so I went groping around for it on the floor. The crown was dented from one of us stepping on it, but I worked it with my hands and it popped right back into shape.

In the darkness around us, people had already calmed down, and I didn't hear any moaning as if someone was hurt. Toward the front the driver was saying, "Here, c'mon now, watch your step," and people were moving up the aisle and climbing out through the open door. The bus was like a cave, so dark you could just make out people's shapes, but when we stepped outside there was more light—a clear sky and a quarter moon low in the west. Lily and I stood around with everybody else, looking at the bus. The front end was only slightly stove in, but two tires were flat, so we weren't going anywhere. We were stranded in that ditch like a whale in a shallow creek.

The bus driver's name was Pete something-or-other. He had a cut lip and a sprained or broken ankle, but he was as calm as an old dog—somebody said he'd been a sapper in the Great War, so maybe that accounted for it. Blood was dribbling from his lip, and every so often he spat out what had run into his mouth, but he limped around from one person to the next, checking to see if any of us were hurt and bending down to thank the little kids solemnly for taking good care of their mothers. One old man complained he had a sore shoulder, but his wife said his shoulder was sore before the crash. So Pete himself was pretty much the only injury.

The Chevrolet had gone on across the road, crashed through a fence on the other side of the highway, and overturned in a ditch. When a couple of men headed over to see if anybody in the car needed a hand, I said to Lily, "I better go help out." I think I just wanted to yell at somebody for causing us to wreck.

The Chevrolet's doors had sprung open, and there was nobody in the upturned car. We kicked through the tall weeds looking for the driver, and after a minute we found him lying a good eighty or ninety feet from where his car had ended up. We stood around looking at him without saying anything.

I had seen plenty of dead cows and even a couple of dead horses, but this was the first dead person I had ever seen. My folks hadn't let me see Mary Claudine after she was found, and I used to lie awake in the night imagining the way she must have looked in the days and weeks after she died—the way cows look after the ravens and turkey vultures get into them. When I think back about the wreck, what I remember is how the dead man looked almost alive, his eyes slightly open and an expression around his mouth that was unsurprised, seeming tolerant of what had happened to him. His head was steeply bent back on the stalk of his neck, the Adam's apple bulging out in high relief, and there was a little blood at his nose, that was all. But nobody bent down to see if he had a pulse, because there just wasn't any question that the life had left his body. He looked to be about thirty, wearing a salesman's suit. His pomaded hair had fallen down over his forehead, which gave him a disheveled look that was at odds with the suit.

Finally somebody said, "I guess we ought to cover him up." One of the men found a blanket in the wrecked car, and we put it over him and then we all walked off.

When I got back to Lily, she said in a whisper, "Is he dead?" and I said yes, or nodded. Then she said, "Was it awful?" in a deeply interested way. I can tell you now, this is how a writer views things, but back then it provoked something in me. I wasn't thinking about Mary Claudine exactly, but I didn't think Lily would have said it in that way—as if she was just curious—if she'd ever had somebody die on her, somebody in her family, somebody she cared about.

I said, "Go on over there and take a look, if you've got to know," and I turned and walked off.

A few cars came along eventually and stopped to help. We were twenty people standing along the edge of the road in the dark, and I have to wonder what those drivers thought they saw at first—a crowd of ghosts, maybe, or sleepwalkers, rising up in front of them at three in the morning. Finally a state police car rolled up and the trooper laid a couple of railroad flares in the road. He took a look at the overturned car and the dead man, then talked to a few people who'd been in the front of the bus, the ones who'd been awake and had seen the Chevrolet come straight for us and knew Pete wasn't to blame. A sheriff's car showed up too, and the deputy talked to the state trooper and then took Pete somewhere to get his ankle looked at and maybe set in a plaster cast. The state trooper made half a dozen radio calls and told us the Greyhound station in Bakersfield would be sending another bus to pick us up. He didn't say so, but he must have called for a morgue wagon too.

Just because I needed something to do, I helped a couple of men haul bags and suitcases out of the luggage holds and the overhead caddies of the wrecked bus, and we piled them at the verge of the highway. It was a warm night. Some people pulled blankets from their luggage and spread them on the grass and sat or lay down to wait. Lily was just sitting on the dry ground. Finally I went over and sat down with her. The flares were still burning, and the night was saturated with a red glare.

She was holding a little spiral-bound notebook in her lap and a pencil, and every so often she wrote something on the page. I didn't say anything to her about the dead man, not directly, but I said, "I guess you're writing about the wreck. Making it into a story," and I know there was some judgment in it.

She gave me a look—that deep crease just above the bridge of her nose that I later came to know as one of her regular features and had mostly to do with being dead tired of idiots. It's pretty much the same look she's giving Roy Cohn in the photograph that made the cover of *Time*. "No, I'm not writing about the wreck, but someday I might. Writers are always using their lives, and if you were a writer you'd probably be writing about rodeo."

When we had first started talking, she had been interested in hearing about rodeo. I had told her the rules of calf roping and bronc riding, the way a ride was judged and so forth, and then I'd told her every damn story I could remember, stories about guys getting busted up or stomped on but riding anyway, and haywire bulls breaking loose from the chutes, chased down by a clown on foot, and man-killing horses ridden until they gave up bucking, lay down, and died. I had seen a couple of these things myself, but most were stories I'd heard from other men. I was pretty sure some of them were true, but a lot of them were lies and boasts, which I also knew, and some I had only seen in movies; plus I let her think some of them had happened to me.

If she planned to write about the wreck and the salesman lying dead over there in the high grass, at least it wouldn't be made up: that's what I figured she was saying to me. And this might be a good place to point out that Lily was always smarter than me, more able to see the truth in things, and the untruth.

I don't think we ever talked about the wreck later on, at least not in those months while we were both living in California. But there's a bus wreck in one of her films, it might be *San Luis Obispo,* and after my wife and I went to see it, I wrote to Lily that it had been quite a few years since I had thought about our bus running off the road outside Bakersfield and that her movie had brought it back.

She wrote that she hadn't ever been in a wreck before that one. "And I hadn't ever seen anybody dead—I don't think death was real to me back then. I had a terrible wish to see what a dead man looked like, but I was afraid to walk over there and see him. You know how it is: I had to leave all that alone for a while before I could put it in my writing."

By then we had written back and forth many times about art, about not making demands on your art but just humbly inviting it in, and I knew this was what she meant.

I lay back on the grass with my head pillowed on my bent arms and studied the night sky as if I didn't give a damn whether Lily talked to me or not, and she went back to writing in her notebook. The grass had a dry late-summer smell, like it hadn't rained in weeks, so I don't know why, lying there, I suddenly remembered a time in January or February, right after we buried Mary Claudine, when I went out after dark and lay down on the frostbitten grass in the pasture behind the house. It was cold as hell, but I stayed out there half the night. The stars were thick in a clear sky, so bright and so numerous I couldn't make out the constellations. The slow turn of the earth is what moves the stars in their slow spiral—I knew this—and I tried to feel it, that slow turning, the earth carrying my body on it like a raft. There had been an odd comfort that night in coming to know in some deep part of my brain the immenseness and indifference of the universe.

The moon had set, and when the flares finally went out, there was suddenly enough darkness to uncover all the stars. I wasn't used to seeing the sky this far south, and it took a while to realize I was looking at the whole of Scorpius along the southern horizon. I made a sound of surprise, I guess, and Lily looked over at me.

If I had kept still, I know she would have gone right back to her notebook. And it wasn't in my mind that she and I might get to be friends. I had been keeping to myself for the last year and a half, drifting around without wishing to make any friends, which could have been something I had decided or just the life, the cowboy life, I had chosen. So I can't tell you why I wanted to get back in Lily's favor right then. But I know it had something to do with the way she didn't seem to care whether I liked her or not.

I pointed as if she had asked me something and said, "Up north, Scorpius is down below the horizon by this time of year. Most of it, anyway. But we're far enough south now, you can see the whole thing."

She looked where I pointed.

"Antares is the bright one," I said. "People call it the scorpion's heart. And then, if you look left and down, you can see the curve of the tail and the stinger. You have to use your imagination. There's a couple of star clusters in the tail, but you can't really see them without a telescope or good binoculars. In July the whole constellation would show up over the ranch for a few weeks. I used to go up to the fire lookout near our place and look through the ranger's binoculars so I could see the clusters—the Butterfly Cluster and Ptolemy's Cluster."

I was showing off, which of course she knew. She studied the sky while she made up her mind if I was worth talking to again.

Up to this point, I imagine she had been thinking I was a ranch kid with a backwoods education, a kid without much knowledge of the world. I had gone to a two-room grade school, and I'd never finished high school, so that wouldn't have been a bad guess. But I came from a family of readers, and we'd always had a lot of discussion around our dinner table. My dad liked to read out loud from the newspapers, anything he found of interest. All of us talked about the books we were reading, and Mary Claudine and I were encouraged to talk about what we were learning in school. I'd had a couple of bright and lively grade school teachers and half a dozen high school teachers who brought the life of the mind into their classrooms. This is not to say I was a kid with intellectual attainment, but I could rise to the occasion.

Finally she said, "Who taught you about the stars?"

"I mostly learned it from books. From *The Book of Knowledge*."

"Is that an encyclopedia?"

"I guess it's like that. It's a set. There's twenty books." My mother had bought *The Book of Knowledge* from a salesman at the Harney County Fair with money she had earned from the sale of a horse. I was pretty sure the expense had been hard for my father to accept— there had been a prolonged silence between my parents and then whispered voices from their bedroom late at night. But all of us, even my father, liked to pore over the colored pictures of muscles in the body, and drawings of Borneo people, and step-by-step instructions on building a dry stone wall, and answers to questions like "Why is the sky blue?" There were drawing lessons in almost every volume; I learned a lot about perspective and values and shading from *The Book of Knowledge*.

Lily didn't ask me anything else, but eventually she lay back on the grass herself, and after she had studied the sky a while she said, "There are more stars here than in Seattle."

"That's because cities have all those street lights and neon signs that shine too much light back up in the sky. They wash out the stars."

"I know that," she said. "You don't have to keep on acting so smart." But she didn't sound annoyed.

In *Hard Light*, one of the movies she wrote for RKO, there's a boy who escapes the fighting and shouting in his house—his father's a falling-down drunk—by going out at night to study the constellations. Lily called me up a few weeks before that picture came out to let me know that the boy in *Hard Light* wasn't me. She didn't need to say so. By then I knew that it was Lily who had grown up with family battles—not brutal abuse but slamming doors, shouting; both of her parents drank. She had escaped from it into books and writing and movies.

27

"I'm so tired," she said after a while. "I haven't really been able to sleep in the bus." Well, she had been sleeping, but I didn't call her on it.

I said, "You could try to sleep right now. That other bus might be a while."

After a minute she said, "I guess I'm too keyed up."

We fell silent. Then she said, "When you get down there, have you got a place to stay?"

I said, "I figure I'll just get a hotel." I didn't tell her I only had enough money for a couple of nights in a flophouse.

"You should look for a place around Gower Street," she said. "A lot of the cowboy pictures are made close to there." She knew quite a lot about Hollywood, which she was glad to tell me without prompting, and I was glad to learn from her. She'd learned most of it by close study of *Photoplay* and *Modern Screen*, but I can't fault her for it, since most of what she told me turned out to be true.

When I asked her where she'd be staying, she told me she had a room waiting for her at the Hollywood Studio Club, which was a kind of sorority for women who worked in the movie business, not only the actresses and starlets but the secretaries and office girls. She would be sharing with the other girls who worked in the agent's office, a three-bed dormitory room that had a sink and two closets. One of the secretaries had married and moved over to Santa Monica with her husband, and Lily would be taking that girl's place.

"I hope I can sleep when I get there," she said, "but it'll still be the middle of the day, so I guess I'll have to wait until the other girls are ready for bed."

It began to gray toward daylight. Some black-and-white dairy cows were standing in the field beyond the wrecked fence, and the state policeman was standing near the dead man as if to keep the cows from walking on the body. I could have told him no cow would ever walk on a human body, living or dead. No horse, either. What I figured he should be worried about was the hole in the fence. If somebody didn't patch it up, those cows would be through it and walking up the highway just as soon as we were gone.

Finally the other bus came from the south, and we watched it jockey back and forth in the road to get turned around and headed back toward Bakersfield. It was still running headlights, which swept across the car lying upside down with its tires in the air and the trooper standing near the dead man. Down there in the dry weeds you could just see a bit of the blanket covering the body.

We shuffled onto the bus without speaking and rode into Bakersfield in silence. At the station a smiling man stepped onto the bus and told us, "Breakfast is on the Greyhound Lines, folks. Step right next door to Betty's Biscuits, they're expecting you all, and the griddle is hot."

So I had a stack of hotcakes courtesy of Greyhound, and Lily ate up every bit of her eggs and sausage — not a word about how it was too much food for a girl to choke down.

4

THE SUN WAS WELL UP IN A CLEAR SKY when we left Bakersfield on a fresh bus. Flat orchard country stretched away on both
sides of the road, and low, lion-colored mountains stood all along
the southern horizon. Around ten o'clock we stopped for gas and
water and a restroom break at the bottom of those mountains, and I
bought some oranges from a stand next to the bus station, not a fruit
stand, but a funny place shaped just like a big orange, with a hole cut
out for the walkup window. This wasn't quite the same thing as buying them right off the tree, but those oranges were as sweet as candy
and so full of juice I had it running down my arms and chin, all
sticky, and had to wash up afterward in the men's room.

By the time we started up the Grapevine, the air was light and dry
and hot. We pulled down the bus windows, and the whine of tires on
the pavement was so loud we didn't bother to talk. The cutbanks on
both sides of the highway were raw red earth, the dry slopes scattered
with scrub oak, chaparral, and cottonwoods — country I had seen in
a lot of cowboy movies. The pavement widened into three lanes, and
cars started to pass us in the middle lane as we ground down into low
gear. Traffic thickened, and there were plenty of cars and trucks and

buses in the slow lane with us, and rigs pulled over with steam boiling out of their radiators.

We stopped for lunch in San Fernando. I still had some oranges left, and I bought myself a piece of butterscotch pie; then I ate most of Lily's chicken-fried steak, which she pushed toward me when she'd barely eaten half.

That last leg into LA, the stretch from San Fernando to Glendale, was mostly groves of oranges and lemons in those days, their big, neatly planted squares bounded by windbreaks of poplars. Every so often you'd see a house with gingerbread trim or a stucco house with Spanish-style balconies and red-tiled roof standing higher than the orange trees but shaded by a big old elm or a beech. Sometimes you'd see oil rigs pumping up and down, right out there in the middle of the orchards, and every so often rows of deep green eucalyptus or palm trees lining a straight stretch of road, or big fields of beans worked by Japanese people.

We rolled through Burbank and then Glendale's rows of little shops and half-built suburbs. What I remember is clean, wide boulevards, palm trees, Spanish-looking stucco houses with bright-flowering vines—orange trumpet vine or red bougainvillea—growing up the porch posts, and fields of pink geraniums in the front yards. You could smell the sweetness of the orange trees even through the stink of exhaust. A kind of fairytale land, I thought at the time. I'd never seen anything like that country in my life.

We crossed the Los Angeles River eight or nine times, although I didn't know it, seeing nothing below the bridges but a mud-caked channel. Somewhere around the last bridge I got my first glimpse of the city of Los Angeles, a knot of tall buildings way off on the valley floor with a grid of streets and dusty trees and houses spread out like skirts around it. We were in baking sun by then, and the whole city shimmered under a yellow-blue dome. One of the passengers started singing "California, Here We Come," as if we hadn't been in California for a day and a half already, and quite a few others joined in. Some of them had become quite friendly after the wreck, as if they'd been in a battle together, and there was some exchanging of addresses. I didn't ask for Lily's, and she didn't offer.

About five years later I would take the grand tour of Europe on the army's nickel—Paris and Rome, the whole shooting match—but at nineteen I hadn't spent any time in a town bigger than Prineville or Burns. Los Angeles in those days wasn't what it is now, but it was every bit the big city, and we began to pass through built-up neighborhoods, places where you could look down the cross streets and see pepper trees arching over the pavement in a shadowy tunnel lined with automobiles, or dry, rustling palms in long rows leaning into the front yards of stucco bungalows. And then we were in swarms of cars and streetcars, the jangle of trolley bells, honking horns, sidewalks packed with people walking fast through a wilderness of billboards and neon signs and telephone poles weighed down crazily with wires. The bus went on threading through the traffic, mile after mile. By the time we got into the downtown proper we were crawling through the shadows of eight- and ten- and twelve-story buildings, and people on the sidewalks were making better headway than the cars.

We rolled into the terminal just after three and milled around in the garage waiting for the driver to haul our luggage out of the hold. Lily disappeared for a minute, walking off to talk to somebody out on the sidewalk. When she came back, I was standing with my bag at my feet, trying to figure out what the hell to do next.

She said, "We have to catch a streetcar that goes to Hollywood from downtown. The yellow cars just go around downtown, but the red cars go out to everywhere else. We have to go to the Subway Terminal Building on Hill Street and catch a red car that goes out to Hollywood."

This went right past me; she might as well have said it all in French. She picked up her suitcase and started off as if she knew where she was going, while I just stood there trying to work out whether I wanted to follow her. When she got to the sidewalk she looked back at me as if asking a question. I guess I must have made up my mind, because I hoisted my bag onto my shoulder and caught up with her.

We walked beside a street with four car lanes and two sets of trolley tracks, and when we got to the corner we had to wait for the electric signal, the first I'd ever seen. When it bonged, Lily took off across the street and led the way up Sixth Street four or five blocks, turned on Hill, and went right to the entrance of the Terminal Building as if she'd been living in the city all her life.

I remember that building as something grand. We walked into a marble-floored arcade flanked with shops and down a sloping floor to a big vaulted lobby as ornate and elegant as the head office of a bank, and I just thought, *Jesus.*

Crowds of people were walking in and out of the branching passageways, so Lily stopped to study the signboards and then said, "We could both take a Santa Monica car," and led the way down a long, winding ramp to a lower mezzanine and a waiting room, and another sloping ramp to the huge cavern at track level.

The banks had closed, and we were in a stream of people headed home at the end of the day. We waited on the platform while three or four red streetcars came and went, and the line of people waiting to get on a car shuffled slowly forward. Around us the men—it was mostly men in that crowd—were dressed for the office in gray or brown suits and fedora hats with narrow brims. If I expected them to take note of my wide-brimmed buckaroo hat and high-heeled boots and maybe mistake me for Ken Maynard, I was disappointed; they went on reading their newspapers and magazines without giving me a second look. The fact is, if you lived in Hollywood in those days you were used to seeing men like me hanging around on street corners hoping to get a day's wages loafing on a movie set. And I guess if I were Ken Maynard I would've been riding around in a limousine, not waiting in line for a streetcar.

When we finally got onto a Santa Monica car, a man gave up his seat to Lily. She had been full of energy when we walked over from the bus station, but now she slumped down, resting her chin on the suitcase standing in her lap and looking out the sooty window with a dull stare. I stood in the aisle, hugging my duffle to my chest to keep from bumping people with it. Standing was fine by me, after sitting in buses for close to thirty-six hours. When the car jerked and started rolling, we went out slowly through a subway tunnel black as night. The car was lit up inside, but the light made a mirror out of the window glass. I could see my face, a skull mask, looking back from the darkness.

After a mile or so we came out in bright daylight, rattling right down the middle of a boulevard, past tough-looking palm trees, drugstores, movie theaters, a bank with a clock that stuck out over the sidewalk. The car stopped and started, squealed its brakes, jangled a harsh bell. A few people got off, but others got on, so it never came to the point of empty seats. After a while the tracks cut away from the busy street and up a short alley, past the back yards of stucco houses that looked parched and yellow in the afternoon light. Overalls and house dresses hung from slack wires in the side yards. Kids playing on the scraps of dried-out brown lawn hardly gave us a look; I guess at that time of day streetcars must have rattled past every five minutes, and the novelty had worn off.

Lily, for all her tired staring, had been keeping track of where we were, and when the car rolled out onto another busy street, she looked up at me and gave my sleeve a yank. "This is Santa Monica Boulevard," she said. "I think you ought to get off somewhere along here."

I didn't see how that could be right. The street was clogged with four lanes of traffic and hemmed in on both sides by two-story buildings. We had already rolled by a J. C. Penney store, grocery fronts, cocktail bars with their neon signs lit up for the evening business. I wasn't so ignorant as to think the town of Hollywood would be the open sagebrush land I'd seen in the cowboy pictures, but I sure hadn't thought it would look like this, and I wondered where all the horses were kept. Every so often I saw a roof off in the distance that I took to be a barn roof, but even back then you wouldn't have been able to see any of the stables from a streetcar on Santa Monica.

I didn't make a move to get off the car—I was sure she was wrong about where we were. After a few blocks Lily picked up her suitcase and stood. "I'll get off with you. I can catch the next car."

I started to argue, but she pushed past me, yanked on the bell rope, and as soon as the car stopped she hopped out onto the street. I felt like I had to follow her. The tracks ran right down the middle of the boulevard, so the trolley stop was just an island between the lanes of traffic barreling by on either side. We stood there a minute, but I was irritated with her and I guess embarrassed that I had let myself be bullied into getting off, so as soon as I saw a break in the traffic I took off without saying anything to her, just bolted across the car lanes to the sidewalk and started walking along like I knew where I was going, which I sure as hell didn't. She didn't try very hard to catch up, but I could hear her shoes on the sidewalk behind me.

That particular stretch of the boulevard was lined with bars and pawnshops. Several of the bars had opened their doors to the warm afternoon, and the smell when I walked by was familiar, a stale, concentrated perfume of beer and cigarettes and men's sweat. A few men were hanging around in doorways or going in and out of the saloons. Some of them looked past me to Lily trailing behind, a brief look before moving their eyes along to something more interesting; she wasn't a head-turning beauty on a good day, and this was at the end of a long ride on an interstate bus. But every so often a fellow would give her a harder stare, which put me on edge. A guy leaning against a parked car smiled in her direction and muttered something under his breath, and if I'd heard what he said I might have started something with him—I had the idea that Hollywood was a dangerous place compared to the towns I'd come from, and I was operating on a fairly short fuse. I gave him a look, and he looked back and smirked slightly and went on leaning there.

So then I stopped at the corner to let Lily catch up to me. She had grown up in Seattle, which was closer to a big city than anywhere I'd ever lived, and in any case, Lily being Lily, she had this way about her, like nothing could throw her for a loop. She was walking along, looking at the storefronts and the street signs like it was all run-of-the-mill, and when she passed the man leaning against the car she gave him a brief look without any interest, and something in her manner must have shut him down, because he turned his head to look up the street like what was happening there was deeply interesting.

When she got to the corner, Lily tipped her head back to look up at me and said, "What's the matter?" I must have been scowling.

It didn't sound like a real question to me, so I didn't bother to answer. I turned and looked down the block and said, "I don't see any hotels."

"Maybe we should go into one of these shops and ask whether there's a hotel or a rooming house anywhere close by. And make sure Gower Street is somewhere around here." The signal light at the intersection glittered in her glasses.

We were standing in front of a window with the words THOR'S NEEDLE painted on it in fancy script. A fat man with his sleeves rolled above his elbows sat behind the dusty glass reading a newspaper. His fleshy forearms were dark with inked designs. He gave us a look and then went back to his newspaper.

I had gotten over being sore at Lily by then, but I sure wouldn't have let her push me into a tattoo parlor to ask about hotels. I said, "There might be something further along. We ought to walk another block or two."

She didn't argue. We walked on up the street, and at the next corner she said, "What's that?" and pointed across the lanes of traffic and halfway down the next block, to a neon sign in looping letters, SAINT JAMES. Under the sign a dirty glass door was propped open, and a couple of men sat on chairs along the front wall, taking in the afternoon sun or the passersby. We crossed the street and walked down to the building, and Lily went right up to the men sitting outside and asked, "Is this a hotel?" Both of them straightened up and said yes it was.

We stepped just inside. There was a stairway at the back of the lobby and a desk to one side of it under a shadeless floor lamp. The man sitting behind the desk was studying a magazine spread out on the desk. He sat with his elbows propped and his chin resting on his upturned palms; he glanced at us briefly and then returned to his reading. The rose design in the flat-grained carpet was faded and worn through in a broad track from the front door to the stairs.

Lily turned to me and said quietly, "It's not very clean," lifting her eyebrows as if she'd asked me a question.

I said, "It's all right, the rooms are probably okay." But I didn't want to go in and pay for the room with Lily standing at my elbow; I didn't want the desk clerk or the men in front of the hotel to get the wrong idea. For that matter, I didn't want Lily standing there while I figured out if I had enough money for the room. So I said, "I'll walk you to the streetcar stop and then I'll come back here and get settled in."

I thought she might argue. But she looked around the lobby once, then up and down the street, and after a little silence she said, "Okay. Thanks."

I walked her up the street to the next streetcar island and stood there with cars whizzing by within a couple of feet of us. We didn't talk much. I asked if she knew where she needed to get off, and she said, "I'll get off at Vine. They said the club is only a couple of blocks from there." We were the only ones waiting, but there were people on the sidewalks, men and women going in and out of grocery stores and laundries. It looked safe enough, now that we were away from all those bars, but at this moment I was the only person Lily knew in Los Angeles, which you will notice works the other way too. So I said, "Listen, I don't know if you should be walking by yourself. Maybe I should walk you to that place where you're staying."

She tipped her head back to look at me. "It's only a couple of blocks from the streetcar stop. Those other girls walk it all the time." She looked up the street. "But thanks anyway."

I might have tried harder to persuade her—maybe she would

have been persuadable—but when we saw the streetcar coming she picked up her suitcase and said, "Well, good luck," and reached out to shake my hand.

"Same to you," I said. We were suddenly a little shy, both of us, and that's what comes back to me—our sudden shyness with each other and how neither of us said anything about staying in touch.

5

I'VE HAD A FEW BROKEN BONES over the years, from horses that fell on me and horses I fell from, one of which you'll hear about, and at the tail end of the war I broke my leg when a transport truck I was riding in was hit by a mortar, which is not part of this book except to say that my body gave me enough trouble in later years that I had to give up riding horses by the time I turned fifty. There's something to be said for ruminating with an animal eye to eye, which I've done more of since I quit climbing onto a saddle, but here I am now, getting up from this desk every half hour to keep my hips from stiffening, and every little while limping into the kitchen to pop an ibuprofen. If I had known I would live to be this old and still be using the original equipment, I wonder if I'd have steered clear of stunt riding when I was nineteen and twenty years old.

Although I guess I already know the answer, because I sure as hell had plenty of warning.

The Saint James turned out to be crowded with men trying to break into the movies and scraping by on what they could make as extras. A few others were retired bit players, old men who had always put their earnings in a sock instead of a bank, and after the Crash still had enough to cover the rent in a cheap place like the Saint James. One of the old guys I talked with that day was Ray Mullens. He was not anybody whose name you would recognize, but he'd ridden in a bunch of cowboy movies, mostly in the silents, and fallen off plenty of horses before he got too stove up to keep doing it.

Now that I'm looking back, I have to wonder why Ray didn't try to talk me out of getting into the business. He'd shattered both his ankles when a horse fell over backward on top of him, and when I met him he was gimping along with a pained grimace, it hurt him that much to walk. But he was happy to talk to me about every gag he'd ever done, some so dangerous and wild he might have been making them up. He bragged about every wreck too—he'd broken an arm and four ribs, had his lung punctured, two or three concussions. When he broke his ankles, he was on location up at Lone Pine and had to be driven a hundred miles to a hospital, loaded into the back of a station wagon. Somebody gave him a quart of Old Crow to kill the pain—he was grinning as he told me this. Now he was coming up on seventy years old and he couldn't stand straight to piss, but he was tickled pink to send me down that same road. And the truth is, I had come to Hollywood looking for some danger, so I was happy to follow his lead. You could get busted up doing almost anything on a ranch—hell, you could die while you were rounding up cattle. But I had the idea that if I was killed making movies, maybe I'd go out in a blaze of glory trying to stop a runaway stagecoach.

Ray said the studios making all the cheap cowboy pictures had their offices clustered around Gower Street—Lily had been right about that—but he called it Gower Gulch, which was a slap at the fellows parading around the neighborhood in their cheap cowboy clothes. I guess Ray could see how green I was, because he made a point of saying I wouldn't spot any horses tied up along Gower Gulch. The pictures mostly got made elsewhere; he was just sending me to the studio offices. He fished out a piece of paper and wrote down a few names—casting directors he was friendly with and second-unit men who might hire me as a rider. And in case I didn't get on with any of them, he gave me a telephone number to call, a switchboard for people wanting day work as an extra. If I hit it lucky, they might be looking for riders, he said.

It was after four-thirty by then, too late in the day to hop on the streetcar and start looking for work. I should have been holding on to what money I had left—the Saint James, cheap by Hollywood standards, was still more than I'd counted on. Instead I went around the corner to a diner and spent four bits on a bowl of clam chowder. I must have figured I'd be on some studio's payroll by the next morning and shortly riding a horse alongside Buck Jones.

The day had been hot, and when the sun went down it didn't get any cooler. In my room I peeled off all my clothes and lay down naked on the bed. I could hear voices through the thin walls, toilets flushing and the rush of water in the pipes, cars going by and streetcars squealing their brakes, people calling to each other and banging the lids of trash cans, and every so often an ambulance or police siren or somebody laying on a car horn. I had learned over the last year to sleep in a room full of snorers, but I'd never had to sleep with all this racket of a big city at night; plus I was used to sleeping in the dark, not with neon signs flashing and street lamps pouring light through the paper shade on the window. I don't know if I ever did fall asleep completely. It seemed as if I was always in a half-dream, riding a Greyhound bus as it swayed up on two wheels, or lying on my back in a field of dry weeds, looking up into the broad faces of dairy cows.

I had saved a couple of oranges from the Grapevine fruit stand, which I ate for breakfast, but I was stale from lack of sleep, so I went back to the diner and paid for coffee in a thick china mug before I caught the streetcar. I was still thinking I'd have a day's pay in my pocket and be moving into a better hotel by nightfall, so I took my duffle with me.

It turned out Gower was ten or fifteen minutes straight down Santa Monica Boulevard, and if I'd stayed on the streetcar the day before I would have landed right at it. But as I watched the neighborhood get more expensive by the block, I began to realize it was lucky that Lily took us off the trolley where she did, because I didn't see anything west of there that looked as low-rent as the Saint James. What I did see was a cemetery so big the tombstones and crypts marched out of sight to the horizon, and big glossy pepper trees in front of a row of baroque office buildings, and every so often a two-story Spanish-style apartment building painted coral pink or pistachio green. I had only ever laid eyes on such things in the movies.

They used to call the part of Hollywood where the cheap studios had their offices "Poverty Row," and when Ray Mullens was working in the business dozens of them were making movies on a shoestring with not much more than a camera and a truck and a rented vest-pocket office. The ones making westerns were strung out along Gower Street and one block over on Beachwood. They'd shoot for a few days at one of the small movie ranches close to town or up in Griffith Park, or in their own back lot if they had one, then rent a sound stage or an empty warehouse for the wrap-up, add gimmick effects and short ends, some canned music, and call it good. They could turn out an hour-long picture for the bottom half of a double feature in little more than a week, which is why people called them "eight-day outfits." But when I looked up the addresses that Ray had sent me to, quite a few were vacant buildings sporting for-rent signs. A lot of the smaller places had been eaten up by Republic, which had moved its operation out to the valley. Most of the studios still doing business along Gower Gulch were making either three-day serials or singing-cowboy pictures, neither of which had any call for riding extras: they used songs in place of action and rented stock footage from film libraries for the chases and stunts. I did find a couple of studios from Ray's list that were still doing it the old way, but his leads were no help at all—nobody remembered Ray Mullens.

I wandered up and down the streets and saw a lot of fellows wearing cheap ten-gallon hats that wouldn't stand up to a light rain and shop-made footgear that hadn't ever toed a stirrup. I didn't want to ask any of them about picture work, and anyway they were lounging in front of bars or leaning on parked cars appearing to be out of work themselves.

The day had started warm, and by lunchtime the heat was shimmering off sidewalks and the roofs and hoods of cars. The duffle began to feel heavy against my shoulder, and my feet were sweating in boots never meant for walking. Finally I hunted up a telephone booth and called the number Ray had given me, and I told a girl who answered that I was looking for work riding horses. She asked me for a phone number so she could get in touch if a job came up, and when I said I didn't have one she wasn't interested in taking my name.

It's a funny thing: when a man is broke he's always hungry. The coffee and oranges I'd had for breakfast had worn off hours ago, and when I walked by an air-conditioned diner the question of money was the only thing that kept me from going inside. But I saw an Indian with long braids sitting at the lunch counter in there, eating a hamburger. He was hatless but otherwise not dressed much different from me, jeans and a button-up shirt, boots with stack heels worn down at the corners. I figured he must be an actor or at least a movie extra, because I'd only ever seen long-haired Indians in pictures; the ones I had met riding rodeo wore their hair cut short like anybody else. I circled the block, thinking it over, and when I came back around I went in and sat on the stool next to him. I studied the menu while I let the sweat cool, and then I ordered a bowl of chili and some saltine crackers. I ate slowly, eyeing blackberry pie under a glass cover on the counter and enjoying the cool air blowing down from a box on the wall. I had to sit there thinking for quite a while before I came up with something to say to him.

"My uncle Jim, he saw Jackson Sundown ride at the Round-Up the year he won the All-Around."

What shames me now is that I thought my knowing about a famous Indian rodeo champion who had died before I was born was somehow a compliment to the whole Indian race.

Well, this fellow was polite about it. He looked over at me, nodded, and said, "Did he," and drank some of his Coke. Then he said, "Your uncle Jim, he a bronc rider?"

My dad's brother had died before my parents ever met, but I had heard enough about him from my grandparents and my dad that I sometimes forgot I hadn't known him. I said, "No, he did some law work for the city of Pendleton and for the Round-Up, so he happened to be there that time Sundown got the silver-trimmed saddle."

He nodded again and took another swig of his Coke. I could see his hands were callused from rope burns and three fingers were bent—maybe they'd been broken and healed crooked.

I was mulling over what else I could say to keep him talking—maybe something about Chiloquin, which was the last place I had rodeoed before heading south to Hollywood. It was the biggest town on the Klamath Indian Reservation, so I had met quite a few Indians there. I might have been preparing to ask if he knew any of them. But then he glanced down at my boots and said, "I guess maybe you're the bronc rider."

I tried to hold on to a sober expression. "Yes sir, I've rode a few. But I'm looking for picture work right now."

I don't suppose he was surprised, but he lifted his eyebrows like he was. "Is that right."

"I thought there'd be a lot of work down here, but I haven't had much luck. You in pictures?"

He'd probably known from the first word I spoke that this was where I was headed—that I was new in town and hoping he might be able to give me a leg up in the movie business. He took a minute making up his mind how to answer, and then he passed me a dry smile and said, "I've shot up a few wagon trains."

"Yeah? You ever been shot off a horse? I heard that's mostly what the work is."

He gave me another look, another slight smile. "That there is called a saddle fall. You get on a picture, you'll be falling two, three times every day. That and just straight hard riding, that's what the work mostly is for the fellows in the posses and such."

44

Then this fellow—his name was Lee Waters—must have decided I was worth a little bit of coaching. I was to learn over the next few months that stunt riders were naturally proud of the work they did, and most any of them would open up and talk about it if you looked interested and gave them half an opening. If they had a specialty, they might not tell you their secrets, but they'd be happy to let you in on the ordinary tricks and tell you the story of how they got started working in pictures. Lee told me he'd been riding for a wild west show, and after the outfit went broke in the Depression he came down to Gower Gulch. This was when things were still booming along Poverty Row, and he picked up work pretty much every day just by showing up at the cheap studios wearing his own moccasins and buckskin leggings, with a crow feather stuck in his long braids. In the wild west show he had learned the trick of hanging off the far side of a horse, shooting a bow and arrow from under the horse's neck, and when word of this got around to the second-unit ramrods, they took to calling him whenever they needed somebody to ride that gag. For the last few years he'd been working regularly for Republic and Monogram, the studios Ray Mullens had called "the big guns."

Ray had told me it wasn't worth my time to try those outfits. The Monogram office was quite a few miles to the east along Sunset Boulevard, and Republic was a long streetcar ride up Cahuenga to the valley. "You'd waste half your day getting out to one of them and back, and I just wouldn't do it if I was you. For them places, you got to know somebody or been around the business a while."

When I said this to Lee Waters, he nodded. "Ray Mullens told you that? Hell, I know Ray, I rode with him a time or two. Yeah, you got to fall off a few saddles for the eight-day outfits, pay your dues, so to speak, before them guys at Republic will give you a ride." He leaned back and lit a ready-made cigarette and took a couple of drags before he said, "Ray got busted up, I heard, and had to quit the business."

"He's pretty stove in."

"Where's this list he give you?"

I pulled out the list and handed it to him, and he smoked quietly as he studied it a couple of minutes. "A lot of these places been bought out or gone broke," he said.

"That's what I'm finding. I guess Ray didn't know it."

Lee took a pencil out of his shirt pocket and wrote down a couple of places he knew about that had their offices in some other part of town. "I ain't sure of the addresses, but I'm writing down the cross streets as I remember, and you can ask around and maybe get yourself there."

Then he said, "You sleeping in the park?" He meant Griffith Park, although I didn't know it at the time. "I slept a few nights up there myself when I first come to town. At least you're out of some heat, being under the trees." It didn't occur to me at the time, but now that I'm thinking back I imagine he meant this as mild advice. He said it as if money wasn't the consideration at all, but he must have known I was flat broke—that if I wasn't already sleeping behind trash cans in an alley I would be before long.

The last year or so following rodeos and picking up itinerant ranch work, there'd been plenty of days and weeks when I had been stone broke, but I could almost always count on some winner buying me a sandwich and some rancher who didn't care if I bedded down in an empty stall in his dry barn. Here in Hollywood it was just starting to sink in that this was a different sort of place.

I nodded. "Well, the room I had last night was hot as hell. Maybe I'll try sleeping out."

I asked him where the park was, and he told me the bus that would get me up there. Then he took back Ray's list and wrote down where to find Diamond Barns, which he said was a stable that supplied horses to the cowboy movies. "It's right up there in the park, so if you're already in the neighborhood you might see if Harold is doing any hiring. That's if you're not too high-hat to go to work pitching hay and mucking out stalls. Wrangling might get you started in

46

the business anyway, get you onto some movie sets where you might meet a few ramrods, get yourself an opening to ride."

We walked out of the cafe together and shook hands, and he said, "See you around," before climbing into a Model A and driving off. I never did see him again, though at the end of 1942 I happened to catch a glimpse of him in a motion picture. That was after I had joined the army and finished up training and was waiting to ship out from New York. It was all over the papers that the cowboy star Buck Jones had died a hero trying to save people in the Cocoanut Grove fire, and a bunch of men from the barracks decided to go see a Buck Jones picture playing at a theater in town. I had stayed away from westerns after leaving Hollywood, but Buck was one of the cowboy stars I'd admired when I was working there; before getting started in the movies he'd been a horse breaker for the French during the Great War, and I knew he was a real horseman. So I went along with the others to see his last picture. When Lee Waters came up on the screen, I recognized him right away. He had a small speaking part, delivering his lines in that clipped "Injun" style that the movies always used back then—not a bit like when I'd met him at Gower Gulch. I waited through the credits at the end to see if I could spot him. Well, there wasn't any Lee Waters, just "Injun Lee."

I spent the rest of the day hunting up the places he had written down for me. I didn't have the damnedest idea how Hollywood was laid out, and I was too stubborn to ask anybody, so I wound up going lost a good part of the afternoon and hoofing it more than my boots were meant for, and in the end I ran into the same trouble I'd had in the Gulch: a girl behind a desk who barely looked up before saying there wasn't any need for a cowboy.

By the time the shops and offices had started closing for the day, my feet had come out in blisters and the sweat was rolling down the back of my shirt in itchy streams. I stood on a street corner counting up the money I had left, which was a buck-eighty, and then I limped up Sunset to Western and caught a city bus going into the park.

6

IN 1938 THERE WAS ALREADY AN OBSERVATORY at the top of Griffith Park, and a Greek amphitheater and an aerodrome, but as soon as the bus started climbing north of Hollywood Boulevard we were in empty hills grown over with manzanita and chaparral, and steep gullies thick with oaks and big old sycamore trees. Even now, most of that park is still undeveloped, still rough country, but back then it looked as if it was unchanged from when Indians had walked those ravines. I was in a black mood about the way things had gone that day, and when I saw how wild the park was I began entertaining a little fantasy about living like an outlaw, camping in the park, and coming down into town to rob a bank now and then. I was thinking if I had my .22 with me to shoot rabbits and threaten bank tellers, I'd be all set.

When I stepped onto the bus I hadn't made up my mind whether I was going up there to find the horse stable Lee Waters had told me about or to find a place to camp, but partway up the hill I caught a glimpse of what might have been water in one of the ravines, and I guess that was when I made up my mind I was camping out. I yanked the cord, and the bus pulled over to let me off, nowhere close to anything—just trees. The driver didn't remark on this, which I took to mean I wasn't his first cowboy looking for a place to spend the night.

It was a relief to be away from concrete sidewalks and under the shade of those big old canyon oaks. And a shock, almost, to hear quiet for the first time in two days. Once I left the road and hiked down into the gully, there was almost no traffic noise, no rattling streetcars, no buses whining through the gears, no muttered voices through cheap hotel walls, just a lot of bird chatter—California birds, their strange songs not the ones I recognized—and the understory buzz that crickets and grasshoppers make, and every so often the dry rustle of a snake or a squirrel or a gopher moving off through the brush. I think that may have been the point at which I realized I'd been taking such things for granted my whole life.

The water turned out to be not much more than a stagnant thread, scummy with algae, but I found a couple of deeper puddles I could dip my hands into, and I was thirsty enough it didn't matter to me. I drank some tepid, fusty-tasting palmfuls, took off my shirt and hat and sluiced water over my sweaty head and chest, and then took off my boots and soaked my feet. The sun hadn't quite set, but the gully was in deep orange shadow, and the air at the bottom of the ravine was cooler than it had been in the city. Sitting with my sore feet in water, my chin resting on my bare chest, I just about went off to sleep. So I found a level spot with plenty of leaf duff, rolled out my blanket and lay down on it, and then, the way it happens sometimes, I was wide awake, staring overhead into the crewelwork of dry oak leaves while the sky slowly darkened.

I should have been making a plan for the next day, but what I thought about was the dead man, his open eyes examining the night sky, and it wasn't far from there to my sister. The stars came out slowly. The only constellation I recognized in the wedge of sky above the ravine was Aries. Finally it got a little chilly, so I sat up and put on my shirt and walked barefoot into the darkness to take a piss.

When I lay down again and rolled up in the blanket, I guess the long day finally caught up with me, because I stopped thinking about anything, and when I came back to the surface it was gray morning.

The oak leaves over my head were faintly moving shadows. I looked up into them a minute, listening to the quiet rustle, and then woke all the way up and turned my head and saw what I'd been hearing, which was a couple of men rummaging through my duffle bag. One of them was hatless, his dirty shirt torn out along the shoulder seam. The other guy was wearing my hat pushed far back on his greasy hair. The one in the torn shirt had my good boots clasped under his arm while he squatted down watching his pal poke around inside my bag.

I yelled, "Hey," which was probably not the smartest thing I could have done. My legs were tangled in the blanket, and before I could get to my feet both men startled upright, and the one with my hat on his head grabbed up my bag and swung it at me. Something hard inside, probably my dad's old steel spurs, clipped me on the eyebrow. It wasn't much of a blow, but I recoiled from it, and then the other one swung out with his hobnail boot and struck me on the side of my neck; all the feeling went out of that side of my body.

They weren't toughs—I imagine they were just hobos looking for money or something to eat or trade for money or food. But at that point they could have taken off running with my boots and my bag, leaving me there in my sock feet with nothing but the clothes I was wearing and a thin blanket. I don't know why they didn't. But once they started, they just became set on beating the living daylights out of me.

I had been in fights as a kid, the kind that ended when somebody got a bloody nose, and in the year and a half since I'd left home I'd been in a few drunken fistfights outside rodeo arenas or bars. I could take a hit and throw one, and I was on my way to being what we used to call a scrapper, but I was on the ground and the two of them were standing over me, kicking with their boots. I couldn't get any leverage to fight back, and one side of my body was nothing but a buzzing numbness. It's interesting how, in a situation like that, you're not thinking about anything, not even feeling fear, you're just trying to protect your soft parts and your head, trying to get out of range of the kicks or grapple with an ankle or a foot to keep the kick from making contact. And your head is too full of the hammering of your own heart, the furious pumping of blood, to have room for feeling much pain.

Finally I managed to get hold of a boot. It was an army boot from the last war, a trench boot too big for the man's foot and with the laces missing. When the boot came off in my hands, he lost his balance and went flailing backward and landed on his butt, and as he went down, the other guy tried to grab hold of his windmilling arms to keep him from falling, which gave me a couple of seconds. I scrambled to my feet and barreled into the one still standing and knocked him flat, knocked my hat off his head, and followed him down to the ground and went to pounding on him with my fists. I was in a rage suddenly, the world gone red through the scrim of blood behind my eyes.

It's probably a good thing I was already beaten up myself, that I didn't have the arm strength to put heat behind the punches. This is something I've thought about off and on over the years.

I don't know how many times I hit him, but at some point the one who had lost his boot got around behind me and struck me on the shoulders and back of the head with a stick of wood or something, hit me two or three times. It didn't knock me out, nowhere close to it, but it stunned me, and I rocked over and brought up my arms to protect my brains. The one who'd been hitting me helped the other guy to his feet, and the two of them took off staggering down the ravine.

I yelled something after them, half-articulated and breathless, something childish like "You better run, pally!" which I think I'd learned from the movies.

I almost stood up, then sat right down again. I looked to make sure they'd left my stuff behind, the boots especially, and the hat, and then I just sat there a while. My mouth was full of blood, there was blood in my eyes. Now that the fight was finished, I had feeling all over my body, throbbing pain in my shoulders and arms, my hands, my neck. Every breath hurt. I lay down for a while, my bloody cheek resting on the dirt, and maybe I even slept for a few minutes. Woke up with a jerk, thinking those two guys were walking up on me again, but I was alone.

I was so stiff I had a hard time climbing to my feet. I went over to the little rill of water and gingerly washed my face—I had cuts on my eyebrow and chin that had already scabbed up, and this got them bleeding again. I felt around inside my mouth to make sure I had all my teeth. The inside of my lip was torn, so when I took a drink of water it tasted of salt and iron. My hands were bloodied and swollen. I soaked them a while, and then I rolled up my shirtsleeves and washed the dried blood off both elbows. I was bruised and sore all over, and it felt like I might have a cracked rib. When I looked through my duffle bag I found I was missing a few things—a pair of socks, a razor, things they must have pocketed before the fight started—but my dad's old spurs were still there, wrapped in a rag at the bottom of the sack. So they hadn't made off with anything important. It could have been worse. I had wakened thinking about Arlo Gantz, who had given me the Hamley saddle, and regretting that I had sold it, but if I'd had the saddle with me the bums might have picked it up quietly and walked off without bothering to rummage through my duffle. Even if they didn't know the worth of a Hamley, they would know that a guy sleeping outside wasn't likely to own anything more valuable than his saddle.

I pulled on my boots and lay down with my hat and duffle resting on my chest, but I didn't sleep. I didn't have a plan for the coming day, but I wasn't drawn to the idea of walking around the Gulch again, looking for work on an empty stomach and sore feet. On the other hand, I knew if I stayed there and tried to sleep off the fight, I'd be jerking awake every few minutes for fear somebody was coming at me again.

The day had already warmed, and I could see some sunlight at the top of the ridge, so after a while I stood and limped my way up there, found the road again, sat down beside the pavement, and waited until a bus came along on its way down to town.

I hadn't had anything to eat since that bowl of chili with Lee Waters the day before, so I got off somewhere along Western, walked to the first diner I saw, and spent most of the money I had left on coffee and a short stack. I sat on the stool for quite a long time afterward, moving crumbs around in the last dab of syrup, until the waitress made a point of picking up the plate and wiping off the counter underneath it. By then the studio offices on Gower Street were open, so I limped around to the same ones I'd been to the day before.

My face all beat to hell like I'd been in a bar fight didn't improve my prospects any, and by noon I had run out of doors to knock on. I walked by a few men standing in the shade, leaning against lampposts, trying to look as if they were waiting for a limo to pick them up, and I tried doing that too. But finally I hobbled over to Western Avenue and caught a bus back up into Griffith Park.

7

LEE WATERS HAD TOLD ME to look out for a dirt road with an arch over it, which was the ranch gate for the stables, but I was slumped down in the seat, half asleep and not paying much attention, until the bus driver called back to me, "You getting off at Diamond?" I guess I didn't look like I was headed up to the observatory to look at stars. I said, "Yeah," and he pulled the bus over where a dirt road poked back into a side canyon. The ranch sign didn't have any lettering on it, just a big diamond carved into the flattened face of a log.

It was half a mile up the road to the Diamond Barns corrals and sheds, which was about as far as my blisters would carry me. By that time, I had pretty much decided to quit the whole movie-cowboy enterprise. I would muck out stalls if I had to, just long enough to get the money for a bus ticket back to Klamath County. And what bumped me off this plan was Harold Capsen, who owned Diamond Barns. Harold was the first person I worked for in the movie business, and I want to say right here that he was also the best.

I came around a turn in the road to find a bunch of corrals and sheds spread out under the trees. From twenty yards off I could see that the fellow leaning on the rails looking over some horses was wearing a hat with a Montana crease in the high crown, an honest-to-god Stetson that had already stood up to some weather; his boot resting on the lower rail was the sort my dad always wore, scuffed brown leather with a worn, steep-cut heel that had been resoled a few times.

A black mutt was lying down on the straw right under the horses, his chin on his front paws, as if he and the horses had come to an understanding of peaceful cohabitation. When he saw me he hoisted himself off the straw and came up the road to meet me. He didn't bark, which I thought was a bad sign—I stood where I was, deciding if it was time to get out of range of his teeth—but he'd been taught that barking riled up the horses, that's all it was.

The man standing at the corral took a look over his shoulder and saw me coming, but then he went back to studying the horses. I spoke to the dog before he got all the way up to me, told him he was an ugly son of a gun and too stupid to find his own way home, and he studied my face and the tone of my voice before he walked up to my hand and let me touch him around the ears. He wasn't a pup, he had some gray around his muzzle.

I walked on toward the man and leaned on the rails next to him. The dog followed me, then went ahead into the corral and wandered amidst the legs of the horses. He waved his tail slightly as he let various horses snuffle him thoroughly. I learned later that he had a bed of feed sacks in a corner of the tack barn. I guess he must have slept on them, because there was always shed fur and a dent in the folded-up sacks in the morning, but when we went out to the corrals he was always there ahead of us, hanging around the horses before the sun was up. No one knew what his history was, because he'd been a stray before he found his way to Diamond. Harold figured he had grown up around horses and was pleased to find himself among them again.

There were about a dozen horses in that corral, a few of them big draft horses, most of them various shades of brown, and they stood around in pairs, head to tail, engaged in the serious late-afternoon business of swishing flies. They'd eaten up the morning's hay pretty thoroughly, but a chestnut with a long head snuffled through stray bits of chaff, looking for morsels. The corrals and barns at Diamond didn't look a bit different from all the corrals and barns I'd been around, and the horses standing in them were no fancier than the horses Mary Claudine and I used to ride to school when we lived on Echol Creek. I don't know what I'd been expecting, but this was a mild surprise and a relief to me.

The fellow under the Stetson hat, who looked to be about fifty years old, said, without turning his head, "You ought to get off those feet before they get so swolled up you have to cut them boots off."

I had been thinking I'd done a good job of walking the last few yards without a gimp, but I guess not. My face got warm, as if he'd caught me doing something shameful.

He glanced down. "Those are good boots, but they was meant for hooking into a stirrup, not walking around Gower Gulch."

I was somewhat testy, so when I said "Yessir, I know that," I imagine he heard a small note of indignation.

After another minute he said, "You get into a quarrel with somebody recently?" and he made a slight gesture with one knuckle toward my beat-up face.

I didn't feel like going into the whole damn story, and there wasn't any part of it that I could brag about, but I said, "A couple of bums tried to rob me."

He didn't say anything to that, didn't even nod. A while later he asked me, "Where you from, son?"

I might have told him Klamath Falls, inasmuch as I'd ridden the Greyhound from there, or I guess I could have said Bly, since that was where my folks were living at the time, but what popped out was somewhat closer to the truth. "I grew up in Harney County," I said, "which is up in Oregon."

"I know where Harney County is. That's where Pete French built that big round barn so he could break out his horses in the winter out from under the weather."

That round barn was pretty famous where I came from, but I was surprised anybody in Hollywood had heard of it. I said, "Our place was quite a bit north of there, we had a couple of sections on Echol Creek and a government lease up in the Ochocos."

He said, "I heard of the Ochocos, matter of fact I went bear hunting up there once upon a time. There's a Nicoll Creek runs around up there if I remember, which is where we were hunting, but you didn't say Nicoll, did you? I sold some horses once to an outfit on Nickel Creek, up in Grass Valley. They used to pan gold up that way." He made a slight sound of amusement. "I guess somebody must've panned a nickel's worth of nuggets out of that there creek." I knew Nicoll Creek, which was maybe ten miles west of our place. It didn't have a thing to do with nickels, it was named for the family that settled there in the early days, but I didn't see any reason to set him straight. Then he turned to me and said, "I'm Harold Capsen," and stuck out his hand. We shook, and I told him my name, and he said, "Well, come on into the house, Bud. I wasn't kidding about you getting those boots off, and I guess you're looking for work, but we can talk that over while you're soaking your feet in Epsom salts."

When I was in high school over in Hart, I'd lived in the school dormitory during the week and spent Friday and Saturday quartered with Dean Dickerson's family. Dean's father was a banker, and they lived in a big stone house on C Street behind the Hotel Regent, a house with a sawdust furnace in the cellar and two bathrooms and oriental rugs in the living room. They had a corner lot with a big elm tree and a lawn edged with flowers, and when we sat down to dinner Dean's mother set the table with plates that matched. But I had never seen a house like the one Harold Capsen took me into.

It was a low, Mission-style stucco that, judging from the spread of the bougainvillea growing up the posts of the veranda, looked to have been there since sometime before the Great War. It was cool and dim inside, behind wide shaded porches and thick walls. The living room must have been twenty feet long, with a big plastered fireplace in one corner, its heavy cypress mantelpiece carved with a phrase I thought at the time was Spanish, but I now know was Latin: *Bene qui latuit bene vixit.* The actress who had built the house was a famous recluse, and "To live well is to live unnoticed" was evidently her personal motto.

The rooms were floored with big reddish tiles, the lines of grout almost black, and the deep windowsills were tiled also. There were heavy wooden lintels over every doorway and window. The living room was filled with oak and leather furniture, floor lamps with mica shades, heavy mesquite-wood or oak tables, and woven Navajo rugs. Mexican landscape paintings in heavy oak frames hung on all the walls.

It was an elegant house, but a bunch of uncivilized men had been living in it, so strips of flypaper were hanging everywhere, black with flies, and the furniture and rugs were tracked with mud, furred with horsehair and dog hair, and most everything had a coat of dust on it. Dirty dishes were piled on all the tables and on every surface in the kitchen. Plus Harold had a habit of dropping dirty clothes wherever he happened to be standing when he shucked them off, so there were jeans and shirts and underwear on the floors in every damn room. Harold had been divorced for ten years when I met him and was apparently uninterested in marrying again. I always wondered if his habit of dropping his trousers any-old-where was the reason for his divorce or something he discovered as a benefit of living alone.

The condition of the house didn't surprise me much; in the past year and more, I had become acquainted with the habits of bachelors who lived close to horses. What surprised me was the remarkableness of this big, fancy place tucked up in the hills, half a mile down a dirt road. I guess Harold had been asked about it so often that he didn't wait for the question to come up. While he was running hot water into a pan in the kitchen sink and stirring Epsom salts into it, he told me that some silent-movie actress—he said her name, but it didn't mean a thing to me—had built the house up here to get away from her adoring public. He had bought it cheap right after she died, bought it fully furnished from money he'd made selling his ranch up in Napa Valley when his wife divorced him. He built the corrals and sheds and opened Diamond Barns in 1929, a couple of months before the Crash. "I was just lucky that the cowboy movies never did crash," he said, "or not much. And when they started pumping out all those second features and chapter pictures, the horse-renting business took a nice upswing." He said this as though his luck was all still a surprise to him.

After I went to work at Diamond, I learned there were plenty of bigger stables scattered around the valley and in Culver City and up in the Hollywood Hills. Lionel Comport had a stable that specialized in renting swaybacked nags for those occasions when you were looking for an easy laugh; and Fat Jones had a big place that supplied the studios not only with horses, burros, and mules, but oxen, Spanish longhorn cattle, and every kind of wagon, even chariots. Over at the Hudkin Brothers, and maybe at some of the other stables too, star horses and specialty horses had their own box stalls with their names on the door.

Diamond was more of a shoestring outfit, without a single trick pony and nothing in the way of fancy props or silver-trimmed saddles. Harold had just six or seven acres and thirty or so horses and mules in a handful of corrals, plus a stagecoach and a couple of wagons. This wasn't much, ranked against the big stables, but he was close to town, tucked into a corner of the park, where penny-pinching studios could shoot their outdoor scenes cheaply, and he was handy to a couple of the smaller movie ranches in the Santa Monica Mountains. Singing-cowboy pictures were on the rise back then, heavy with actors who hadn't ever put a boot in a stirrup, and Harold staked his reputation on renting out livestock that was thoroughly broke, horses that were proof against even a tenderfoot actor without a bit of riding experience. This meant that Diamond Barns, small as it was, had about as much work as it could handle.

Harold might have had even more business if he hadn't had a rule against renting out his horses for stunts and falls. In those days, whenever stunts were involved, you could just about count on horses being tripped with a Running W or run into a pitfall or galloped through a candy-glass window, and Harold didn't want his horses used roughly. He always said he was running things on a tight budget and didn't want to be hauling dead horses to the glue factory or selling off the lamed animals and buying new ones all the time. But I think that was only part of the reason; Harold had concern for his animals is the rest of it.

While I sat there in a kitchen chair soaking my sore feet, he put together a couple of roast beef sandwiches and asked me a few things about the ranching I had done and whether I could drive a truck with a horse trailer behind it. I didn't tell him any wild tales—I figured he'd know if I tried to sell him one. I told him my folks raised cows and horses, and I'd done pretty much everything around their place and I'd driven our old truck, which had been cobbled together from an International drive train and a homemade box. I had driven it with a cow or a colt riding in the bed, but we never had owned a livestock trailer. A few times in the last year I had driven a truck towing a one-horse trailer, but only to move the rig around a rodeo ground, never out on the highway, and I hadn't ever tried to back the thing up. I told him I'd been working around rodeos for a while, but I didn't brag about it. Mostly what I had done, I said, was calf roping and working the gates. When he asked me how come I was down here in Hollywood, I told him I'd heard there was plenty of work for anyone used to being around cows and horses. I didn't say anything about expecting to ride alongside Buck Jones or Ken Maynard, and he didn't ask me why I wasn't still working for my folks.

He told me he had two trucks, a Dodge Brothers pickup and a big GMC cab-over, plus a two-horse trailer he ran with the Dodge and a big livestock trailer he pulled behind the GMC. "One of the fellas that works for me used to work for a freight hauler, so he's the one always taking out the big rig. It's the principal reason I hired him on. He ain't the best horse handler, but that truck and trailer is a goddamn beast, and he's the only one of us can lick it."

When he had a bunch of horses rented out, they had to do a lot of shuttling, dropping off horses and wranglers and then picking them up later. "Hugh took eight horses out to the park this morning, and Jake's got four out at The Canyon, and I just brought one in from a little shoot in Culver City. Along about four o'clock I need to go pick up Jake and those horses from The Canyon, but Hugh has the big rig, so I've got to do it with the Dodge and make two trips."

He said, "Days like today, it's a hell of a lot of driving, and I wish I had another truck, but I'd rather be busy with two rigs than slow with three. Feed ain't cheap, I guess you know, blacksmiths and vets neither. I don't have a lot of leftover money to invest in new equipment. Anyway, hell, the bottom could still fall out of the cowboy-movie business. Where I grew up, we learned to rub the picture off a nickel"—he cut his eyes to me and raised his eyebrows like he'd just had a surprising and amusing thought—"Shit, maybe that's why there's no damn nickels in any of those creeks. So anyway, I'm holding off on a third rig until I see if this keeps up being busy."

I was of the opinion that the bottom would never fall out of the cowboy movies, but I didn't say so.

He handed over one of the sandwiches. It had his big dark thumb-print in the bread, which didn't stop me from biting into it. When we were just about finished with the sandwiches, he went rummaging around for something that turned out to be a pair of socks, which he handed to me without saying what for. Well, I had worn holes in the heels of both my socks from walking around Gower Gulch, which he must have seen. Given my stiff neck in those days, I might have said something ungrateful to him if I hadn't had my mouth full of bread. In any case, I didn't get the chance, because right then he said he had two men wrangling for him and business was good enough he was in the market for another, "which I guess means I'm giving you a try. I don't know where you're staying, but there's a room at the back of the house you can move into with Hugh if you don't mind listening to him snore. I'll dock your pay three bucks a week for the bed and board if you want it. Or if you want to stay down in town, you'll just have to get yourself up here every day, good and damn early in the morning, which is what my other fellow is doing."

Later on I heard from Jake that Harold had more or less made up his mind to hire me when he first saw me walking up the road. He'd been on the lookout for somebody for a while—tired of the long days and feeling shorthanded. Plenty of men were walking around town hoping for movie work, of course, and every so often one of them would find his way up the road to the barn, but a lot of the rodeo riders and cowpunchers were hard drinkers, illiterate, work-shy about anything they couldn't do from a saddle, and many of the others didn't know a thing about horses—they thought the way to get hired as a wrangler was to dress up like a movie cowboy. Harold was always polite, and he would ask a few things to make sure he wasn't missing something—that was how he'd come to hire Jake, who didn't look the part—but he could always spot a dime-store cowboy. And I guess he could see right off the bat that I was a ranch kid who'd grown up knowing the work and knowing how to work hard.

I imagine he also knew that I wouldn't be in his employ for very long, that I had come down to Hollywood expecting to ride fast horses, not stand around holding the reins for greenhorn actors. That as soon as an opportunity presented itself I'd be gone.

I went on chewing my sandwich for a bit, so as not to appear eager, and then I said, "I've been staying in a hotel, but I'd like to take you up on that room."

"I thought you might. Have you got anything you need to pick up at the hotel?"

"No sir, I don't. I've got everything in this here bag."

"Well, all right. We got a couple of hours before I need to pick up those horses from out at The Canyon, so after we finish with these sandwiches you can go on down the hall there and make up the other bed in that room and take a load off your feet for a short while."

I gave myself half a minute, then said, "I sure appreciate the work."

He grinned. "Well, you might want to hold off the appreciation until you know what I'm paying, which ain't much, and whether this job mostly involves shoveling horse crap, which it does."

§

THE ROOM HE SHOWED ME TO had been the servants' quarters when the old movie star had lived there. It was a small, airless bedroom behind the kitchen, smelling of grease and onions and dirty clothes, with just one small window looking out on a feed shed full of hay, but it had twin beds with fancy carved-oak headboards and oak bureaus carved to match, and a bathroom to itself, which I guess was meant to keep the servants from using the movie star's bath. There was a permanent dark yellow stain at the base of the toilet and on the front rim of the bowl, and the bowl was almost black inside. The tub had a thick ring of grime and shed hair, but there were fancy coral-colored tiles on the walls and on the plaster arch over the bathtub alcove, and a pair of paintings on the wall, a couple of Mexican kids with round faces staring solemnly out at the world. I had grown up in a house without indoor plumbing, and I'd lately been camping in the hills, fighting off bums, and considering the prospect of sleeping in alleys, so when I saw the fancy beds and that bathroom I felt like the pig who lands in slops.

Harold gave me some limp, worn-thin sheets and a couple of blankets he pulled out of a cupboard and left me alone to settle in.

One of the mattresses was bare ticking, the other one a tangle of wrinkled, soiled bedclothes with crumbs of hay and dry mud stuck in the folds and furrows. I was so damned tired and sore I lay down for a few minutes on the bare bed, but after a while I stood and found an empty drawer in one of the bureaus, emptied my duffle into it, went into the bathroom and peed and washed up as well as I could without running a bath, then made up the bare mattress and lay down again. I didn't think I'd sleep—I was pretty wrought up and my whole body ached, and I could hear Harold moving around in other parts of the house. But the next thing I knew, Harold was tapping on the doorframe.

"I'm going out to start up the truck. If you can stuff your toes back in those boots, I'll take you with me to pick up the horses."

It was getting on toward dusk, and some cars were already running their headlights by the time Harold had us pointed up Cahuenga in the Dodge truck. That truck wasn't more than three or four years old, but the gearbox was already half shot because Harold had never learned to drive with any facility, and he had managed to strip the gears pretty well. Every time the traffic slowed or a signal light stopped him on a hill, he double-pumped the clutch and roughly manhandled the stick to get it to shift down and muttered, "Jesusgod get outta my way." But after dealing with the downshift, he'd go right back to what he was telling me, about the work I'd be doing for him, not shoveling manure, or anyway not as the principal thing, but trucking horses to wherever they were needed—nearby in the park usually or over to one of the small movie ranches—then getting them groomed and tacked up, ready for the actors, and leading them to and from the camera setup. You had to make sure the horses had some shade and water when they weren't in a scene, he said, and since nobody else on the set would give this a single damn thought, you might have to be the one to figure it all out and probably haul the water yourself. Keeping the horses fit and getting them to where they were needed, ready to ride and on time: really, that was the gist of it.

The Canyon was a little movie ranch off Mulholland with about twenty acres of chaparral-covered hills and a couple of bare dirt fields decorated with hauled-in boulders and some tumbleweed. Harold parked the truck and told his dog, who'd been riding in the back end, "Jack, you stay put." We walked past a few trailers and cars to where a tarp was strung up for shade over a couple of saddled horses. In the field in front of us they were finishing up filming a scene, so we stood a minute, watching. There was a big two-reel camera on a heavy tripod, and several people stood near it talking, surrounded by silver reflector boards and big spotlights and umbrellas on tall poles. One of the fellows had a megaphone, and after a while he said something that sounded like "Quit" but I guess must have been "Quiet," and then a shrill whistle blew and everybody fell silent. A couple of cowboy actors who'd been lounging on horseback a few yards away suddenly looked alert, jumped off their horses, and crouched down studying a cold campfire on the dirt. Their mouths moved, and the words must have been picked up by a microphone on a long fishpole-like thing, but we were too far away to hear what they said. Then they jumped back on the horses, wheeled around, and trotted off. That was all there was to it. The whistle blew again, and the people who'd been bunched around the camera began to talk and scatter. The actors pulled up their horses before they'd gone twenty yards, hopped off, and just walked away. The horses were evidently used to this; they stood there waiting until somebody walked over and took their reins and led them off.

Well, it turned out the fellow who picked up the horses wasn't one of the movie crew but was Harold's wrangler, and he brought the pair of them right over to us. He was wearing a cloth cap like newsboys used to wear and flat-heeled workman's boots and a Levi's jumper, all of which caused me to wonder whether I'd been wrong about Harold being a fellow of savvy judgment.

Harold introduced us: he said I was Bud, from Oregon, but he pronounced it "Or-ee-gone," and he said, "This is Jake, from Ohio," making Ohio sound like three words too, just because he thought this was amusing. He didn't say I was the new hired help, but I suppose he thought Jake could figure that out. We shook hands, and Jake took a look at my cut-up face, but he didn't ask about it. He said to Harold, "Boss, you can have these two. It's King and Skippy they want for the sundown shot."

"Okey-dokey, we'll see you in a while," Harold said, and took the reins from him. I followed Harold back to the truck and helped him load the horses into the trailer, still saddled. We didn't talk much, but as we were driving back to Diamond he said, out of the blue, "That there's my best hand. Jacob Reichl. He's a Jew, which in his case don't signify. He's the best hand with horses that I believe I ever have seen."

I'd never met a Jew before in my life, or anyway none that I knew of. Without a clear idea what a Jew was, I must have imagined there wasn't any such thing as a Jewish cowboy. Harold saying he was his best hand wasn't enough to settle me on the question, because no horse handler of my acquaintance would walk around in those clothes, looking as common as any shoe repairman or grocery store clerk. I didn't argue with Harold, though, or ask him about it. Now that I seemed to have a toehold on the bottom rung of the movie world, I intended to keep my mouth shut and hang on until something better came along.

At the Diamond ranch gate Harold pulled over and let me drive the half mile of his dirt road to get the feel of the truck with that swaying horse trailer back there, and the tricky gearbox. I did all right—our old truck was a son of a bitch too—but I was already worrying about the highways and the Hollywood traffic that I knew I'd have to get used to; I was more than glad that somebody else would be driving the big GMC, hauling the other trailer with eight or ten horses in the back.

We unloaded the horses, stripped their tack, turned them into one of the corrals. Then Harold drove us all the way back to The Canyon on dark roads streaming with headlights. I was so tired I fell asleep for part of the way. We loaded up the other two horses and headed back to Diamond, all three of us crammed together in the front seat. I was in the middle, getting cozy with that gearshift, and Jake at one point said, "Boss, quit playing with the new kid's balls." I had been thinking a Jewish cowboy must be different from the rest of us, but this was the kind of ribbing I was used to hearing from ranch hands and bronc riders.

It must have been close to ten or eleven by the time we got back to Diamond and turned out the horses. Jake got into an old Chevrolet parked in the yard and drove away into the dark. Harold and I took a piss off the veranda, and then I went down the long hallway to the room I'd be sleeping in. Harold's other hand, Hugh Rovzar, had come back from the shoot in Griffith Park quite a long time before and was already asleep and snoring in the other bed. I stripped to my underwear and climbed under the sheets, and I think I was asleep before Harold made it to his bedroom at the other end of the house.

9

EVERY SO OFTEN in those first days looking for work, I'd thought about Lily Shaw. The Studio Club, that girls' sorority she had told me about, was somewhere close to Vine Street—I remembered that much—so walking around Gower Gulch I had looked for it, and I kept an eye out in case I might bump into her. I wondered how she was making out.

It would be January before we met up again, and I never did ask her much about those months when we'd been out of touch. But a couple of years before she died, she wrote about that time in a piece for *Vanity Fair*—she'd been working on her memoir, and this was part of it. She always let me know whenever she used my name in a piece she'd written, so she called me up one day and said, "You're in this, Bud, but you're not the star."

And then she read the whole thing to me over the phone, a story I had never heard from her before, about how she went into the Studio Club that first afternoon right after we split up at the streetcar stop, then went out to buy a pack of cigarettes.

"This woman, Miss Legard"—Lily's voice was husky, reading it to me, the way smokers' voices get after a few years—"walked me upstairs to the linen room, piled my arms with towels and sheets, and led me to the bedroom I would share with the other agency girls. It was four o'clock, they were away at work, so when she left me to get settled in I found myself standing alone in an empty room. There were rumpled clothes scattered on the floor and the furniture and on the two mussed beds and on the bare mattress that I surmised was mine. Pots and tubes of makeup lay open on the dressing tables, damp towels were draped over closet doors, henna stained the bowl of the sink. I sat down on the bed, holding the stack of folded linens in my lap. I was quite tired—I thought of lying down and trying to sleep—but after a while I stood and made the bed, found an empty drawer in which to put my things, walked down the hall to use the bathroom, and then went downstairs to one of the parlors off the entrance hall.

"It was an enormous long room, with chairs and sofas upholstered in mohair in groupings of two or three. A proscenium stage with maroon velvet curtains took up the whole end wall. The only people in the big room were a young man and woman sitting near the fireplace talking quietly, their fingertips touching. I sat down in a wicker rocker in a far corner close to a window, took a notepad out of my pocket, folded it to a blank page, and wrote *letter to folks* and, underneath that, *buy cigarettes*.

"Making lists of things I planned to do was a habit from childhood. I've kept lists sometimes for weeks—it's satisfying to look at the rows of chores and errands and see all the things crossed out, what's been accomplished, the unwasted days. The summer before, when I was still arguing with my parents over my plan to move to California, I had decided to take up smoking as soon as I was living away from home; it was in some unstated way part of my larger plan to become a famous Hollywood screenwriter. I must have imagined that to be famous a woman needed to be bold and shocking.

"That first afternoon at the Hollywood Studio Club, I wrote a short letter to my parents, crossed that off the list, folded the letter inside the notepad, and then at the bottom of my list wrote *buy stamps.* By then it was nearly five o'clock. Some of the girls had begun to come in from their jobs, but when I went back to the bedroom it was still empty. I picked up my purse and walked out in search of a place to buy stamps and cigarettes and to mail the letter.

"A man wearing a big cowboy hat and denim trousers tucked into shiny boots was lounging against a parked car at the corner of the block, and though I knew perfectly well it wasn't Bud Frazer, this gave me a start. I had left Bud at the streetcar stop only an hour earlier, and in any case, he was someone I had known for just a day and a night. So I couldn't account, and can't even now, for the sudden pang of lonesomeness when I saw this cowboy who was not *my* cowboy."

Lily drew on her cigarette: I could hear the slight, soft *puck* and then the slow exhale. "That's it for you, Bud. It's a walk-on part. Day rate is all you get."

I laughed. "Let's hear the rest."

She must have known I would want to hear it all, but she fell silent for a minute, maybe reading ahead. When she started again, her voice was flat, without inflection.

"When I reached the corner I said to him, 'Do you have a cigarette?' I had seen women in films approach a stranger for a cigarette and then lean in for the flaring match. They were being flirtatious usually, though sometimes a certain kind of woman was signaling something else, something like confidence or casual bravado, and that was what I meant to show. I didn't smile, and I looked the man straight in the eye.

"He seemed only slightly surprised that a girl he'd never seen before had asked him for a cigarette. He straightened up and fished one from his shirt pocket and offered it to me. He struck a match and cupped it in his hands and waited for me to lean in for the light. I touched the cigarette to my lips but didn't quite put it in my mouth. 'I'm just starting to smoke. Am I supposed to puff on it as you're lighting it?' This, too, I meant as a sign of self-confidence. A woman who was bashful or meek wouldn't just boldly say, *Show me how to do this.*

"He made a slight sound of surprise. 'Here,' he said, 'I'll get it lit.' He took the cigarette back and put it in his own mouth, lit it, and exhaled a thick stream of smoke through his nose. When he handed it back to me, I took it between my thumb and forefinger as I'd seen men do.

"I didn't really want to put the cigarette in my mouth after it had been in his, but this was necessary. I took a brief puff. The smoke in my mouth was warm and tasted a little like raw almonds. When I took a deeper breath, the hot air went down into my chest and I had to suppress a cough.

"I was aware that the man was examining my figure or looking over my clothes. I hadn't changed out of what I'd worn on the bus, and I knew there were sweat fans under my arms, deep folds across my lap, a map of wrinkles where the bodice fit loosely under my slight breasts; the collar of the dress had darkened along the neck edge from the oils in my skin. I was aware, too, that my hair was oily and unkempt, bent in odd directions around my ears and at the back of my head. If I had cared about any of this, I might have explained to him that I'd only just arrived in town after three days and nights on a bus—then he might have held me to a looser standard. But really, I didn't care what he thought.

"From an early age I had known that I was smart rather than pretty, and although for a while I hoped that intelligence would make up in some way for not being attractive and popular, by the time I was thirteen I knew that it mostly did not. Intelligence added an extra dash to a girl who was pretty, but by itself wasn't enough to interest most people, especially men. At fifteen I decided that no man would ever wish to marry me, and I laid out a plan for my life that included that fact. I saw no reason to wear makeup or wave my hair. I kept myself tidy when it was convenient or necessary for employment and didn't worry about it otherwise. Now that I was twenty-two, almost twenty-three, I didn't really care if a stranger looking me over thought I was not much to look at, as the phrase goes.

"The man said, 'You're new?' He thumbed back his hat in a calculated gesture, an imitation of the boyish cowboy heroes in movies. The front of his hair showing beneath the brim of the hat had been cut very straight across with scissors. He was about forty and had a soft belly above his shiny leather belt.

"I knew what he meant: new to Hollywood, new in town. 'No, I've been here a while,' I said. The lie came easily to me. Hollywood bubbled with newcomers, it was a city where their yearnings were almost palpable in the air. I hadn't minded being one of the hopefuls when I was riding on the bus, but I had seen and read enough melodramas to know that even a homely girl could be seduced if she landed in town wearing innocence and gullibility on her face.

"I took another little puff of the cigarette, blew out the smoke, and walked away casually, the way Joan Crawford would have, or Marlene Dietrich."

When she finished reading, I said, "I always figured you had your first cigarette that time we ran into each other in front of the hardware store. Before we started going to the movies together. Back before you went to work for Sunrise."

She laughed. "I wanted you to think I'd been smoking for years. I must not have faked it very well. I don't remember how many cigarettes I'd had by then, but it wasn't a whole pack."

"You looked about thirteen when you smoked. A little kid playing grownup."

"Did I?" She made a small amused sound. "Jesus, I thought I was up-to-the-minute."

At the time the *Vanity Fair* piece came out, Lily was half a year into treatment for cancer. She wrote that story about her first cigarette without making any mention of the cancer raging in her throat or of the surgery that in another year would take away her voice.

TWO

Echol Creek

1923–1925

◆

WHEN THEIR SON BUD WAS BORN, Henry and Martha Frazer were living in Elwha County, buckarooing cows and breaking horses for two old spinster sisters who had a big cattle ranch in the foothills of the Whitehorns. In 1923, when the sisters died six days apart without either of them leaving a will, their ranch went to a cousin living in Spokane, who sold it to a local fellow, who then sold off the cattle and logged off the trees and put most of the cleared land into wheat and sugar beets.

The Frazers might have gone to work for some other rancher in the valley, but a friend of theirs, a woman named Louise, who was related in some way to Elbert Echol, pointed them toward Harney County. Elbert was sixty-five at the time, and his wife had died in the flu epidemic. The Echols had been childless, so he was looking for somebody to take the ranch off his hands, now that he had arthritis and a weak heart. Martha and Henry had been saving up money in a coffee can with the idea of one day buying a few cattle and some acres of their own. They thought it would be long years before they could do that, but Louise told them Elbert was looking for a way to support himself in retirement and he might just carry the paper for somebody he approved of.

It was 140 miles from the Elwha Valley to Echol Creek on rough backcountry roads. The Frazers bought a spring wagon from a farm family moving back east, packed it with everything they owned, hitched it to a team, and drove six days to get there, camping each night by the side of the road. They mounted a chuck wagon on the tailgate and had their meals there. Henry drove the wagon, and Martha, with several horses in a pony string, rode ahead and kept a lookout for automobiles or wagons approaching. Their boy, named Ernest after Henry's stepfather but always called Bud, was not quite three years old. He rode on the saddle in front of his mother. Most of the roads were no more than one lane. When she called a warning and nosed her horses over to the shoulder of the road, Henry pulled the wagon in behind her and waited until the other rig had passed. There wasn't much traffic—a wagon every hour or so, a car two or three times a day.

This whole adventure must have struck some of their friends as foolhardy. They went without knowing whether Elbert Echol would approve of them or whether they would even want his place after looking it over—they wouldn't have been surprised if it turned out to be one of those dryland spreads that couldn't support a cow to fifty acres. But if the Echol place didn't pan out, prospects for finding ranch work in Harney County were no worse than where they had come from, and they had both knocked around a bit before settling in Elwha County and weren't opposed to doing it again. Martha, especially, had the idea they might like to roam the West as itinerant cowhands, along the lines of heroes in the romantic novels she had read. She didn't think a three-year-old child would upend this idea so long as the child could sit a horse.

The Echol ranch, they had been told, was north of Foy, a town that sat on the cross-state highway roughly twelve miles west of the county seat at Burns. Foy wasn't much of a town even in its heyday, but it had a post office and a Grange hall, some buildings around an old rock quarry, and a store offering hardware goods and groceries, a refrigerated case for soda pop, and a gasoline pump for folks driving cars east and west on the highway. While Martha waited with the horses, Henry went into the store to ask the last part of the way to the Echol ranch and came out with an ice cream cone for his son. Then they went on as Henry had been told, north up the Bailey Creek Road five miles to where Elbert Echol's rutted ranch lane veered off to the northwest.

The greater part of Harney County is high desert, a flat basin four thousand feet high and running mostly to sagebrush and juniper, except for the marshland around the shallow basin sink that is Malheur Lake. But it's a big county, sprawling all the way from the California border across the big dry middle of Oregon into the southernmost reach of the Ochoco Mountains. At that far north end of the county there's a clear boundary between the sagebrush flats and the forested uplands, as if somebody has drawn a line as level and straight as a ruler, and most of Elbert Echol's place lay on the high side of the line—foothills country, timbered and steeply cut by draws and canyons.

Martha and Henry didn't know any of this when they first went up there, and the flat sagebrush and scrubland around Foy and the lower part of the Bailey Creek Valley didn't look at all promising to them. Then, after the road forked and they turned off along Echol Creek, the way quickly became nothing more than bad ruts climbing up through a narrow canyon between shelves and steps of basalt. The roadside was choked with dry scrub that hid the creek except at the five or six places where they had to ford. This was in early October, and it hadn't rained, or anyway not to speak of, for more than three months. Dust rose up listlessly behind the tailgate and settled on the underbrush in thick, pale cloaks. They could hear the creek still faintly running, which was the only good sign.

There were no cattle guards in those days, but post-and-wire fences crossed the road three or four times. At each one Martha climbed down and dragged the gate across, waited while Henry drove the wagon through, then brought her horses through and dragged the gate shut again. At the fords where the road crossed the creek, they could sometimes drive straight to the other side, but at other places they had to travel up or down the creek bed to find a low bank where they could drive out.

They weren't particularly aware of the road climbing, but after a mile or so they began to see pines and a few aspens clinging to the rock benches, and knew they must have gone above five thousand feet; gradually the canyon widened and flattened, and the creek came clear of the scrub and fanned out, branching and braiding back and forth in a lacework of shallow channels and sloughs. The road wound for half a mile alongside this watered marsh, through willow groves thick with birds, and then, at the far edge of the park where the land began to rise again toward a ridgetop of big pines and scattered white fir, they came to the last gate. Beyond it was the Echol home place: an old-fashioned log barn, three or four outbuildings, and a small one-story board-and-batten house, its porch rails made of deer and elk antlers.

Elbert had title to just under thirteen hundred acres—not very large as ranches go—and it was remote and half-wild at a time when most parts of the country had been domesticated. The yard was full of discarded and broken equipment, and in recent years the old man had let a lot of things go. His fences and buildings were in need of repair—doors and some of the wall boards were missing on the barn, corral posts were leaning and wouldn't hold an animal for very long. When Martha and Henry rode over the place with him, they saw how skittery and reclusive his mountain-bred cattle were, bolting off through the woods when anybody got close. His hay fields were small and oddly shaped, none of them more than two or three acres, strung out along the creek between steep ridges and scattered on the benches among stands of pine and skinny-legged aspen.

But Elbert had spent years picking those small hay fields clean of rocks, and the water on the ranch was soft and clear and cold from springs and a hand-dug well barely ten feet deep. He had a rain gauge, and he'd been recording the measurements for years, as well as the yields from his fields. If his records could be trusted, most of the ranch could count on twenty inches of rain a year, whereas neighbors down on the flats and along Bailey Creek—the sagebrush country Henry and Martha had driven through on the way up from Foy—were lucky to get eight or ten. In a typical season his small fields planted to wheatgrass or left in wild rye grass and blue joint grass made one heavy cutting of hay, which was enough to feed his cows through the three or four months of winter, and most years he got enough summer rain to regrow the fields for fall grazing or even a second cutting. Above his deeded land was the Ochoco Forest Reserve, where he grazed his cattle most of the summer. Elbert had the senior water rights on Echol Creek, its headwaters far up in the reserve, and the Frazers could see for themselves that this part of the creek was still alive even at the end of summer in a dry year. In the winter months, Elbert told them, there were redband trout and tui chub in the cold flood. And the annual spring overflow of melting snow off the Ochoco Mountains was the water source for all those acres of slough and parkland in the narrow valley below the house.

Neither Henry nor Martha had ever lived as high up as the Echol place, but they were used to gathering cattle from the foothills of the Whitehorn Reserve, and those steep pine ridges behind the Echol home place were more familiar and agreeable to them than the sagebrush flats. Elbert's place was more ranch than they had expected, which they both had known almost as soon as they came through the canyon and caught sight of the wetland park and the ranch buildings.

And it was more ranch than they could expect to pay for. But the old man took a shine to Martha, at least that's what Henry always claimed, and he let them have the place more or less on a handshake. Elbert and his wife, Etta, had built up the ranch together, buying neighbors' farms and homesteads bit by bit, and when they surveyed their land, it was Etta who dragged the chain while he handled the compass — everything they did, they did equally. So it was true that Martha put him in mind of Etta, who had buckarooed cows until she was fifty years old. But also he just wanted the ranch to go to somebody who would take care of it. He could see for himself that these were the right people, and Louise, who was Etta's sister, had told him as much before the Frazers ever showed up in his yard.

In Elwha County they had been just three miles by road from Bingham, a town of a thousand people. The Echol ranch, by those lights, was remote and isolated: they were now three miles up a badly rutted ranch lane from their mailbox, eight miles from any kind of store, twenty miles from Burns, the only town of any size.

They were not cut off from the world. A postman delivered mail all up and down Bailey Creek Road, and Henry or Martha or in later years one of the children rode horseback down the long ranch lane through the canyon to their mailbox two or three times a week to collect what was sometimes a heavy sackful. Henry took the weekly *Burns Gazette* to keep up with county news and stock prices, and Martha, who was a reader, took the monthly *Reader's Digest* and the *Saturday Evening Post* and ordered books from the state library. There were always letters from Henry's family in Baker City and from friends back in Elwha County, and once or twice a year a short note from one of Martha's brothers up in Pendleton.

Even in those first years before they acquired an auto-truck, they made the eight-mile trip to Foy almost every month to buy groceries and goods they couldn't grow or make for themselves. And three or four times a year in dry weather they drove on from Foy to Burns, to take in the Harney County Fair or a livestock auction and to buy goods they weren't able to get at Foy. Every so often on one of those trips they'd see a film at the Desert Theatre on Main Street. They ate popcorn, ice cream cones, hot dogs.

They acquired a motor truck in 1926, shortly before Mary Claudine was born, and around that time Martha traded one of her horses for a two-cycle gasoline-powered washing machine. But for all that, compared to how people were living in most American cities and towns in the 1920s, their life was something out of a western romance, rough and primitive.

A couple of prosperous neighbors—Arlo Gantz was one—had light plants to generate electricity, but power lines wouldn't make it out to the remote corners of Harney County until the 1950s, so the Frazers and most of their neighbors had no electric lights. For the fourteen years they lived on Echol Creek, they relied on kerosene lanterns. Elbert had piped the creek to bring in running cold water to the kitchen sink and the water tank on the back of the stove, but they had an outdoor toilet and no refrigeration. They rented a frozen-food locker from the grocer at Foy, but sometimes in winter they would shovel snow up high on the north wall of the house and bury cream cans filled with meat and milk in the snowbank.

The county graded and oiled the cross-state highway and plowed it after heavy snow in winter, and every so often a farmer or rancher in the valley would take his tractor out to the Bailey Creek Road and blade off a stretch of the ruts that ran north from Foy, but the three miles from the fork up the canyon to the Echol home place had been carved out back in the 1880s, when Elbert first settled there, and it was rough going even in a wagon. At the places where the road crossed the creek, they had to watch out for rocks that had shifted or come down during the last storm in the mountains. The ruts swung wide around the marsh where the canyon opened out, but in spring the lower road through the canyon was a running stream, a branch of the creek, and later in the season, when the creek drew back into its channel, there were washouts and water bars in the road, and certain places stayed muddy for weeks.

Back in Elwha County, when they were first married, Henry had been the foreman for the old spinsters' cattle ranch and Martha broke horses for people up and down the valley. After they moved to Harney County and onto the Echol Creek property, they divided up the ranch work more or less along those same lines.

Henry handled the books — he had a better head for numbers — and since he was the cowman he bought the bulls and decided which of the yearling calves to sell and what price to go with. He particularly set out to make Echol's wild cattle easier to handle: when he sold animals in the fall, he culled the renegade cows and the fighting bulls and kept back the gentler heifers. In his opinion a good cowboy on a good horse ought to be able to turn a cow or calf back without roping it, but he thought there must have been a lot of roping and choking at the old man's gathers, which had made those cows leery of a man on horseback. Henry made it a point to ride through the herds every day so the cows would grow accustomed to him — he wanted to be able to slip through and get a good look at them without stirring them up, and if he saw a sick cow he wanted to be able to ease it out of the herd so it could be doctored without raising a big ruckus. At roundup and when he was making the rough cut to shape the herd for market, he left his rope on the saddle for the most part until he got the cattle penned. And over the years his cattle grew more manageable.

Martha had a particular understanding and knowledge of horses. She'd always had a gift and a preference for breaking them to saddle and training them to work cattle, but the foothills of the Ochocos in the 1920s were thickly settled with homesteaders — farmers who didn't have much use for a saddle horse but were still plowing, harvesting, and logging with horses and mules, using them to haul wood and pull wagons. So on the Echol ranch she gave up her cowboy bias, began training horses and mules to drive and harness, and in some years the sales of her animals amounted to half their income.

The other job she took on was calving the heifers, because Henry didn't have much patience for the young cows delivering their first calves: "It ought to be natural, but sometimes I think they're just too stupid to do it right," he liked to say, which she took more or less personally.

"Well, if you had ever been through this, you would be more understanding," she told him. She had labored for almost twenty hours to deliver their son, and she wondered if, in Henry's opinion, she had moaned and complained more than was seemly.

In the calving season she brought the heifers to the pasture close by the home place and walked among them every couple of hours in the daytime and went out at least twice at night with a lantern. Most years they calved just twenty-five or thirty heifers, and Martha became acquainted with each one. She walked every corner of the field and looked under the brush, because some heifers would try to find a hiding spot to have their calf. She learned to look and look again and to watch especially for ones who seemed distraught or confused— this was something she was sympathetic to. When they were close to calving she brought them into the pen and talked them through it.

She could pull the easy ones, but she called on Henry if she ran into trouble. He could usually figure out what to do if a calf was hung up, but every so often one would be stuck, too swollen to pass through, and then it was Henry who handled cutting it up and pulling it out in parts—which Martha could hardly bear to watch. She didn't like to see any of them die. Whenever she lost one, she tried to think if there was anything she could have done to save it. She became better and better at the calving each year, and she grew adept at getting orphan calves to drink from a bucket of milk, but there were always some who died in spite of her best efforts. When she was tired from lack of sleep, the death of a cow or calf would sometimes cause her to sit down and cry. In the beginning, Henry tried to tease her out of it. "Your babies," he called the heifers. But when he saw how it bothered her, he let her be. "That's just how it is," he told her every year. "You're doing everything right, honey, but that's just how it is."

The Echol Creek hay fields were too small and scattered to warrant machinery, so all the years they lived there they had a horse-drawn mower and rake pulled by a pair of half-Belgian mules. In August 1925, just after Bud turned five years old, Henry was getting a second cutting off one of the hay fields along the creek bottom when an owl flew up from the grass underneath the mules. The bird beat its wings right in the eyes of both animals, and they half-reared and then bolted. This was ordinarily a steady old team, and the mules might have slowed and calmed before going very far, but they ran the mower into a shallow ravine at the edge of the field and the wheels came up hard against the side of it, which threw Henry from the seat. He kept hold of the lines, which would have been the right thing to do if he hadn't fallen in such a way that it yanked the mules, who were already upset, and this caused them to back up the mower in worry and confusion. Henry went to some trouble to keep away from the sickle bar, but one of the mower's wheels went over his leg and one of the mules stepped on his shoulder. He let go of the lines finally, and when the mules found themselves free they took off straight for the house.

Martha was working with a young colt in a pen behind the barn, and Bud was riding up and down the roadway on his mother's old mare, Dolly. He was pretending that certain rocks and clumps of trees were cows and trying to get Dolly to pretend to herd them. When the mower and team clattered into the yard, he turned Dolly to head them off, just for practice, but when Martha shouted at him to get down from the horse he slid right off and stood there waiting while his mother came quickly out of the pen and across the yard to him. He was afraid he had done something wrong—she was particular about Dolly, in consideration of the mare's age and old injuries.

She hardly looked at Bud, though; she went straight to the mower and bent over the sickle teeth looking for blood. Then she straightened and said, "Bring the team into the barn, Bud, water them, and then go in the house and stay there." He was too little to unhook the mules from the mower and she didn't have the time to do it herself, but she didn't want the mules to have to stand there in the hot sun in the yard. She didn't know how long she'd be gone.

She took the reins from him and walked Dolly to the big stump her son used as a mounting block. The saddle he was riding wasn't child-size, but the stirrups had been shortened way up; she had to hoist herself onto the horse from the mounting block and then let her legs hang down stirrupless. She was five months pregnant. Henry didn't like her to ride when she was carrying a child so she hadn't been on a horse for more than two months. Her belly rested uncomfortably against the swells and horn of the saddle.

"Go on now, Bud, take care of Mike and Prince. I'll be back in a little while." She put Dolly into a trot up the creek trail to the hay fields, but then right away she had to slow to a walk—the baby inside her just couldn't stand the jouncing.

It wasn't a long way, no more than half a mile, and when she came through the willow brush at the edge of the half-mown field she could see Henry standing on one leg, leaning hard on a stick he must have picked up off the ground. From the way the grass was roughed up, she knew he had managed to hobble only a couple of yards from where the mower had thrown him off.

"I wish you wouldn't ride," he called to her before she had quite reached him.

"I wouldn't have to ride if you'd managed to keep your seat on the mower," she called back. His face was dirty and a bruise had started on his chin, and the frown he was wearing was one he brought out only for broken bones and serious money worries, but he was upright and all his limbs were still attached. There wasn't any blood, but the lower half of his pant leg was dirtied and torn. She said, "I hope you didn't break your leg."

"I guess I might have. Damn mower ran me over. And one of the mules stepped on this here shoulder."

She swung a leg awkwardly over the saddle and slid off the horse. "Can you get up on Dolly?"

"I could if those stirrups was let down."

He stood on one leg, leaning against the horse, while she worked the stiff leather straps. Henry had punched extra holes with an awl so the stirrups could be shortened enough for a four-year-old boy, but those holes were so tight they gave her trouble. When she finally got both sides down, she said, "Can you get yourself up now?" She was a strong woman and tall as a man, but Henry wouldn't have wanted her to boost him onto the horse. He wasn't the sort of husband who ruled his wife, but he stood his ground on a few things, and he was adamant that she wasn't to do any heavy lifting—nothing heavier than a saddle—now that she was five months pregnant.

He couldn't put his weight on his bad leg, so he had to lean into Dolly and lever with his arms until his chest was resting halfway onto the horse's back, with both legs dangling off the ground, before he could toe the stirrup with his good foot and lift himself onto the saddle. It was a hell of a job, and all that wrestling around wasn't good for his shoulder. A swearword Martha's dad had been partial to, a word she had never heard from her husband, popped out of his mouth in the middle of a string of more familiar curses. When he finally got his bad leg over and settled himself onto the saddle, he was pale and sweating. "Well, hell. Now that I'm up here I don't know if this is the best thing. That leg is gonna bang against the horse when she steps out."

Martha went around to that side of Dolly and took hold of Henry's pant leg near the hem and lifted gently until his leg was held in a kind of hammock well away from the horse. "I'll walk along like this," she said.

It wasn't a perfect arrangement. Henry sat crooked on the saddle, hunched over and grimacing every time Dolly took a step. He could feel the broken bone in his lower leg wriggling loosely, which made him slightly sick to his stomach.

At one point Martha said, "I wish we had a truck. We'll have to go to town to get your leg set, and it'll take all day and half the night in the wagon."

Martha had been advocating for an auto-truck almost from the day they moved onto the ranch. It was nearly twenty miles to the nearest doctor and the hospital in Burns, and a motor would shorten the trip by half. But sometime before she and Henry met, Henry had been riding with his brother in his brother's brand-new Model T Ford when the car overturned on an icy road and Jim was killed. Now, a dozen times a year, Henry found a reason to say that horses always started right up and they never ran out of gas and you didn't get greasy fooling around with them. It had come as a surprise to him, and in some way an affront, that his wife didn't mind getting greasy and didn't mind fooling around with machines. She always had had a gift for working with animals, and it seemed to him that her interest in machinery stood at variance with that.

"Well, I won't be much use to you with a broke leg, so maybe you ought to just shoot me and save yourself the long trip to town."

He was peeved at himself, which she knew. She said, "I would, but I guess you can still stand at the stove even if your leg is in plaster, and I like your cooking better than mine." After a moment she reached up and cupped her hand around the fist he was holding against his thigh. He opened his hand and squeezed her fingers briefly. Then he let go, and made a loose, unhappy gesture in the air.

"Owl flew up right under them. Scared the hell out of me too. What the hell! An owl in broad daylight, sleeping on the ground." It wasn't a question.

When they got back to the yard, Bud pushed open the screen door and came out of the house, but when he saw his father's face he stayed on the porch, shy of coming nearer. He had one time seen his mother thrown from a horse so hard she turned white and her eyes rolled back in her head, and he'd seen his father bleeding from a deep cut in the meat of his hand. In coming years he would see his parents hurt often enough to grow almost accustomed to it. But at this point in his life he was still badly scared by any such thing.

"Bud, go in the house and get the quilts and blankets off our bed and the pillows and bring them out to the porch and then you go make some sandwiches and bring those out too. Make three. Do you know how many three is?"

"One for me and one for you and one for Dad."

"That's right. Now go on. Don't cut yourself, slicing the meat."

She walked Dolly close to the porch so that when Henry got down from the horse he would be able to sit right down on the steps. He swung his good leg over and came off on the mare's wrong side and rested his weight briefly on Martha's shoulders to steady himself before he sat.

"You'd better help me get this boot off," he said, "before the foot swells up and we have to cut it off."

There wasn't any way to do it without hurting him. He gripped his leg at the knee and she squatted down in front of him and took hold of his boot in both hands and eased it off slowly. He didn't yell, but he hissed through his teeth, and his knuckles turned white from squeezing around his leg. When she finally had the boot off, he leaned back against a porch post with a glazed look and she watched him for a minute to be sure he didn't pass out. Then she stripped the tack off Dolly and turned her out to the pasture, went into the barn and unhooked the mules from the mower, hitched them to the spring wagon, and led the team up to the house. She gathered up the blankets Bud had piled on the porch and spread them on the floorboards behind the wagon seat.

By the time Bud came out again, carrying the sandwiches in a lard tin, Henry had managed to get himself into the back of the wagon. He sat crosswise with his leg propped on the pillows and his back against the sidewall, which was how Bud himself often rode. The ordinariness of it reassured the boy somewhat.

Martha took the lard tin from him and helped him climb to the high seat, and then she climbed up beside him. "Can I drive?" he asked, because he had recently driven the team for the first time, going into Foy for groceries. She didn't answer him except to shake her head. She took the reins and clucked to the mules, and Bud twisted around to look at his father, who smiled slightly and said, "Hey there, Buddy," but nothing about letting him drive the wagon, nothing about the reason they were heading off to town at this time of day, late in the afternoon and near suppertime.

The ranch lane in the month of August was hardened ruts, a rough ride, and Martha drove the three miles at a deliberate walk, but when they got onto the Bailey Creek Road she coaxed the mules a bit faster, quick-stepping so the wagon rumbled and bumped. Henry held on to the sideboards and gritted his teeth. At Foy, Martha pulled over and went into the store and phoned ahead to the hospital. It would be after dark, maybe as late as ten o'clock, she told the woman who answered, but could a doctor wait there to set Henry's leg? Then they turned east onto the highway.

She had accustomed the mules to the roar of car engines and the honking of horns, but she didn't trust drivers to give up the middle of the road, so she slowed and pulled to the side whenever a car came up behind them or passed them going west. A broken shinbone wasn't a matter of life or death, but she didn't want the doctor to get tired of waiting and go on home, so when the road was clear of cars she asked Mike and Prince for a jog-trot. When she could, she kept this up for a mile or so, then walked them three or four, then trotted them again. The mules were in good shape and had good feet, and they would have been able to go on trotting longer, but the old wagon made so much racket, even on the graded road, that she worried a wheel might come off. And there was Henry in the back, who wouldn't have said so but couldn't stand the jarring for very long. And for that matter the baby inside her, forcing a sour bile behind her breastbone whenever she trotted the team.

When Bud said he was hungry, Martha didn't stop the wagon but let him bring out the lard tin and pass around the sandwiches, which were thick, uneven slices of roast beef between thick slices of biscuit smeared with too much butter. The biscuits were stale—Henry had made them two or three days earlier—and Martha knew the sandwiches would have gone down easier if she had thought to bring cider or milk or a jar of spring water.

Henry didn't eat much of his, and when he offered half to his son, Martha looked over her shoulder and studied her husband. It was dusk already, and in the failing daylight he looked about as white as skimmed milk. "Are you feeling sick to your stomach?"

"I just don't have an appetite."

"If you want me to slow down, I will."

"It's all right." He winked at her. "But if you'd've let me buy a truck like I wanted to, we'd already be there."

She tightened her mouth. "You think you're joking, but if you were dying instead of just stubborn we would never get to a doctor in time in this damn wagon."

She turned back around, and for several minutes neither of them said anything. She had been tired and cranky almost from the beginning of this pregnancy, and Henry thought she was mad at him for being hurt. This wasn't true, although she was dreading the long night ahead without any sleep. She wasn't in any mood for his joking.

"Bud, if you're about to fall asleep I want you to climb in back with your dad and get under the blankets."

"I'm not," he said, but he didn't straighten up from leaning into Martha's side.

"Come down here with me, Buddy." Henry patted the rag quilt spread across his lap.

Martha nudged the boy away from her, and he made a glum sound and climbed over the seat and down to the floorboards. He had forgotten all about his father's leg by this time, and when he started to climb into Henry's lap, Henry made a sharp hissing sound and pushed him off. "Damn it, Bud, watch out."

The boy scrambled back and made himself small in a corner of the wagon bed, his thin arms wrapped around his knees.

Martha turned and looked at them both. Her son hadn't been yelled at very often. He wasn't crying, but his mouth was puckered, holding it in. She thought of reaching a hand down to stroke the top of his head but made up her mind not to. Henry was hunched over, rocking slightly, and she could hear his breath, the shallow panting effort as he waited for the pain to ebb. After a minute she said, "Bud, be careful around your dad. He got hurt when the mower ran over him," and she turned back around and gave her attention to driving.

In another few minutes, after Henry's breathing had slowed and quieted, he said, "Bud, come over here now, I need you to reach one of these blankets up to your mother. She'll be cold when the sun gets all the way down." The boy looked sidelong at his dad without lifting his head, and then he stood and loosely bunched the gray wool blanket and pushed it up to his mother. When he sat again, Henry held out the edge of the rag quilt to make room for the boy next to him. He had to wait a minute, but finally Bud scooted in.

The streets coming into Burns were entirely empty and dark, but several windows at the front of the hospital were still lit and some of the Catholic nuns were working inside even at half past nine. No doctor was waiting, but the nuns behaved as if these proceedings were commonplace. They brought Henry inside in a wheelchair, and one of them took an x-ray of his leg and of his shoulder where Prince had stepped on it, and a different nun then set his leg in plaster. Afterward, when she pushed the heavy sleeves of her robe above her elbows and washed the wet white plaster from her hands, Henry saw that her forearms were ropy with muscle, and it crossed his mind to wonder what the life of a nun was like.

She then explored the lurid bruise on his chest to satisfy herself that the x-ray had not missed a crack in the clavicle. He sat meekly, half-naked in his underwear, as she ran her cold, wet hands across his chest and back. He was suffering too much to be embarrassed. She was very strong, and she pushed her fingers so hard into the sore places that he couldn't hold back grunts of pain.

Finally she stood away from him and rolled down her sleeves. "I think it must be pointless to say so, but you shouldn't sit on a horse until the cast comes off your leg, and you ought to do no lifting or pulling with that shoulder for six weeks." She was accustomed to men who did ranch work, men who hardly waited for the plaster to dry before climbing back in the saddle. Of course she knew there might not be anyone else to get the work done — she had grown up in a family like that herself.

While all this was going on, Martha waited in the lobby with Bud, who rested his head in her lap and fell asleep. A man was also waiting there with two small girls who might have been twins. The man's face was drawn down with tiredness, and the girls too were heavy-eyed. Their father tried to coax them to lie down on the bench and sleep "like that little boy over there," but they squirmed and whined restlessly. Finally the man took hold of both girls, gripping each by a shoulder, and shook them roughly and bent close to them and said something Martha couldn't hear, and after that they sat on either side of him on the bench and stared dully down at the floor and were quiet. Martha leaned back against the wall and closed her eyes, but she wasn't able to get comfortable enough to doze off.

Around midnight one of the nuns came out and spoke softly to the man, and he nodded his head with an expression of relief and then herded the girls out the door into the night.

It was after two o'clock before a nun rolled Henry into the lobby in a wheelchair. They had cast his leg from the ankle to just below the knee. His bare foot was bruised-looking and swollen, childishly vulnerable. His pant leg had been opened up to make room for the cast, but Martha saw that someone had been careful to pick out the stitching along the inside seam so the pants could be sewn back up afterward and the pants not ruined. The heavy denim was torn where the mower had caught him, but not so much it couldn't be patched.

The woman pushing the chair said, "Here is your husband, Mrs. Frazer. You will need to bring him back to have the cast off in two months. And keep him from hard work until then if you can."

Martha thought Henry might make a joking remark about leaving the hard work to his wife, but he only looked at her, apologetic and miserable, and shook his head. *Two months.*

Martha had been sitting there worrying about the four horses she was breaking for Arlo Gantz, none of them finished yet, and the haying only half done, and the fall roundup not even started, and only half as much stove wood cut and split as they would need to see them through the winter. She would keep Henry off a horse as long as she could, but that would mean finding chores to occupy his time. She hadn't really been joking when she said she'd put him to work cooking supper, and if he could stand and hobble around a little, she thought he could wash the dishes. As soon as he could limp out to the sheds, she'd make him a chore list: sharpening sickle teeth for the mower, feeding the chickens, sorting bolts, washers, nuts, and whatnot into coffee cans, fixing broken harness, finishing up some minor carpentry that had gone undone for months or years.

She could finish the mowing herself, though it meant she'd have to put off breaking the horses. And without two of them to do the work, it would be a battle to get the hay put up and hauled down to the home place before the elk got into it. She could hire one of their homestead neighbors to split firewood if he would take a steer in payment. Arlo Gantz was their neighbor on the northeast side, and they had always traded help with the Gantz family at roundup. She hoped when Arlo got word of Henry's broken leg he would show up with his boys to help her with the fall gather without expecting any of the Frazers to show up for theirs. But Henry wouldn't want to sit by and watch them doing everything, and if there was early snow she knew he would be wanting to ride up into the Ochocos to look for any stray cows they might have missed.

Her mind went to the hay field up at Lindsey Bench. It was so remote from the home place that Henry always left the stack right there. This meant feeding some cattle there as well, so he scattered salt on the ridges and in the side canyons all summer to keep cattle nearby, and when winter came on Martha brought some of her horses up there. Henry left a team and sled at the bench all winter, in a small corral with a three-sided shelter, and every day he rode a saddle horse up to the bench, harnessed the team, pitched a load of hay onto the sled, and then forked it in a loose oval. The cattle and horses spending the winter there would come up to feed when they heard the sled. Then he watered the team at a spring down in the draw, fed them, left them in the corral for the night, and rode his horse back home. Every day.

Two months.

She slipped out from under Bud, laid him down gently on the bench, and stood. She was dressed in men's overalls and boots and a man's work shirt that fit too closely across her belly, but the nun's face did not register any bit of disapproval. "I don't know what the bill is," Martha said quietly to the woman, "but we came away from the house without a bank check." She didn't say that they would need to sell some calves in order to raise the money.

The front of the nun's habit was spattered with gobbets of plaster. Her white wimple, fixed close around her chin and cheeks, made her face look pinched. She said without inflection, "Come with me. We'll tell Sister Louise at the desk that you will try to pay when you come in October." She tucked her hands into the folds at the front of her costume and walked back down the corridor. Her shoes on the floorboards made no sound at all.

Martha followed her, while Henry waited in the wheelchair beside his son asleep on the hard bench. When Martha finally reappeared, he got himself up from the chair and stood on one leg with a hand braced against the wall while she woke Bud. The boy wanted to be carried, but she stood him on his feet and then went over to Henry so he would have her shoulder to lean against. They shuffled a couple of steps, but then the nun who had cast his leg reappeared, walking swiftly toward them with a pair of crutches. She held the door for them as they went out.

On the long drive home Martha kept the mules to a plodding walk. The night was clear and cold, the sky thickly peppered with stars, and a quarter-moon lit up the sagebrush on the hills. Henry and Bud slept in the back of the wagon, and Martha might have been able to doze on the seat—the mules would have been all right on that straight road—but she felt awake now, gone past the point of needing to sleep. She looked out at the dark land and turned a few things over in her head.

The doctor who had delivered Bud was back in Elwha County, and now that they were living so far away from any town, she didn't know how she would find a doctor near enough to help her when this one was ready to be born. She wasn't mad at Henry for being hurt, but she wanted him to get over his fear of machinery and of learning to drive a motor.

She had seen trucks that were nothing but a cabin and a cargo box cobbled onto an automobile chassis. If she could find a chassis and motor and get it running, she thought Henry might be able to build the rest. She wondered if he might be able to start on it even while his leg was still in a cast.

THREE

◆

10

IT WAS STILL DARK, must have been four or four-thirty, when Harold turned on the light in the bedroom that first morning. Hugh just rolled out of bed and put on his clothes in silence without asking who the hell was sleeping on the other bed, so I got dressed too and followed him out through the dark kitchen to the yard without either of us saying a word. Harold had already turned on a couple of floodlights mounted high up on the feed shed and on the house, and he was out there with a clipboard, looking over the horses. He didn't say anything to me, so I followed Hugh and helped him pitch hay to all the animals. Hugh finally did say half a dozen words to me, but they were all about how much hay to toss and where to toss it. I thought his silence had to do with us not knowing each other, but it was just that he never had much to say in the morning until he'd had five or six cups of coffee. Well, I was used to that with my parents, so it wasn't hard for me to leave him to his quiet.

While we were feeding the horses, Jake showed up in his Chevrolet. He went right over to Harold, who handed him the clipboard, and then the two of them walked around the corrals eyeballing the horses and talking together quietly about which ones should go to which places. They had orders for three horses at one place and seven at another, which meant the Dodge would have to make double trips again; I guess they were also talking about where to send the new kid, which was me. When Hugh and I finished up with the hay, Harold called over to us, "Go on in and have something to eat. I'll be there in a bit." So we went into the house and ate a couple of slices of toast and bolted down two quick cups of coffee as we hunched over the filthy breadboard in the kitchen.

Harold never did come in to eat, and when we went back out to the yard he said, "Hugh, go fetch me the leathers for Dewey and Betty, and while you're at it show Bud the tack barn and get him acquainted with what's where."

What Harold called the tack barn wasn't strictly speaking a barn but a three-walled windowless shed with the most saddles in one place that I had ever seen. Wooden saddle trees were nailed three high along all the walls, and harness of every kind hung from knobs and hooks wherever there was space. Saddle pads and blankets were piled high on a stool in the corner. Most of the saddles were just trail saddles, nothing meant for roping or cutting out cows. There were little faded pencil notes written on the butt end of each tree naming the two or three horses a particular saddle would fit, and names written right on the wood walls next to the bridles. "Here's Dewey's saddle," Hugh said, "but see here, the names are writ down so you know it'd fit on Lewis or Injun too. Harold finagles things so he's not sending out two horses that need the same saddle." He hoisted Dewey's saddle and pointed at another. "Grab that one, it's Betty's. Get her bridle too, it's hanging there somewhere. And a couple of saddle pads off that stack there."

The shed smelled strongly of dust and leather and pitchy wood and bat guano. There were dust webs everywhere, even on certain of the saddles, and white bird shit on the crosspieces of the rafters. In that respect it was like every barn I'd ever been in—you sure wouldn't have known you were ten minutes by bus from Hollywood and Vine or the neon front of Grauman's Chinese Theatre. That was how I always felt, living in Hollywood, working with horses: the strangeness of those two worlds occupying the same ground.

Harold's horses knew the routine: when he pointed to the one he wanted, any of us could walk into the corral and slip a bridle on him and lead him out, it was that easy. Mostly they were easy to load, too, but I would learn later that every so often it could get tricky. The big trailer had a wide ramp with no sides, and you'd start a horse up the ramp and then just toss the rope over his neck and he'd trot on inside to join the others. Most of them even knew to arrange themselves tail to head. But every so often you'd get one who was new to the whole business, or one who'd decide he just wasn't in the mood to go in. Halfway up the ramp he'd make a sudden U-turn or jump off the side, and he could be right back on top of you before you had time to move out of his way. That happened often enough to keep all of us looking out for it.

Which was almost, but not quite, the trouble I got into that first morning.

Harold rattled off the names of the horses he wanted Hugh and Jake to load into the big livestock trailer, and then he pointed to a gray horse named Guy and said I should put him in the two-horse rig. Well, I didn't have much experience loading horses, which might have been the problem, or Guy had made up his mind he wasn't going anywhere that day. I led him partway up the ramp and then he just planted his feet. The trailer was small, but it was an open-roofed contraption with side rails, so it wasn't like I was leading him into a dark hole. I wrestled with him a while, pulling and coaxing until I just got tired of it. I waited until nobody was looking and then tied the shank of the lead to the front bar of the trailer, took a couple of steps down the ramp and swung my boot up in a short, sharp kick to Guy's belly. It wasn't how I'd been taught, but I had picked up some bad habits lately. Bad habits and a dark outlook. Animals might as well get used to hard times was more or less what I thought. Suffering went along with being alive.

Guy squealed and lunged ahead into the trailer, and when I

jumped out of his way my boot caught the edge of the ramp and I went down hard on the trailer floor with the horse over me, spooked and snorting. He was trying to keep from stepping on me, which I knew, but it amounted to a lot of dancing and banging around. Then he started backing himself out of the trailer and his left hind leg went over the edge of the ramp, which panicked him, and he began throwing his head up, fighting the tie and rearing off his front feet. I was underneath him, half on my back, trying to roll out of his way, but I couldn't get any purchase, squeezed in there along the wall of the trailer, and I was still pretty banged up and stiff from the fight the day before. I had one time seen a bronc rider stomped almost to death when the saddle slipped loose and he went down in the chute, caught between the horse and the sideboards, and I guess that's what went through my mind.

Just about then Jake climbed over the side of the trailer and dropped down in front of Guy and began making a crooning noise, words that weren't quite words, or maybe words in another language, and he cupped both hands around the horse's muzzle, sort of cradling his big head with his knuckles, and Guy suddenly quieted. In fact, he put his jaw on Jake's shoulder and closed his eyes. I had seen my mother work a kind of magic with unbroke horses, but I'd never seen anything like what Jake did, and it was then I decided a Jew could damn well make a cowboy.

I crawled out of the way and stood up leaning against the side of the trailer, and Harold called out, "Everything all right over there?" and I yelled back, "Yeah." I was trying to quit shaking, although that's not how I would have put it at the time. Jake stood there a couple of minutes, holding Guy and talking to him in a low voice with his mouth right up against the blaze on the horse's head, in that language I never had heard before, which now I'm thinking might have been Yiddish. Then he backed Guy out of the trailer, bent down to get a look at the horse's hind leg where he'd scraped himself on the edge of the ramp, and finally raised up and looked over at me and said, "You okay?"

I had a pretty good bruise where the horse had stepped on my thigh and a scraped-up elbow from hitting the side of the trailer—the same elbow I'd bloodied in the fight. But I had grown up ranching, and in that life you learn early that it's not worth complaining unless you think you might need an ambulance or a surgeon. I was used to my dad asking, "Where does it hurt?" and then, no matter what I said, nodding like this was good news, and saying, "Lucky it's a long way from your heart."

I told Jake, "Yeah, nothing broke."

He looked tired already, like we were at the end of the day instead of the start. "Well, good. I'm gonna bring up another horse to load. Guy's had about all the excitement he can stand today." He walked off toward the corrals with Guy leaning up against him, pressing his head into the bend of the man's arm.

I was only at Diamond about four months, and I never got to know Jake Reichl that well—we were usually working different locations, and he always headed down the hill to his family as soon as the horses were put up at night. But I remember him.

He had grown up in Cleveland, I think it was, and his dad had a drayage that still used draft horses even into the twenties and early thirties, so he'd been around horses all his life. I guess that didn't make him a cowboy, but Harold hadn't been kidding about his touch with horses. He was the best goddamn one of us when it came to calming a kinky horse. He had been working for Harold better than five years and was unofficially the boss when Harold wasn't around, but I never did know if he got paid more than Hugh and me. If he did, it couldn't have been much. He and his wife had two little kids and lived in a bungalow apartment somewhere around Silver Lake—they must have always been worried about finding the money to pay the phone bill or the water bill. But you never heard Jake talk about money troubles or gripe about hard times. I think he was just grateful to be doing work he didn't mind, for a boss who was easy to get along with.

One thing I remember pretty well: when I'd been at Diamond six or seven weeks, he had all of us to his place for Sunday supper. He didn't give a reason for it, except he said his wife was cooking a pot roast.

Their apartment was at the end of a row of six, the other five places occupied by families like theirs, the men all grips or carpenters or electricians working in the movie business. The wives worked as extras and bit players when they could—they needed the walk-on money to make ends meet—but it meant listening for the phone every day in case Central Casting called with a part. The women kept an ear out for each other's telephones if one of them had shopping to do or a doctor visit, and they watched each other's children when they had a casting call.

Leah must have been thirty years old, which I thought at the time was on the way to middle-aged, but she had a mane of curly dark hair and she teased me about being tall and handsome and having to fight off the girls, which embarrassed me some and made me fall in love with her the way boys fall in love with their pretty schoolteacher.

Their kids, a boy named Noah and a girl, Miriam, whom they called Mimi, were around five and six years old. Jake was easy with his children, wrestling and playing with them, hugging and loving them up, unselfconscious about it, even with all of us sitting around the living room watching him. When I saw Jake with his kids, it brought up things I had just about forgotten: my dad holding me on his lap when I was maybe four years old, his work-rough hands and the hay-and-cow smell of his shirt, the feel of his stubble when he nuzzled his face into my hair, and a cold-weather memory of sitting on a horse in front of my mother, buttoned inside her coat, leaning against the warm pillows of her breasts and peering out through the gaps in the wool. Her arm coming around me when the horse stumbled.

There was ease and kindness in our family, and tenderness that we all understood was love, but I don't think I ever heard my parents tell each other "I love you," and I know they never said it to their kids, at least not in our growing-up years. In our family, and all of the families I knew, you could pet and kiss puppies and kittens, foals and young children, but a child who was eight or nine was too old for that kind of open affection. When I watched Jake with his children, I remembered being ten, a big kid finished with cuddling, watching Mary Claudine, who was not quite five, snuggling into Dad's lap. I remembered a longing I couldn't then have articulated.

Along about 1946, a year or so after I mustered out of the army, I got in touch with Harold to thank him for some things that had gone unsaid while I was working for him, and he told me Jake had died on Okinawa. He'd been dead a couple of years by that time, but I wrote to Leah anyway, a few clumsy lines about being sorry and not knowing what to say. I was living up at Vanport at the time, going to school on the GI Bill, and by then I had started to get serious about drawing. I sent her a little sketch I had made, of Jake holding his two children in his lap and Leah sitting next to him. It wasn't a good likeness—I only had memory to go on—but Leah wrote right back.

She said good things about my drawing and nothing at all about the war or Jake's death, but I guess my letter must have opened up a window. Maybe she didn't have anybody else to talk to about Jake, because she wrote quite a bit about those years when Jake had worked for Harold. She told me he would leave the apartment at half past three every morning while she slept, and she always tried to wait up for him in the evening if the children hadn't tired her out too much. When he came in, she heated up his supper and they sat at the kitchen table while she told him quietly whatever funny thing Noah or Mimi had said or what they'd been doing that day, and she'd ask about his work; then they'd pull down the wall bed in the living room to sleep—they let the children have the one bedroom so Jake wouldn't wake them when he had to rise so early.

He often saw his children only one day a week because Harold had us working the other six. I didn't know back then that Jews went to synagogue on Saturday, but Harold had us working most Saturdays so if Jake was a religious Jew, he couldn't have been much of one during the years he worked at Diamond. Leah said they both knew he was lucky to have steady work—a lot of men were out of work, there were camps of jobless men in the city parks, and families living in tents. And Harold always treated Jake with respect. But in Leah's own childhood, her father had been a ghost in the house, going out in the early morning and coming in late at night—he had worked a grocer's long hours—and Leah didn't want that to be her children's memory.

"Jake didn't want it either. On Friday nights he tried to get away from Diamond early enough for the Shabbat blessing, and I tried to keep the children up late to wait for him; but lots of times he had to lay his hand on our sleeping children's heads and whisper the prayer in the darkness of their bedroom."

She wrote that Jake's clothes always smelled of horses, and when he undressed for bed he set his folded pants and shirt on a wooden chair in the corner of the room: he didn't want his clothes stinking up the closet.

In my letter I had brought up the time we all went to their apartment for dinner. She remembered it. "I made pot roast, and sent you all home with chocolate cake wrapped up in waxed paper." None of us had known it, but she had made the cake for Jake's birthday. He was thirty that day, and he had told Leah that he wanted to have a little celebration, a dinner party. She didn't say why he wanted to invite the men he worked with. She didn't say if he had any better friends than the three of us.

And she wrote about horses, the Belgians Jake had grown up with in Cleveland, how they had big feathery legs, and in the winter when they got sweaty, each one of the hairs would frost, and they'd get icicles hanging down around their mouths and noses. "Jake always said they were beautiful when they were frosty all over. It never got cold enough for that in California, and I think he missed it." His father kept the horses in a barn just off the south-side rail yards, but there was a drayage company over on Pike Avenue that kept horses in a bare field, and when Jake was a boy he had wondered what those horses thought about when they were left outside in the middle of a winter night or standing in deep mud in the spring when the ground thawed out. He always wondered if Hollywood horses were grateful for the mild weather. When he saw a horse standing in a pasture alone, looking off toward the horizon, maybe looking toward the sun setting behind some trees, he wondered what they were thinking, whether they felt lonely. "Jake had a love for horses," Leah wrote in her letter. "I guess you must have known that."

11

THAT FIRST MORNING, when we had all the horses loaded, we threw the saddles and the rest of the tack and gear in the back of the two trucks, and then Harold had me ride along with him in the Dodge while he sent Hugh and Jake in another direction with the bigger load. The dog jumped in the bed of the truck with the saddles. It wasn't quite daylight but already growing hot, and we rode with the windows rolled down. Harold didn't talk much except to say we were going up to Bronson Canyon, where one of the Poverty Row studios was setting up to shoot in the park, and he planned to leave me there with the two horses while he went back to Diamond to pick up a third one. I didn't know Harold at all yet, but he seemed to be brooding about something, and shortly I started brooding too, thinking maybe he'd seen the whole business with Guy and was feeling he'd made a mistake taking me on. I didn't know where the hell I'd be sleeping that night if Harold decided to boot me out of the house.

I guess the TV shows still use Bronson sometimes when they want to give an impression of rugged wilderness without bothering to leave town—I spot it every so often on a show I'm watching. There are a couple of caves up there, left over from when the place was a quarry, plus a small, bowl-shaped piece of ground with a lot of rocks, a few trees, a small stream, and some quarry rubble. It's tucked into the west side of Griffith Park, and you can see the big HOL-LYWOOD sign on Mount Lee if you stand at certain places in the bowl—they always have to angle the camera to keep that out of the shot. It was a favorite location for the cheap studios making westerns back then, when the sign still said HOLLYWOODLAND. Diamond hauled horses up there a couple times a week.

We unloaded the horses and took them to some skimpy willow shade, and Harold said darkly, "Try to keep out of trouble until I get back." I thought this was a jab at me, but then he gestured toward an actor in fancy boots and a pale blue pearl-button shirt, sitting in his car with the door propped open. "That's Dick Hayes. If he's drunk, he'll be mean. Keep the horses clear of him if you can, but don't lose me any business. If push comes to shove, you let him shove. To a point, anyway."

I imagine this was what he'd been brooding on in the car. The horses had been hired out to Merit Pictures, and Dick Hayes was Merit's big star. Harold had had dealings with Dick, so he had the view that leaving me alone with him was the same as throwing me into the deep end of the pool. Hayes was a genuine horseman, you could say that for him, but when he got into an argument with the producer or the director about how a picture should be made, he'd show up drunk and take out his frustrations on the horses. Well, I didn't know any of this yet, but I'd watched Dick Hayes lift a flask to his mouth half a dozen times in the few minutes we'd been there, and now Harold was the model of an unhappy man about to see trouble, so I was able to figure out more or less what was up.

After Harold drove off, I got busy brushing dust and dried manure off the horse Harold called Bingo and picking rocks and dirt clods out of his feet. I was saddling him when Dick Hayes wandered over. The horses seemed to know what was up too. They had had their own dealings with him, or they could smell the booze and the anger coming off him like fog. Both of them shifted their weight and twitched their hides nervously, and Bingo bumped my sore thigh as I was reaching under him to grab the cinch. I swore and shoved him over hard with my shoulder, which maybe had something to do with Guy, or was in some obscure way a show for Dick Hayes.

"That's the same goddamn plow horse you brought me last time," he said. "Goddamn plug. You get me? Every goddamn picture I've made for Ferret," and he paused over the sarcasm so I wouldn't miss it, "they rent me this shit-ugly crowbait."

I said, "I don't know anything about it, Mr. Hayes, I just got hired today," and went on saddling the horse.

"You mean to say you don't know plug-ugly when you see it?" He was standing at Bingo's head, and he grabbed hold of the horse's jaw and shoved the muzzle up until it was pointing at the sky. "That's ugly right there, see? Don't tell me you don't know ugly." The horse snorted and tried to shake his head loose, and I could see Hayes's thumb whiten as he held on and dug into the hinge of the jawbone.

I said, "You could be right. I guess I've seen prettier." I tightened up the cinch and dropped the stirrup and stepped over to the other horse, the one called Blue, even though he was as red as the king of hearts. Hayes let go of Bingo's jaw then and grabbed hold of the halter up close to the throat. The horse rocked his head up and down, rattling the metal D-ring.

"I'm asking for a particular reason. Why I always get the ugly horse." He wasn't looking at me when he said this. He yanked on the halter, forcing the horse's head toward him so he could look Bingo in the eye, like he was daring him with a scowl. Hayes's face was smeared thick with makeup, his cheeks rouged. Up close, I could see the bristles of his beard through the pancake batter.

"I don't know. I'm just the hired help. I'm supposed to get these horses cleaned up and saddled, that's all I know." I was brushing out Blue, who kept shifting his feet and shaking his head up and down. I took hold of his ear and twisted it, leaned in, and said, "Quit."

"I get an ugly horse because they're making ugly pictures, and they don't give an ugly goddamn," Hayes said, breathing the words directly into Bingo's flaring nostrils. The horse's eyes showed white all around, and I could hear a low groaning vibrato coming from him, the kind of sound a cat makes when he's deciding whether to put up with you or take a bite out of your hand.

I didn't say anything. I didn't want Harold to fire me on the first day, and I figured from what he had said—*you let him shove*—that he didn't want me to get between Hayes and the horse unless I thought the horse was about to stomp him. I wasn't a bit sure what I ought to do in that case, but while I was grooming Blue I started thinking that if I had to, I could step back and land a boot or a knee in the damn horse's belly.

Hayes cuffed Bingo on the muzzle lightly, as if with affection, and the horse snorted and pulled back as far as the rope would let him. But then Hayes let go of the halter and made a sound that I thought might have been a word, stepped back, and dug his flask out of his back pocket and drank from it. "Probably you'd like me to leave you and these horses alone, mind my manners, is that it?"

"It doesn't matter to me. But if a horse stomped you, I'd lose my job. And I just got hired."

He laughed. "That horse hasn't got the balls to try to stomp me. He hasn't got any balls, period." He leaned against one of the trees and watched me, taking a long pull every so often from his flask. He wore black trousers with red piping along the pockets. His shirt had red piping on the pockets and along the edge outlining the pearl buttons. There must have been a hat and a fancy gun belt to finish the look, but he wasn't wearing them.

"What's the name of the picture you're making?" I asked, thinking if I started him talking it might take his attention off the horse.

"Hell, I don't know. They don't give this crap a name until it's ready to ship. They give it a number, and then they just pull something off a list, Burning Cheyenne Hills or Filthy Flaming Arrows or some other shit, when they're slapping a label on the cans. Don't matter if there's no arrows in it or no Cheyennes. They give it a name without even looking at it."

Lily Shaw had shown me a list she kept in her notebook, titles for scripts she hadn't yet written. At the time it hadn't occurred to me to wonder if this was a good idea, but Dick Hayes sure made it sound stupid. And I was pretty certain Flaming Arrows had been on Lily's list.

"The boss went back for another horse," I said after a while. "A buckskin that looks pretty flashy. You should make sure they put you on that one."

He was drunk enough now to turn sentimental. He leaned forward and made a kissing sound and touched his lips lightly to the horse's muzzle. "Naw," he said, leaning back again. "This here's the horse I always ride. Ain't that right, Bingo?" He rubbed the horse on his blaze, and Bingo, like a goddamn lap dog, stretched his neck toward him, everything forgiven.

12

AT FIRST I JUST RODE IN ONE OF THE TRUCKS with Harold or Jake or Hugh, learning the ropes, but sometimes, for short trips that didn't go through downtown, Harold took the shotgun seat and had me drive the Dodge with the two-horse trailer; he wanted me to start getting used to the traffic and how the city was laid out. We worked the same locations over and over, and before long I was acquainted with most of them. I learned where to find water and where to string up a picket line out of the way of the cameras. In hot weather I knew to loosen the girth to let air under the saddle, so a horse wouldn't get too sweaty between shots; and I learned to tell, from the way people stood around idly in small groups and then suddenly got animated, that they were about to want the horses brought up for the scene. As soon as Harold was sure I could get them in front of the cameras on time and get them to the right spot, he started dropping me off with a couple of horses and leaving me all day, and shortly after that he started sending me out in the Dodge on my own if he didn't need the truck to make another run.

All the horses were six, seven, eight years old—young enough to get the job done but old enough to be well broke. Harold had a good eye for smart, sound horses that had lived a little and learned a lot. They were all experienced picture horses — they hardly even twitched when guns went off right by their heads. The trouble wasn't with the horses, usually, but with actors who didn't know a damn thing about riding a horse but liked to pretend they'd grown up with Tom Mix on a ranch in Texas. A fellow who couldn't ride but thought he could was a dangerous nuisance, which I already knew, having learned it the worst way. A lot of the job was just figuring out how much an actor could really handle and matching the horse to the rider. Before I took a horse over to an actor I might have to get on myself and ride him until he settled down — taking the top off is what we used to call it.

Harold wanted us to stay close to the horses all the time. We had to watch out for an actor doing something stupid that might cause a horse to misbehave, or a crew member walking up behind a horse who wasn't expecting it or thinking it might be funny to play a prank involving a burr under a saddle. Diamond had a reputation for reliable horses, horses safe for any greenhorn actor to ride, and Harold didn't want that reputation wrecked by one of his horses going suddenly wild, bucking off some handsome hero wearing a fancy shirt.

When a horse was in front of the camera, I sometimes had to crouch down out of sight and hold his leg to keep him standing still while they were getting a close-up shot of the guy on his back playing a guitar and singing. Or I might have to poke a horse in the hindquarters when they wanted a shot of him tossing his head and snorting. I was the pickup man, too, which was what I had seen Jake doing that first evening, walking out to where the horses had been left standing and leading them back in. Wranglers for the big studios sometimes were called on to ride out and grab the traces of a buckboard or stagecoach, but the cheap studios we were working for filled in those scenes with cut ends, so I never did get to stop any runaways.

I had come into this job with a vague notion that moviemaking would be like watching a movie, but I got over that right away. For one thing, the scenes that used our horses were pretty tame: the actors would amble along speaking their lines with the boom mike overhead, or they'd gallop a short way straight toward the camera, then pull up hard, jump down, and crouch behind a plaster rock, something like that. Since Diamond Barns mostly rented out horses for chapter pictures and cheap features, all the fast action—the chases, stampedes, and horse falls—were clipped from older movies and then spliced in with the new film in a cutting room.

When there was action, it was mostly away from the horses—saloon brawls that broke all the furniture and sent the whiskey bottles flying, gun battles between the bad guys and the hero. When you saw them up close, the fistfights looked pretty phony: long, looping punches with unclosed fists, and some guy off camera slapping a boxing glove against a big pink ham to fake the sound of knuckles hitting a jaw. The gun battles, if they weren't using a long lens and rubber pistols, could look more like the real thing—squibs full of fake blood and real pistols and rifles shooting blanks—but they didn't let the camera run the whole time the scene played out. They were always stopping, moving the camera setup, then starting again in short overlapping runs, so it never felt like I was watching a movie. After a week or two I stopped paying much attention to the filming except when I had to, when Diamond's horses were in the shot.

Even on the sets where they were shooting very fast and wrapping up the outdoor work in two or three days, there was a lot of waiting around. The background extras would get together and play cards, and I guess I could have joined them; it would have been all right with Harold so long as I kept an eye on the horses. But I was into the habit of keeping to myself, so I spent the loose time mostly reading paperback books I borrowed from Hugh, who had a collection of Tarzan adventures and lurid stories about tentacled monsters grabbing hold of buxom young women. If I found a newspaper lying around, I'd read through every bit of it. I remember that was the year the Yankees swept the Cubs in the World Series, and Seabiscuit beat

War Admiral in a match race. I read about a ballet called *Billy the Kid* opening in Chicago. And that was the year France and Germany signed a treaty promising neither of them would attack the other.

On movie days we didn't have time for anything but toast and coffee for breakfast, and the box lunch every studio put out was never much more than a stale sandwich and an orange. At night we ate a lot of canned meat and canned tomatoes and peaches, or peanut butter and crackers, right before we headed for bed. I wasn't exactly going hungry in those first couple of weeks, but it didn't take long to get tired of crackers. So one time when we got back to the house earlier than usual, I rummaged around in Harold's kitchen and cooked up a pot of soup from dried peas, a hunk of canned ham, and a couple of onions and spuds that had softened and started to sprout. Jake had already gone back to town to have supper with his family, so it was just Harold and Hugh and me. When Harold finished his soup, he leaned back with a cigarette and asked, "Where'd you learn to cook? Your mother teach you?"

I had learned to cook mostly from my dad and my grandmother—my mother worked outside with the cows and horses—but I wasn't interested in getting into any of that with Harold. I said, "I was helping out the cook on a dude ranch last summer," which wasn't quite what he had asked me. "I'm not any kind of fancy cook, but I know enough to put food on the table if I have the groceries."

He considered this for a minute, then pulled out his wallet and unfolded a couple of bills and laid them on the table in front of me. "Groceries," he said.

After that, while the others were feeding and watering the livestock in the evening, I was usually in the kitchen putting supper on the table. My cooking was pretty plain and ran mostly to what I could fry up in a hurry, but it was better than peanut butter and crackers.

When we weren't hauling horses to a movie set, Harold kept us busy with the sort of work I had done all my life: fixing fence, grooming horses and doctoring them, repairing leather goods. But most days were movie days, and we put in such long hours I was always tired out by the time I got to bed, and then I'd have trouble falling asleep. I wasn't thinking about home, or not often, but my mind would fasten on something—it could be anything, not even a worry, just something that had happened that day or a remark one of the others had made—and circle around and around it, the way you rub your thumb over a ragged hangnail. When that happened, I was lucky to get three or four hours' sleep at night. Some nights I'd get to sleep right away, then wake up an hour later. I envied Hugh, who could sleep anywhere—in the truck, or lying on the grass with the hubbub of moviemaking going on around him. Sometimes, as we sat talking in the living room of Harold's house, Hugh's chin would just drop to his chest and he'd nod off.

Hugh and his brother had been homesteaders up in eastern Colorado before a string of dry years drove them out. They had drifted south to Los Angeles, where Hugh landed a job driving truck for a heavy hauler, and after the hauler went out of business he wound up working for Harold. He'd been there about a year before I showed up. I guess you could say he was one of those sodbusters I had so much disdain for, and he wore the same filthy pants every damn day and snuffled annoyingly from an adenoid problem, plus he had a loud, high-pitched voice to make up for being a little bit deaf. But he was a hard worker, tireless as hell, and he didn't seem to mind giving up half his bedroom to me.

I shared that bedroom with Hugh for four months without making much effort to get well acquainted, but a lot of nights after we turned out the light, we'd lie in those twin beds swapping dirty jokes and grandiose plans. Mine were all about being a movie cowboy, but Hugh's plan was to save up his money so he and his brother could buy a tourist court. They had a particular one in mind, a place near Yellowstone Park where they had stayed one time on their way to California. Well, they never bought the motor court, but years later I heard from Harold that Hugh had wound up writing for the smut business.

It didn't surprise me much. The dirty stories he used to tell weren't so much jokes as elaborate tales of sexual conquest. On the wall opposite our beds there was a painting of a young Mexican woman with long black braids and a white dress embroidered with red and orange flowers, a dress that showed off her round bosom. Hugh would start out saying that the girl in the painting reminded him of someone he'd met that day on the movie set—a different girl every day, no matter what location he was working at. "She was wearing an outfit like that," he'd say, or "She was wearing one of those Injun wigs with braids like that," and then he'd describe how the two of them had wandered off behind some bushes, where he'd persuaded her to open up the front of her dress and show him her "bumps" and then lift up the hem of her skirt and show him what was down there between her legs—"turned out her hair wasn't dark at all, the wig had sure fooled me"—and eventually, of course, let him touch her in all sorts of places and then have sex with him in various ways. He spun it out, describing every bit of the girl's body in detail, and everything the two of them did, and what both of them said, imitating the girl's virtuous refusals in an accented falsetto voice, and then her giggles and sighs as she gave in to his persistence.

A few years back I tried to find that painting, or one like it, to buy for Hugh—I had heard he was sick with emphysema and living in a nursing home in Encino. When I couldn't find that Mexican girl, I sent him one like we'd had in the bathroom, a solemn child in a serape, and when he called me up to thank me for it, he laughed and said, "But what the hell, Bud, did you think I was too sick to want that little senorita to fuck?"

Hugh was a few years older than me, but I don't know how much actual experience he'd had in those Hollywood days—I'm guessing not a lot. I only know I learned quite a few things about women's anatomy from those bedtime stories of his.

13

AFTER HAROLD HAD PAID ME A FEW TIMES, and I was pretty sure I had the job nailed down, I phoned my folks. I called at suppertime, when I thought they might both be in the house, but when Mom answered she said Dad had driven into town to pick up some hardware for the pump. I told her where I was and what I was doing. She was surprised, and interested to hear about the horses, but the names of the actors and the things I told her about moviemaking didn't mean much to her. She had read more than a few cowboy romances, but I could remember only half a dozen times when she'd gone with us to see a picture show.

We talked about the weather. When I told her it was still hot and dry down in California, summer weather in the first week of November, she seemed not to know what this meant—as if I'd told her about a strange dream that made sense only to the dreamer. It had snowed on them twice already, five or six inches, and they'd been seeing hard frost just about every night. She said the house they were living in had a bad roof that leaked onto the porch, and when the wet places froze overnight you had to be careful not to slip and fall when you stepped out in the morning or went out to the toilet at night.

I said, "Maybe Dad should roof the house," and after a little silence she said the owner wouldn't pay for a new roof, but Dad had climbed up there and patched the part that overhung the porch.

She asked me where I was rooming, and I told her about Harold's house and the silent-movie star who used to live there. When she asked if I was eating right, I told her about the lunch they put out on the film sets, and about cooking supper for Harold and Hugh. She said, "You always did like to cook, Bud. Your dad liked it more than I did, so I guess you take after him in that way." This was something she'd said often, and it was my dad who always said, "Well, honey, Mary Claudine takes after you."

I asked her about the hay crop and the rainfall and the calf crop, but I didn't pay much attention to the answers. It frankly didn't matter to me if the hay was poor or the calves weren't putting on weight, because the place wasn't theirs, they were just hired help.

When we ran out of things to talk about, I said, "Tell Dad hello," and she said, "He'll be back in a couple of hours if you want to call again."

I was standing in a telephone booth in front of Santa Ana Pictures, down in Gower Gulch. We'd been shooting in a quarter-acre vacant lot behind their office, and I knew we'd be there the rest of the day, but I said, "Well, we're about to head out to a movie set over in the park." When she didn't say anything to that, I said, "Maybe I'll call next week."

"That's all right, Bud," she said after a moment. "He'll be sorry he missed you, but I'll tell him you're doing good."

It would be years before I heard the real story about the icy porch. Mom didn't see him fall, and Dad never did remember how it happened, but she had come in from the barn and found him lying there with a plum-colored egg on his forehead, eyes open but not able to speak or get up. She couldn't get him to his feet by herself, so she bundled him in blankets and just sat there talking to him until he came back to himself. She never gave a thought to phoning the neighbors,

and of course after he was able to stand up and walk around and answer what year it was and who the president was, neither of them
considered that he should have been brought to a doctor.

Even if she had told me all that when I phoned her up, I wouldn't
have considered it a reason to go back home. More likely I would
have thought it was another reason to stay away, which maybe she
knew, and maybe was the reason she didn't tell me about it at the
time.

A couple of weeks after that phone call, when Harold brought in
the mail there was a letter from my mother. I hadn't given her an ad-
dress, but she had sent it to Diamond Barns, Hollywood, California,
and that was all it took.

I thought her letter might have something in it, something that
she hadn't been able to say on the phone, but what she wrote was
just a few short lines about everyday chores, and bits of news about
animals and people I had never met—a bay colt she had finished
and sold to a Mr. Tallman, who ran the hardware store in Bly, "and
now I am starting the paint which is half Arab and belongs to Don
Pollock's daughter, they are people living west of here. Your Dad is
reseeding the Cougar Bench hay field that was burned out last summer."

When I was boarding at the high school in Hart, my mother
wrote to me once a week, but this was the first time since we'd all left
Echol Creek that she had known how to get a letter to me. Her large,
looping, childish hand kicked up some familiar feelings. I kept the
letter and reread it a few times.

Another letter came from her a couple of weeks later, and regularly after that. Every now and then my dad wrote something as well,
folded into the envelope with hers. He had had a high school education, and his handwriting was schoolboy neat. "Take care, son," he
wrote at the bottom of every letter. Neither of them said much in
their letters except the humdrum happenings of their life.

I didn't write back. I thought I would call them on the phone every couple of weeks, but sometimes it was six or seven weeks before I got around to it. The calls were short—none of us liked to use the phone much, and there wasn't a whole lot I could think to say.

A package came for me right before Christmas, a purple polka-dot neckerchief like one Arlo Gantz always wore. I went out and bought a souvenir plate painted with a likeness of Grauman's Chinese Theatre and mailed it off to them.

On Christmas Day I went into town and found a tavern that was open, drank a few beers, then went to a phone booth and rang up my folks. It was late. Probably they were already in bed, or I had dialed the wrong number. Anyway, nobody answered. While I was standing there listening to the rings, I leaned my head back and studied the sky. The stars over the Echol ranch were always at their brightest in December, the cold winter nights bringing them out crystal clear, but here a brown haze—nobody called it smog in those days—had been hanging over the Hollywood Hills and the whole Los Angeles valley for the past few weeks, and I couldn't see a damn thing above me except the blurred disk of the moon.

14

A WEEK OR SO INTO THE NEW YEAR, I ran into Lily Shaw. I had been down around Gower Gulch more than a few times doing movie work, and the Studio Club where Lily lived was just a block from there, but we bumped into each other not at Gower but over on Sunset.

Harold had us putting up a perimeter fence around his property, tackling the work a little at a time whenever we had half a day, and he had sent me down to the hardware store to pick up a couple of buckets of creosote for the posts. While I was hoisting them into the back of the Dodge, I heard a voice call out "Bud!" I had parked the truck right in front of the building where Lily worked, just up the block from the hardware store. She had seen me from her window on the second floor and had come down the stairs to say hello.

In recent weeks the Greyhound trip had begun to seem as if it had happened a long time ago—I had been thinking Lily Shaw was someone I'd never see again. So when I turned around and saw her standing there, I was caught off-guard, surprised by how glad I was to see her. As if I'd unexpectedly bumped into somebody from back home, someone in my family or a friend I'd known all my life, down here a thousand miles from where I'd left them—that was the feeling I had. It seems to me now that I had set out on purpose to put myself as far as I could from everybody I knew, so this was not what I expected to feel.

It was raining that day, which is why we weren't hauling horses to a movie set. I stood with Lily at the front door of her building, and we talked for a few minutes with the rain rattling on the metal awning over our heads. She had thrown on a cape coat before coming down the stairs. Her hair was combed, the bangs pinned back with a barrette shaped like a bow, and the blue dress under her unbuttoned coat looked as if it had kept a morning appointment with an iron. She was tidy, in other words, compared to how she'd looked when we were on the bus. She had ink on two fingers, though, and a smudge of it on her lower lip, and I almost wet my thumb and reached out to rub it off, as if we knew each other that well.

I figured Lily would ask me if I'd met Buck Jones yet and what movies I'd been in, so right away I told her I wasn't chasing any stagecoaches, that I was just working as a wrangler. But I must have been coloring it as if wrangling was what I had come down to Hollywood intending to do. She didn't let me off the hook. She wrinkled up her brow in disappointment and said, "You'll probably be riding in the movies before long, Bud. You just have to keep trying."

She wasn't doing what she'd hoped, either. Her job, she said, was reading through the screenplays and treatments that writers sent to the agency, then typing up a little summary of each story. After her boss looked those over, she typed up the letters that he dictated back to the writers. A lot of the stories were terrible, in her opinion, but it turned out the boss didn't want her opinion, and he didn't want her to do any editing, he just wanted the plot boiled down to a few words. She'd written a summary of her own story, *Death Rides the Sky*, and slipped it in with the others, but he'd never said a word to her about it.

She was a bulldog even then, and she had come down to Hollywood with an unshakable ambition to be a screenwriter. It was clear to her that being a secretary at a talent agency wouldn't ever lead to a writing job, so she was already looking around for something else, some work at one of the studios. She didn't want to quit the agent, though, until she had another job, which was more or less the same situation I was in, holding on to the work at Diamond Barns while I kept my eye out for a riding job, hoping to bump into a second-unit ramrod every time I came on a new movie set.

When I told her about Diamond Barns, that it was up in Griffith Park, she said, "Do you know there's a telescope at the top of the park? Have you been up there yet? You could look for the star clusters in Scorpius." She had remembered every bit of what I told her that night after the bus wreck.

I said, "I was up there Sunday, but I couldn't make out much of anything. The sky was too dirty. They said the haze is from dust, but I don't know if that's right."

She said, "Well, it's been a dry year."

I came from a dry part of the world myself, but the only time the sky turned brown in Harney County was in late summer, when wind picked up the topsoil. I didn't know enough to argue about it though.

Lily told me about the Studio Club—that the room she shared with the other girls was unremarkable, but the public rooms were a great deal fancier than she'd expected. When she had walked through the doors the first time and seen that grand staircase descending from lofty regions into the big entrance hall, she had thought she was in the wrong place.

The club took up a whole block just off Santa Monica Boulevard and west of Gower, and as she was describing it I realized which place she was talking about. I'd seen it when I was walking around Gower Gulch that first day looking for work: a big Mediterranean-style building with three archways at the front under a painted frieze, full-length arched windows, and balconies with iron balustrades and decorative brackets. I had thought it was a mansion where some

movie mogul lived, or maybe the headquarters of a big motion picture studio—Paramount Pictures, maybe, or 20th Century Fox. I
hadn't figured it to be a girls' hostel.

"It's even prettier inside," she said. "I could show it to you if you
want. Not all of it, but at least the fancy front rooms. They let boys
come into the front rooms when they visit." She said this as if she
didn't care about it one way or the other, which in some other girl
might have been romantic cunning. But I hadn't figured her for cunning, and I was pretty sure she didn't have any romantic interest
in me.

I shrugged as if it didn't matter to me either. "I could come over
there on Sunday if you want."

On Sundays, our only day off work, Harold took care of the animals himself, then went out to Glendale to call on a woman he was
seeing. Hugh took the bus to visit his brother over in the commer-
cial district, and Jake spent the time with his wife and children. I
had tried once staying put at Diamond, but when there's too much
silence it's easy to wind up in a dark place; so usually I rode the
streetcar into the city and killed the day aimlessly, walking around
looking in shop windows, eating in a diner, going into a pool hall to
drink a few beers. The rest of the week I could keep from thinking
too much: even when I wasn't handling the horses or reading one of
Hugh's trashy books, there was always some sort of hubbub going on,
and it kept me out of my own head. But Sundays there was too much
empty time and I had nobody to spend it with.

"Good," Lily said, without any particular emphasis. "Come around
two o'clock. Just come into the lobby and I'll meet you there."

Over the years she and I rarely talked about the beginning of our
friendship. Only that it was Hollywood where our lives had inter-
sected, and if we had met at any other time and place we might not
have become friends.

But once she said something else about those early days. This
was after her dad had died and I had taken the train up to Seattle

for his funeral. We met in a hotel bar and spent an hour or so sipping scotch and talking. Somewhere in there she told me that all the girls she lived with at the Studio Club and the girls she worked with at the agent's office had been fixed on becoming wives, "which left me outside the picture." It was a state of affairs she was used to, but a girl with no romantic expectations, a girl who never planned to marry, was ironically a girl that many boys found easy to be with, and at college she had always been able to make friends among the boys. But living in a women's sorority and working with women, "I wasn't lonesome exactly, or friendless, but I guess I felt solitary." She gave me a slightly amused look. "You weren't much like the boys I knew at college, but this was Hollywood and I had cast you as The Cowboy with a Tragic Past. You'd get a look in your face, Bud, a look I used to see in my dad."

The bit about my tragic past was mostly her writerly invention, but I guess some part of it was real. Her dad had been a soldier in the Great War and had come up against some terrible things, so I know she must have picked up something in me that, at the time, I thought was well concealed.

That day in front of the hardware store, she looked out at the rain puddling in the street and the wet dog in the bed of the pickup. "Whose dog is that?" she asked. Jack was watching every move I made. Every so often he stood up to shake himself off, but he was enough of a ranch dog that it didn't occur to him to make a show of being pathetic.

"He's Harold's."

She suddenly left the shelter of the awning, crossed over to the truck parked at the curb, and petted the dog's wet head. "What's his name?"

"Blackjack. Or Harold just says Jack."

She scritched the dog behind his ears. "Good Jack," she said quietly. Then she looked over at me again. "I had a black dog once, his name was Rags." She was squinting, her glasses already spotted with rain. "Don't you hate how dogs always die before people do?" She said this as if it was a curious question she'd been pondering for a long time.

When we were still living on Echol Creek, a neighbor gave us a shepherd pup that Mary Claudine named Quinn. He was now about eight years old, living up at Bly with my parents. I thought of telling Lily she was wrong about dogs always dying before people, but I didn't have the words for it.

She gave the dog another little pat on his head and then came back across the sidewalk to stand under the awning. While she wiped the rain off her glasses with a handkerchief, she said, "They don't let us smoke in our rooms at the Studio Club; we have to go down to the living rooms to smoke." As if this was a hardship she had learned to live with. Then she pulled a pack of Lucky Strikes from the pocket of her coat and offered me one.

I had known only a few women in my life who smoked, and I hadn't thought Lily was one of them—I hadn't seen her smoking on the bus. But I acted like I wasn't surprised. I had smoked a few cigarettes myself in the last year without yet making it a habit, so I took the cigarette from her and lit us both up. Lily drew some smoke into her mouth and blew it out, then tucked her elbow into her waist and held the cigarette out from her hip. I had seen movie stars strike that pose, but she looked to me like a child play-acting with a candy cigarette.

15

I GOT TO THE STUDIO CLUB ON SUNDAY about a quarter of two and waited in the lobby for almost half an hour, watching pretty girls come and go. Lily, it turned out, was still in her night-gown. While the girls she roomed with were primping for a picnic, speaking slyly about being "crazy" or "gone" for young men they had met the week before, she was sitting up in bed writing. She had the opinion that a screenwriter had to learn to write with distractions — telephones ringing and directors charging in and out of your office and actors standing over you demanding that lines be changed. So while the girls chattered, she kept her pencil moving across the page. When one of them said, "You should come too, Lily, and bring that boy Bud," she didn't look up from her work. "He's just coming to get a look at the club," she said. "He's not my boyfriend."

When she finally woke to how late it was, got dressed, and came down the curving staircase, it was twenty past two. But she just said, "Hey," and I said "Hey," and then she led me around the public parts of the building, those big front rooms and the library. The parlors flanking the hall were each a good thirty feet long, sporting tall fire-places with tile surrounds and ceilings with heavy plaster arches and oak box beams. I was fairly awestruck by the place, but it wasn't in Lily's nature to be awed. Anyway, she had grown up in circumstances considerably more embellished than I was used to—her dad was a ferry boat inspector for the state of Washington, and her mother was an opera singer and a music teacher who used to play the organ for silent films at the Orpheum Theatre in Seattle—a gilded building more opulent than anything in my experience. Lily stood back and let me gawk.

We could hear somebody practicing vocal exercises in one of the music rooms down the corridor. She said there was a dance studio where girls could rehearse their auditions for musicals, utility rooms with ironing boards, sewing machines, and machines for doing up laundry. A makeup room with shelves and mirrors. Even a typewriter room for aspiring screenwriters, although Lily hadn't used it yet. She liked to write her early drafts in pencil in a notebook.

When we walked out through the gardens and the loggia, girls were sitting under the bougainvillea drinking coffee and talking, and girls in shorts were stretched out on the lawn, reading movie scripts or magazines. I had been holding my hat in my hand inside the club, but as soon as I stepped out to the loggia I put it on, and several of the girls looked up at me when we came by, at least partly, I imagine, to see if I was a cowboy actor they recognized. I was wearing my good boots, a bib-front white shirt, and the purple polka-dot rag my folks had sent me for Christmas, knotted at the side of my neck.

Lily said quietly, "That girl in the pink shorts is crazy for you."

I was nineteen years old, and I had never seen a naked woman or touched a naked breast, which is probably all you need to know about my sexual experience. But I wasn't bad-looking in those days, which I was not unaware of, and of course Lily knew, although she was also perfectly clear—we both were—that she and I were pals only.

I looked around and spotted more than one girl in pink shorts. "Which one?"

Lily laughed and said, "All of them."

When we walked back through the big dining room, the tables were already set for dinner and the kitchen staff was at work—we could smell onions frying. The Studio Club served two meals a day, but the girls were on their own for lunch. During the week Lily sometimes bought a sandwich or a bowl of soup from the Dutch Diner around the corner from the office, but on weekends she usually wrote all day and would forget to eat lunch at all. She hadn't even come down for breakfast that day, and when we walked past the kitchen she was suddenly hungry. She said, "Do you want to get an ice cream cone?" so we walked out to an ice cream store on Sunset and bought a couple of cones and walked around eating them and talking.

When I asked about her war movie, she told me she'd finished that one and now was writing a cowboy picture. She gave me a sidelong look as if she thought I might disapprove. "I have to start somewhere, and I heard Mr. Buchanan on the phone the other day saying to one of his writer clients that a shoot-'em-up was an easy sell." She'd been reading a bunch of "giddyuppers" to get a feeling for the form, and she was reworking one of her New York plots, moving it to the wide-open range and throwing in a couple of chases. She didn't know a thing about ranching, but I understood even then that it didn't matter much. Her movie was about a Texas Ranger wounded by an outlaw, and the outlaw's daughter who saves his life and nurses him back to health.

"Rose gets killed later by one of the rustlers, and the Ranger wants revenge. He plans to go out and shoot them, but in the end he knows he has to follow his duty, and he takes them all to jail."

Well, I'd seen that plot a few times, but Lily might not have known how common it was. She said, "People think honor is simple, but it's really not." She meant this seriously. Even in those days, she always wanted to write important stories—stories that mattered. The pictures that later made her famous were gritty, unsentimental melodramas—women and men wrestling their way through tough situations—and noir thrillers with an understory of political shenanigans. Movies not out to change the world, maybe, but always trying to mean something.

We passed a billboard for a Mickey Rooney picture, which got us talking about movies we liked. Lily had been taking herself to the pictures a couple of times a week for years, so she had seen pretty much every movie that showed up in Seattle. This put me at a disadvantage. Every so often a bunch of us kids from the farms and ranches around Echol Creek and Bailey Creek would meet up to ride our horses to the movie theater in Burns, which was twelve miles by trails and backcountry lanes. We'd just turn the horses into a vacant lot next to the theater and ride home late at night after a double feature and not think anything of it. And when I was in high school, Dean Dickerson and I saw a picture most every Saturday at the theater in Hart. But those were small-town movie palaces that showed cowboy pictures, jungle adventures, popular melodramas. Lily had no trouble keeping up with me when I started talking about Wild Bill Elliott—she had seen enough cowboy movies to know some of the plots and the names of the heroes—but I didn't have anything to say when she brought up *I, Claudius* or *The Life of Emile Zola.*

"Did you see *Grand Illusion*? That's a war movie."

It didn't sound to me like a war movie. "Who's in it?" I asked her.

"Jean Gabin is the most famous one. He's really good. It's a French movie."

"Well, I don't go to foreign pictures." I'd never heard of Jean Gabin. I didn't say anything to her about the kinds of movies that came to small-town theaters.

"No foreign movies at all?" She said this as if it was not to be believed.

"I guess I saw a picture about Pancho Villa once."

"That doesn't really count. You should see *Grand Illusion*. I think it's just about the greatest movie ever made."

We were walking past a line of shops with apartments on the second floor and a row of palm trees along the curb. It was the middle of January. In her last letter my mother had written that there was a foot of snow on the high pastures, but in California we had had a string of days as warm as summer. It must have been about eighty that afternoon, and the shade under the palms was a relief from the sun. When we came out again into the heat and glare, what popped into my mind was that my parents hadn't seen more than a dozen motion pictures in their lives.

"Well, I didn't see it. I guess that makes me a shitkicker raised in a barn."

She looked at me to be sure I wasn't teasing her. "I don't know why you're mad."

"I'm not."

"You are. I just think you would like it if you saw it. I could tell you the whole story if you want."

"No thanks."

She looked at me again. "Well, sometime I will."

She didn't say so at the time, but *Grand Illusion* was the reason she had decided to be a screenwriter. She had been fourteen or fifteen when she first saw it, and up to that point she hadn't thought of films as involving writing. She hadn't thought of the stories she'd been writing since she first learned to use a pen—stories spooling out behind her eyes as she wrote the words on the page—as a kind of movie. It was when she saw *Grand Illusion* that she suddenly understood *somebody wrote this story and then somebody else turned it into a movie.* And the whole concept of filmmaking hit her.

When we finished our ice cream, she brought out her Lucky Strikes, and for a while we walked along in silence, smoking. Then she said suddenly, "I want to go to Paris. The French make the best pictures. I want to meet Sacha Guitry—he writes movies and directs them too. That's what I plan to do. If you want to have any say over what you write, you really have to become a writer-director or a writer-producer." If she knew the odds against such a thing, she didn't let on. She spoke as if it wasn't in question—as if it might have already happened and she and Sacha Guitry were old colleagues.

I didn't know the difference between a director and a producer, and I didn't ask her to tell me. The cigarette had gone straight to my head, the slight buzz that can happen when you're new to smoking or haven't done it in a while. I said, "Sacha sounds like a girl's name. I guess he doesn't make cowboy pictures." I meant for her to hear it as a wisecrack.

Lily looked at me to see if I was still mad, but then she just changed the subject. "Is that a new scar?"

I had a few scars, but the new one was the bright pink line running through my eyebrow, which I had got when those bums robbed me in Griffith Park. I told her, "A horse tossed me into some barb wire." I guess I didn't want to admit to her that I'd been sleeping in the park. And anyway the fight didn't make a very heroic story.

"There's barbed wire up at Diamond where you're working?" Of course, that's the trouble you get into when you start lying.

I said, "It was on a movie set."

She took in this information and nodded. "When you get into the movies, they'll probably want you to play one of the bad guys, because the hero never has a scar on his face. He should, though, shouldn't he? Because he's always getting in fistfights, and wouldn't he get scars?"

My dad always joked about how nobody's teeth got knocked out and nobody's nose got broken when men fought in the movies. I had been in enough scuffles, even as a kid, to know he was right, but it annoyed the hell out of me every time he said it.

I just said, "I guess," and kept walking.

When we went by the Marcal Theater, Lily stopped to look at the posters. They were showing *White Banners* in a double feature with *The Big Stampede,* and Lily said, "Oh, I like Fay Bainter. I saw this movie last summer."

I didn't know anything about *White Banners* or who Fay Bainter was, but *The Big Stampede* was a cowboy picture, and the show was about to start. I said, "If you want, we could go in and see *Stam-*

pede. We wouldn't have to sit through the other one if you've already seen it."

She gave me a scornful look. "I wouldn't let you see your cowboy picture without making you see my weepy."

It was seven or eight months later, while I was laid up in the hospital, that Lily one night started telling me the whole story, scene by scene, of *Grand Illusion.* This was long after the floor nurse had given up trying to kick her out. The room stank of pain and sickness. The three other men in the beds near us in the darkness were listening too, although she spoke pretty low and sat so close to the bed I could feel her breath on my neck and cheek. I was in poor shape, and I imagine she meant to take my mind off my miseries. Well, just about any movie could have served the purpose, and *Grand Illusion* wouldn't be the first one you'd think of. There are some lighthearted, even comical things in it, but people are shot and killed in that movie, people that you wish had gone on living, and it doesn't end with the lovers together.

That night Lily said, "Remember when you came down to the Studio Club that first time, and we walked around eating ice cream and talking about movies?" Something—I don't know what—had brought that into her mind. And then she began telling me the story of *Grand Illusion* in such a way that I could almost see it playing on the inside of my eyelids. She always had that gift for telling a movie, her own or somebody else's.

I wouldn't get around to seeing it myself for another twenty years. When it finally played at the art house here in town, I took my wife to see it, and I know she was afraid of what it might dredge up— something about the war, my war. But what it brought back into my mind was the movie Lily had been writing when I met her on the bus, that World War One story about a guy who goes behind the lines to rescue a French girl. And it brought back to me that year in Hollywood, every part of it, including Lily Shaw and the night she sat by my hospital bed and told me the whole damn story of *Grand*

Illusion, as well as Steve Deets, Cab O'Brien, and all the horses I'd seen killed when we made *The Battle at Valverde Ford.* Every part of that year. And for two or three weeks after seeing the movie, I'd wake up in a sweat, dreaming of jumping a horse through a candy-glass window, falling twenty stories to the street. Dreams that mixed up Lily with my sister, long nightmare searches going lost in the dark maze of a movie lot.

Now that I'm writing what I remember of that year, I have begun to wonder if we only invent the past. When we think back over our lives, maybe we just take a few things remembered out of so much unremembered and stitch those bits together so they spool out like a movie and make a kind of sense.

That night when Lily told me the story of *Grand Illusion* she got a few things wrong. She left out Boeldieu's death, for one. He had planned an elaborate ruse to help the others escape from the prison, and he was shot before he could get away himself, but when she told the story, Lily said he made it out with the others. I don't think she rewrote it deliberately for my sake. I think she just remembered it that way.

16

ABOUT THE MIDDLE OF JANUARY, Harold sent me up into the Santa Monica Mountains to Las Cruces Ranch, where an outfit called Sunrise Studios was shooting a picture. This was the first time I'd been up there. Las Cruces had once been a Spanish cattle ranch, and it ran close to a thousand acres—everything from salt lagoons and beaches to chaparral hills and wooded uplands. The studios we usually worked with couldn't afford the rental at a place like that, but Sunrise was a couple of cuts above Poverty Row. They weren't one of the majors, but they were known for using better locations and staging the action scenes instead of cobbling together stock footage and gimmicks. Sunrise had rented the horses for this picture from White Oak Stables over in Culver City, but White Oak was short of draft horses that day, and they asked Harold if he'd help them out. He wouldn't have taken the job if it had involved a runaway stagecoach or anything tricky like that, but they just needed a pair of horses pulling a farm wagon, clopping along in the background of a scene. Las Cruces would supply the wagon, so Harold sent me up there in the Dodge with a couple of his color-matched Belgians.

The ranch had a permanent little western town with dummy

fronts and some roofed three-wall and four-wall buildings where players and crew could stay overnight if they needed to and a livery barn with a small tacked-on corral for horses to stand in the shade under some cottonwood trees. A dozen White Oak horses were already saddled along a picket line when I got there, and another dozen were loafing in the corral. The White Oak wrangler, having nothing better to do, helped me get the Belgians unloaded, and then we stood around talking while we waited for our horses to be called up for their scenes.

This other wrangler, Verle Miller, was a little guy who had been a jockey until he got tired of starving himself to make weight. He was wearing calf-high jockey boots and a Spanish beret, which didn't impress me, but he knew horses, and he'd been around the movie business for three or four years. He knew a fair bit about the nutty studio goings-on and the tricks of the trade, and he was full of stories about the parties he'd been to and the famous stars who were his pals. I thought at the time this was mostly bullshit, but I heard later that going to the races was a popular pastime for the upper-crust Hollywood crowd, and a lot of actors cozied up to Verle because of his inside knowledge about horse racing.

What they were shooting that day was a Wichita Carson movie. Nobody remembers those now, but I had seen a couple of them. Wichita went around masquerading as a desperado on the run from the law, which was a trick to fool the bad guys. In some movies he was secretly a marshal or a sheriff, but in others he was just a stranger riding into the middle of a local feud. He would seem to take up with the outlaw gang until the crucial moment, when he'd drop the pretense and fight on the side of the outgunned homesteader and his pretty daughter.

In this particular movie Wichita had to prove his mettle by mastering a wild horse the outlaws had set him on. At the cheaper studios where I'd been wrangling horses, they would have filled in the bucking-horse scenes with short ends clipped from other oaters. I've seen some where they didn't even bother to try to match the horse's color or the shirt the cowboy was wearing. But Verle pointed to a pair of black horses stabled in the barn that he said were stunt horses brought in for that scene. One was a trained bucking horse and the other one was trained to rear up and paw the air or toss his head and paw at the ground like he was looking for somebody to trample.

I had the opinion, after working with rough-broke ranch horses over the last year, that a lot of horses would buck and rear for just about any reason you could name or no reason at all, so I wondered why the hell anybody would go to the trouble of teaching them to do it. Why not just bring in a rodeo bronc, is what I wondered. But of course this was the movies, and they needed a horse who would rear up on cue and one who would start bucking at a signal and buck just enough to look good but not so much as to toss the rider. Plus, they didn't want a mean horse rampaging around the set or running off when they were filming him outside a fence. Later I heard people say it could take a year to train a horse to buck and act wild at a signal, maybe bare his teeth and look ready to fight but then calm right down and go back to being gentle when the cameras quit turning. There were only four or five horses in town who could fill that bill, and White Oak didn't have one. The ramrod had hired these two horses straight from their trainer, a guy named Dale Rybert.

Rybert had his own small stable out in the valley, half a dozen horses trained to do all sorts of tricks, and he had trained some famous horses belonging to movie stars. In those days it was common to see a horse's name and picture on the lobby card alongside the cowboy star, and I had always thought those horses were trained by the actors who rode them. But the actual trainers were men I'd never heard of until Verle rattled off some of their names; it was Verle's opinion that Dale Rybert should have had his name on the billboard right up there with the horse.

Rybert was hanging around the barn that day keeping an eye on his animals. He must have been about fifty, balding in front, wearing wire-rim eyeglasses and carrying about twenty pounds of spare tire around his middle. If Verle hadn't told me who he was, I wouldn't have guessed him for a horseman. He was hatless, sporting tan trousers with neat creases and turned-up cuffs, and a crisply ironed white shirt buttoned to the throat and closed with a little bolo tie. The two-color steep-heel boots showing under those trouser cuffs looked handmade, though, which saved him in my estimation.

After a while a couple of men came over to where he was sitting tipped back in his chair at the front of the barn, and the three of them put their heads together. One of the men was the ramrod — the guy in charge of the horse stunts — and the other was the film's director.

The ramrod on this movie was Cab O'Brien, a hard-drinking redheaded Irishman from Mississippi who had stunted for ten years before moving up to boss. I would get to know Cab pretty well in the next few months, but that day I knew only what Verle told me. "That's Cab O'Brien over there," he said, pointing him out. "He's a son of a bitch."

Directors liked to hire Cab because he had a great eye for action and he could crank out the scenes fast, but among the crew he was known for taking risks with his stuntmen and for being hard on horses, which was more than likely the reason Rybert was staying close to his valuable animals that day.

Cab's specialty as a stuntman had been transfers — jumping from a horse to a stagecoach or a train. A lot of stuntmen could do transfers, but Cab was known for a fancy one: he'd stand right up on the saddle, which is a trick-riding stunt, before leaping over to the tailgate of the coach. After he became a ramrod, a young guy got busted up trying to run Cab's stunt. The kid had been training with Cab, and some people — Verle was one of them — thought Cab might have intentionally coached the kid to fail so he could go on being the only guy in the world who could do that trick, even now that he was a boss and no longer doing the stunt.

Well, I didn't care about Cab's reputation. I hadn't come down to Hollywood for the chance to ride herd on a bunch of horses. If that was all I wanted, I could have stayed up in Oregon and kept working for P Ranch or someplace like that. The Indian I'd met, Lee Waters, had told me that working for a stable might eventually put me in the way of a riding job, but Diamond was the wrong outfit for that. Any stunt director who wanted to goose up the action just knew to get his horses from some other stable; they all knew Harold was dead set against any of his horses taking a fall. I'd been with Harold more than three months at this point, and until that day at Las Cruces I hadn't worked on a picture that had a ramrod—somebody I could hit up for a riding job.

The wild horse scene was being set up on a patch of bare dirt about twenty yards from the livery barn, so I hung my heels on the top rail of the corral, where I could still keep half an eye on Harold's draft horses like he wanted me to but get a bird's-eye glimpse of some real moviemaking for a change, and maybe, if the chance came up, put myself in front of Cab O'Brien.

The star of the Carson movies was an actor named John Barlow. A few weeks later I made a picture with Barlow and found him to be a decent sort of guy who didn't know much about horses and didn't pretend to. At Las Cruces he showed up for only a couple of shots and wasn't there more than five minutes. They filmed him hauling back at the end of a long rope, with one of Rybert's trained horses at the other end going into a stiff-kneed crow hop as Rybert, off-camera, gave him a hand signal; then they shot a close-up of Barlow smiling out of the side of his mouth and saying a few honeyed words to the "tamed" horse as they stood eye to eye. Then he was gone as quick as he'd appeared, and the stuntman stepped into the setup.

The stuntman that day was Steve Deets, who didn't look much like Barlow up close but had roughly the same build and the same dark brown hair, and when you put him in the Wichita costume and shot him from behind, or a few yards off with his hat pulled low, the camera couldn't see the difference.

The crew played around with the reflectors to take shadows off the scene, and then they repositioned the camera right down on the dirt and aimed upward, so when they filmed the horse rearing off his front feet, his hooves would seem to just about scrape the clouds. From that angle Deets, playing Wichita, would appear to be right up under the horse's big chest as he hung on to the shortened rope. They filmed that shot in one take, then broke the setup and scurried around preparing for the next shot.

While they were getting set up, O'Brien and Rybert stood off to the side arguing over something to do with how much Deets weighed, and when they rolled film again I saw what the argument must have been about. The scene had Deets pretending to wrestle with the horse to get him saddled, and at one point the horse reared back and lifted Deets off his feet and slung him around, as if to try to shake loose of him, and then Deets brought his legs up and hooked them on top of the horse's withers so he was hanging upside down under the horse's neck.

Rybert didn't want his trained horse injured, that much was clear—if something happened to make the horse afraid of rearing up, he sure wouldn't have been as valuable for movie work. And it looked to me like the horse wasn't happy to have Deets hanging on him that way—he flattened his ears and widened his eyes until the whites showed. But this was a stallion about sixteen hands, and he didn't look delicate; he was muscled through the neck and shoulders, might have had some draft horse in his bloodline. And as soon as the camera quit rolling and Deets let go of the horse, Rybert went up and fed him a handful of something he fetched out of his pocket, maybe an oatmeal cookie, and right away the horse relaxed his neck and ears—such a quick switch that I had to wonder if I'd been wrong, and his wild-eyed look had been faked for the movie.

Then they brought around the bucking horse, who was smaller, a gelding, and not as good-looking as the rearing horse. He wasn't even quite the same color—a dark blue roan, not black—and he didn't have much more than a snip of white on his muzzle; they'd painted his face white to match the other horse. Up close, anybody would have known the difference, but they wouldn't be using him for close-up shots, and he'd be in motion the whole time.

They ran a bunch of shots of the horse bucking Deets off or seeming to—Deets would stick for a couple of jumps and then bail off, brush down his clothes, and climb right back in the saddle again; the horse would stand quietly under him until Cab called "Action!" and Rybert gave the signal to start a new round of bucking. They ran half a dozen shots one after the other, with Deets varying the way he came off the saddle each time. This seemed like plenty to me, and when Cab said he wanted one more, Deets smiled slightly and said, "You bet," and I thought I heard something in it. Maybe Cab did too, because he ran three or four more takes before he gave Deets a look and said, "I bet that'll do you."

The last thing they filmed was Wichita riding the wild horse to a standstill. I never did see the finished movie, but I expect that at the end he'd have been handing over that horse, meek as a housebroken dog, to the sodbuster's pretty daughter. The gelding was a straight-up bucker who circled slowly to his left, no head spins or fakes, nothing rough or fancy, and Deets was able to make it look pretty, his body in perfect rhythm with every jump, his left arm swinging in a high arc and his spurs raking from high on the shoulders to well behind the cinch. He had a throat latch on his hat and he let the hat come off so it billowed out behind him on the jumps. They ran the camera slow for the bucking scenes so the film could be speeded up to make it all look wilder and rougher than it was. If I haven't already said so, this was a trick they used a lot in those old cowboy movies.

If this had been a rodeo show, I imagine almost anybody could have stuck on that horse until the horn blew—it wasn't the kind of ride that would have put you in the money. But Cab, standing next to the camera, twirled his finger in a silent gesture to keep shooting, and they ran film for nearly two minutes. Even a straight-up bucker would begin to hammer your spine on a ride that long—my teeth started to ache just watching it—and I could see the horse looking more and more annoyed, beginning to get serious about bucking Deets off. Rybert stood off to the side, frowning. But when Cab finally signaled the end of the shot, the horse settled right down.

Deets climbed off the saddle, brushed the dust and horse hair off his costume, and walked off deliberately on his boot heels without a sign of a limp. There might have been a little color in his face, but it didn't look to me as if he'd broken much of a sweat. He found a bench under the awning of one of the false fronts, sat down, and lit up a cigarette.

That was all they needed for the wild horse scene, so the crew went off to set up in another part of the ranch. Rybert led his winded horse back to the barn, and Cab climbed into a car with a couple of other men and drove off. I had been hoping to get a chance to talk to him, but he was gone too quick.

Verle was over at the corrals saddling up a lot of horses for the background players, and I knew I should have given him a hand—I had some time to kill until they were ready for the Belgians—but I went over to where Deets was sitting and parked myself on the other end of his bench.

I wanted to say something admiring about his long ride, but I couldn't think how to do it without sounding like I was after something. Which of course I was. Finally I said, "I heard Rybert's religious about that horse, so I guess you had to be pretty careful how you put spurs to him." There hadn't been a bit of blood showing on the horse, even after a two-minute ride, so I figured he must have blunted the tips of the spurs and then, with Rybert standing there watching him, been careful not to plant them in the horse's hide.

He gave me a sideways look and a slight smile and exhaled a stream of smoke from his nostrils. "They're rubber," he said. "They don't hardly tickle him." He tipped a boot up and showed me how the spurs were nothing but soft props. "Rybert's finical about all his horses. He had these fake spurs made up special. I'll be walking them back over to him in a minute."

The spurs I wore for rodeo were hand-me-downs from my dad, shop-made the old way from battleship steel, and I was pretty proud-minded about them. When Deets showed me those rubber ones, I shouldn't have been surprised—by now I had gotten used to seeing all kinds of moviemaking fakes, even rubber guns and rifles and knives—but I must have looked a little bit scornful, because he said, "Kid, everything about the movie business is phony except the broken bones and dead horses."

I hadn't seen any dead horses or broken bones yet, not here in Hollywood, but I shook my head as if this was a regrettable fact that wasn't news to me.

When it looked like he wasn't planning to say anything else, I said, "You ride rodeo?"

He smiled, not entirely in amusement. "Used to, but this here's a more dependable payday. And the movies pay you more for falling off than for staying on. What about you, kid?" He pointed a knuckle at my flat-crowned hat. "That there looks like prize money." His own hat was part of the costume, the hat Wichita Carson always wore, a high-crowned Texas-creased Stetson. I had thought his chin strap was a rawhide string, but up close I could see it was elastic.

I didn't think my profound knowledge of bucking broncs was likely to impress him, and my hat had been a gift from my parents, but I said, "I rode some horses."

"You go up to Newhall, do you?"

I didn't have the least idea what this was. I thought about pretending I did, but finally I said, "Newhall?"

"Yeah. It's up the valley not too far. They got a rodeo every Sunday." He smiled again. "There's a lot of fellows in the Hollywood posse that think bronc riding is church." He took a long drag on the cigarette. He blew smoke and then, in a slow, droll way, said, "If you draw a horse called Pretty Dick, tell him Steve Deets said hello."

After a bit I stuck out my hand and said, "I'm Bud Frazer."

We shook, and then he made a gesture toward the Belgian horses loafing in the shade. "You wrangling for Harold Capsen?"

I said I was.

"Well, he's a good one to work for. Jesus, that house of his is something, ain't it? Used to belong to that old movie star. I went to a couple of parties up there fifteen, twenty years ago, before she went half nuts." He tapped the ash off his cigarette. "She never liked the business, I guess." He leaned forward, resting his wrists on his knees, and studied the smoke rising up from his hand. "I'll be getting out of pictures myself, here pretty quick. I've got my eye on a dude ranch over in New Mexico."

Steve was about forty when I met him. A Texas boy, he'd left home at thirteen and worked his way west, riding for different cow outfits, until he hit California and fell into the movie business. He'd been making his living as a stunt rider since sometime in the silent twenties. But in the months I knew him, he talked all the time about his plan to get out of stunting before his body was broken for good; if it wasn't the dude ranch over in New Mexico, it was an orange grove east of Glendale. He always talked like he was a few months away from having the money for it, but every dollar he made was bet in poker games—his friends sometimes had to pay his electric bill when he ran into a losing streak at cards. He didn't have much of a life outside of his work and playing cards. He lived in a rundown furnished apartment in West Hollywood, didn't have a wife or kids. When he died, a bunch of us had to put money in a hat so he could have a cemetery plot and a tombstone.

That first day at Las Cruces, though, I didn't know a thing about him except he was dressed up like a cowboy hero and doing the kind of work I wanted to be doing. I let a little time go by, and then I said, "I don't mind working for Harold, but I guess I'd rather be riding horses than saddling them for other people."

He gave me a brief look. "Yeah? Well, I don't recommend it—Cab ain't nothing like Harold—but you could go talk to him. One guy didn't show up to work today, maybe he'll let you fill in." He pointed his cigarette at my hat. "You're dressed for the part."

He was all decked out in that Wichita Carson costume, fancy blue embroidery on the yoke and cuffs of the shirt, but he meant I was dressed like any of the riding extras, the men riding behind the leaders in a posse or a band of outlaws. Most of the riding extras in those days were men who had come off the ranches, like me, and they just showed up to the set in their own Levi's and a faded work shirt, their own hat and boots, sometimes a neck scarf. I didn't look much different, although I guess my flat-crowned buckaroo hat must have looked old-fashioned.

I didn't have any idea how to find Cab, which I said to Steve Deets. "Anyway, I've got to stick around until they shoot the scene with Harold's plow horses."

He stood up. "Well, when you get done with it, we'll likely still be working. We're shooting a couple of chases today and a bulldog fall. I expect Cab's already headed out to Cow Rocks to get set up. Ask somebody where that is." He dropped his cigarette and stepped on it and started to move off.

I said, "That ride you made was something."

He looked back at me. "Yeah? Cab run the shot so long, that horse like to beat me to death. I can still feel I got blood behind my eyes." He looked pleased about it, though, so I was glad I spoke up.

17

IT WASN'T MUCH LONGER before they called up the Belgians, and then it wasn't much of a scene, just pulling a farm wagon down the western street, clopping past John Barlow in his Wichita costume and a pretty actress in a suede skirt, the two of them saying their lines on the steps of the sheriff's office. When they cut me loose for the day, it was just past noon. I turned the Diamond horses into the corral with Verle's stock, unhooked the trailer from the truck, and drove up a rutted dirt track about a half-mile to the Cow Rocks location where O'Brien's crew was filming. There weren't any permanent buildings out there, just a bunch of trucks parked next to a clump of dry trees, and some picnic tables under a shade cover. They were breaking for lunch just then, and a guy in a caravan was doling out sandwiches and soda pop from the back end of his rig. I asked a guy in the lunch line where I could find the ramrod, and he pointed to Cab standing over by the camera truck with three other men. I guess if I'd listened for a minute I could have found him just by following the sound of his Mississippi drawl. That voice could charm the quills off a porcupine, but he was swinging it like a club just then, shouting past one of the men without waiting to hear what was said back. I stood off from them and tried not to look like I was listening in. The fellow Cab was arguing with gave up after not too long and just dropped his chin and stared at the ground. Cab stuffed his hands in his pockets, rocked on his heels, and went on talking in a gradually lowered voice. Every so often one of the others nodded, but none of them said anything. After a couple of minutes Cab broke it off and headed for the lunch truck. He walked right past me without giving me a look.

I said, "Mr. O'Brien, I heard you were short of riders today."

He didn't stop walking.

I caught up and walked with him. "I was wrangling a wagon team this morning, but I'm done for now and I thought maybe I could ride for you."

He didn't slow down or look at me, but he said, "Who the hell are you?"

"I'm Bud Frazer, I've been working for Harold Capsen at Diamond Barns. But I was riding rodeo broncs before I came down here. I've been riding horses since before I could walk."

If he heard any of this, he didn't act like it. He bulled right to the front of the lunch line, picked up somebody else's box lunch, sat down in a camp chair, and unwrapped the waxed paper from a sandwich and started eating. I could feel the heat building in my face. I wasn't about to stand over him, begging for work. I said, "Well, just so you know, I can ride anything with four legs and a tail. I'll be around if you want to give me a try," and I turned on my heel.

I sat a minute on the running board of the Dodge and didn't look his way. I was too steamed up to be hungry, but then I got up anyway and walked over to the caravan and got myself a box lunch and sat in the open door of the truck to eat it. When Cab finished his lunch, he went off without looking in my direction.

About the time the lunch truck was packing up to leave, a guy carrying a clipboard came over to me and said, "If you can get yourself a horse and get back here in ten minutes, Cab says you can have half a day's work."

He meant get a horse from Verle. I raised a big rooster tail of dust driving back down that dirt road. Verle half laughed and shook his head when I told him what was up. Actors and extras familiar with the White Oak stock had already taken his good mounts, so he didn't have much left. He brought me a sorrel with a flaxen mane and tail, a good-looking horse except for the long scar on his off foreleg, and while we were tacking him up he said, "You might have to strong-arm the son of a bitch. He's opinionated, and he's got a cast-iron mouth." Well, I felt half-naked getting on a horse without spurs, but I had left Diamond that morning figuring I wouldn't need spurs for a wagon team, and my dad's rowels were lying where I'd kicked them, in a corner of the bedroom. When I climbed on the sorrel and booted him in the flanks, he just flattened his ears and chewed the bit. It wasn't until Verle whacked him with a buggy whip that he finally broke into a jog-trot, and then I had to plow-rein him with both hands to get him steered back along the rutted road.

When I got to Cow Rocks I could see some men on horseback lounging about a hundred yards off and a bunch of people gathered out there around a camera and boom mounted on a dolly. I was about to head that way when the guy with the clipboard waved me down and called out, "Go see the prop master, get yourself a gun."

I had been around enough sets to know what a prop master was, but I hadn't ever needed to ask one for a gun. I found him sitting under a shade umbrella next to the grip wagon. He wrote my name in his ledger and held out a rubber six-shooter and a vinyl holster and belt. I had to get down off the horse to take them from him, which I knew was a bad idea, but there wasn't much I could do about it. When I buckled on the gun belt, the whole outfit was light and stiff, nothing that felt real, but I liked the way it looked hanging from my hips.

When I tried to get back on the sorrel he got cagey, pivoting side-ways to keep the stirrup out of reach of my boot. I yanked on him and cuffed his nose, which caused him to act aggrieved and let me mount, but as soon as my back pockets hit the saddle he broke into a hard trot and tried to head for the corrals. I had to seesaw the bit in his mouth to get the son of a bitch headed the right way, out to where they were getting ready to shoot.

Steve Deets was there, still dressed up like Wichita Carson. When they'd filmed the bucking scene he hadn't been wearing a gun belt, but now he wore a fancy tooled leather belt with a big buckle and two pearl-handled pistols that looked real. He gave me a glance and then inclined his head to point me toward where I should be, at the back of the posse of eight or nine riders. A couple of the other men glanced at me, but nobody said anything about the way I had come in, steering with both arms like a greenhorn.

The dolly track started right there and ran straight out in front of us across a hardpan plain tufted with clumps of sage and greasewood. Cab was standing on the dolly with two camera operators, looking through a small eyepiece across the flats toward a line of scrub willows more than half a mile away. When he turned back around to us he didn't notice me, or he acted like he didn't. He said to Steve Deets, "I want you charging like hell, and you better get this in one shot," as if it was a warning, and Deets said, "You bet." I couldn't see his face, but he sounded like he was smiling when he said it. Then a shirtless grip rolled the dolly out along the tracks, with Cab and the two cameramen riding on it. Halfway to the willows, they anchored the dolly and Cab stepped off and walked around behind, and you could just see his head peering at us past the shoulder of one of the camera operators.

Half a dozen crewmen were standing way off to the side of us, one of them the man that Cab had been arguing with before lunch. He called to us through a megaphone, "Y'all let Deets get out about thirty yards and then go. Everybody stay in a tight pack." I guess he thought this was enough instruction even for the greenhorn, because he gave me a short look without adding anything else.

Deets glanced back at all of us. He was wearing long-shank Mexican spurs this time, and I could hear the rowels jingle lightly when he straightened around in the saddle. I thought the horse he was riding was the one Wichita Carson always rode, a big white stallion called Sunday, but I heard later he was a stunt double that looked like Sunday. The saddle was decked out with silver conchos, and there were long, silver-trimmed tapaderos over the stirrups. Deets settled his hat and made a gesture with his head to signal he was ready.

The guy with the megaphone called, "Quiet on the set," and I guess seasoned picture horses—chase horses, they were called— must know the sound of those words, because all them, even that cross-grained horse I was riding, went still. I don't think I'd ever heard things fall so suddenly quiet, the only sound the kind of clicking whisper that insects make moving through dry grass. Then there was a shout from out at the dolly, and the man with the megaphone, maybe echoing the word lost to distance, shouted, "Action!" and Deets whooped and spurred his horse into a flat-out run. The rest of the horses were savvy enough about movie work that they didn't quite bolt after him but nervously shifted their weight, and I felt the sorrel shiver underneath me and give a little crow hop of excitement. Then the fellow with the megaphone called "Go!" and we all took off in a bunch.

I had thought I might have trouble with the sorrel, that he might veer off in his own stubborn direction or not have the legs to keep up with the others, but he lit out at a hard run—I lost my hat on the first jump—and he wormed his way into the middle of the pack and settled there. I leaned out over his stretched neck, ropes of his slobber trailing back in my face. Clods of dirt and grass flew up in a pelting rain. We were galloping so close together that I could have reached out and touched the man on either side of me. We raced out along the dolly rails, chasing the dust plume of Deets's horse, and when we swept past the camera I saw it swivel to follow us, the grip pushing the dolly along the rails a short way to give the scene more of a rush.

The whole chase didn't last much more than a minute. Deets pulled to a stop at the edge of the willows, and the rest of us barreled up to him and brought our horses on their tails. I don't know if I thought it at the time—not in words, anyway—but if I could have kept racing like that until my horse wore himself out and lay down underneath me, I think I would have been glad to do it.

18

EVERY RIDER WORKING THAT DAY was well acquainted with the cold-jawed son-of-a-bitch horse I was riding, which is why he'd been the last one standing in Verle's picket line. Somewhere or other that horse had learned all manner of low tricks, and once you had ridden him you would go to some trouble to keep from riding him again. Somebody had named him Prince, so whoever was stuck with him was naturally dubbed the Prince of Fools, a label that got shortened to Fool and trailed me for most of the time I worked in the movies. But the men had all had plenty of practice keeping a straight face when a newcomer got stuck playing the Fool, so they didn't start ribbing me until after we'd finished the chase.

"Hey kid, since you need both hands to steer that horse, maybe you want me to scratch your ass when it itches."

"Nah, Jerry, he don't need your help. He bounces on the saddle so much he can scratch his ass on the horn."

And so forth.

In my experience hanging around rodeos and ranches, men wouldn't bother to razz a green hand or a dime-store cowboy, so I took this to mean I had measured up. I said something along the lines of *go-to-hell-why-don't-you,* which seemed to make them happy.

I had been ready to beat the damn horse with a piece of pipe earlier, but by now I was feeling almost warmly toward him. I steered him back along the dolly rails to hunt up my hat, and when we went past Cab he looked over but didn't say a word to me.

They set up the camera at a new place, right at the bottom of a long hill. What Cab wanted for the scene was the outlaw gang exploding over the top of the rise, racing in a tight bunch downhill straight toward the camera, then scattering apart at the last minute, the horses flying by close enough to throw dirt on the lens. He sent a guy out to tie a strand of orange ribbon to a clump of greasewood so we'd know where to swerve off—"and no damn sooner." He didn't want all of us breaking in the same direction, so he told each man which way he wanted him to swerve. When he got to me, he said, "I want you to follow Wes there, when he heads off to the right," and he pointed out a guy sitting on a broad-barreled chestnut. "But if you can't muscle the fucking horse where I'm telling you, just be sure you don't run over the fucking camera. Got the idea?"

I could feel a little blood come into my face. Cab's foul mouth shocked me a bit, to tell the truth. I had grown up in a part of the world where men just didn't swear that much, and even hanging around rodeo grounds I hadn't often heard worse than *son of a bitch.* But I was feeling pretty cocky right then, so I said, "You bet," trying to get the same tone I'd heard Steve Deets use, and this made a few people crack a smile. Cab was one of them. I didn't know him yet, or I might have seen this as a reason to worry.

We started our run a few hundred yards back so that when we cleared the top of the hill we'd be going flat out. The sorrel liked to gallop, I'll give him that, but for his own inscrutable reasons he wanted to put himself shoulder to shoulder with a big red roan in the middle of the pack, nowhere near Wes's chestnut, and I had all the work I could handle trying to get him lined up behind Wes so we could veer off the way Cab wanted us to. When we came pounding down that hill, the ground streamed by in a blur and I never did see the orange ribbon, but when Wes peeled off to the right I yanked the reins hard over. The sorrel flung his head around, fighting the bit, and cut so close to the camera I think he wound up jumping one of the splayed legs of the tripod. The camera operator's head was down, his eye fixed to the lens—I don't think he knew how close we came to running him over—but I caught a glimpse of Cab perched on a stool behind him, arms folded and shoulders leaning out almost in our path, and Cab didn't flinch a bit. I never got to like Cab much, but I sure admired his nerve.

He was known for keeping a tight schedule and shooting his scenes quickly, but he made us run that chase twice more—he wanted us breaking over the hill faster, he wanted us bunched up tighter, he wasn't happy with the way we were veering off. When he finally had something that suited him, we brought the horses into the shade under a couple of valley oaks and took a break while the crew got busy setting up for a new shot.

Verle had come out to the field by then, driving a truck with a water tank, and he started making the rounds with buckets, watering all the horses. When he got to mine he petted the sorrel's forehead and said sweetly to the horse, "I hear you and that Fool over there are getting along real swell."

I made a scoffing sound, and Verle looked my way and grinned and said, "I told you he was opinionated."

I said, "If he was mine, I'd think about shooting him." I wasn't joking, which I guess Verle could hear.

He ran his hand down the horse's shoulder to the scar on his leg. "Well, he got tripped one too many times with a dubya, and he took a grudge about it. Next thing we knew, he was making up his own mind about what he'd do or not do."

What I'd heard about the Running W had come mostly from Harold—the dubya was the principal reason he wouldn't let his horses be used for stunts. I hadn't seen one in action yet, but I knew a horse could wind up lamed or dead. Or you'd get a horse like Prince, who had so much hatred for the people who'd tripped him he was ever afterward looking for ways to make a rider's life miserable.

The horse had his nose buried deep in the water bucket. When Verle stroked his long neck he sighed and shifted his hindquarters as if he was making ready for a cow kick, and Verle laughed and took a step back. "He's pigheaded," he said, "but he looks good on camera and he still likes to run, so we keep him around." He gave the horse a couple of pats and walked off. Verle was never sentimental about the horses he wrangled for the cameras, but he could find something to like in just about any horse he came across.

Some of the riders were lying on the dry grass, catching a little rest while they could, so I lay down too and pulled my hat over my face. Almost as soon as I shut my eyes I heard Cab call out, "Hey kid, you, what's your name, Frazer." When I sat up he gestured that I should come over where he was powwowing with Deets. I figured I was about to get my walking papers for some reason, but that wasn't what happened. Cab was sitting in a canvas chair, and he leaned back in it and said, "Have I got you wore out yet?"

My arms and shoulders were aching from fighting the damn horse, but I wasn't about to own up to it. I said, "No sir, I'm doing all right."

"Well, we're about to shoot this here bulldogging gag, you know what that is?"

I would have known what bulldogging meant if he'd been talking rodeo, but I didn't figure it meant the same thing here. I acted like I knew, though, and just gave him a little nod. He said, "I was gonna let Epps play the bad guy, but now I'm thinking you might could do it. It's an easy gag, you'd get a little extra paid. You want it?"

Deets was looking at the ground, frowning slightly, so I knew Cab wasn't giving me a prize for good riding. But I figured this was a tryout, and if I passed I might get on steady with him, so I said, "You bet," which caused Cab to give me another of his little smiles.

"Good. Go back over there to the trailers, find the wardrobe guy, and tell him I want you dressed up like Gillis, and then get back here pronto."

Gillis was the outlaw leader, so the costumer dolled me up in a high-crowned black hat and black leather vest and spurs duded up with copper trimmings. I remember feeling stupidly self-admiring, as if it meant something to be wearing those clothes. Walking back to the setup, I happened to think about Lily, that the next time I saw her I'd be able to say I was riding in pictures now. That in half a day I'd gone from the back of the posse to doubling for one of the principal players.

Lon Epps, the one who had been set to do the gag before Cab gave it to me, and Steve Deets were waiting for me. Epps had a high-bridged nose and a face so deeply tanned that I took him for part Apache, although I heard later he was Dutch or German and came from a tank town in Oklahoma where he had sold barbed wire for a living before he moved over to California and got into movies.

He said to me, "This here bulldog is Carson chasing the outlaw leader, jumping him, knocking him off his horse. But this here won't be like getting bucked off a bronc, if that's what you're thinking. This here horse will be going at a dead run when you bail off. You got to land right, and then you got to hope the other man don't land on you. There ain't no rehearsal, kid, so listen to what we're telling you and maybe you won't get killed." He looked over at Steve. "Or kill my friend here."

He and Deets had worked together quite a bit, and they'd done plenty of bulldogging falls. I hadn't known what the gag was called, but as soon as Epps laid it out I knew I had seen plenty of them on the movie screen—a furious chase on horseback and then one rider coming alongside the other and knocking him out of the saddle, both of them hitting the ground together. Deets and Epps had done so many they could almost have done the gag blindfolded, but just because something is routine doesn't make it less dangerous, which they had learned the hard way. And of course I was dangerous on account of I didn't know a damn thing. In the movies, as my dad liked to point out, you never saw anybody break any bones—both men always scrambled to their feet, fists swinging—but in the real world fellows were always being carted off to the hospital when something went wrong with the gag.

Prince wasn't any kind of horse to use for a bulldog—if his rider bailed off, he'd have kept right on running out of LA County—so Verle brought around a couple of horses who were trained for the gag, who knew to run at a steady gallop in a straight line. Deets's horse was another one of those doubles for Wichita Carson's good-looking white stallion, and Verle put me on a plain bay gelding like the one Gillis rode.

We'd be racing along a dirt road with a grassy sloping shoulder, and I only had to make sure the bay ran close to the edge of the road so when I bailed off I could land on the grass and roll downhill. "When we're in our run, look back once or twice like you're worried about me catching up to you," Deets said, "and then just lean forward like you're urging the horse faster. But don't spur him. Let him set the speed." The bay knew to keep to a straight line—"He runs true," is what Verle said—and I could count on him to keep to a regular pace. He knew he was supposed to let Steve's horse catch up and pull almost alongside. He'd be at a gallop, but nowhere near the lickety-split I had seen in so many movies. As I've said, this was a movie trick: they cranked the camera at a slower speed while they were filming, and when they played it back at normal speed it made everything fly by faster than the real thing.

Steve would be the one timing the fall for the camera. When I felt his hand on my shoulder or back—getting ready to grapple me out of the saddle—I was to kick loose of both stirrups and pick a landing spot, point my left shoulder at it, relax everything, and tuck into a somersault roll. "Don't stick your arms out to break the fall or you'll wind up breaking an arm." And if I could manage it, I should roll to the right when I hit the ground, and Steve would try to roll left so as not to land on top of me.

They went over the gag with me pretty fast because Cab was just about set up, and everybody knew that when he called for action he wanted you right there ready to ride. Then Steve and I jogged back along the road a few hundred yards and waited for the signal to start. The muscles in my shoulders and legs were tight and sore from the riding I'd already done, and by this point I was on edge about the whole thing. I could feel the horse under me picking up on my nerves. Maybe Deets picked it up too. He looked over at me and said, "You know you don't got to jump to your feet afterward like they do in all the pictures. They put that in later with the real actors. I don't know if you had that idea. You just keep rolling—it takes some of the bang out of it—and then you just lay there and get your breath, that's what I do. These falls ain't no cake and pie."

I had seen guys knocking each other off galloping horses, going sideways or ass over teakettle, in every oater I ever sat through, and they always jumped right up to fight. So I had ideas, for sure. Growing up on horseback, I had fallen plenty of times, been thrown from horses when they stumbled or fell, been rubbed off under trees and clotheslines, been bucked off when a horse was scared or feeling frisky. And I'd been falling off rodeo broncs for more than a year. I hadn't ever deliberately jumped off a horse that was running full out, but I think I shrugged at Deets's warning. I was nineteen years old, putting on an act like I was already an old hand.

We didn't have long to wait. From the bunch of people around the camera, I heard somebody with a bullhorn shout, "Quiet," and then, a couple of ticks later, "Action!" I clapped my legs against the bay, and he took off running. The road was hard packed, and the booming of his hooves against the dirt drove everything else out of my head. When I finally remembered to look back at Steve, I could hardly see him through the cyclone of dust we were raising in the dry road. I turned back around and leaned over the bay's neck and remembered not to spur him.

"Pick a landing spot," Lon had said to me, but a horse at a gallop covers a lot of ground in one stride, so how the hell was I supposed to pick a landing spot I couldn't even see until I was running by it?

Steve came up quickly on the off side—I could feel him there more than see him. But when his hand touched my back it sent a shock through me just as if I hadn't been expecting it, and I must have twitched, which threw the bay off his rhythm. He shied toward the middle of the road, not much, but enough to cause trouble, and by then my boots were already out of the stirrups and I was half out of the saddle and I knew the stunt wouldn't end well—I was headed for a landing on the hard road instead of the grassy shoulder. Steve must have seen it too, because he gave me a shove in the middle of my back while we were both still in the air.

I don't remember much of anything else except crashing into the ground, and the jarring that went all the way up my spine into my skull. They had coached me to fold my arms up against my chest and keep my body rolling, had warned me to shut my eyes and mouth tight against the dust and dry grass. I don't know if I did any of that. I hit on the grass and rolled downhill a couple of times without re-membering to roll to the right. All the breath went out of my lungs and my head rang with noise. I lay there a minute, as stunned as a roped and thrown steer. I couldn't see much of anything through wa-tering eyes, but shortly I heard Lon Epps say, "You okay, kid?" and I realized he was leaning over me, his face a dark blot in a field of sunlit dust.

I staggered to my feet and stood there swaying. "Yeah. Sure." My head felt loose on my neck.

Steve Deets was on his feet, but standing like a hipshot horse with all his weight on one leg. He offhandedly brushed the dust off his costume and then reached down and massaged his knee. He said, "Pardner, that just about undone us both." I wasn't sure if he was talk-ing to me or to his friend Epps.

He had timed the stunt so that we bailed off the horses right where Cab told us to, not more than twenty feet from the camera.

A bulldog stunt was run-of-the-mill, an everyday shot for the crew, so they were already hauling things to the next setup. Cab, though, stepped over to me to have a word. He was smiling as he clapped me on the shoulder, a light blow that rattled my wobbly neck and almost sat me on the ground again.

"I figured you'd need an ambulance or a priest," he said, "but you fooled me. You ready to go shoot another one?"

I had been thinking the bulldog gag was a test to see how much I could do, but now it occurred to me that Cab might be trying to drive me right into the ground. Neither Deets nor Epps looked my way, but I could feel them waiting for the answer. I was so beat up and sore and weak in the legs I wasn't sure I could climb onto a horse without help, but I was dead set on showing I could take whatever Cab dished out. I gave him a little nod and said, "Yeah, you bet."

He laughed. "I'm just joking with you. That's it for today. Put your phone number on my clipboard, kid. I got more work coming up if you want it."

He started to saunter off, and I called after him, "Thanks, Mr. O'Brien." He didn't turn around—he seemed not to have heard me—but Lon Epps made a grunting sound I thought was a laugh.

Steve Deets, still kneading his leg, looked over at Epps and smiled slightly. "Well, if nothing's broke, it's a good day's work."

Epps glanced at him, then down at the ground and then up at me, and said, "Anything broke, kid?"

I shook my head, which set off a shower of red sparks behind my eyes. Epps grunted again, and that time I knew it wasn't a laugh.

The others in the posse were still lounging under the trees, so I walked over there and squatted down on my haunches to loosen up my hips and knees without being too obvious about it. It had been a long time since I'd ridden that hard or taken a hard fall, and they all must have seen me wobble a bit. One of them, a fellow named Wally Gilbert, fished a tube of liniment from his pocket and held it out. "Kid, if you're like the rest of us you'll be sore in the morning. This'll do you better."

I shook my head and said, "I'm not hurting yet."

Wally didn't quite smile. "You young bucks can take a licking, I guess."

After a bit, I said, "I just don't care for that stuff, the stink of it."

That part, at least, was true. The smell of Absorbine could always throw me back to Arlo Gantz and the weeks we had spent scouring the mountains looking for Mary Claudine.

FOUR

Echol Creek

1926–1934

WHEN BUD WAS A BABY, back in Elwha County, Henry had made a blanket-lined box with wire hangers to hook on the top rail of the corral so Martha could keep an eye on the baby and keep him out from underfoot while she worked with her horses. And when she was riding to help Henry at roundup or hauling salt to the pastures, she put the baby in a papoose contraption slung from the saddle horn; later she just rode Bud on the saddle in front of her, buttoned inside her coat. When the boy was old enough to listen and mind what he was told, they laid some logs on the ground in a big square near where they were haying or building fence, set him down inside the logs, and told him, "Don't get out," which worked pretty well. They gave him a stick for digging in the dirt and a bucket of water, and he spent his time making and destroying little rivers and dams and ponds.

Mary Claudine, who was born on the Echol ranch, was a different sort of child, more given to mischief. Some of the methods they'd used with Bud worked for a while, and later they put him in charge of watching the baby—and then became more liberal in their definition of mischief.

Most of the women Martha knew took a great deal of pride in their homes and their cooking, but she had never had much interest in either—she preferred working outside, which was all right with Henry; the Echol place wasn't big enough to support a hired hand, but it was big enough that he needed her help getting everything done. Anyway, he had made her a promise before they were married—it was a famous story in their family—that she would always be able to work outside and he would always help with the housework and cooking.

Martha learned the trick of giving the house a once-over so it looked presentable when a neighbor stopped by, and Henry was the sort of man who picked up his clothes and didn't make more of a mess than he had to—he was careful not to come into the house with manure on his boots. From a young age, their children made the beds, washed the dishes, swept the floor.

Martha always liked to say she couldn't boil water without scorching it, but the truth was she could fry eggs and steak, and the Woodruff sisters had taught her to can meat. She could roast a chicken if she had the time. It was just that she would rather be working outside than standing over a stove. The only cooking she was particular about was coffee. She kept a big graniteware coffeepot on the stove almost all the time, and her children woke in the morning to the sound of their mother grinding coffee at a hand grinder on the wall. She mixed the grounds with a whole egg, shell and all, dropped this mess into the granite pot, poured boiling water over, let it settle, and then poured in a cup of cream—they didn't have a milk cow, but bought milk and cream from one or another of their homestead neighbors. She taught both children to make coffee this way so that in the haying season they could bring gallons of it several times a day out to the fields where she and Henry were working.

Henry, who had lived a bachelor life for twelve years before he and Martha were married, could make a proper stew and baking powder biscuits with red gravy, so in the first years of their marriage Henry did most of the cooking. They didn't ever go hungry—there was plenty of food—it was just that it was plain and unvaried. And when Henry got to the end of a long day, he could wish for somebody else to put supper on the table.

One day when Bud was maybe six or seven years old, he pulled up a chair and stood on it to help his dad make bread. Henry let him deliver the sourdough sponge in spoonfuls from the heavy crock into the bowl of bread makings. The sponge hissed slightly when he dug down into it with the wooden spoon.

"That sponge is older than you are by a long shot," Henry told him. "Your grandma is the one who taught me to grow it and use it. It's got to be watched over, kept alive."

Bud watched his dad bearing down, beginning to stir the stiff dough. "It's alive?"

Henry pointed at the crock with his chin. "If it was dead it wouldn't bubble and fizz like that. It'd go flat and gray."

It seemed a kind of magic to the boy, the way flour, salt, and milk could become bread, the loaves rising up golden and fragrant. After Henry taught his son to feed the sponge, keep it warm, not stir it too much, he learned to make pancakes, and then doughnuts firm enough for his mother to dunk in her coffee.

His grandmother, when she heard that Bud had taken up this interest in cooking, gave him *The Better Homes and Gardens Cookbook*. He read through it but never relied on it much. The book called for too many things they didn't have on hand, and anyway he had his own notions for how things should be done, and no sure idea what some of the terms in the book meant. What was "simmer" or "baste"?

When Mary Claudine was four or five years old, she pulled up a chair and tried to help Bud roll out the biscuit dough. A good many of the people he knew, especially his friends, considered cooking the province of girls and women, but it didn't occur to him until much later that he might have begun shifting this chore to his sister. He did teach her a few things, but he went on doing most of it himself. Mary Claudine was more a nuisance than a help to him, and he had seen his dad at the stove more often than his mother. He didn't give his friends' point of view much credit.

Mary Claudine was a daredevil who liked to ride bareback at a flat-out gallop, liked to slide in a dishpan down steep, gravelly banks. She was a monkey when it came to tree climbing, light enough to crawl out on the thinnest branches, and she liked to taunt her brother, who couldn't climb as high. Her favorite pastime, even on a windy day—especially on a windy day—was to scale a tree and sway in great arcs, singing "The Bear Went Over the Mountain" at the top of her voice.

She collected snake skins and the bony skulls of dead creatures. She liked to catch toads and softly stroke their bellies. She often kept a living field mouse in a lard tin lined with straw in the bedroom she shared with Bud. And she collected birds' eggs; she had learned from *The Book of Knowledge* how to poke a hole and blow out the innards, then clean and mount the hollow shell with a neatly labeled card. She scrupulously gathered only one egg from each nest, because it was a scientist's responsibility to conserve as well as to study.

But she was afraid of black widow spiders, which liked to hide in the darkness under the toilet seat in the outhouse; she worried about being bitten on her fanny if she had to sit there very long.

When she had to use the outhouse at night, she whispered to Bud without leaving her bed, "Bud, Bud, Bud," until he made a waking sound, and then she told him desperately, "Bud, I have to use the toilet."

This was when she was a coming five-year-old and Bud ten. It pleased him that Mary Claudine, who in most ways was bold as brass, had a few things she was afraid of. Sometimes he made her ask him three or four times, "Bud, go with me. I'm scared. There's spiders in the toilet. Bud, Bud." But some nights he just sat up in the darkness and went out with her to the back porch. In silence they slipped their bare feet into barn boots and trudged across the dark yard, the loose laces on the boots slapping faintly.

While Mary Claudine watched him through the open door, Bud went into the outhouse and gave the seat boards three or four hard kicks. He didn't think it made any difference to the spiders, and Mary Claudine could have kicked the boards herself. But she was afraid and he wasn't.

"Okay, they went way down," he told her when he came out.

"Are you sure?" They were both careful to speak quietly so as not to wake their parents — the night seemed to carry sound farther than the day. Neither of them ever thought about the booming sound his boot made, kicking the boards.

For good measure he'd piddle into the hole. He told her, "I drowned a few and the rest legged it down to the bottom." This wasn't true, or anyway it was information he couldn't have been sure of. The hole was pitch-black even when a full moon laid down a bar of light through the door. The time or two when he had shone a lantern down the hole to reassure Mary Claudine, they had been able to see the bottom of the pit, but not the first couple of inches along the underside of the seat.

"Okay. But wait for me, Bud," she said when she went in, and she left the door cracked open slightly in case she had to make a fast escape.

She always had to screw up her courage before she sat down. Bud waited until he heard the faint sound of her pajama bottoms sliding down and then he scratched the wall of the outhouse with his thumbnail to scare her. This had worked a few times, but by now she was used to it. She said, "Quit it, Bud, I know it's you." So he walked off a couple of steps and stood there looking up at the stars.

Whenever he was outside at night, Bud tried to pick out constellations he had memorized. They were easy to see on the star charts, with lines that connected the stars and made recognizable shapes, but the Milky Way was a vast blurred wash through the middle of the sky above the ranch, and there were so many stars and planets that it had been hard at first to single out any but Orion and the Plough.

He had recently made a cardboard planisphere, and when he held it over his head and lined it up with the night sky he could sometimes find the dimmer constellations, but he had forgotten, this time, to bring it with him when Mary Claudine woke him for her trip to the toilet.

"Which one is the Bear?" she asked when she came from the outhouse. She craned her head back in imitation of her brother.

"Find the Plough first," he said, pointing. "Then see? Those three pairs of stars are the big bear's paws. The paws are up high right now, like he's walking upside down. Or rolling on his back, like a horse does."

She was silent, frowning as she peered up. He had shown her the Great Bear and the Little Bear a few times, but she was never sure if she really saw them. She liked the idea of bears roaming around the night sky, but she wasn't as patient or as interested in the constellations as Bud was. She wished the Bears really looked like bears.

"I'm cold," she said suddenly, and ran for the house, clomping in her loose boots.

Bud went on standing there a while longer, looking for Hercules. It was a big constellation but hard to find because the stars weren't bright. "Look between Draco and Ophiuchus," the book said, but he couldn't always find Ophiuchus either.

When he went back into the house and got under the blankets, Mary Claudine whispered to him, "Bud, I wish we were Indians."

This was a recent obsession of hers. She had been studying pictures of Iroquois houses in *The Book of Knowledge*, and their mother had read to them *Strongheart of the Prairie* and another story about two boys who lived as Indians. She had declared her wish to be not only an Indian but a boy and to live in a longhouse with her clan totem—a bear—painted above the door.

"We're not," Bud said matter-of-factly. "Anyway, the Indians are a vanishing people." He had heard this in school and read it besides.

He longed, himself, to be a cowboy, though it seemed possible that cowboys had had something to do with vanishing the Indians.

"If we were Indians we wouldn't have an outhouse, we could just go in the woods."

"There's spiders in the woods. And snakes. You'd still be afraid."

"I'm not afraid of snakes." She considered, for a moment, whether black widow spiders, who lived in dark holes in the woodpile and in outhouses and cellars, might also like to live underground, and whether they might come out to bite someone who was squatting to piddle. But she didn't want to argue with Bud about spiders, she wanted to think about being an Indian. "If we were Indians we could ride bareback and wear moccasins and put feathers in our hair."

"You can already ride bareback. Anyway, I'd rather have a saddle." He wanted a saddle heavy with silver ornament like the one Tom Mix had, and a bridle and breast collar studded with silver conchos, but he was old enough now to know the impossibility of such a thing. He hoped for silver conchos on his hat someday. And a horse like Tony, a good-looking dark sorrel with white stockings on his hind legs, who had saved Tom Mix's life more than once. Bud's mother was always buying and selling horses, and if she ever took in a horse that looked like Tony, Bud planned to claim it for himself.

"If you were Indian, you'd have to scalp people," he told his sister.

"Strongheart never scalped anybody."

"He did. They just didn't write about it in the story." He said this just to throw her for a loop.

She was silent a short while. "Well, then I would scalp people," she said, "but only the bad ones."

When Elbert Echol had first settled there, the scrubland to the northwest was all open range, and the few ranchers and wheat growers living at the north end of the county sent their children eight or ten miles down Bailey Creek Road to the schoolhouse at Foy. But by the time Henry and Martha moved onto the place the hillsides were crowded with homesteaders, and a two-room grade school had been built at the upper end of Bailey Creek Valley for the children of all those farmers. It would have been four miles on bad roads from the Echol ranch to the schoolhouse, but it was less than half that on a trail over the ridge, so from the time he was six years old Bud rode horseback to the Bailey Creek Grade School, and when Mary Claudine was six she followed behind him. They carried their lunches in lard pails—a hunk of roast beef, a handful of dried apples, a jar of milk. In winter the milk would just about freeze, and they'd eat it with a spoon like ice cream.

The school had two teachers and as many as thirty students in the first years Bud was there, but by the time Mary Claudine started first grade the school was down to one teacher and twelve or fifteen students. The second classroom standing empty was a testament to failure: most of the homesteaders who had come into the countryside in the 1910s and 1920s had been trying to make a living from seed crops on 160 acres of poor soil and less than ten inches of rain a year. By 1930, even before the Depression made itself felt, a great many of them had gone bust and walked away from their farms, and the number of schoolchildren had dwindled.

The upper valley was always remote, even in its heyday, and over the years a string of teachers came and went, dismayed by the solitude and discomforts of the place; Bud and Mary Claudine's education was erratic at best.

In Mary Claudine's first year at school, the teacher for a short time was a woman who was deeply educated, with a degree in biology from Stanford. There were, of course, no job prospects or research fellowships for women in the sciences, so Miss Goodell had taken up rural school teaching because it gave her opportunities for unfunded field research. To her way of thinking, the Bailey Creek School, situated at the edge of the Ochoco Forest Reserve, was very nearly at the center of the natural world. She kept a horse in pasture behind the school and rode it into the hills on the weekends in all sorts of weather. At school Miss Goodell wore shapeless brown dresses with a watch pinned to her bosom, but for her weekend excursions she wore lace-up boots and knee-high breeches, a man's shirt, and a floppy khaki hat with feathers and fishhooks stuck in the band. She said to the girls in her class, "Who would want to play with dull old dolls stuffed with sawdust when you could keep a snake as a pet and catch live toads and collect birds' nests?" Mary Claudine was smitten from that moment.

Even by the lights of the remote Bailey Creek Valley, Miss Goodell's behavior was bold and strange, verging on disreputable. Allowances were made for ranch women like Martha Frazer, who wore men's clothes and worked out of doors in all weathers, laboring alongside their husbands; Martha herself was known to be a gifted broncobuster, which was an acceptable if not respectable reason for a woman to don trousers. But schoolteachers were held to a different standard. There were seven men on the school board, including Henry. Miss Goodell was let go halfway through the school year, by a vote of six to one.

The woman who replaced her was Miss Ruedy, who had been teaching domestic economy and rules of decorum for young women in the city of Medford, and might have gone on doing it if the Depression had not cut such a big hole in the Jackson County budget. In Miss Ruedy's view, the Bailey Creek School was at the end of the earth, its students an alarming band of oafs and ruffians. Mary Claudine, in particular, was at odds with her teacher from the first weeks of Miss Ruedy's tenure, and in mid-March Miss Ruedy sent a letter home to the girl's parents.

At six Mary Claudine was as small as some four-year-olds, too little to saddle and unsaddle a horse herself, so her mother was doing this for her, lifting the saddle off and setting it on the rack. Mary Claudine was in her school dress, her long wool stockings dusty with horse hair and scabbed with dry mud. She unfolded the letter from the pocket of her coat and reached it out to her mother with her fingers curled around the damp edge of the envelope. Bud was stripping the saddle from his own horse. He shrugged slightly when his sister threw him a beseeching look.

It was a letter cataloging what Miss Ruedy saw as the girl's peculiarities and wildness: Mary Claudine had captured a litter of baby mice living under the schoolhouse and made pets of them in the pockets of her jacket; had antagonized a porcupine with a flat board and captured its quills to make darts from the hollow stilettos; and every day at recess flopped down on her back in the dirt of the schoolhouse yard, worked up a lot of spit in her mouth, and whistled through the spit—practicing, she said, a screech owl's call. "These are interests and behaviors that I consider more rightly the province of rough farm boys," Miss Ruedy wrote, "and I should like you to speak seriously to her about the proper conduct of a young lady."

Martha folded the letter and put it in her own pocket. "Mary Claudine, go on in the house and set the table for supper. Bud will be in after a minute."

Mary Claudine threw her brother another quick glance and made a beeline for the house. Martha looked toward Bud too. He was making a show of picking up his horse's foot, studying it as if there might be a stone lodged in the shoe. Martha waited until she heard the screen door slam, then said to her son, "I don't know what sort of teacher Miss Ruedy is."

Bud understood that this was a question.

He had recently turned twelve; by now he was used to teachers of strict expectation and vicious discipline, teachers who rapped children's hands with stove wood or wooden rulers. He had learned the trick of staying out of their way. Miss Ruedy on her first day at the school had upbraided the boys for their dirty shoes, and Bud had not gotten over his feeling of humiliation; plus she had gone on calling him Ernest even after he had told her to call him Bud. But it was Mary Claudine who was always in trouble, who had taken to hiding her bruised hands from their parents. It was vaguely unsettling to him that his sister, who was just about fearless, was on her way to being afraid of Miss Ruedy. He didn't know what to make of that, and he didn't know if it was anything he should say to his mother.

Still bent over studying the hoof, he said, "She doesn't like it when any of the kids come to school with dirty fingernails."

Bud raised up from the horse and glanced at his mother. Color had come into her face. After a moment she said, "Well, I have known teachers like that." She petted Bud's horse briefly and then walked off toward the house.

She had grown up in a house without running water, a house where you walked out to the pump in the yard in all weathers, and she had a thorough acquaintance with teachers who humiliated the children from farms and ranches, children who came to school with dirty shoes, dirty fingernails.

She didn't show Miss Ruedy's letter to Henry but considered her reply carefully and then wrote it out in small, neat print on a lined sheet of paper from the pad that Henry used for keeping track of hay yields. "I have spoken to Mary Claudine about her proper conduct, which is to stop hiding her swolled hands from me which I know are swolled on account of being hit with a stick of firewood. I spoke to her seriously that she should not think the wrong was hers. I am only a rough farm girl myself and never hardly wore a dress until I was married but have not thought that a teacher hitting a child with a wood stick is proper conduct for a grown lady. If you say I am mistaken I will come there and hear it right from you. Sincerely yours, Mrs. Henry (Martha) Frazer."

Martha's native shyness could rise up when she was in the presence of one of her children's teachers—she felt sure that whatever she said would point up her own lack of an education—but Miss Ruedy was a special case. Martha had a world of patience, more so than Henry. But she had been the one teaching Mary Claudine to imitate a screech owl's call, and she could be roused to fury by cruelty.

Arlo Gantz had one of the bigger ranches in that part of Harney County. Arlo had grown up in the buckaroo tradition—his grandfather had been Basque, and his father had been part of the *vaquero* crowd that came north from California with Pete French. Arlo had a toothbrush mustache and a flat-top hat with a stiff brim, and he usually wore a tight wool vest and a silk square around his neck that he called a wild rag, and chaps that quit at the knee that he called chinks. A lot of buckaroos liked to sport silver conchos on their hatbands and on their saddles and bridles, but Arlo never took the fashion that far. He liked to say, "I don't think my cows would be unusually impressed by all that silver, and they're the ones would mainly see it, the cows and maybe the sagebrush." But he had big fancy tapaderos on his stirrups and great big silver rowels on his spurs, and he wore leather cuffs on his wrists to save himself from rope burns. He liked the old silent movies because William S. Hart wore a Mexican sash around his hips, which Arlo did too, for tying up the hooves of a steer after roping him. Such things had gone out of style by then, but Arlo kept to the tradition.

Henry could throw a good rope himself, but Arlo was a master rawhide worker—he could lasso pretty much anything on the first throw, either hand. And he was famous for knowing his stock. He kept all of their histories in his head, could tell stories about each of his cows, which everybody who knew him liked to test. When Henry helped Arlo brand his calves, he would point to a cow and say, "What about that one?" and Arlo never had to consider. He'd say, "Well, she lost a calf last year and then didn't breed back, and I thought I might ought to sell her. But I give her another chance, and now she's got that nice heifer calf—see it there? The one with a white patch on its left shoulder? Good healthy calf—and she's a real good mama." And he could do that for every one of them.

Both Martha and Henry admired the old man. One spring, after they had been on the Echol Creek ranch three or four years, Martha sold a pair of twin calves she had bucket-fed and raised up from sickly orphans and spent the money on a red silk wild rag to knot around her neck and a handmade silverbelly hat with a stiff flat crown; the next year, with the money from another dogie calf, she bought the same hat for Henry and chaps that quit at his knees. She might have

encouraged her husband to grow a mustache and wax it, except she
didn't think she'd like the bristle against her face.

Even in the 1920s and '30s there were still some wild horses living up
in the Ochoco Reserve. The Ochoco mustangs ran small, as a rule,
but they were tough enough to keep well fleshed through the winter,
when there might be snow on the ground for weeks at a time. They
had good feet and, as Arlo Gantz liked to say, "good smarts." It was
Arlo's idea that his quarter horses could benefit from the mustangs'
toughness, so one year he and his sons ran down and captured a
young Ochoco stallion, a liver chestnut with a lot of black on him, no
white markings at all, and turned him in with half a dozen of their
Hancock brood mares. They sold the little stallion at auction later on
that year because he was a troublemaker around their other horses,
but before that he sired seven foals.

Arlo and his sons weaned the foals, gelded the colts, accustomed
them to being handled, taught them to lead, and to pick up their
feet for the shoer. Then, when they were coming four-year-olds, they
brought the young horses over to Martha Frazer to start them under
saddle.

The horses were small but agile and alert. Martha liked the way
they moved, the bright look to their eyes, their good muscling, and
good strong legs. They weren't the easiest horses to break, some of
them headstrong and stubborn, but not one of them was lazy, and
once they understood what was expected of them, they were willing
and mostly reliable.

Mary Claudine, who was then seven, began begging for one of
the young half-mustangs, a little dun gelding with a wavy black mane
and forelock standing out against the gray-brown hide, and a black
tail so long it dragged the ground. "He's just like a gypsy horse," she
told her mother, which was not from knowledge but from one of
Bud's drawings, of a gypsy caravan pulled by a horse with a heavy
forelock and a black tail that touched the ground.

Bud and Mary Claudine had both learned to ride on Martha's old mare, Dolly, but this was the year Martha had retired Dolly to pasture, and Mary Claudine lately had been riding a big bright chestnut named Tippy, a levelheaded horse that never bucked but had a fast lope and clumsy feet. The girl liked to ride bareback and play at being an Indian, galloping over ditches and windfalls, racing through creeks so the splash made a big noise and sent all the birds flying up from the willow brush. She wore a hat with latchstrings so that when she rode fast the hat would flutter behind her on its tethers. Martha had been a daring rider herself as a girl, but she had a different view now with respect to her own children and especially her fearless daughter. It always gave her a start to see Mary Claudine on Tippy, the girl so tiny and the clumsy-footed horse so huge underneath her.

She hadn't planned to keep any of Arlo's horses, as Henry thought they already had too many to feed through the winter. But all the half-mustangs were more sure-footed than just about any horses she had met, could pick their way through rocks and brush and badger holes, loose shale rock or steep bare places without stumbling. And the dun hadn't minded at all the first time Martha sat on his back; in fact he had reached around and nuzzled her foot. It had moved her almost to tears at the time. So when she brought the horses back to Arlo that fall she took the gypsy horse as part trade for the work she'd done that summer. Mary Claudine named him Sugarfoot.

When Bud was fourteen, he began trapping muskrat for the little bit of extra income. His trapline was in the upper reaches of Echol Creek, and on a Sunday in late October he went up there to check the sets. He was riding a dark sorrel with white hind legs, a horse he had named Tony.

It was a cold morning. There had been a thunderstorm overnight, but now the sky was as blue as a robin's egg, with just one big white cloud above the mountains to the north.

The first of his traps was at Cooks Bench, where the creek widened and wound itself in lazy curves through a field of bent grass. This was one of the hay fields where his mother grazed horses in the fall after rain greened the stubble, but the damp field that day was sunlit and empty. Bud's trap was at the upper end of the field where the creek went under the edge of the trees, and as he headed there a little breeze kicked up a smell of burnt hair, a smell he knew from years of calf branding. And then another smell he understood vaguely to be burnt meat and death.

Tony carried him a few more yards and then flared his nostrils. He didn't quite buck, but he took a spraddle-legged stance, his sides heaving. "All right," Bud said to the horse. "You stay right here," and he came off the saddle and dropped the reins and walked the rest of the way to what he could see now, a dark shape along the creek bank, in shadow under the trees.

Lightning wasn't overly common in their part of the world, but Bud was acquainted with it. He had several times seen a cow dead on the ground with scorch marks on its hide and had heard stories from Arlo Gantz about entire bunches of cattle or sheep killed by lightning. Sugarfoot was the first horse he had ever seen killed in this way.

He came up close enough to be sure it was Mary Claudine's horse lying dead, his hind legs in the creek, his long black tail floating out gently on the current. Then he went back to Tony. The horse had waited, but he was standing nervously, his ears flattened all the way back, and he gave Bud a baleful stare as if he thought the boy had done him a great disservice.

Bud mounted and turned back toward home, and after a minute he asked the horse for a jog-trot. When he came through the gate into the pasture, he saw his father digging out one of the old rotted posts along the east side of the fence. Bud had been going over and over in his mind the words to tell his sister what had happened, but now he headed for his dad.

Henry straightened up from his work and called to his son, "That was quick. You checked all those traps already?"

"No, I came back," he said. "There's a dead horse up at Cooks Bench. It's Mary Claudine's."

"You don't mean Sugarfoot."

"It was him."

Henry looked off toward the creek and then back toward Bud. "Could you see what killed him?"

"Lightning, I'm pretty sure. He had a burnt mark all down his back."

"I think your mother turned some of her horses onto that grass a few days ago. Lightning didn't kill none of the others?" He was thinking it was a good thing she'd been keeping Dolly in the home pasture and not with the horses grazing on that bench.

"I think the lightning must have spooked the others off. There weren't any horses up there at all."

Henry set aside the shovel he'd been using and wiped his hands on his bib overalls. "Well, your mother took the truck into Foy to pick up some staples for this fence, and Mary Claudine went along with her. They won't be back for a while." He looked at his son. "Where's the horse at? I know you said Cooks Bench, but is he laying out in the middle of the hay field or where?"

"He's laying in the creek."

"Well, we better pull him out of there before he poisons up that water. You go in the tool shed and rummage up some logging chain, and I guess I'll go harness up one of the mules."

Bud dug a long, heavy piece of chain out of the box of chain goods and then helped his dad buckle the plow harness on Mike.

"Grab that can of kerosene there, too," Henry said.

They rode up the creek trail single file. Bud rode Tony with the chain piece doubled up and draped across the horse's withers, and Henry, carrying the can of kerosene, rode Mike with his legs clamped around the plow harness. He was still wearing his overalls and his chore boots.

When they came near the place where Sugarfoot had died, the mule and the horse both got agitated, so they left them standing twenty yards off and walked on up to the carcass. Bud stayed back while Henry squatted down next to the horse and examined the wide streak where the hair had been burned off right down to the hide. The horse's eye was as pure white as the albumen of an egg. "I think it must have entered through his eye and traveled down his back," he said over his shoulder to his son.

A horse might live to thirty or better if well cared for. Henry was thinking about something Martha had said to him once, that she had often thought of her life in terms of how many good horses she would love. He knew that Dolly was the first horse his wife had loved, and he was afraid that Sugarfoot had been his daughter's first. Mary Claudine was nine years old that year, her horse just about six.

He stood up. "Well, let's have that chain," he said to Bud, "and then you might see if you can get that mule to come any closer."

Bud handed him the chain and went off to see to the mule. Henry stepped out on the rocks so as not to get his feet wet in the creek; he looped an end of chain around the dun's hind fetlocks and then walked away from the creek bank, pulling the chain out to its full length, waiting while Bud talked to the mule and petted him. Bud didn't have his mother's gift for working with animals, but he was patient, and horses generally trusted him. Finally the mule agreed to come close enough to reach the end of the chain. Henry bent down and hooked the logging chain to the heel chain on the plow harness, and when he rose up again Bud said, "Okay?" and Henry nodded.

Bud walked the mule out until the chain pulled straight and tightened around the dead horse's fetlocks. Mike was a big half-Belgian; they had used him to drag dead cows and logs and stumps. Sugarfoot weighed maybe eight or nine hundred pounds, but some logs the mule had dragged must have weighed at least that. Bud chirped to him and asked him to put his hindquarters into it. He scrabbled and dug his hooves into the soft ground of the stream bank. The chain rattled and then tautened, and the mule moved ahead, his big muscles clenching, his neck bowed; the horse's body began moving by inches, trailing a mud smear. His long, coarse tail swept over the water and then over the mud like a bead curtain as the mule went on pulling.

When the carcass was fifty feet from the creek, Henry said, "That ought to do it." He came up and unhooked the heel chain and then went back to unhook the drag chain from the horse. The links had bitten through the hair and hide, and the left cannon bone had broken, which he thought must have happened at the beginning when the carcass had twisted on the ground. The unnatural angle of the leg and the fractured white bone poking through the hide briefly sickened him, made him turn his head away.

He loosened the links from the fetlocks and gathered up the chain and carried it over to where Bud was waiting with the mule. "Go ahead and take him out of the way," he said. "It'll be smoky." He waited until Bud and the mule and the sorrel were well out in the open field, then picked up the kerosene can and went over to the carcass and poured out the kerosene and lit it afire and walked off a dozen yards before looking back. Then he walked the rest of the way to where his son was waiting.

They stood and watched the fire burn. Dark smoke rose up and smudged the sky above the edge of the field.

"Mary Claudine . . ." Henry said, but then wasn't sure what it was he had started to say.

"I wish it wasn't her horse that got struck," Bud said.

Henry tried to think how to answer. "I don't imagine he felt it," he said finally. "It probably didn't hurt him at all."

It seemed to Bud that his dad didn't understand what he was getting at. "She'll feel awful about it, Dad." His sister had a soft spot for runty barn cats and crippled birds, baby mice, toads with ill-formed legs. In the fall, when they weaned the calves she hid in the barn and wept to hear the bawling of the bereft babies and their mamas. She had always hated knowing that the young steers they sold every fall after roundup were doomed to be butchered and made meat.

"I know she will," Henry said. "But that's just the way it is sometimes, Buddy. Things happen." He looked tired and unhappy, watching the fire burn. After a moment, he said, "She'll just have to make peace with it."

When the flames had died somewhat, they headed back down the hill. The blue sky had turned dark in the northwest, and soon a wind came up, thrashing the branches of the pine trees. It was the sort of wind that always signaled a change in the weather, and maybe a little rain. They heard thunder two or three times, a long way off, but never saw any lightning.

Henry watched the sky and finally said, "It's moving off southeast," in case Bud might be worrying about it.

They were all the way down the hill, passing through the gate that let into the home place, before Bud remembered his trapline.

"Dad, I didn't ever finish checking my traps."

Henry made a tired gesture. "Well, you might as well wait until after dinner now."

The truck was parked in the yard. Henry and Bud went on across to the barn and were stripping the tack off Mike and Tony when Martha walked out from the house.

"I thought you were working on the fence," she said to Henry.

"Well, something came up."

She took in the thing unspoken underneath his words. She didn't ask Henry anything, just watched him pull the harness off Mike and hang it on the sawhorse. She waited through his silence until finally he turned to her and said, "There was a horse killed by lightning up at the bench. Now, honey, don't cry, but it was Mary Claudine's horse, it was Sugarfoot."

Bud had seen his mother cry a few times—she was sentimental about her heifer calves—but *Now, honey, don't cry* was so unexpected that it brought a little heat to his ears and his cheeks, a feeling of shame, as if he had eavesdropped on his parents in an intimate moment.

She didn't cry. She looked at Henry without speaking, then turned from him and looked off toward Dolly and the other horses in the home pasture. What occurred to her, standing there, was how many times she had called Mary Claudine to the window when lightning flashed, just to say, *Isn't it beautiful?*

"I've seen lightning enough times," she said. "I don't know why I never thought to worry about it killing a horse."

Henry was silent for a while, and then he said, "Worrying about it wouldn't have changed anything. There wasn't anything you could have done to keep it from happening."

Martha looked over at Bud. "Was it you who found him, Bud?"

"He was up at Cooks Bench where I set one of my traps."

"There were some other horses up on that grass. Was Sugarfoot the only one struck?"

"The others must have took off. We might have to go looking for them."

Henry said, "Where's Mary Claudine?"

"She's in the house with her nose in a book. We stopped by the Forbeses' place and Evelyn gave her a book about birds. She was reading from it all the way back."

"Well, when I get this mule here turned out, I guess I'd better go in and tell her about the horse."

Martha reached out to touch Mike on the neck, and the mule leaned, pressing himself into her hand. "We'll both go," she said, looking over at Henry. Then she looked at Bud again. "After dinner maybe you could help me find those horses. If they went uphill they probably got stopped at the fence line above the old Troxle cabin."

He didn't say anything about checking his trapline. He said, "All right," and then he said to his dad, "I can take Mike," and he led the two animals out to the pasture fence. He watched them trot out to join their friends, and he watched as his horse rolled around on the ground and then stood up and shook himself off. He was still standing there looking out at the animals when he heard his parents cross the porch and go into the house.

FIVE

19

AFTER I RAN INTO LILY in front of the hardware store, and after we sat through that double feature at the Marcal, we started going to the picture show every Sunday. I'd meet her at the Studio Club and we'd walk to the Iris or the Victory or the Marcal, see a double feature, then go back to her dormitory and play a few hands of cards in the living room, gin rummy usually, or pinochle, hunched over the cards, smoking and talking. What we mostly talked about was movies.

Now that I had some understanding of how the cheap cowboy pictures were made, I had become scornful of them. I told Lily they were cranked out in a week without anybody even knowing what the title was; I was especially bitter about the short ends they spliced in to save money on action scenes.

Well, she had read and studied about the movie business, but Lily had never been on a movie set, never seen a movie camera turning. Her magazines carried plenty of photographs of movie stars lounging on the set or chatting with directors but none of actual moviemaking. So it didn't matter to her that I was only working on Poverty

Row pictures. What mattered was that I was watching movies being made every day.

She would pump me to tell her the details of everything I'd seen that week. If I had been near enough to hear what the director told his camera operator, or what the gaffer told the electrician, she wanted every word of it. She wanted a description of the big klieg lights on telescoping stands, how many there were and where they were placed in relation to the camera and the actors. Why did some of the lights have metal earflaps but others didn't? Did I know why the grips built a tall platform and mounted the camera on it for this scene but not for that one? What about the shiny boards and umbrellas that kept shadows off the scene, and the white butterfly nets that softened the daylight, where were those? And where was the director standing when he said "Action"?

She was always pressing me for a better account. I didn't have answers to most of her questions, and I wasn't much good at the meticulous descriptions she wanted. She would have loaned me her little folding Kodak camera, but all the studios had rules against picture taking.

So one day I filched some paper and a stub of pencil from somebody on the film crew, and I drew what they were shooting at the time, which was a cowboy star and a pretty girl standing next to the cowboy's tall horse. I put in the boom mike overhead, and the camera with as much detail as I could capture, and the little crowd of people standing behind it, watching the actors deliver their lines. Once I'd started, I made another quick sketch, a cowboy actor taking a nap on the grass, with his high-crowned hat over his face and his fancy boots crossed at the ankles, and a jumble of light standards and grips' boxes in the background. I didn't have an eraser, so I just moved the pencil in fine scribbles where I wanted to reshape part of the drawing. To my eye the blurred line could seem intended — an impression of the horse restlessly shifting his weight or wind lifting the fringe on the star's fancy shirt.

When I gave Lily the drawings, she studied them quite a while, her dark brows pulled down to her nose, and then looked up at me. "You never said you could draw, Bud. These are really, really good."

I wasn't exactly embarrassed. I had always liked to draw, and all my life I had been praised for my drawing. But I should probably make it clear right here that becoming an artist was not a notion that had yet taken hold. Back then it was obvious to me that art wasn't related to real work—work you could earn a living at. I had grown up believing that I would make my living on horseback. I was just killing time and helping Lily out, is what I thought when I made those first sketches.

I said, "Well, there's a lot of waiting around on the set. I had the time, and I figured it might be easier to sketch what was going on than tell you about it afterward."

She pointed at the drawing of the actors being filmed, the tip of her finger not quite touching the paper. "Who is this woman sitting with a big notebook in her lap? Is she the screenwriter?"

"That's the script girl. I don't know what a script girl does, exactly, but she's usually on a stool right there next to the camera. She makes a lot of notes. I'm pretty sure she didn't write the story."

She frowned again—I imagine she had been hoping to see actual proof that a woman could be a screenwriter—then went back to studying the drawing. Two men were standing by the camera, and she pointed to the one who had his hand lifted as if he was supporting its weight. "Who's this?"

"That's the focus puller. I guess he's kind of holding the camera steady or something."

She went on frowning. "No, no, I know what a focus puller is, he helps the cameraman keep the picture sharp when the actor moves around. He's turning the lens with his hand, I bet."

It went back and forth like that, until she had learned everything I could tell her about the people and equipment in both drawings. She didn't compliment me again, which I was glad of, but she said, "This is better than a Kodak picture."

Mostly, as a little kid, all I had to draw on were the margins of the

Saturday Evening Post or the backs of old ballots from the last election; for Christmas I always asked for a brand-new tablet of drawing paper. My folks bought me tablets now and then when they could afford it, but it wasn't until high school that one of my teachers made sure I had all the paper, pencils, and paint I could want. The last couple of years, working on ranches and hanging out at rodeos, I was stone broke most of the time, and if I had any spare coin I spent it on beer, not paper and pencils. And I guess after Mary Claudine died I lost some of my inclination to draw.

But after I gave those first sketches to Lily I bought a box of soft lead pencils and a couple of pads of paper, and whenever I was waiting around on the set, I sat down on the ground or in a folding chair close to the picket line and sketched whatever was going on in front of me: the actors, the equipment, the horses lounging about. I bought an eraser too, but I didn't use it much. And then on Sunday I'd hand the drawings to Lily. And after we had talked over what was in them, we would head for the theater to see a double feature and walk out afterward, arguing over what we'd seen.

Before I met Lily, it had seemed to me that movies were fixed, unchangeable, they just existed in the world. I didn't much care for the singing-cowboy pictures, the silliness of the damn things, with a full orchestra suddenly backing up a guy on horseback strumming a guitar, but I hadn't realized that a series of decisions had made it that way, that the movie would have turned out differently if somebody else had been making those decisions.

Lily, on the other hand, was always thinking of how a movie could have been better, which for her meant better written. To her way of thinking, every time a cowboy broke into song the writers were getting away with not writing a real story. Her complaint about the singing cowboys and the eight-day oaters was that they always had a bare-bones plot and not much dialogue. In the lobby at intermission, and later when I was walking her back to her place, she'd be rewriting for me whatever we'd just seen—shifting things around, dropping things out so they'd be less predictable, making up dialogue for the scenes where they'd sidestepped it with a long shot and sentimental music.

She was game to see just about anything playing in town, but she made sure we saw all the major studio melodramas and foreign films dubbed in English or with English title cards. When I didn't like a picture, she would press me to say why, which to my way of thinking was like asking "Why don't you like the way those stars are arranged up there in the sky?" I had thought she was too proud of her French films, but it turned out she was a bit like Verle with his horses: she could find something to like in almost every picture we saw. She judged each one by its own standards. She measured a cowboy picture against other cowboy pictures and not against *Captains Courageous* or *The Good Earth.* "You can't expect a cowboy movie to be *Grand Illusion*, Bud. People call them horse operas because they're like grand opera but more American. Opera has silly plots too." This didn't mean much to me. I didn't have a clear notion what an opera was.

She'd get just as exercised arguing the fine points of a cliffhanger in a chapter movie as picking through the themes in Fritz Lang's films. She'd ask my opinion of whatever we'd seen and then argue with every damn thing I said. I was used to girls who tried to make you think you were smarter than them even if you weren't, but Lily never in her life cared whether a boy knew she was smarter than he was.

When we started going to the pictures together she was still working on her Texas Ranger script. I had seen more hay-burners than she had, so she wanted me to tell her if she was plowing up ground that was too familiar. Familiarity was one of the things I liked about the cowboy pictures—knowing from the outset that Tim McCoy wouldn't be shot dead, that he'd only ever be winged in the shoulder. But this was Lily. Even then, when everything she was writing was more or less pulp work, she kept trying to wrestle the usual stories into something fresh. When we were at the movies she'd lean over and whisper what she thought would happen next, and how it would end, and she was almost always right. So when she read part of her script to me, she would stop every so often and ask me to guess what I thought would happen next. Whenever I guessed right, she took it as bad news. She'd study the script, her eyebrows bunched over her nose, and then scribble something in the margin, and the next time she read it to me that part of the story would be heading off in another direction. I can tell you this: in those early movies Lily wrote, you never saw a cowboy hero save his sidekick at the last minute by cutting the hangman's rope with an unerring shot from halfway down the street.

I had a pretty clear idea that the cowboy hero stood for being brave and true, a man with a strict moral compass, and in those days even Lily hadn't thought too deeply about what else the cowboy hero might stand for—she was the first person I ever heard talk about Buck Jones, Tom Mix, all those top cowboys, as if they were America's version of Galahad or Lionheart, as if the cowboy were a chivalrous emblem of our national character. But she always wanted any picture, even an oater, to be about real people and their problems, so it annoyed her that all the heroes in westerns were rootless loners, lacking a childhood history and a family—no parents or brothers or sisters, never a wife.

A few years later, in *Bent Grass,* the only western she wrote for RKO, she gave Ted Barstow a sister living back in North Carolina, a sister he had broken with for reasons that were never quite spelled out. Toward the end of the film Lily put him at a desk writing a letter to her, a letter full of loneliness and regret and tender affection. John Ford always said he couldn't have made *The Searchers* without RKO having first made *Bent Grass.* I don't know if that's true—those pictures don't seem at all alike to me—but I know the studio tried to cut that letter-writing scene out of the film before it hit theaters, and Lily had to dig in her heels to keep it.

20

I HADN'T SAID ANYTHING TO HAROLD about the work I'd done for Cab O'Brien up at Las Cruces—I figured he wouldn't want to know I'd been stunt riding while I was supposed to be wrangling his horses, and anyway I wasn't sure anything would come of it. But I told Lily.

I didn't have to do any bragging to impress her. She hadn't seen any of the Wichita Carson movies, but she knew Sunrise was a real studio, not a two-bit outfit making serials on Poverty Row. And she had seen enough cowboy pictures to know what a bulldog fall was when I described it to her. Walking back from the theater, she pressed me to tell her everything I'd done and seen, and she acted interested in it all, which inflated me somewhat. And I guess this must have been about the time I started thinking about kissing her.

Hugh had been needling me about her from the start, as if the two of us were courting, which I knew we weren't—I hadn't been thinking of her in that way at all. When I told him Lily wasn't a girl I would want to marry, he just started talking about her in a smutty way, as if the only other reason to spend time with a girl was

if you were taking her to bed. I should have stood up for Lily's reputation, but his ribbing carried a strong whiff of congratulations, of
admiration, and the truth was, I didn't want to let on to him that I
hadn't ever bedded a girl. So I went ahead and let him think what he
wanted.

And then I did start thinking about Lily differently. She was
older than me by a few years, so I thought she might have had serious boyfriends and maybe even some experience. And I had begun
to think she was interested in me after all. When she had got me
talking that day about the stunt riding I'd done up at Las Cruces,
it had felt like the kind of thing a flirting girl might do to nour-
ish a boy's ego. Now that I've got some distance from it, I can see
that I was feeling itchy, the way young men get, and Lily was the
girl at hand. Anyway, I started to think she might be fair game for
some kissing and nibbling and touching. Of course in the dirty stories Hugh was always spinning, this was the kind of thing that led to
sexual relations, and I guess I was starting to get serious about having
some.

I worked up my nerve for a couple of weeks, and then when we
happened to see a movie with some romance in it, and when the
movie stars went into their clinch, I made a clumsy move, trying to
plant a kiss on her lips.

We bumped heads, and she whispered, "Bud, what are you doing?"
and rubbed her forehead.

"I was about to give you a kiss," I said.

The movie theater was dark, but not so dark I couldn't see her
frown.

"Well, don't."

"I just felt like it. I still feel like it. Why don't you let me kiss you?"

For some reason, she took off her glasses and squinted at me nearsighted. "Why do you want to?"

"I just do. I've been thinking about it for a while."

She was still frowning—it was a look full of suspicion—and it
took her a minute to say anything else. "On the lips?"

"Sure." I leaned in again, but she pulled back and turned her head so my kiss brushed the side of her mouth.

"Bud, quit it. I don't know why you want to kiss me. We're just friends. Anyway, I'm older than you."

"You're not much older, and anyhow, what does that mean? Have you got a lot of boyfriends or something?"

She threw me a look I couldn't read. She didn't answer, and after a moment she put her glasses on and turned toward the screen and studied it. I was embarrassed for reasons I couldn't have put into words, which I guess is why I started to say something else, something about her boyfriends. She stood up suddenly and put on her sweater.

I wasn't sure what was going on. I stood up too and said, "Are you mad?"

She said, "No," with her face turned away from me, but she sounded mad, and she walked up the aisle and into the lobby without looking back to see if I was following.

When we got out to the sidewalk I caught up to her and she said calmly, "That was really stupid, Bud. I'm not interested in having sex with you."

I was stunned for a minute. I hadn't been clear in my own mind whether I was after sex or after Lily, so it was a shock that Lily herself seemed to know which it was and had spoken right up about it — had called it "having sex," which wasn't what any of us said back then.

I know I must have turned color — my face was hot. I said, "It was just a damn kiss," like I was the one entitled to be mad. We walked a block or two without talking. I shoved my hands in my pockets and kept my head turned from her, studying the shop windows.

Then she said, "We don't love each other, we're just friends. And we can't be friends if we're having sex, Bud. You wouldn't want to be friends with me if you thought I was fast." She said this in almost a matter-of-fact way, but her eyebrows had closed in a hard frown, the same expression I had seen on her face when she was thinking about how to fix a bad movie.

I said again, with a hell of a lot more force, "It was just a damn kiss. You shouldn't get so het up about it." And then I said, "Well, I changed my mind about it anyway," like I was sore at the whole idea. Like I had all the girls in the world to choose from, and Lily Shaw didn't even make the list.

I had kissed a few girls in high school, and once a woman I met at a tavern had let me pet her breasts through her brassiere, but I hadn't ever talked to a girl about sexual matters—I hadn't ever heard the word "sex" spoken by a woman before—so I had by now come to the belief that Lily knew a good deal more about these things than I did.

Well, I was wrong about that. What I would come to know much later was that she hadn't kissed a single damn boy yet, and she was still trying to figure out the whole confusing business of her crushes on girls. Up to now, she had thought I was harmless, not a boy she might need to be careful of; but she hadn't ever been the object of anybody's sexual attention, which I think must have accounted for some of her fearlessness. And I believe it came into her mind that day that she might not want to go on being friends with somebody she had to be on guard against.

I didn't know any of this at the time, and I was inflamed with a particular kind of embarrassed anger. Rummaging around in my head looking for a way to get off the track we were on. After we'd walked a while in silence I said, "Well, we skipped out on that movie, so I hope you already figured out what happens at the end." Like I was still mad at her but ready to forget the other stuff that had happened.

For a minute she thought about whether to answer me. Then she said, looking straight ahead, "He runs after her and finds her in front of the museum. It's nighttime and it's raining, so when they kiss we can't tell if it's the rain on her face or if she's crying. She's crying, though, and we know it's from happiness."

She said it deadpan, and by this time I'd had a few weeks' education in film clichés, so I answered with a sound that wasn't quite a dry laugh but almost.

We didn't talk much more on the walk back to her dormitory. We went ahead and played cards without saying much, and when the lights in the front rooms blinked—a signal that guests should be heading for the door—we both stood up right away. Lily hesitated, but then she said, "See you next Sunday." I dipped my head and said, "Sure," as if we hadn't come near to calling it quits a few minutes earlier.

I didn't catch the bus back to Diamond right away—I was full of unspent, inarticulate embarrassment and a yeasty tension that I didn't know what to do with. It was after dark, but the weather was dry and not cold, so I just started out walking, weaving around through the neighborhoods and staying off the boulevard, figuring I'd walk to the bus stop on Western, the last one before the road goes uphill into the park.

In those days, even in the cities, you hardly ever saw a dog on a leash—dogs would be roaming around loose, hanging out with kids playing ball under street lamps. But halfway along my route there was a brown dog on a six-foot rope tied to the front porch of one of those California bungalows you still find in the neighborhoods, stucco with peeling paint and a sun-faded, half-rotted awning over the living room window. The dog, ribby and filthy, was lying curled up on the dirt below the porch. A dog doesn't like to shit in his den, so it looked like he'd been going to the end of the rope, squatting to take a dump, and then curling up to sleep as far from the piles as he could get. But I could smell the stink of his shit from yards away, and there were clouds of flies swarming around the feces.

When he saw me, he stood up and walked toward me as far as the rope would let him. He didn't raise his hackles. After we had stood looking at each other a while, he moved his filthy tail. He had a long narrow snout and one ear folded over, and his legs were too short to balance his long body—not a good-looking dog by anybody's standard.

Even now I can't tell you why I went up to him and untied his rope. I can't tell you what this had to do with trying to kiss a girl and being rebuffed, but I know it did.

The dog crouched and curled his lip while I was working on the knot. He didn't get the idea right away. I waved my arm to send him off, which made him shy and cower, but when I kicked my boot toward him, he finally figured out what I was saying and he loped down the street without looking back.

There were lights on in the house, but nobody came out to the porch. I stood there a while, thinking about going to the door, but finally I went on up the street. I hadn't even gone a block, though, before I heard a guy coming up behind me, calling something I couldn't make out. I turned around and waited for him.

"What the hell!" he yelled. "You the bastard that loosed my dog?" This was Sunday, but he was wearing dirty overalls, his face and hands sooty, as if he'd worked all day in a metal shop maybe, or sweeping chimneys.

"Dog didn't want to be sleeping in his own shit," I said, and he sang out, "The hell if it's your business!"

He was close to me by then, and I got ready to hit him if he came at me. Or hit him even if he didn't come at me. He was heavier than me, but I was taller: I figured I had more reach and he had a softer gut. But he was still a couple of yards off when he stopped and took a wide stance and shook his hands in front of his face as if the fingers were burning. He said, "The damn dog might have got the rabies! I been tying him up since he got bit by a coyote. What the hell I tell my kid, heh? Tell him his dog's gonna get shot?"

There had been a rabies epidemic in Los Angeles the summer before I got there, people dying of dog bites, and for a few months any dog running around loose had been suspect. A lot of dogs had been shot. It was one of the first stories I had heard when I got down there.

My face went warm. I said, "Tell him his dog didn't like sleeping in his own shit," and I turned around and walked off.

He yelled after me, "Ah, go to hell!" but it didn't have any great force in it, and he didn't make a move to follow me. At the time I guess I thought he was chicken. Now I think he was just tired, and this was the end of a long day.

When I got to the middle of the next block, I took a quick look back. He was standing in front of his house, looking down the street. His damn dog was trotting toward him, tongue lolling in a big smile.

21

THE PHONE NUMBER I had put down on Cab O'Brien's clipboard was the number for Diamond Barns, so for the next three or
four weeks every time some two-bit studio called up to rent horses I
thought it might be Cab. Finally, early in the week after that whole
thing with Lily, the kiss, and the dog and all, I got a call.

The woman on the phone said if I wanted to ride for Cab I should
show up at Corriganville in the morning, be there by six. I didn't
know how the hell I'd get out to the Corrigan ranch by six—it was
clear out in the valley, and buses didn't run that early. But I said I'd be
there, and then I told Harold I had something else to do the next day.
And I asked him if he'd loan me the Dodge because the something
else was clear out in the valley.

He and Hugh were sitting in the living room playing dominoes
when the phone rang, and he had heard my side of the phone call.
Maybe he didn't know exactly what the hell was up, but he could
guess, and he gave me a look. "As it happens, we got an easy day
tomorrow, so take the Dodge, but get it back here by six." Then he
gave me another look, tipping his hat back so I could see his face
and know what he was getting at. "And don't figure this for a regu-

202

lar thing. The rest of the week we got plenty of jobs to keep us busy. If this gets to be a regular thing, you'd better figure out where you're gonna live when you quit working for me, because this here isn't a boarding house and I need somebody who can show up for work every day."

Harold was always straight with me, and fair, which at the time I didn't appreciate as much as I should have.

So I drove out to Corriganville the next morning, where it turned out they were shooting a Republic picture starring Wild Bill Elliott. I didn't see much of Cab that day, I guess because he was overseeing a saloon brawl on an indoor set. A second assistant named Mike Tifflin was in charge of the humdrum stuff, and he put me in with a dozen men riding in a sheriff's posse hard on the trail of some badmen.

Steve Deets and Lon Epps were riding in the posse too. I had been thinking they were unhappy with how I'd handled the bulldog fall that day at Las Cruces, but now that we were working together again they seemed to think I was worth a little help. One or the other rode alongside me most of the day and gave me a rundown on some of the gags—what a transfer was, and a pony express mount. If you bailed off a running horse, that was called a saddle fall, and if a Running W or a pitfall took your horse down and sent you flying off him, that was a horse fall. And they gave me some tips on how to do it without breaking my neck. In a few hours I learned things it would otherwise have taken me weeks of movie work to pick up, if I didn't kill myself first.

That day at Corriganville none of us did any falling, but we did a lot of riding at breakneck speed, the horses crowding stirrup to stirrup. It was a long day, and then we had to wait in a long line to get paid. I was tired but feeling as if I'd done real work for a change, and then Mike came along and told all of us that the movie they were shooting would be ten days' work if we wanted it.

I didn't have to think too hard about it. I figured this was my chance to get on steady with Cab, and I was pretty puffed up about riding for Republic, one of the so-called big guns when you were talking about westerns. So when I got back to Diamond I went ahead and told Harold I was quitting. And I'm ashamed to say I didn't give a single thought to whether I was leaving him short-handed.

He wasn't surprised. He and Jake had the hood up working on the GMC when I told him, and he just said, "You got somewhere else to bunk?" without looking up from what he was doing. He didn't say he was planning to kick me out that night, and I imagine if I had said I didn't have a place yet, he'd have let me stay on until I found one. But I'd been talking that day to a fellow named Dave Keaton, who shared a rented house with a couple of other riders. Dave had said I could sleep on their living room sofa for a few days if I needed to, so I told Harold I was moving in with some other stunt riders who lived down in Los Feliz.

Harold didn't look up. "Well, good."

I watched him and Jake work on the truck for another minute or two. Harold's dog was sitting on the porch staring out at something in the middle distance. I looked, but couldn't see anything in particular he was staring at. After a minute I turned back around to Harold. I felt like I had to say, "I came down here looking to ride horses, not to haul them around in trucks and hold the reins for other men."

Harold straightened up and ran his greasy hands down the front of his shirt. "I know that," he said, then stuck his hand out. "You take care. O'Brien's got a reputation for wrecks."

We shook, and I said, "Thanks for everything, Mr. Capsen," and he said, "You need a ride downtown?"

It was a half-mile hike down the driveway to the road, and then probably two or three buses to get to Dave's place, but Harold's offer shamed me a little, and maybe I would have said no. Then Jake spoke up and said, "I can drop him off, boss. It's on my way, more or less."

I went into the house and packed my duffle, then walked down to the shed where Hugh was trimming hooves on one of the horses. I told him I was leaving Diamond to work for Cab O'Brien. Hugh shook his head and grinned. "Riding stunts is a good way to get yourself wrecked. You'd be better off sticking with Harold."

When I told him I'd be making more money in one day than Harold paid me for a week, he just shook his head again and laughed. "You'll be spending them big bucks on hospital bills maybe." We shook hands, and he said, "Don't get killed if you can help it."

I climbed into Jake's old Chevrolet, and we bumped down the half mile of dirt lane in silence. When we were on the pavement and headed downhill into town, Jake said, "So you're gonna be riding for O'Brien? I heard he's hard on horses."

I said, "What I've heard, he's hard on his riders."

He kept his attention on the road. After half a minute, he said, "Well, the way I look at it, those riders are lining up to take the work, but the same can't be said for the damn horses. Nobody asks a horse if he wants to get tripped or run off a tilt chute. You heard about that horse that died making *Jesse James*? They ran him off a cliff, he broke his back or something, rolled over and drowned."

This had been in all the newspapers, and Lily said that everybody at the Studio Club was talking about it. Horses had been dying in the movies since the early silents, but nobody had noticed when it was the cheap oaters, the serials and cliffhangers pumped out on Poverty Row. This was a Tyrone Power picture, though, so the story about the dead horse had raised an unholy outcry.

I was gone from Hollywood by the time they quit running horses off cliffs, but while I was down there the major studios were just starting to get back into cowboy pictures after a decade or better of leaving them to the low-budget blood-and-thunder outfits—*Jesse James* was the first in a string of them coming out that summer—and the stars at the big studios, big stars like Tyrone Power, didn't want their names connected to the death of a horse. If the western had never moved off the bottom half of the bill and over to the major studios, maybe they'd *still* be running horses off cliffs—that's something I've thought about once or twice.

I hadn't ever seen a tilt chute in action, but I had seen plenty of pictures where the hero, escaping the bad guys, rides his horse right off a cliff into the water, so I acted like I knew what I was talking about. "He just landed wrong is what I heard. They run horses off cliffs all the time and they don't usually get hurt."

Jake cut his eyes to me, then looked back at the road and was silent.

At the time I thought Jake was sentimental about horses. The truth was, he just had a good opinion of them and strong views about how they ought to be treated. He was like my folks in that way, and it was how my folks had raised me. But a horse had played a part in Mary Claudine's death, and if I wasn't exactly holding a grudge against the whole horse clan, I was at a point in my life where I was intent on being unsentimental about horses and everything else.

When Jake dropped me off in Los Feliz, I thought the odds were pretty good I wouldn't meet up with him or Hugh or Harold again, because Harold's horses hardly ever worked one of Cab O'Brien's jobs. I was wrong about that—I ran into each of them a few more times before I left Hollywood for good—but when I shook Jake's hand and stood on the sidewalk holding my duffle, watching him drive away, I had the same hollow, butterflies-in-the-stomach feeling I always got when I was about to climb into the chute with a saddle bronc. I had come down to Hollywood expecting to fall off horses for the cameras, and I'd been looking out for that kind of work all the time I'd been wrangling for Harold. But I hadn't actually thought through the part where I'd leave Diamond Barns, leave Harold's employ. I could count on the fingers of one hand all the people I had come to know in California, and now I was cutting myself loose from three of them. That's what I happened to think.

22

THE SOFA I SLEPT ON in the Los Feliz house turned out to be too short and plenty lumpy, and it smelled like cat piss—it was a long way from the servant's bedroom in Harold's fancy house. But I was riding in movies and not sleeping in an alley somewhere, and all of us were working on the same job, so we could ride out to the location together in Dave Keaton's old Franklin sedan. In the mornings I just folded up the blanket and shoved my duffle in a corner, brushed my teeth, and climbed into the back seat; that was it. No need to feed, groom, and load horses into trailers before heading to the set at five in the morning. And they always stopped at a diner on the way back to the house at night, so I never let on that I knew how to cook a pork chop.

Pretty much the only thing I knew about movie riding was the coaching I'd had from Steve Deets and Lon Epps, but I picked up a couple more things from Dave in the few days I lived in that house. Before he came to Hollywood, he had done some trick riding for wild west shows—double vaults and side cartwheels and what-all. He liked to use an extra stirrup—he called it a step—that he'd made out of scraps of leather, which he buckled above the stirrup so he'd have something to push off on when he was doing a saddle fall or a bulldog. And he had some polo stirrups that hinged on both sides so they'd break open and release his foot quickly when he was the one being bulldogged or when he was flying off a horse fall. I never did get myself any polo stirrups, but I found some scrap leather and made a step like the one Dave used, and I know it saved me from getting hurt a couple of times.

For the first couple of days on that Wild Bill Elliott picture we mostly did a lot of fast, hard riding. We would do a chase scene, then maybe change wardrobe and horses, and film another one. I learned that any time you were in a posse or a gang of outlaws or a bunkhouse crew, they wanted you bunched up, riding flat out, even if all you were doing was riding from the ranch to the saloon. And when you got where you were going you were supposed to pull to a stop and jump off the horse like the saddle had caught fire. So they had to keep bringing in fresh horses for the ones that were wearing out or pulling up lame, which I learned was typical. I had always thought Harold was too fussy about the people he rented his horses to, but I began to see his reason for it.

It was Mike Tifflin who ran things when it was just straight riding, but Cab showed up toward the end of the week to ramrod a running gun battle. The crew was setting up to shoot in a big field that Corriganville used for saddle falls. It was about fifteen acres of old farmland that had been disked with a tractor and the earth mixed with peat and sand to make the landings softer. We were dressed in itchy, hot costumes that day, pretending to be a cavalry troop, and Cab looked us over like he was the inspector general. Then he pointed at a man I didn't know—it was Ralph Foster, the fellow I later roomed with in Arizona—and at me. "You and you. I want you shot off your horses."

Some phony sagebrush had been set out for markers, and Cab walked us through the field so we'd know where we were supposed to be when we took our falls. Then he said he wanted one of us falling head over heels off the rump of the horse, and he didn't care which one of us it was.

If I haven't already said so, every gag was priced out. For straight riding it was a flat day rate, but on top of that the studios paid an "adjustment" for every saddle fall, bulldog, transfer, horse fall, what-have-you. It varied with the movie budget is what I was told, but the ramrod usually was the one setting those prices, and he could be generous or tight in how he doled out the adjustments. The interesting thing is that Cab was one of the generous ones, and this might be why he had a lot of men willing to work for him, even when they knew he took risks with his crew.

I hadn't done any falling since Las Cruces, but a backflip was worth eleven dollars in those days—damn near a fortune to my way of thinking. I didn't have any idea how to do one without breaking my neck, but I might have stepped up and said I wanted it, except Ralph got his name in first. I wonder now whether Cab would have let me try it. He knew I was green and I might have made a botch of it, maybe gotten myself killed or crippled, but knowing Cab, he could have been hoping to catch a spectacular wreck for the cameras.

Then he pointed at me again and said, "So that means you're taking the first fall, kid." I knew from what Steve Deets had told me that this was not good news: the first one to fall has to lie there and play dead while the rest of the horses run by him. "You got to quit rolling as quick as you can," Steve had said to me. "It's easier for a horse to keep from kicking you if you're not moving. If you stand up before all the others have come through, you're liable to get run over."

We walked back to where the rest of the riders were waiting, and as soon as we were mounted up, Cab called for action. The whole bunch of us, fifteen or twenty, went galloping across that field like lives were at stake, pretending to shoot our fake guns back over our shoulders. I was at my mark so fast I didn't have time to get worked up about it, I just bailed off like I'd been shot, smacked the ground hard with my arms tucked into a hedgehog roll the way I'd been coached, and then lay on the ground like a corpse while all the horses went flying by me and over me in a rain of damp clods. A man I had known when I was growing up, a cowhand who worked sometimes for Arlo Gantz, had a divot in his head the size of a golf ball where a horse's hoof had stove in his skull, and that dull-minded fellow came into my mind while I was lying there.

When the whistle finally blew, I wobbled to my feet, and I was standing there half-dazed when Steve walked up to me. "You're getting the hang of it," he said, which made me stupidly proud of myself.

Cab worked all of us hard that day. Right after we did the running gunfight, the crew moved everything over to a long, low slope and got set up for a shot of cavalry making a downhill charge toward a bunch of Indians who'd taken cover in a ravine. While the prop master was doling out rubber sabers, Cab said he wanted some horse falls to goose up the action, and who wanted to volunteer? I hadn't seen the Running W in action yet—I should have kept my head down when he looked around for riders—but I thought it over and then nodded and touched my fingers to my hat, and the only reason I didn't get killed or busted up that day is because Cab wasn't looking in my direction, and other men got their hands up first.

A bunch of grips came along while we were getting our horses sorted out, and they set about burying a bunch of heavy truck axles in the ground, each one hooked to a big coil of airplane cable. Then the wranglers hooked the other end of the cable to cuffs on the fetlocks of several horses, and through a complicated three-ring apparatus— this was the W—on a surcingle around each horse's body. When they were set, we all mounted up and waited for the whistle and took off racing down the hill.

One of the horses rigged up and hooked to the cable was a rangy chestnut who must have been tripped before—he'd been edgy when they put the cuffs on him, and his muzzle and the white blaze on his face were crisscrossed with scars where the hair had grown back a different color. So I guess he had it figured out. He was running behind me, so I didn't see what happened, but they said when he got to a spot about thirty feet from where he was set to fall he came to a hard stop, planted all four feet, and stood there. The man riding him jabbed in the spurs and whipped him, but that horse just groaned and flung his head up and down and wouldn't budge.

The other rigged horses were out in front of me, though, so I got a good look at how the Running W worked. We were riding at a pretty fast clip, and when the cables suddenly played out to their ends they snatched the horses' front feet up to their chests in mid-stride and flipped them over on their heads and shoulders in a cloud of dust and shattered sagebrush, and the riders went flying off in spectacular fashion.

If it had been up to me, I probably would have put my horse on his butt and stopped right there to keep from running over the men on the ground, but we were supposed to keep racing downhill, brandishing our sabers, which meant I had to trust the horse I was riding, a horse I had known all of ten minutes—had to trust him, in a flat-out run in a crowd of running horses, to jump the men like windfall logs and veer out around the tripped horses, who were already lunging to their feet and shaking off blankets of dust, had to trust him not to lose his footing or get spooked and start bucking and throw me off into that mess. But when the whistle blew for the end of the scene, the other men just pulled up their horses, and several of them lounged back and took out their smokes as if nothing unusual had occurred. I looked back up the hill and saw the tripped horses all standing, looking dazed and confounded, like they were surprised to still be alive. I was frankly surprised by it too.

Mike Tifflin was up at the crown of the hill, yelling through the bullhorn that we should come up there and regroup for another shot, and when I started my horse in that direction I passed Wen Luett-gerodt, who had been one of the men riding a horse fall that day. He was walking along pretty slowly, smoking a cigarette, not showing any signs of wear, except his cavalry uniform was all brown with dust and he was missing his hat and there was a lot of chaff in his hair.

When I went by him I said, "I guess you've done that a bunch of times."

He kept walking. "A few." He looked up at me and smiled a crooked smile, and I saw he had blood around his teeth. "Another day another dollar."

When we got up to where Mike was waiting, Cab was standing a few yards away chewing out the rider who'd been on the chestnut horse, and Mike told us the whole thing had to be run again because the horse stopping in his tracks had ruined the scene.

The horses who'd been tripped were wobbly and shaking, not in shape to do it again, so the wranglers brought in a fresh bunch, and the same men who had fallen the first time went ahead and rode the gag again, which saved me from giving it a try.

But I wound up doing three saddle falls that day, and it was after dark by the time I got back to the Los Feliz house. I was covered in dust, had grit in my teeth, my legs and back were aching, and my shoulders were purple with bruise. I fell asleep on the couch without the energy to wash up. I guess I thought I had pretty much arrived at being a movie cowboy. Although from where I am now, this strikes me as a belief grounded in a lack of information.

23

I WASN'T SURE where I stood with Lily. Now that I was riding for the cameras, there wasn't as much waiting-around time, and it was hard to find a place to stash a drawing pad and pencil when we got called for our scenes, so I didn't have any sketches for her when we met up that Sunday. But the stunt riding gave me something to talk about, some chatter to keep the quiet from taking hold. She asked a lot of questions and seemed pretty interested in the answers, which suited both of us. I didn't take any of this for flirting, I took it to mean she was interested in every part of moviemaking and happy for me that I was finally riding in the movies. And for the time being, I took it to mean we had got past our dustup. Or mostly past it.

A couple of weeks later she started working as a reader for Sunrise Pictures, which gave us something else to talk about.

In those days, the head of the Story Department at Sunrise was Marion Chertok, a Russian woman of about forty who spoke with a heavy accent. People said she had ridden with the Cossacks during the Great War, which may have been somebody's idea of a joke or could actually have been true. What Lily told me—most of it gossip she had heard from girls at the Studio Club—is that Marion had been Ronald Vlackey's secretary in the silent-picture days when Vlackey himself had been the story editor at a tiny studio down on Gower Street, and as he had climbed up the ladder he had brought her along with him. Now that he ran Sunrise, Marion was his number two.

No one thought Marion and Vlackey were lovers—Marion was mannish and dour in her shapeless dresses, and Lackey was one of those studio heads who auditioned young actresses on his office couch—but everybody knew she was the only person whose judgment Vlackey trusted unreservedly; Marion Chertok and Ronald Vlackey together decided on every picture that was made at Sunrise. Marion wasn't the only female in Hollywood who had risen that high, but all of those women could have squeezed into a single booth at the Brown Derby, so it made Lily happy to be working for one of them.

Sunrise wasn't top drawer by anybody's measure, but they put thirty or forty feature films on the floor every year, and their readers were always looking for the next property that might be the basis of a film adaptation. They read screenplays written in-house or submitted on spec, novels and stage plays, galleys of books about to be published, magazine short stories, even opera librettos, newspaper features, court records of trials. You read quickly, and if you liked the story you wrote a three- or four-page report; if you didn't, a single page. Then the report went to Marion, who decided whether to pitch it upstairs to Vlackey.

Lily wasn't supposed to judge anything for literary quality. Marion had stressed to her that they were looking for stories that could be compressed and simplified, stories with a neat resolution. If it required too many trucking shots or establishing shots or expensive camera setups, it was probably out. And some of Sunrise's actors were barely literate, so a story without much dialogue was a definite plus—fewer lines for the actor to memorize. Almost half their movies were hay-burners—the Wichita Carson picture I'd ridden in at Las Cruces had been a Sunrise picture—so they were always on the lookout for a western that kept things simple: one street, one girl, one saloon, one hero, one villain at the head of an anonymous gang of henchmen.

When Lily told me about the illiterate actors and the one-horse stories the studio was looking for, she didn't make excuses for it. She said, "It's not real writing, it's almost the same thing I was doing for Mr. Buchanan. But at least I'll get a better idea what a studio is looking for. And I might be able to get somebody to read one of my scripts." The job wasn't what she had come to Hollywood to do, but at least it was headed that way. She knew you had to get your foot in the door somewhere.

The Story Department that Marion was in charge of numbered at least twenty-five people: readers, stenographers, researchers, a couple of foreign-language translators, and a corps of writers. Most of them reported directly to her, but the writers had their own department head who reported to Marion, and that was Dale Lampman.

The writers' offices were in the back lot, an old wooden building called the Barracks, while the rest of the Story Department was housed in the big stucco building at the front of the studio grounds. The two offices were separated by a cluster of sound stages, shops, storage buildings, and a bunch of outdoor sets—a block-long western street, a two- or three-acre jungle, the false front of a city street. At least twice a day Lampman made the long walk through those sets to Marion's office, where they talked over scripts and story ideas for a few minutes behind closed doors. On his way out, he made a point of passing through the readers' room, where the women—they were all women in that office—turned pages and scribbled notes in a semi-quiet commotion. He liked to remind the girls that he had been a reader himself when he started in the business. Sometimes he paused and rested his hand on a woman's shoulder as he leaned over to deliver some bit of advice—"a little pearl of his wisdom," as Lily said to me mockingly.

I never did see Lampman in the flesh, but over the years I've seen a few photographs. He was thirty or thirty-five then, a big guy, hook-nosed, with a soft face. He was not good-looking, and he had a lot of dark hair at his wrists and climbing up his neck from the collar of his shirt, but he had noticeably blue eyes, he wore well-tailored suits and ties, he combed his hair straight back from his forehead, and Lily said he smelled faintly of good aftershave. He had charmed Marion in some unspoken way—this was something everybody knew—and when Lily went to work there she heard the others speak obliquely about the girl whose position Lily had filled, a girl who'd been fired by Marion because she "hadn't got on well" with Mr. Lampman.

When Lily had been there a couple of weeks, one of the girls in the reading room told her in a lowered voice that Dale Lampman was "dangerous." Lily had been around the picture business long enough by then—we both had—to have heard a few stories: men who claimed to be with a casting agency, holding interviews for new talent in a hotel suite late at night, men sidling up to young women in the dark corners and alleyways of a movie set, men with roaming hands adept at opening the buttons and hooks on period costumes. She knew what was being implied about Lampman.

But after his up-and-down inspection of her the day she started work—too thin and breastless, as she knew, and her thick eyebrows unplucked—he hadn't paid her a minute's notice. It had been clear to her for years that she was not the sort of girl who stirred a man's blood.

On the Sunday after she started at Sunrise, she told me everything that had gone on that week at the new job, the stories she had read and reported on, and what people had said to her. But she left out the part about Lampman being "dangerous."

She may have had a few reasons to keep it to herself, but here is one: I had moved in with True Riddle by that time, had gone out partying with him on Saturday night, and I think when I saw her that Sunday I must have been strutting around like a young rooster. Put that together with the kiss I had tried to give her, and I imagine Lily thought I was not the right person to talk to about lechery.

24

A RIDER NAMED MASON something-or-other had been doubling for the star in most of the stunts on that Wild Bill Elliott picture, but when they got ready to shoot a runaway Conestoga wagon, they brought in a wagon driver to play Bill, and this was True Riddle. He was a young guy, no older than me, but he'd been around the movie business all his life. His dad had starred in about a hundred silents for Mojave Pictures, playing Dusty Jones, a square-jawed cowboy hero, Mojave's version of William S. Hart. In a funny way Hollywood was a company town, a one-industry town. If True had been born in Detroit, he might have followed his dad onto an assembly line at General Motors or Ford, but in Hollywood he fell into the movie business. By the time I met him, True was driving all manner of rolling stock—horse-drawn wagons and stagecoaches, army ambulances, buckboards, Roman chariots, tallyhos.

I'd been driving teams around the ranch since I was four or five years old, and I thought I knew how to handle the leathers, but True Riddle was another story: he seemed to just send his wishes out through the lines so the horses could read them like coded telegrams. He was one of a handful of movie people who could handle a six-up at a full gallop, along with the tricky, dangerous business of cutting the team loose and bailing off the seat as the wagon overturned, which was what they were filming that day in the Elliott picture.

I had seen this stunt more than a few times on film without thinking much about how it was done. They had dug a narrow trench so that when the left-hand wheels rolled into it the wagon would tip over, but hell, I don't know how True could see where the trench was, coming at it from a few hundred yards back with all the dust raised by six horses at a full gallop. And then he had to pull the cable rig at the last minute to set loose the horses, and the wagon was already careening over when he jumped clear.

I had figured that if I got into the movie business I'd be riding horses. I hadn't wanted to drive wagons. But after I watched True do that stunt, and after I heard people talk about the other picture work he had done—driving rigs through floods, flames, and over cliffs, driving blind from a hiding place inside a runaway wagon—I started hanging around him whenever I could, hoping to pick up some advice. Well, it turned out he was like a lot of those specialty stuntmen, not willing to teach anybody else his secrets in case they ended up cutting into his own livelihood. About the only thing I heard from him was a story from the old silent-movie days before Yakima Canutt had invented the breakaway rig that set the horses loose. In those days, when the wagon flipped over it would bring down the horses too, and when True was a kid, watching the movies his dad starred in, he had seen horses tangled up in the wreckage, crippled or killed by that stunt. "My dad never liked the breakaway, he thought it looked phony," he said. And he shrugged, not weighing in on the question himself.

Maybe he didn't want to tell me his secrets, but I was the first person he had met, the first one his own age, who knew how to harness a team and drive them. In southern California a lot of ranchers and farmers had already gone to tractors, and the old teamsters True had known as a kid, the ones who had taught him how to drive, were a thing of the past. I hadn't ever driven our wagon down the road at a flat-out gallop as was always happening in the movies—we'd never had a team run away on us, and there'd been no need to go that fast. On the other hand, True hadn't done any of the real ranch work I had done, the work my folks were still doing, everything handled the old way with horses. So he started pumping me for particulars about how I'd used teams for field work and feeding cattle and logging timber, as if every part of it was extraordinary or exotic. In the end I think he pried quite a bit more out of me than I managed to pry out of him, although now, looking back, I wonder if he ever expected to make use of what I told him.

We were the youngest guys on the set, which might have thrown us together anyway, and when True heard I was sleeping on a too-short sofa in a house with three other guys, he said he had a bed that nobody was sleeping on. I had been looking around for a rooming house I could afford, but at the end of that ten-day shoot I moved out of Dave Keaton's place over to the house True rented on Gordon Street in a little neighborhood off the east end of Sunset. True had the bedroom, but in the living room was a Murphy bed that dropped down from the wall, the mattress thin and sagging in the middle but an improvement over the sofa I'd been sleeping on.

And it was after I moved in with True that I started going to Hollywood parties, met a girl named Margaret, and finally sowed some wild oats.

True had a red DeSoto roadster and that long family history in the movie business, so a lot of his friends weren't the cowboy stuntmen we worked with but a young crowd of junior writers, assistant directors, actors, and actresses who were up-and-coming bit players. Pretty much every Saturday night he went off to one of their parties—a gathering at somebody's house out in Encino or the valley, where everybody stayed up until damn near daylight drinking beer and eating sardines. Or down to the beach at Santa Monica, where they'd stand around a bonfire roasting wienies and passing a flask of booze.

The parties I had gone to in Harney County had mostly been

in barns and community buildings, and the principal entertainment was school kids singing "The Streets of Laredo" or "The Yellow Rose of Texas." And for the past couple of years I hadn't been to any parties at all, just dance halls and bars near the ranches and rodeos I was working at, where the principal entertainment was drinking beer and getting into fights. I felt I was a little rough around the edges for the crowd True hung around with—girls in pastel dresses and boys in suits and ties. But I was working on not giving a damn if people thought I was rough, and I was feeling halfway cocky now that I was riding and falling off horses in the movies.

So the first Saturday night after I moved into his house I rode with True in his DeSoto out to a party in the valley.

He stopped on the way and picked up three girls waiting for him in front of a house in Thousand Oaks. I was wearing my bib-front shirt and my good hat and boots, and when the girls looked me over I guess they all thought I was an actor. One of them, a tall brunette wearing eyebrow pencil and red lipstick, smiled and said, "Hi," and crowded into the front seat with me and True, her thigh pressing up against mine.

When we got to the house where the party was, a couple of dozen people were already there. A pinochle game was going on in the kitchen, and a few couples were dancing to music from a console radio—Kate Smith singing "When the Moon Comes Over the Mountain"—but mostly people were drinking beer and standing or sitting in the crowded rooms talking about the movie business.

True knew enough of the people there that he just waded right in, which left me standing like a post, so I walked through the house until I saw where they kept the beer, and then I leaned against a wall and nursed the bottle and acted like I was watching the card players. I wasn't there very long before the brunette who had smiled at me in the car came up and leaned on the wall next to me. She was drinking something amber-colored in a glass, not beer. She took a sip and glanced over at me and said, "Are you in the cowboy pictures?"

I said, "Yeah, I'm riding for Republic right now."

I don't know if she got the import of my naming a big-gun studio. She peered at me over the lipstick print on the rim of her glass and pretended to look disgusted. "You cowboys are all crazy. I knew one who broke his leg, and now he's got a limp and has to use a cane. You should try to get into real acting."

I looked down at my boots and said, "They were shooting a fist-fight the other day and I was in the scene. Maybe that makes me an actor."

She gave me a coy look and touched the scar in my eyebrow with her pinky finger. "Well, that's better than falling off horses. Did you get hit in the eye?"

I glanced at her and kept a straight face. "I was riding down the street while they were filming the fight, and I'm pretty sure my left boot made it into the picture." I had told this to Lily a couple of Sundays earlier and she had said dryly, "Ha ha ha, funny boy." The brunette gave me a blank look. I finally had to smile to help her get the joke, and then she laughed briefly, her mouth opening to show her white teeth, her salmon tongue.

Her name was Margaret. She had brought a flask of whiskey in her purse, and she was drinking it with a splash of lemonade. I hadn't yet developed a taste for hard liquor, but I thought I could choke it down if it was doctored with lemonade, so when I finished my beer she made me one of her whiskey sours. We sat on the floor in a corner of the kitchen and she told me she was an actress. She didn't say which movies she'd been in, but she talked about various stars as if she knew them. She said she was twenty-six years old—by my lights, an older woman of vast experience. We had two or three drinks, and then we wound up outside, sitting on a picnic table in the dark yard. When I kissed her, I could smell her sweat and our whiskey breath and her cloying lilac perfume. After I'd kissed her a few times, she put her hand high up on my thigh and squeezed. I had to work up my nerve, but I fumbled a hand inside her brassiere.

In the wee hours, True drove us back to town. There were so many of us crammed into the car that Margaret sat in my lap, pressing one of her breasts against my arm. Every so often she wriggled her behind against my thighs, like she was just rearranging her seat, and I was stupid enough to be embarrassed by my hard-on.

When we got to the house where the girls lived, Margaret walked off with the others, swaying her hips, and she didn't look back. Driving away, True said to me, "Margaret likes to fuck."

In the last couple of weeks, I'd heard that particular vulgarity from Cab O'Brien's mouth often enough to become halfway used to it. I just answered, "I figured." I had grown up with certain ideas about girls—the ones who were marriage prospects and the ones who let men do things to them—but there didn't seem to be any judgment in what True had said about Margaret. In his crowd, it seemed, promiscuity just meant you were fashionable.

There were always too many people packed into the houses at those weekend parties, and for the next couple of Saturdays all I managed with Margaret was some furtive groping in dark corners. But then True got hired for a picture on location in Arizona, and he was gone for a couple of weeks. The studio hauled the crew there in a chartered bus, so he left the DeSoto for me to use. I acted the big shot, driving myself to the set all week, and on Saturday I went without him to one of the parties. I picked up the girls as usual and afterward drove them back to their house in Thousand Oaks. When the others got out of the car, Margaret scooted closer to me and laid her head on my shoulder.

We were already drunk, and we drank some more when we got back to True's house, so let me just say that it didn't go as I'd hoped. We managed to get our clothes off, and then, after I'd fumbled around a while, I started to weep in drunken stupidity and frustration. She murmured something pacifying and pulled my head to her breasts and fell asleep, and after a while I did too. But when the sun came up, I woke her and tried again, and she blearily helped me figure out what goes where. It was one of those gifts a woman will sometimes bestow on a boy, and I'm pretty sure it had nothing to do with liking to fuck. It wasn't optimal sex, nowhere near, and it was over in seconds, but I halfway remember the way the daylight came through the blinds and lit up the fine fuzz of hair on her soft belly and breasts.

25

I TOOK MARGARET back to True's house a couple of times, but then she moved on to someone else and so did I. It's not as if every girl at those parties was looking to have sex, but some were, and some of them wanted to have it with me. Most of them were actresses, but one was a stunt girl named Lorraine. She had grown up in North Carolina riding English, and she had a pretty low opinion of cowboy horsemanship. "You boys all ride fast as hell, but you don't have any kind of seat," she told me.

I wasn't sure what she meant by "seat," but I said, "You haven't seen me ride."

She gave me a pinch-eyed look. "All you cowboys ride the same."

At another time or coming from somebody else, that might have rankled, but we were sipping whiskey and sitting thigh to thigh on a driftwood log on the beach at Santa Monica, and I had intentions for the way the night might go.

There weren't many stunt girls back then. In the year I worked in the movies I met maybe three or four. They were always girls who had grown up with horses, and some were the daughters of stuntmen who had gone into the family business, the way True had. A stunt girl would double for the actress when the script called for a fast gallop or jumping a fence or a pony express mount, and they'd step in when the script called for a woman clinging to the seat of a runaway wagon or inside a careening stagecoach, which was the usual trouble females fell into in those movies, but there wasn't much work for them for the simple reason that most of the oaters didn't have roles for women.

Lorraine had doubled for Dolores Waterman for the long wagon chase in *Laredo Days,* which is where she'd met True. A girl holding on for her life on a bouncing wagon seat behind six galloping horses is pretty much at the mercy of the driver sitting next to her, and True was one Lorraine had learned to trust. She had a couple of impressive scars, which she eventually showed me—one on her hip from a bad fall off a Roman chariot—but she complained more about the hot, itchy wigs she had to wear, the skimpy or confining costumes, and the unnecessary risk-taking of some of the men she worked with than about the bones she had broken.

When I met Lorraine, I was still working mainly for Cab O'Brien, but I was hoping to get calls from some of the other ramrods around town. The work I did for Cab was mostly just riding fast and getting shot, and I was ready to branch out, plus I wanted a location job, if not in the Chihuahua Desert or the Rockies, at least up at Lone Pine or Tehachapi. I started saving money with the idea of buying a car so I wouldn't have to rely on buses and streetcars to get to the sets and so I'd be ready to drive myself to Lone Pine when the time came.

Then what happened is Cab needed somebody to ride like hell down a steep canyon wall, and I said I would do it. There were eight of us riding that day, and none of the others argued for it. No rancher in his right mind would have asked a horse to go down the side of that canyon—it was the closest thing to a sheer cliff. But I made the ride in about five or six jumps, steering the horse so he'd land on a bit of ledge just long enough to gather his hindquarters under him before springing down to the next. The horse was a big brown gelding, and he couldn't check himself quick enough at the bottom, but when he sprawled and fell I rolled off him as if it was planned, and as he got to his feet I jumped on and rode him out, right in front of the camera.

Cab lit into me. "I asked you to ride straight down, not go hopping rock to rock. Next time you better do the fucking scene exactly like I tell you."

But he used the shot—I imagine it looked pretty good—and after that the word must have gone around, because I started getting calls from other ramrods. Not location shoots, and I was still doing a lot of straight riding and falling, but every so often I got paid for other kinds of horse work—riding through a burning barn, racing along a wooden sidewalk or up the staircase inside a saloon or a hotel, riding hell-for-leather across streams, the water flying up in sheets. One time I was riding into a river when the horse balked and sent me over his head; I popped up from the water, swung onto him from the wrong side, and we lunged on out. The ramrod used it without saying a word to me about sticking to the scene.

I did some pony express mounts, doubling for Dick Hayes, and I put on a balsa-wood vest under my shirt and got killed with an arrow a few times. For a Three Mesquiteers movie, I rode up to the front of a two-story hotel, caught hold of a rope dangling from a flagpole, and swung up onto the balcony. And I ran a horse through a bank window once, which turned out to be harder than it looked. You had to blindfold the horse so he couldn't see what was coming, then spur him from a standstill to a gallop in about three jumps, and pull off the blinders at the last minute, when it was too late for him to quit. Flying through that candy-glass window in a shower of crystal sugar, I started to think I was some kind of top-notch stuntman.

So I was riding all week, going out to parties on Saturday night, and then taking the bus over to the Studio Club on Sunday to see a movie with Lily. I had told her about the parties without telling her that I was bringing girls back to True's house, but I imagine it wasn't hard for her to guess. I didn't give it a minute of thought at the time, but I know I was acting loutish and rough in those days, out at the edge of wild, which Lily must have seen. I would show up at the Studio Club on Sunday smelling of stale sex, and then I'd make thinly veiled remarks to girls behind the popcorn counter or pretty girls we passed on the street. Acting like a top horse, as we used to say.

I asked her once, about a year after I had gone back to live with my folks, why she didn't throw me over when she figured out what I was up to and the girls I was bedding. She laughed. "Jesus, Bud, you didn't shock me, you made me feel dead on the vine! You were acting in movies, going to Hollywood parties, drinking whiskey, sleeping with pretty actresses, and I was still living in a dormitory with a bunch of office girls. Jesus."

Well, she had come to Hollywood with the idea that a woman who wanted to make it in the movie business had to be as bold and shameless as the men, but the most shocking thing she'd done up to that point was take up smoking. I was nothing but a green ranch kid, but I had managed to fall in with a rowdy crowd of movie people, doing what Lily imagined young people in Hollywood must all be doing. So she didn't think about throwing over our friendship. What she began to think about was finding a way to lose her virginity. "How could I write about sex if I hadn't ever experienced it?" is what she always said about that, but it went along with her belief that a Hollywood life should look more like the one I was living than the one she had settled into.

Right around this time she landed a spot as a junior writer working under Dale Lampman and began working on scripts with Bob Hewitt; the timing was either lucky or luckless, depending on your point of view.

The writers were all men at the time, but Lampman had had women writers working for him in the past, so of course Lily was looking for a way to be noticed. She'd been thinking that if she stopped Lampman as he came through the office and asked him for some advice, she might be able to impress him with her judgment of scripts and the good, crisp prose in her synopses. She was clear in her own mind that he wouldn't take this as flirting.

But then one day when Lampman came out of Marion's office, he crossed through the reading room, came straight to her, and perched himself on the corner of her desk. She was caught off-guard, but she could be pretty unflappable, so she pushed back in her chair as if she was the one who had called him over, and she closed the script she'd been reading and held it up to him. "Don't bother with this one," she said. "It's a Crime Doesn't Pay, very badly written." As if she was Bette Davis in *Front Page Woman*.

This seemed to amuse him. He took the script, glanced at it, dropped it back on the desk. Then he adjusted his seat and said, "I hear you want to be a writer."

She hadn't made this a secret—she had told Marion as much when she was first hired. "I have some stories I've been sending out," she said. She didn't tell him she had brought her Texas Ranger script into the office for one of the other girls to read and report on but had heard nothing about it afterward.

She hoped he'd offer to take a look at one of her stories himself, but instead he pushed out his thick lips like he'd tasted something bitter. "Waste of time. A screenplay done on spec is a sign of weakness. You're letting everybody know you're too young and green to land a contract. Or a failing writer trying to hold on."

She knew too little about it to argue, but this was Lily. She frowned and argued anyway, because his tone provoked her. "A good script should rise to the top of the pile, no matter if it's on spec."

He made a slight scoffing sound and shrugged—her opinion was nothing to him. "A woman can make it as a writer in this business, but she needs to get her foot in the door first. You want to get on as a writer, you ought to find somebody else's piece-of-crap script, polish it up, and show it to whoever heads up the writers. Show him you can put lipstick on any damn thing—that'd be one way to get in the door." He smiled slightly, stood, and strolled away. But then he stopped at another girl's desk, a girl named Elaine, and leaned in close, speaking too softly for anyone to overhear. Elaine's hair was blond, she wore bright lipstick and skirts that showed off her legs.

He might not have been serious, Lily knew, but she took home the Crime Doesn't Pay—it was badly written, but the plot had promise—and stayed up all night in the typewriter room at the Studio Club, rewriting the whole thing. She brought the old version and the freshly typed pages back to the office in a paper folder, and when Lampman walked by her desk again she held it out to him. "I heard you're the one who heads up the writers," she said.

He laughed, took the folder from her, and went away without saying whether he would read it. But he brought it back the next day, threw it loosely into her lap, and sat again with his hip resting on the corner of her desk. "It ain't great, but it's pretty good," he said—out of the corner of his mouth, like George Brent in *Front Page Woman*. He smiled briefly, then leaned back and looked around the room as if he had lost interest in her. It was half a minute before he looked down at her again. "I told Marion I'm giving you a try as a junior writer. If it doesn't work out, you'll land back here. Tomorrow, come over to the writers' building and I'll give you some other piece-of-crap thing to start on." He leaned in and touched his knuckles lightly against her chin. "Good girl," he said.

In the morning, when she tapped on the door of his office, he yelled out something that could have been an offer to enter. He was reading a sheaf of manuscript pages, and she stood at his desk a minute or so before he looked up and handed her a four-page scene from a crime drama that Dick Hayes was set to star in. "Something's wrong with it, too grim or something, see what you can do." He went back to his reading without saying anything else.

She went out into the hallway. The Barracks was partitioned into several small rooms, many of them windowless, and she looked into several until she found two men sitting at a desk. One was typing as the other one leaned over his shoulder, smoking a cigarette, frowning down at the words as they rolled off the keys. There was a small window in one wall, but the venetian blind was closed to keep out the daylight.

"Find an empty desk in an empty room," the typist said without looking up. Lily hadn't asked them anything.

She went into one of the small, windowless rooms, and in a couple of hours she rewrote the scene in the Dick Hayes movie and turned it in. Lampman didn't look at the revised pages, just tossed them onto a pile on his desk, then stood up and poked around in the bookshelves behind him until he found the book he was looking for. He reached it out to her. "Write a treatment for a picture," he said, and picked up his own reading again.

What she turned in a couple of days later was not a film treatment but a carefully reasoned four-page opinion that the book would never make a movie. Lampman put the report on top of his pile of papers and said without looking up, "I'm busy. Ask around, find something to work on."

Gradually she learned not to bother him when his door was closed—to turn in her projects to a box on the hallway floor. He seldom offered an opinion about her work. She thought he might send her back down to the reading room when he got around to reading her report on the novel, but one of the other writers told her it was a project several people had already wrestled with—that Lampman knew it would never make a movie. So after a couple of weeks she took his silence to mean she was now officially a junior writer.

She spent some of her time in the Barracks working on her own screenplays, which all the junior writers were doing, and some of the time helping out other writers with their projects. And then she helped Bob Hewitt finish a two-reel comedy for one of Sunrise's minor stars. Movie programs in those days always included a few one- or two-reel short films—newsreels, comedies, travelogues, cartoons—and the junior writers had a better chance of getting a two-reel picture on the floor than a feature. So after they finished work on the comedy, she and Bob wrote and submitted a lot of ideas for short comedies and cartoons. The staff writers were on six-month contracts, but the junior writers were hired week to week, and throwing a lot of ideas out there was how they kept themselves employed.

Well, this wasn't what she had hoped for. Lily wanted to be writing about real human conflicts, real people and their problems, but was stuck writing trivial scripts with dancing animals and idiotic plots for pratfall comedians. The Dick Hayes crime drama she had written a scene for was filmed without her scene, and as far as she knew, none of the two-reel stories she and Bob wrote or proposed ever made it onto the screen. She wrote an audition piece for a young actress Lampman had said was in line to be the studio's new star, but the ingénue's name never made it into lights.

Still, she was working — *writing* — at a busy studio. And while she waited for an assignment or a reaction to a script, she and Bob visited the outdoor sets and the sound stages, and they went into a cutting room and watched an editor at a Moviola machine, cutting strips of film and splicing them together, shaping the first rough cut into something resembling a picture. Lily wasn't star-struck — she knew that the actors and directors she was watching were nowhere near Hollywood's best. But she kept a notebook in her pocket and wrote down everything she saw and heard. In later years, whenever she talked about her beginnings in Hollywood and the seven weeks she worked at Sunrise Pictures, she rarely mentioned Marion Chertok or Dale Lampman. She talked about those second-rate directors and what she'd learned from watching them make their second-rate movies.

I only saw Bob Hewitt one time, when he brought Lily to the hospital after I was hurt; I don't think we spoke a word to each other. I can tell you Bob wasn't much to look at. He had russet hair and a chin that sloped back to his neck. The most interesting thing about him, as far as Lily ever said, was that he got her jokes.

When Lily met him, Bob had just come out of college in Chicago or Boston or someplace like that. He had ambitions to be a story editor at a big studio, but while he waited for one of the periodic shakeups at Warner Brothers or Paramount to open a door he could walk through, his uncle, who was an attorney for a couple of studios, had finagled him the job at Sunrise.

Lily told me he was a decent-not-great writer but a top-drawer critic, with an ear for good dialogue. After she showed him *Death*

Rides the Sky, he told her his uncle might be able to get the story in front of someone at RKO if she changed a couple of things. And while the two of them were working on the revision, Lily and Bob wound up sleeping together.

Later on, when she wrote about this part of her life, she said Bob was the first man to show interest in her. Well, I had shown interest, and she had told me we couldn't be friends if I thought she was fast. Years later, when I brought this up, she said she didn't care if Bob thought she was fast—her feelings for Bob weren't complicated by friendship. But there might have been more to it than that.

Once she had made up her mind to lose her innocence, she wanted to get it over with: she thought she might not have another chance unless she married, which she didn't plan to do. But she had ruled me out: I was acting pretty reckless in those days, and though Lily would never have admitted it, she was a little bit scared of the whole "having sex" thing. So it's not hard to guess why she picked Bob Hewitt to give her a past—he was genial and safe, and he was the boy at hand.

Lily always sounded perfectly clear on her reasons for just about anything she did.

26

AFTER SEVEN WEEKS AT SUNRISE, Lily got fired the same day
Steve Deets got in a wreck, which we'll get to next. When she told
me she'd been let go, she said it was on account of the studio not
having enough work to keep the junior writers busy, but this was
a lie. Later, when this all came out, she said, "Bud, you were such
a goddamned cowboy back then." I guess she had good reason to
think I was inclined that way—that I might go after Lampman like I
thought I was Tom Mix or Buck Jones. We both knew a cowboy hero
wouldn't let a man get away with molesting a woman.

I didn't hear the real story until about 1949, and if I thought Lily
would have wanted it to stay off the record, I wouldn't be writing
about it now. But she went ahead and wrote about it herself, more
or less, in *Dangerous,* the first picture she and Mike Beahrs produced
together; and she told it again in her Hollywood memoir, though she
left out all the names; Lampman was the head of Lighthouse Pictures by then, and Lily had become savvy about Hollywood politics.
So both times she told the story she told it slant, and it seems to me
I can only tell it straight, the way she finally told it to me.

After she moved over to the Barracks and became a writer, she saw less of Dale Lampman. She mostly saw him in the commissary where they ate lunch every day, and it was a crowded place, with actors and actresses and extras in costumes—Roman gladiators, cowboys, women in ball gowns—all of them in heavy layers of makeup, streaming in from the sets to grab a bowl of soup or a sandwich. The writers sat together at their own table, but Lampman never joined them: he and Marion Chertok sat together at a small table off in the corner.

Then one afternoon when she was walking through the western street on her way back from lunch, he swung in alongside her. "I've been thinking I might give you a piece of the Louis Jossup script, see if you can do something with it." This was a project she had heard people talking about, a comic western with a lot of problems; several writers had worked on parts of it. "Jossup doesn't like the saloon scene. Thinks it won't work for his slapstick."

"Then the comedy should be in the dialogue," she said, because this was her strong preference anyway.

Lampman shrugged. "The kid's got a rubber body, that's his gimmick. He doesn't go for the jokes." He took hold of her elbow suddenly and steered her toward the saloon. "Here, you need to get a look at the set."

In recent weeks Lampman had barely looked at her, seldom spoken to her; the only woman she had seen him with was Marion. She had just about forgotten his reputation among the girls in the reading department. But with his hand on her elbow, she suddenly remembered *dangerous,* and turned her arm to get free from his grip.

He tightened his hand. "Don't be a girl," he said in a mocking way and pulled her along. She said, "Well, don't drag me," as if that was the point.

He laughed and let go of her arm and walked on ahead. When he went into the dim saloon, he held the batwing doors open for her. She stood a moment on the boardwalk and then followed him in. "Like a goddamned *girl!*" she told me.

There was no one else in the saloon. The set was crowded with unused equipment—cameras, booms, shiny reflector boards, heavy lights on telescoping stands. The air inside was dusty and cold. "All this junk will be out of here," Lampman said, sweeping an arm, "but the kid's right, there's not much room for the camera to follow him if he's throwing himself around like a rubber ball." He brought his arms up and shaped a small frame with his hands. "See? You'd have to keep the action inside the box." He moved his arms back and forth, like a camera following some movement out there. Then he backed up a couple of steps, took her elbow again, and pulled her to stand in front of him. "Here, look here, you'll get the idea."

He brought his arms up and made the small square with his hands again, close to her face. His barrel chest came forward to rest against her upper back—the heat and weight of him suddenly intimate. In that moment she became conscious of him as a big, powerful man, a man twice her size. She took a step ahead to get clear of his arms, but he dropped his big hands to her hips and pulled her back against him—it was almost playful—and then in a single smooth motion ran his hands up the front of her dress and squeezed her breasts.

She pushed at his thick wrists. "Don't!"

He laughed. "You haven't got any tits to worry about, honey." He brought his head down and nuzzled her neck with a wet mouth. As she grappled with him, her own hand knocked her glasses off her face. He pressed and rubbed himself against her and with one hand pulled open several of the buttons on the front of her dress. When his hand came inside her clothes, his breath became harsh and quick, but not from effort. For the first time in her life she had a panicky awareness of her own frailty, her powerlessness. She fought him, but it was a brief, silent wrestling match—she didn't shout or scream or cry out, whether from embarrassment or shame, she only wondered about afterward.

"Miss Shaw!"

Marion Chertok was standing just inside the room, her broad Russian face creased and flushed with anger. Lampman's arms loosened, and Lily bolted to the other woman. She was rabbity with fear, would have hidden herself behind Marion except the woman stepped away, turning a shoulder to fend her off. "Cover yourself up, missy—you are completely indecent. We cannot tolerate this kind of smutty behavior in our girls. Really, we cannot put up with it."

This was so unexpected that Lily was struck dumb. She had not cried for years—she was fifteen when she'd made up her mind she was too grown up for weeping—but she broke into tears now, and her hands jerked and shook, buttoning the dress.

Marion turned from her to Lampman. "Dale—Mr. Lampman—you should get back to your work. I hope this fuss hasn't upset you too much."

His face was bright with color, but he spoke smoothly. "Not at all, Marion. Girls with too much ambition, we both know they'll do anything to get ahead. I should be more vigilant." He straightened his suit coat and walked past them both, through the batwings and out to the street.

Marion spoke to the far side of the room, without a glance at Lily. "Miss Shaw, it is the responsibility of women not to inflame a man's baser instincts. I have overlooked the tittle-tattle about you and Mr. Hewitt, but this behavior with Mr. Lampman is not tolerable, not a bit of it. Turn in your timecard. I don't wish to see you again." She turned and followed Lampman out of the dim, cluttered saloon.

Lily picked up her glasses, bent them straight, and put them on. But it was several minutes before she went out into the sunlight.

In 1948 she was teaching a screenwriting class at a Hollywood night school when she met her first husband, a veteran of the Army Air Corps who might have stepped right out of her screenplay *Death Rides the Sky*. Mike Beahrs had family money, and he'd worked around the picture business before the war, so the two of them bankrolled their own production company, and Lily finally took the reins of a picture.

Dangerous, their first production, was set against a showbiz background—a Los Angeles gangster with a latent moral compass and the salty, tough actress he falls for. In an early scene an assistant director gets the actress into a dark corner of the set and puts his hands on her. When a Russian woman interrupts the assault, it tripped old bells for me—I remembered the story about Marion Chertok riding with the Cossacks. This was ten years after Lily's encounter with Lampman, and I guess she didn't see a reason to go on lying when I asked her about it.

"Oh for Christ's sake, Bud, he groped me, that's all the hell it was. It scared me, that's all."

But we both knew it could have ended differently—that she could have been raped.

She hadn't said a word to me about it when it happened. But she told Bob Hewitt, which even to this day can chasten me when I think of it.

27

AT THE TIME THIS HAPPENED, I was making the movie that
got Steve Deets killed.

When I met him, Steve had been riding in pictures half his life.
He already had bad knees and had torn loose the moorings in one
shoulder, which was a nuisance—his arm would fall out of its socket
at any excuse. He got so he could pop it back into place, but it happened over and over. One of his specialties was being dragged by a
horse, and if his shoulder went out while he was being dragged, he
had a hard time reaching the release catch for the wire that went
down his trouser leg onto the stirrup.

I'm not sure how much of this to get into—this isn't a primer on
stunt riding—but I can't really tell you what happened without talking first about the way things were in those days, men and horses
both disposable.

Being dragged by a horse, in particular, was a good way to get
killed or crippled. There wasn't a lot of protection, just a close-fitting
jacket, and if you bounced around you could wind up too close to
the horse and get your head kicked in. If the horse veered past the
pickup men and dragged you onto ground that hadn't been prepped,

you might get run into a stump or a rock. And sometimes the release would hang up. But the gag paid quite a bit, which is why Steve went on doing it even after he wrecked his shoulder. In those days, skill was less important than nerve, but he had a lot of both.

When we were kids, Mary Claudine and I used to practice the mounts we saw in the movies—leapfrogging over the horse's rump into the saddle or swinging onto a horse that was already in motion, not using the stirrup. I think I was twelve or thirteen when I broke my wrist doing one of those pony express mounts, and we caught hell for it, both of us, because our playing around made my folks short-handed for the spring branding.

Steve Deets laughed when I told him about breaking my wrist. He had broken his, rehearsing one of his showy flying mounts. And he'd cracked a couple of vertebrae doing a second-story mount, which is jumping down onto a saddled horse from an upper porch or a stair-case. I had tried that one, too, jumping off the roof of our woodshed with Mary Claudine standing below me holding the unsuspecting horse by the headstall. I jammed my spine so hard I was just about paralyzed for a couple of days, and when the horse bolted, he tossed me and Mary Claudine to the ground. We told our dad I'd been hurt when a bull took after me in the pasture.

The other thing Steve was known for was riding a horse off a tilt chute into a lake or river thirty, forty feet below. Just about any horse will balk at going off a cliff, so the grips would build a wooden chute at the brink of the bluff on top of a low, seesaw platform and grease the floor of the chute to make it slick. The rider would lead a blind-folded horse onto the chute, and once he was mounted he'd take off the blindfold and signal the grips, and when the platform tipped for-ward the horse would just slide off into space. They'd edit the film afterward so it seemed as if he'd galloped right up to the brink and sailed off gracefully into the water below.

The tilt chute was a risky fall for the rider—Steve had wrecked his shoulder the first time doing that stunt—and it was a notorious horse killer. If the horse hit the water on his back or neck, he'd just roll over once and drown. So no famous horse ever did the stunt—it was always some unlucky stable horse with similar markings doubling for the star. Even if the stunt horse died, the camera would pick up the real actor swimming to shore on his famous horse like nothing had happened.

When I saw Steve get wrecked for good, we were shooting a Wichita Carson movie out at Westerlund, a movie ranch in the Chino Hills, thirty or forty miles from the studio. It was far enough out of town that they put up the principal actors right there at the ranch in pine-walled cabins set down under some big old oak trees, but they ferried the rest of us, all the riders and the extras, back and forth from the studio every day in buses. We had to get to the studio by five in the morning to make the hour-long bus ride, get into costume if we needed to, and sort out the horses in time for first call; we didn't get back to the studio until around ten at night—the days damn near as long as when I'd worked for Harold. The main house had a dining room where they served all of us an elaborate spread at lunch and dinner, which I guess was to make up for the bus ride and the long hours, but most days by the time I staggered in from shooting I was hurting all over, barely able to muster the strength to cut a steak.

I had done quite a bit of riding for other ramrods by then, but this was a Cab O'Brien picture again. Steve didn't have much respect for Cab, but he rode for him anyway because Cab paid pretty well and kept his regular crew busy—he was popular with directors looking to shoot fast and cram in a lot of action.

At the end of the first week, we were filming a pitched battle between Wichita's men and some wild Indians, all of us on horseback crowded together in close combat, swinging at each other with rifle butts and tomahawks and long knives. This wouldn't have been any more risky than usual, except Cab had set it up to film along a dirt road carved into the side of a ridge, a road not even six feet across, with the ground falling steeply fifty feet on one side and rising up sheer rock on the other. The rock was streaked with bands of color and eroded away in weird vertical columns, which was Cab's reason for using the narrow road: he said he wanted the fight pitched against that wild-looking backdrop.

I should say here that besides Cab's reputation for paying good adjustments, he was well known for shaving his budget with "free" falls. He'd set up a situation where the chance of a big wreck was just about certain, but since the spills weren't planned he'd call them "unavoidable accidents" and get away with not paying the adjustment. This was one of those times, one of Cab's damn stunts made to look like straight riding except it was more dangerous than it needed to be. You could look at that narrow road and just know that horses would get crowded and pushed over the side. Before the take, Lon Epps and a couple of other riders had tried to get Cab to move the location or else set up some actual stunts, plan them out so there would be some control over what happened. Cab walked off while they were still trying to talk to him. "Just keep your butts in the fucking saddle like you're paid to. If you can't keep those fucking horses on the fucking road, I'll go look for somebody who can."

Nobody was happy about it, but if you wanted to stay on his call sheet you didn't refuse.

Cab was riding in a crane with the cameraman, the two of them high overhead, when he called for action. Twenty of us were packed into that narrow road, clashing our weapons, the horses nervously jostling each other, maneuvering for footing, bumping up against the rock face, trying to keep away from the dropoff on the downhill side. When the whistle blew for the end of the shot, Cab rained down a storm of profanity: we were a bunch of fucking pantywaists, fucking sissies every one of us. So when the clapper sounded, we went at it again, hard and fast. I was in a scratchy Indian wig, flailing around with a rubber hatchet, thinking that if my horse stumbled I might wind up on the ground in the middle of the melee. I only halfway saw what happened, but I sure heard it, the panicked squeal when a horse slipped off the edge of the road. And then people shouting.

I guess Cab must have whistled for the end of the shot, but what

I heard was the horse screaming—a sound I had never heard from a horse in my life—and I couldn't hear anything but that. It took the rest of us three or four minutes to bring our horses down off the road and around to the foot of the ridge. By then most of the crew was standing around the horse, but nobody was standing too close. This was Monte, the horse Steve always used as a double for Wichita's white stallion Sunday. He had shattered both his front legs, was thrashing his head in panic and anguish, scrabbling with his hindquarters against the rocky ground, raising a cloud of fine gravel and sand. I could feel the horse's screams, like violin strings pulled too tight in my chest and the bow scraping harshly across them. Steve was half pinned under the horse. He was pale and keeping very still out of worry the horse might get a hind leg high enough to kick him.

The prop master had doled out rifles that morning—the real thing, not rubber props—but nobody had a bullet. I was having a hard time just standing there, and I started turning over the question of whether a rifle butt striking the horse's skull just right could kill him quickly. But then one of the prop guys walked up to Lon Epps with a box of ammunition, and Epps jacked in a shell, stepped close, and shot the horse behind his ear. The silence afterward—the echo of the gunshot and the scream, the slow decay as the air absorbed the sounds—I felt that too, a reverberation inside my chest.

I helped some of the others lift the horse off Steve. By then the crane had come down to the ground. Cab walked over and watched us, and then, without seeming to aim the words at anybody in particular, he said, "Well, we got the shot, even with all the fuckup." Nobody said anything.

After we moved the horse off Steve, there was a minute when we all thought he was okay—his legs weren't bent wrong, there wasn't any blood, he didn't look like he was suffering. His shoulder was dislocated maybe, we thought that might be all of it. But when Lon reached a hand down to hoist Steve up, he didn't take it. "I guess I better stay right here," he said.

"Your shoulder's out?"

"Nah, not this time." He was sheepish. "I guess I busted a gut," the all-purpose term for badly hurt.

Cab said, "Christ. You want I should call an ambulance?" as if there was shame in it.

It was Lon who looked over at him and said, "Call the damn ambulance."

Cab blew a wordless sound of annoyance and walked off to the ranch house. But then he yelled back over his shoulder, "Mike, get that fucking horse hauled off and move the setup for number four. The fucking day ain't done yet."

Mike Tifflin made a brief, apologetic gesture to Steve before going off to shepherd the crew.

Lon Epps and three or four other riders who were Steve's friends sat down on the ground to keep him company until the ambulance showed up. I pulled off my wig and sat down too. We took out our smokes, and somebody lit one for Steve. His hand shook slightly whenever he lifted the cigarette to his mouth. It was a long wait. None of us asked him what part of his body was broken. Somebody made a remark about Cab and his "free" falls, and then we started passing around a few entertaining thoughts about how to get Cab himself in heavy plaster, hooked up to morphine in a hospital.

A grip drove over in a forklift truck, scraped up the dead horse, and drove off with it. The horse's head, bumping and dragging along the ground, left a smudged track through the dirt with a little dribble of blood and brain matter trailing through it. The soul that had made him a horse had already gone completely out of him; he was a stiff carcass only.

After a while John Barlow walked over from the house, dressed in his Wichita Carson outfit. He'd been working with the first unit, but he and Steve knew each other pretty well. Steve was doubling for John Barlow a lot in the days when I knew him: he liked Steve to fill in for him not just for the stunts but in any scenes where he was supposed to be riding faster than a jog-trot. And it was Steve who did all of Barlow's fancy mounts and dismounts.

Men moved aside to make room, and Barlow crouched down with us. He took off his high-crowned white Stetson and turned it a couple of times in his hands before he said, "Steve, what's this I hear about you busting a gut?" It was a pretty strange moment. I hadn't seen anybody who'd been badly hurt until now, and when Barlow spoke, it felt like we were all acting out a scene from a Wichita Carson movie.

Steve smiled slightly, a crooked movement of his mouth. "Ah shit, John, I'll be riding for you tomorrow."

He went on lying there quietly smoking his cigarette, as the rest of us, even Barlow, started up again with ideas for staging an accident, mowing down Cab under a runaway wagon or a bunch of stampeding horses. I don't think Steve was in pain. What we heard afterward was that he had broken his back or maybe his neck and couldn't feel anything below his hips.

I went to see Steve just once when he was in the hospital. A week or so later they moved him to a nursing home on Melrose Street, half a mile or so from True's place. This was in the middle of a slow week, and I was sitting around with no work, but I put off going over there to see how he was getting along. A couple of days later True told me Steve had blown out his brains with a pistol stolen from a movie set, loaded with real bullets. Nobody knew how he had gotten the gun.

Steve didn't have a family that anybody knew about, and he sure didn't have any money. Lon Epps passed the hat for the funeral and a tombstone. I chipped in more than I could afford, but while the funeral was going on I was in a bar in North Hollywood, looking into a glass of beer.

SIX

Echol Creek

1935–1938

◆

SOME RANCH AND FARM WOMEN living in remote parts of the county moved to town in the winter when their kids were in high school, but Martha never did—she still had horses to care for and Henry relying on her for help with the cattle. The high school in Burns was twenty miles by road from the Echol ranch. A school bus came out from town to pick up the farm and ranch kids at Foy, where they waited out of the weather in a building that had been part of the old rock quarry offices, but Henry or Martha had to drive their son from the ranch to the highway junction every morning on winter roads and make the trip again in the afternoon to bring him home.

Even in dry weather, getting up and down between the ranch and the bus stop, sixteen miles round trip, could take an hour or better. In some places they had to gear down and take it slow, the truck's thin tires bouncing heavily, and the ridge between the ruts sometimes scraping the axle. If the truck hit something hard enough to mash the oil pan, they had to stop and crawl under, take off the pan and beat out the dents with a hammer, put it back on, and add fresh oil. In spring, when the parkland flooded the road, they had to drive wide, veering off through the trees and willow brush, and even then sometimes the truck mired down, and they had to walk the rest of the way home and bring back the mules, hook a chain to the axle, and haul the rig out by brute force.

For Bud, the ride to Foy was only half the trip, as the bus made six or seven stops on the twelve miles of gravel highway between the quarry and the school. He left home in the dark and got home in the dark. And there were quite a few times that year when the snow was too deep to make it out to the highway. When he stayed back at the ranch, Martha, who was dead set on making sure her children got an education, pestered him to read aloud to her in the evenings from one of his schoolbooks, and she asked Henry, who kept the accounting ledgers for the ranch, to pose arithmetic problems that Bud had to solve in his head—a pointless exercise, since Bud had already moved on to algebra.

By midway through that first winter she had begun to fret over the number of days her son had missed school, and she and Henry both were pretty fed up with the long drive taxiing their son to and from the bus stop. So the next year they sent Bud over to Hart, eighty miles away, where there was a public boarding school that drew students from the far corners of Harney County and Malheur County.

The students lived in a dormitory building next door to the school, boys upstairs, girls downstairs. The dormitory was shut from Friday noon until Sunday evening, as most of the ranch kids went home for the weekend, so the handful of students who lived too far away to make it home were housed around town with the families of local students. Bud spent the weekends with a family named Dickerson, whose son, Dean, was in Bud's grade. Bud went home only in the summers and at Christmas, and for spring roundup.

Hart wasn't a city, but for a few years in the twenties it had been an up-and-coming community. Even now, with the drought and the Depression emptying out the countryside all around, the town still boasted three restaurants, a hotel and dance hall, a newspaper, a bank, a movie theater. Bud hadn't liked the long commutes to Burns on the school bus, but at the Hart school he was homesick for the ranch. The countryside around Hart was flat and dry, and the town noisy with car traffic and the rumble of grain cars and cattle cars switching back and forth in the rail yard behind the school. He hadn't ever spent a night away from his family: it took a while to get used to living in a dormitory with a bunch of other boys. And he was uneasy and self-conscious about spending his weekends in the Dickerson house.

He had grown up without indoor plumbing or electricity, in a house without a foundation, a house with worn-out linoleum covering all the sloping floors. The Dickerson house was of another order altogether. No one in that family had to put a pot under the bed or hike through the snow to the outhouse or heat water on the stove to take a bath—there was a bathroom down the hall from the bedrooms, with a flush toilet and a deep porcelain tub with taps that ran hot water. The living room and dining room had chandeliers that could operate on gas or electricity—Mr. Dickerson had ordered them from a store in Chicago to light his house reliably in those days and weeks of winter when the lines sometimes went down and the whole town was without power.

Dean Dickerson's father was a bank executive who had moved the family west from Philadelphia just the summer before, and what Dean knew about ranching, horses, and cattle had come mostly from the movies. He had the romantic idea that Bud's life on the Echol ranch must be something close to the cowboy life in westerns. An outhouse, to his way of thinking, was a thing to envy. So when it became clear to Bud that Dean put him in the same class as Tom Mix, it had the effect of easing his awkwardness and raising his opinion of himself.

Dean was skinny and small, a well-dressed newcomer and a town kid, which made him an object of ridicule among the boarding students at the Hart school. It fell to Bud, living in the Dickerson house every weekend, to educate him in the rough values of the other boys, who were almost all from second- and third-generation ranch families. If Dean couldn't ride or rope or shoot, he could at least fight, and when his nose was bloodied he could smile grimly and take his beating without crying. Dean and Bud weren't much alike to start with, but they grew to be friends.

In December Henry drove over to Hart and brought Bud home for the Christmas recess. Mary Claudine had been waiting on the porch since shortly after breakfast, anxiously standing on tiptoe and peering down the lane to spot the first sign of the truck. Her dog waited with her, excited by her eager jitters. But when she saw the truck coming through the gate at the bottom of the slough she was suddenly shy. She sat down on the front steps, took hold of her dog by the loose skin of his neck, and pulled him against her chest. He squirmed and squirmed and whimpered to be let go. The truck pulled up alongside the barn, and finally she let the dog wriggle free. He ran right up to Bud, waving his tail and barking, and Bud bent down and scratched him around his bony head.

"Are you teaching him to work cattle?" Bud asked his dad, above the dog's high barks.

On the long drive from Hart, Henry hadn't said anything about the dog—that he had brought a pup home for Mary Claudine because she'd been lonesome without her brother. Now he said only, "Well, he's your sister's dog. She'll have to teach him to be quiet and mind first."

Bud looked over at Mary Claudine. "I hope you're teaching him not to sleep in my bed."

She ducked her chin and studied her shoes. "He doesn't come in the house," she said.

Dean Dickerson had two younger sisters, one of them about Mary Claudine's age. Bud and Mary Claudine, without other children nearby, had each been the other's chief companion, and it had struck him as odd that Dean had few dealings with his sisters. In the evenings, while Dean was finishing his homework, Bud sometimes went down to the dining room and played charades or pinochle with the little girls. Now it seemed to him that he had been gone from home a long time, and he had expected his sister to come flying off the porch and jump onto his back with a wild cry. He didn't know why she acted shy to see him, as if he had become someone else, a stranger.

Martha came out of the house and went to her son in the yard. She smiled and said, "Your hair is long, Bud." She pushed it back from his forehead, and as she brought her hand away she let the tips of her fingers brush his ear and his cold cheek.

He reached up and smoothed his forelock where his mother had ruffled it. "I don't like how that town barber cuts it. I'm used to you cutting it."

"Well, I'll cut it while you're home."

In the house, everything looked exactly the same, which was in some vague way a surprise and a relief to Bud. "That smells good," he said, for something to say.

Martha laughed and said, "Well, you shouldn't have to cook the first night you're home," which was not quite a joke. She and Mary Claudine had pored over Bud's *Better Homes and Gardens Cookbook* looking for a meal to mark the homecoming, something they could make with foodstuffs they had on hand. They had cooked a pot roast in canned tomatoes.

Bud went through to the bedroom he shared with Mary Claudine at the back of the house. His sister followed him and sat on her bed, watching him empty his duffle and put away his things in a drawer.

"What did you name the dog?" he asked her.

"Quinn." This was the dog's name in a story they had both read, about a heroic dog who carried messages back and forth in the trenches during the Great War.

He nodded. "Good."

After a moment she said, "He already minds me. He just barks and gets excited when somebody comes that he doesn't know."

"Well, he'll get over that."

"That's what Mom said."

He looked around the room. The two beds were neatly made. Mary Claudine's collection of snake skins, bones, and birds' eggs still covered the windowsill and the top of the dresser, and now a dozen or more of his drawings, the ones he had sent home from boarding school these past three months, were pinned to the wood walls.

When he looked at his sister, the light coming in through the one window outlined every stray hair on her head. Her braids were tied off with bows of colored ribbon. He had an impulse to get out a pad of paper and sketch her, right that minute, posed just that way, sitting on her hands watching him.

He hadn't taken off his coat—he wanted to go out to the pasture to see Tony and Dolly and the other horses. He said, "I thought I'd go out and see the horses. You want to come?"

The young dog was waiting on the porch. He didn't bark but made a low whining noise in his throat as he pushed and wriggled his way between the two of them.

There wasn't any snow on the ground, but the grass was brittle with frost. They walked out to the pasture, the dog trotting with them, and at the fence Bud called to Tony, grazing alone at the far edge of the field. The horse lifted his head and came partway toward them but then got interested in the grass again, so they climbed through the fence and walked the rest of the way out to him.

Bud had brought a couple of windfall apples with him, apples he'd picked up from the Dickerson yard and saved for his horse. He brought one out of his coat pocket, and when he was still a few yards off he held it out and waited until the horse moved up to him and examined the apple with his whiskery, soft lips.

Tony, in his winter coat, was shaggy and muddy, but when the apple was gone Bud rubbed the horse on his poll and behind his ears and then climbed onto his muddy back and took a handful of tangled mane. "Let's go over there and see Dolly," he said. He reached down to Mary Claudine and swung her up behind him, then started the horse ambling toward his mother's old mare, who was standing with one of the mules in another part of the pasture. Mary Claudine's dog trotted ahead of them, calm and assured now.

"Do you like that school?"

"It's all right. I'm used to it now."

"Will I have to go there? I don't want to."

"You wouldn't want to ride the bus to Burns either. It takes too long."

"Aren't you lonesome? Don't you miss Tony? And Mom and Dad?"

His sister had put her arms around him, and when she spoke he felt her breath tickling the back of his neck. He looked over at the house and the barn and the line of willow brush where the creek ran along the edge of the pasture. It was overcast that day, and a cold fog obscured the timbered ridges where the Ochocos rose up behind the house.

At the boarding school he had felt lonesome much of the time. He had, in the beginning, told himself it was because of the flat, dry landscape around Hart—he had told himself "homesick" meant he was missing the mountains and the sloughs around Echol Creek, missing the ranch house that was the only home he knew, and the place he felt safest. He had not thought it meant he was missing his parents and his sister.

"Well, I'm used to it now," he said.

Mrs. Dickerson had a maid who did most of the cooking, and their house didn't seem to have many chores that needed doing. In the fall Bud and Dean raked the leaves that piled up under the elm tree in the front yard and the apple tree in the back. In the winter they stoked the sawdust furnace and shoveled snow off the steps and the paved walk from the porch to the street. In the spring they took turns pushing a lawn mower through the new green grass. But otherwise they were free to spend the weekends however they liked.

Dean had a bicycle, and Bud learned to ride double with him, straddling the rear fender and resting his feet on the axle rods, with his hands gripping the back of the seat. In good weather they rode everywhere around town, up and down the graveled residential streets and the three paved business blocks, out to the lumber yard and the gravel pit, and often to the railroad yard, where they hung around watching the men load freight and the switchman coupling and uncoupling cars and switching the rails to shuffle them back and forth. There were stock pens behind the depot, and sometimes they were lucky enough to watch a crew on horseback loading cattle, driving steers up the alley between the pens and the rail cars. On the eastern edge of town Hart Creek ran through willows and cottonwoods, and Bud and Dean rode the bicycle out a bumpy dirt path to the creek to catch crawdads or go fishing for chub. After the weather turned cold they spent their Saturday afternoons at the matinee show at the movie theater.

No money ever changed hands between the Frazers and the Dickersons, but Henry saw to it that a steer was butchered and delivered to the Dickerson house. And at the end of the school year, when Bud came home to the ranch, Dean came along and spent a couple of weeks with the Frazers, learning to cowboy.

Martha put him on a gentle gelding named Pumpkin, and the two boys rode into the hills above the ranch and shot at tin cans with Bud's .22 rifle. They helped Henry blast out some stumps from a hay field and rode out with him when he was hauling salt up to the benches where cattle liked to graze in the early summer. They rode up to the fire lookout at the top of Rough Butte, where a cabin had been built in the twenties, with the lookout perched on wooden stilts about fifteen feet high. They climbed the ladder to talk with the ranger, Ferris Cantlin, and they looked out over the vastness of the country, miles of canyons and forest, through Ferris's good binoculars. Ferris could name just about every creek drainage and summit in every direction, clear to the horizon.

Once, with Mary Claudine, they made the long ride to Burns to see *Charge of the Light Brigade,* and when they were crossing the sagebrush flats east of Foy, an airplane buzzed them and set all their horses bucking. Dean went off on the first buck and bloodied an elbow when he landed hard on the rocky ground. Before Mary Claudine could quit laughing and before Bud could get over to help him up, Dean had taken hold of Pumpkin, remounted, and headed off as if nothing had happened. He had caught on to the cowboy code. That fall, when school started up again, he strolled in wearing boots and Levi's and affecting a bowlegged walk.

The Frazers rode for cattle every spring and fall. In spring it was to gather the new calves, get them branded and castrated, and then move cows and calves up into the reserve, where they'd be on summer pasture; in fall it was to collect them from the high canyons and benches, bring them down to the ranch, and then wean the calves, sort out calves and dry cows for market, and herd them down to a holding pasture in the valley, where they'd be sold and shipped out. Everything they did all year led up to those roundups.

When Henry was foreman for the Woodruff sisters over in Elwha County, the sisters hired four or five extra cowboys, a cook, and a cook's flunky to help out for the roundups. The Echol place wasn't anywhere near as big as the Woodruff ranch, but the reserve, where the cows spent the summer, was rough country, cut through with ridges and canyons, and Henry was always grateful to have Arlo or one of his boys pitch in, in trade for Henry lending a hand at the Gantz roundup. And as soon as Bud and then Mary Claudine got to be more help than trouble — six or seven years old — they began to ride for cattle with their parents.

On a lot of ranches the size of theirs, the wife would have cooked for roundup, but Martha wasn't one of those wives, and even after Bud became a pretty good cook Henry felt that his son was more help to him gathering livestock than standing over a stove, so Henry paid a neighbor woman to do the cooking. Mrs. Stanich was a homesteader's wife living in the foothills just west of them. She would walk to the house every day to cook and serve the noonday dinner and wash the dishes, and then before she walked home again she built a pile of roast beef sandwiches and left a fresh pie in the kitchen for when they came dragging in at sundown.

For roundup they got up early every morning—by three or three-thirty. Martha had to prod the children awake while Henry went out to the corral to saddle the horses by lantern light. Mrs. Stanich wouldn't be at the house until after sunup, so Bud and his sister moved about the kitchen, heavy-eyed and silent, putting together the breakfast, and Martha made gallons of coffee, enough for breakfast and to portion into canteens and jars to carry along and keep them going until noon or one o'clock, when they went back to the house for dinner.

They ate in silence, all of them half asleep and trancelike, and it was still dark, barely four-thirty, quarter of five, when they finished up and headed out.

In a country without fences, it was hard to know where your cattle were. The most you could hope was an intelligent guess. In general, the cattle ranged within an hour or so of water or salt, so in March and April Henry hauled salt up to the reserve and left it on certain hillsides and ridge points, and after the spring roundup he dropped off cows and calves near the salt and near springs where ponds had formed. Then in the fall, searching a different part of the allotment every day, they worked inward toward one of those salt blocks or ponds, collecting the cattle they found in that area. They brought them down in pairs and small bunches, counting as they went, and when they had enough to handle, took them to whatever place had been agreed upon that day, where they could be held or corralled for a few hours until everybody had come in. Then they drove that morning's gather—a couple of dozen pairs on an average day—down to the fenced pastures at the home place, where the herd grew bigger day by day.

When they sat down in their dusty clothes to eat Mrs. Stanich's dinner, they hardly spoke except to ask for a plate to be passed. Afterward they saddled fresh horses and headed out again to comb for cows around another salt cairn.

Fall roundup was twelve or fifteen sleep-starved, backbreaking days.

The Echol place had always had water flowing in the creek, water in the wetlands at the lower end of the property, and half a dozen springs that never failed, but in the thirties a string of dry years hit everywhere in the West. The Frazers had more water than many of their neighbors: a couple of springs that kept trickling, and water in the upper reaches of the creek, enough to keep the livestock watered and the kitchen faucet running. So they gave away what they felt they could spare, to ranchers down on the arid flats who were trying to save well water for their cattle and to nearby homesteaders whose springs had dried up. All through the dry summers of 1934 and 1935, neighbors came and went, driving up the canyon with a team and wagon or a motor truck and hauling back water in buckets to keep their kitchen garden going and maybe wash clothes every other week. But late in the summer of 1936, with no rain to speak of since March, the wetlands below the house shrunk until they were mostly mud beds. Echol Creek in places became a necklace of still puddles. That year the cows ran out of grass in July and began shedding pounds, so Henry and Martha started the fall roundup in early August, a good month sooner than usual.

Sandy Gantz, the youngest of Arlo's boys, was helping them that year, and Bud's friend Dean Dickerson had come over from Hart to help out. He wasn't much of a hand—Henry was afraid he would make more work for them all—but the boy was eager to prove himself a cowboy, and Bud had spent so much time at the Dickerson house over the last couple of years that Henry felt obliged to let him try.

Every morning Sandy, who was twenty that year, came into the yard on a motorbike with his saddle tied onto the back of the seat, and then they all sat down to eat. Bud and Dean and Mary Claudine had been up since three, cooking biscuits and sausage gravy, stewed prunes, bacon, pancakes.

Even in August the early mornings had a bite of frost, so when they rode out around four-thirty they were bundled in coats and scarves they would shed when the heat built up later in the day. There had been fires in the valley all through that summer—the grass had dried up so early in the season it took no more than a cigarette butt tossed out along the highway or a horseshoe striking a spark against a rock to get hundreds of acres burning black. The night sky was a starless smudge, and the air smelled faintly of ash and charcoal. The only sound was leather squeaking and bits jingling and the horses sometimes huffing breath.

On the fourth day of roundup that year, they were still working the highest part of the allotment, sweeping the ridges and ravines around Shoestring Canyon, a rocky place about eight miles long, with mountains rising steeply above the canyon bed. Two side canyons fed into it, Crow Canyon from the east and Lost Sheep Canyon from the southwest, and the gathering place was at the outlet of Crow Canyon, where there were some old corrals. They planned to be working cows down the side hills into Crow in the morning, and Lost Sheep in the afternoon.

It was six o'clock when they got up to the corrals, the sky overhead lightening to pearl gray but the sun not yet risen high enough to clear the eastern ridge. This was country so rough and wild that even Henry had sometimes wandered around up there without knowing for sure where he was, so he wanted them working in pairs: Sandy and Martha together, and Dean with Bud, who was charged with keeping his friend out of trouble, though nobody said so. Henry, who had been rounding up cattle for more years than any of them, would get along with just the dog, Quinn. He told Mary Claudine, "I want you to wait right here and help run in the cows as they come down to the canyon bottom."

Mary Claudine gave Henry a glance of wounded outrage. She

was ten that year, old enough in her view to be riding for cattle on her own, and she was waiting every day for her dad to say so. It was hours of boredom, hanging around the corrals until the first cows were brought down, and it was her opinion that her brother's friend knew less about the work than she did—that it should have been Dean made to sit at the bottom and wait. She sent a beseeching look to her mother, but Martha merely shook her head. *Don't argue with your dad.* It was Martha's own opinion that Mary Claudine could chase cows better than Dean, but she knew Henry had made up his mind to let the boy play at being a cowboy.

They talked about how to split up the terrain, and then they rode up Crow Canyon and scattered up the side hills out of sight, leaving Mary Claudine alone with a long time to wait. She was riding Goldy that morning, a chestnut mare with one floppy ear. Goldy was too tall for her to climb on without a stump or rock or some other high place to mount from; earlier that week she'd had to stay in the saddle all morning. But at Crow Canyon she had the corrals to climb on, and she was too cold and bored to sit on the horse for long. There was sunlight at the top of the ridge, so she slipped off the horse, took out the book she had carried in the saddlebag with her jar of coffee, and hiked up the steep side of the ridge.

Mary Claudine, like her mother, had a great love of books and reading. She had learned to read at four, and by six had worked her way through several of the books that were her mother's favorites— *Black Beauty, Call of the Wild, A Dog of Flanders.* She had begun *The Dark Frigate* at the start of roundup. When she reached the top of the ridge, she sat on the ground in the warming sunlight, opened the book, and found where she'd left off reading.

She didn't have any way to measure the passage of time. Every so often she looked up at the sun in the great bare sky, then went back to reading about the *Rose of Devon* taken over by pirates, and the orphaned Philip forced to join their crew. But she wanted to be ready when the first cows came down to the canyon floor, and when she began to worry that she had spent too much time with the frigate, she hiked back down the steep hill and climbed onto Goldy. She forgot to piddle before getting back on the horse, and before long she desperately needed to. She dithered, not wanting any of the others to show up while she was squatting by a rock with her bottom hanging out of her overalls. But finally she got down and crouched a short way off and relieved herself on the dirt, then boosted herself onto Goldy again, in such a hurry that she was on the horse before she finished doing up her shoulder buttons.

She hadn't needed to rush—the waiting went on. The sun broke over the ridge finally and warmed the bottom of the canyon. When she grew hungry she drank from her jar of milky coffee. It seemed to her that the sun hung overhead without moving. She began to ride Goldy a hundred yards up the narrow canyon and back again, just to keep them both from falling asleep in the sunlight. And she sang to herself, one of the songs she'd heard Gene Autry sing the last time she had gone with Bud to the movies in Burns.

She had been counting on the bawling of cows to warn her when somebody was coming down, but Bud rode in unannounced from the outlet of Crow Canyon and caught her unprepared—she was singing loudly and pretending to strum a guitar. She was mortified, but Bud didn't even notice. He was riding Tony that day, and he came on at a slow walk, with Dean behind him on Pumpkin. It took Mary Claudine a minute to realize that Bud had Pumpkin on a lead and that Dean, pale as milk, was hunched in the saddle, seeming to hug himself.

She called out, "What happened? Did he fall off?"

It was Dean who answered her. "I didn't fall off. A damn cow butted the damn horse and he went over on me. I busted my arm."

Mary Claudine knew he wouldn't have used swearwords if her parents had been there; he might not even have said "busted." And he sounded proud of himself. She hadn't ever broken a bone—she was the only one of her family who hadn't. She sometimes took this as proof of her superior horsemanship and sometimes as evidence that she hadn't yet proven herself. She gave Dean a look that was partly envy, but then, just to let him know where he stood, she said righteously, "I hope you didn't get Pumpkin hurt."

Bud said irritably, "We wouldn't be riding him if he was hurt." He was in a bad mood about the way things had gone, upset that he hadn't been able to keep his friend from getting into trouble, upset that his dad would be short-handed now and the roundup made to drag on longer than it should.

"I've got to take Dean down the hill. Tell Dad and Mom I'm driving him to town in the truck."

"Did you find any cows? Should I go bring them down?"

He was abreast of her by then, and as he rode past her he looked over and frowned. "We had half a dozen we brought in to the bench around Rim Springs, they might still be there. You know where that is?"

Her excitement was bright in her face. "I'll find them." She jigged Goldy and trotted off.

Bud called after her, "If they're not there, don't go looking for them. Just come on back."

She flung back over her shoulder, "Okay," and went out of sight up the Crow Canyon trail.

They found Mary Claudine's horse on the third day, in among a band of wild horses at the far northern edge of the reserve. The saddle was still cinched up, the mare's hide rubbed raw under the girth and along her back, her mouth raw from the bit. The reins were broken off short—they'd been stepped on or torn from some entanglement. It looked as if the horse had been on her own, roaming the mountain, since the first day Mary Claudine went missing. The broken jar rattling around in the saddlebag had spilt its coffee on the book she'd had with her. The pages were soaked and swollen, the illustrations almost indecipherable under a scrim of brown stains. The saddle was badly scratched, but there was no blood on it, which Martha and Henry both took as a good sign. They would find their daughter lying up with a broken leg, they felt, or limping out of the mountains on sore feet.

But then, after the horse was found, there was no further sign.

In the first days after the girl went missing, fifteen or twenty neighbors pitched in to help them search, but this was roundup, and most of them couldn't go on neglecting their own places after it became clear that Mary Claudine wouldn't easily be found. Arlo Gantz, though, was in his seventies and he had three sons who had taken over the work on his ranch. He had time on his hands and a desire to feel useful. Before sunrise day after day for weeks, Arlo drove up in his blue Oldsmobile, dragging a pale rooster tail of dust. Every day Martha was out in the yard saddling horses, and he would nod as he stepped out of the car and say a few words to her before going into the house.

A hardened old-timer like Arlo might cry a few tears at weddings and christenings but never at a funeral, and perhaps for that reason, or some other one, he never said a word of sympathy to any of the Frazers, and he never speculated about what could have happened to Mary Claudine. Most mornings he called out, "Lucky it wasn't cold overnight," or, if it had been cold, "Lucky it didn't rain," which he meant to carry an unspoken solace. And then he went on into the house, where Bud was packing the lunches—sandwiches and doughnuts, maybe big squares of cake from pans their neighbors had brought—and he sat down with Henry at the kitchen table so the two of them could go over the map. They had started the search at Rim Springs and widened out from there, but the Ochoco Reserve was hundreds of square miles of rough land. The network of penciled crosshatchings marking off the places they had searched never seemed to be more than a small island in a great sea.

They put in long days—ten or twelve hours on horseback. The woodland up in the reserve was mostly open, and they stayed in sight of one another but spread out to cover as much ground as they could, closing the distance only when there were windfalls or clumps of brush—places where a child could be lying out of sight and unable to call out to them. They got down and walked in the steep draws and wherever the horses couldn't get through. Quinn was always with them, sticking close to Martha or Henry and seeming confused when they ignored the cows and calves they came across. He wasn't any help with the search—they knew this—but when he got down low on his belly and pushed into a thicket, investigating whatever was in there, one of them would dismount and pick up a stick and feel around, just to be sure. The first time Martha found a dead animal that way—it was a calf that had been gnawed on by coyotes and buzzards—her head filled suddenly with white noise; later, when she lay down on the bed, so tired she thought she might not be able to pull off her socks before falling asleep, her mind went right to the dead animal she had poked with her stick. And then to her daughter, a wheel of images, most of them unbearable.

They didn't noon up but ate lunch in the saddle. They went back to the house after dark and heated the soup or stew Mrs. Stanich or one of the other neighbors had brought by and left on the porch in a dishpan. Arlo often went on to his own place to eat supper with his wife, but every so often he stayed to eat with the Frazers, and while the supper was warming he stripped his shirt off and sat on the front porch rubbing Absorbine into his shoulders and arms, the pungent smell of it overtaking whatever was heating on the stove. Arlo didn't have an ounce of fat on him, and you could still see the lean muscle in his upper arms and back, though age had loosened the skin from his bones so it hung in slack folds around his nipples and above his elbows.

Some of the neighbors who had helped out with the early search tried to finish the Frazers' fall roundup, or as much as they had time for. But they got around to it late, and a good many of the ravines and canyons in the allotment were lightly combed or not combed at all. Anyway, by then a lot of cows and calves had moved off the range, looking for feed, drifting north or west, away from the Echol ranch. The Gantz boys weaned the calves, but they didn't know how many of the heifers Henry wanted sold. All over the country the drought had driven ranchers to sell off more stock than usual, earlier than usual, and this had pushed down the prices. But if you held back, hoping for a better return in the spring, you might not have enough hay to see the herd through the winter. When Chuck Gantz, Arlo's oldest son, took Henry aside and tried to talk to him about shaping up the herd for market, Henry said, "Do whatever's easiest," and walked off. So they made a rough cut, turning back onto pasture just about half the heifers and driving the rest to the sale lot, along with a few of the long yearlings and old bulls. It wasn't a big payday, and fall sales were their income for the year.

Arlo Gantz had heard of children lost in the mountains and never found, or the bones stumbled on by accident a year later, two years, ten. By the end of September it was clear to him that Mary Claudine was such a child—that she wouldn't be found, or anyway not by one of them—and it was his opinion that Henry needed to get back to the business of running his ranch. This was something he couldn't say to the man except roundabout. What he finally said was just "I think it's best if I get back to my own place, Henry. We been at this a while and I been letting a lot of things slide."

Henry knew what the old man was getting at, but it didn't make any difference to him. He shook Arlo's hand and thanked him for helping, but then he and Martha and Bud went on doggedly looking for Mary Claudine right into October. Of course by then they were looking for her body, her bones, although none of them said so.

One afternoon when Henry rode down into the yard, Mr. Dickerson's big gray Cadillac was parked next to the barn under a heavy blanket of dust. Dean and his father were waiting on the porch. Henry lifted a hand briefly in greeting, but he rode on across the yard to the pasture fence and unsaddled the horse there and turned him out, then he caught up another horse and saddled him.

By the time Henry finished this business with the horses and walked to the house, Mr. Dickerson had changed his mind about what he had planned to say. He had not seen any of the Frazers since the whole thing started, and though he had pictured them grief-stricken, distraught—he had prepared himself for that—Henry seemed to him only drawn down with exhaustion. His face was deeply burnt, his cheeks and lips cracked into deep, scabbed-over furrows that had bled and healed and broken open to heal again. But there wasn't a trace of the sorrow that Mr. Dickerson had been expecting. He had thought he might speak to Henry about his son's broken arm, even apologize for the small part this had played in what happened, but when they shook hands he only said a few words about how sorry he was "for what happened to your daughter."

Henry nodded but didn't reply. He glanced briefly at Dean, who had been looking down at the ground while his dad spoke.

It wasn't how Mr. Dickerson had imagined things would go. Not for the first time, he wondered if Henry blamed Dean for getting hurt. He wondered if Henry understood how much pain the boy had been in, and how hard it had been for Dean to carry on his life with his good arm in a plaster cast.

"Well, you know it's the boys' last year in high school," he said. "And school has already started up." He smiled regretfully, as if this might be something Henry had overlooked. "So we came to see if maybe we could bring Bud back with us to Hart."

The truth was, Henry had forgotten about the start of school. Martha was ordinarily strong in her feeling about her children's education, but she hadn't said a word about it. "I guess we lost track of it," Henry said. He didn't have any idea what Bud would say about going back to Hart to finish school. He himself didn't have an opinion about it. In the first days after Mary Claudine had gone missing, his brain and heart had raced along, but by now he was hollowed out, body and soul, too tired to give his attention to anything but the map and the search.

He took off his hat and scratched the dry scalp. "I don't know how long you've been here waiting for Bud," he said, "but I imagine he won't be in until after dark. It was just luck that I come in early; I had to swap out a horse with a bruised foot. Anyway, I'll talk to him about it and if that's what he wants I'll bring him over to school myself in a day or two."

Mr. Dickerson nodded. "Well, all right, you talk to Bud. He's a smart boy, he ought to get a high school education. He hasn't missed but three weeks so far. He'll catch right up."

They shook hands again, and Henry walked with them to the car. Both Dean and his dad wore shoes meant for hardwood floors and sidewalks. The cuffs of their trousers were colorless with dust from walking across the dry yard.

Dean hadn't said a single word. Before they drove off, Henry reached in through the open window and briefly cupped a hand to the boy's shoulder. "You take care," he said. Dean flashed him a look that Henry couldn't read. He didn't blame the kid for wanting to make a cowboy. He blamed himself for letting him try.

There had been so many grass fires in the valley that summer and on into the fall, well past the usual fire season, that whenever the wind came up in the long afternoons of their search they could smell smoke and ash, taste it on their tongues. For many years afterward, whenever any of them smelled wood smoke or burning grass they would fall back suddenly into a memory of those fruitless long days on horseback looking for Mary Claudine.

But the weather finally rounded a corner in the first week of November, days of rain and then a wet, heavy snow. They should have welcomed it after the long drought, but the wet weather turned the steep slopes in the reserve muddy and slick. When Bud's horse slid and rolled off the side of a ravine, it scared Martha and Henry both. He wasn't hurt, but he might have been—might have been killed, which they didn't speak of.

They kept on a little longer, riding wet and cold through the shortening days, but one morning, a week after Bud's fall, Martha left off saddling the horses and went back to the house. She had come inside to tell Henry something that was still unformed in her mind, something about how tired she was. Or something else, something about Mary Claudine. She found him standing in the front room staring out the window at the rain. He didn't turn around, but he must have heard her, because he said, as if she had asked him about it, "I haven't been down to pick up the mail in a while. I'm thinking I ought to go do that before the creek floods the road."

After a silence she said, "All the horses need their feet trimmed. I guess I'll do that."

"You hate trimming hoofs."

"Well, it needs doing."

Henry nodded. When he turned to her, she saw nothing in his face but empty exhaustion. She looked over at Bud, at his narrow shoulders and back, the way he moved slowly, deliberately, making three sandwiches. He hadn't yet turned eighteen.

"Bud." She waited until he quit what he was doing and looked at her, and then she said, "Arlo and his boys stacked some hay at the Germany Bench. You need to go up there and fence the stack yard so the elk don't get all of it."

He understood what his mother meant: that they were quitting the search for his sister and were picking back up the work they'd been neglecting.

Mary Claudine had always been prone to close calls and narrow escapes — she had come near drowning in the creek when she was little, and she'd been stung by a hundred hornets once when she poked a stick into their nest. He was used to feeling more annoyed than worried when she got herself into trouble. But in the past few weeks he had stopped going over in his mind all the many ways in which Mary Claudine could still be alive in the world. And he'd been waking up in the morning as tired as when he went to bed. He wanted to argue with his mother, to accuse her of losing courage. But no words came into his mouth.

· · ·

It was a couple of men hunting a mountain lion early in January who found Mary Claudine's bones in a part of the reserve that had been searched back in September.

They buried her in the Bailey Creek Cemetery, a place that had been laid out maybe fifty years earlier with the first rush of home-steaders. It was a quarter acre of leaning tombstones, cow-fenced from the sagebrush all around it. No one had ever bothered to plant trees there, or maybe they had, and none had survived. It was by now a place of desolation and despondency. There had been rain in recent days, but the ground was dry below the top couple of inches, and dirt striking the casket made a hard, rattling sound. D. L. Winslow, a homesteader and part-time preacher from down around Foy, read a verse from the Bible, the one about the shepherd in the valley of the shadow. None of the twenty or twenty-five people standing around the grave wept. This was 1937, and it seemed to all of them that the barren cemetery was a sign and symbol of their life and times.

The neighbors had done what they could to finish the roundup, but nobody had finished the Frazers' haying, and it had been a skimpy year for hay anyway. By February their cows were half starved, and a heavy snowstorm killed off a great many of them. That same month Elbert Echol, who had a weak heart, died suddenly, and in the spring his nephew called the loan on the ranch. Martha saw the heif-ers through the calving season, and right after the spring roundup Henry sold off what was left of the herd and paid what he could, but they had always lived on a thin edge and by now they didn't have anything in reserve. The nephew was strapped himself and in need of his inheritance.

In June, almost a year after Mary Claudine was lost, Martha and Henry Frazer gave up the ranch where their daughter had been born and died. They hired themselves out to Arlo Gantz's cousin, a new widow who needed somebody to run her husband's ranch until she could figure out what to do next.

The widow's place was on the Umpqua River in Klamath County, and if Bud had been willing to move over there with them he could have finished his last year of high school in Roseburg. Or he could have gone back to the boarding school at Hart. But he had already missed a year because of all that went on with his sister, and he didn't have the patience for going back. Or, to tell it clean, he didn't know how to fix his parents' unhappiness, or they his, and he was looking for a reason to get out from under their roof. So when they moved out of the house at Echol Creek, Bud headed out on his own.

There were some big ranches around Harney County, and he picked up work here and there that summer, mostly delivering groceries to the cow camps or putting in fence. A lot of the men who worked for the big spreads would buck horses on their off-days, just for the hell of it. They'd bring an unbroke horse into a pen and ear him down while they got the saddle on, then turn him loose after the rider climbed up. No gun to sound the end of the ride, you'd just ride until the horse quit or the men watching said get down. And every so often a bunch of them would pile into cars and find a real rodeo somewhere and spend their wages on entry fees. Bud Frazer tagged along.

The horses he had grown up with had all been started by his mother, and they hardly ever bucked. When you're a kid dreaming about riding at Madison Square Garden or Calgary, this can be somewhat of a disappointment. You look for horses that might buck, or you climb on a young steer, and when he goes wild-eyed and throws you off, you find another one and try again; after you manage to stay on one or two, you start thinking you're some kind of bronc rider. By the time he was thirteen or so Bud had kept his seat on some unbroke ponies at Fourth of July picnics around Harney County, and he thought he was hell on horseback.

But he was not quite eighteen when he left home and not done growing—he was five-nine and weighed about one forty soaking wet. When he started hanging around rodeos that summer, those big saddle broncs just shrugged him off like a burlap sack. He was too slight to bulldog steers, but he could work the gates and haze the calves and steers. The riders and stockmen paid him for that, and if there was a wild horse race he could sometimes stick on long enough to finish. And he could rope calves: once in a while, if he had enough money for the entrance fee and if the competition wasn't too fierce, he'd come in third and pocket a few dollars, enough to pay for the beer he had started to drink.

In the fall, when roundup got under way, Arlo Gantz's old Hamley saddle was enough credential to get him a few weeks of steady cow work. But after roundup the ranches laid off all the itinerants, and shortly after that the rodeo season was done. He managed to pick up a little more work here or there, but by the middle of winter he was out of work and out of money, so he found a ride to where his folks were living—they were running a small ranch for an absentee owner in Jackson County by then—and spent a few weeks helping them feed cows. But as soon as the weather broke that spring, he took off again.

He spent most of the summer of 1938 working as a cook's flunky for a dude ranch in the Chiloquin Valley. And in September, two years after Mary Claudine was lost, he rode a Greyhound bus to Hollywood.

SEVEN

28

WHEN I SAW LILY that first Sunday after Steve Deets got hurt, I didn't say anything about what had happened, nothing about the screaming horse, nothing about Steve putting a gun to his head.

This was the same day Lily told me she'd been laid off from Sunrise—told me her lie about the writers not having enough work, leaving out the part about Lampman and the Cossack. So we were both steering clear of some things that day.

I could see she was down in the mouth about something, but I figured it was about money and being out of work, so I asked if she wanted to play cards instead of spending two bits on a movie. But we wound up going to the theater anyway because we both wanted to see *Stagecoach*.

Lily had a high regard for John Ford, who had made a big impression on her with a show called *The Informer;* and I had a high regard for Yakima Canutt, who had doubled for John Wayne in the new movie. Before I came down to California I hadn't ever heard of Canutt, but after I got into the stunt business I heard his name damn near every day, and people had been saying there were tricks in Ford's movie that nobody but Yak could have pulled off.

Whenever people talk about "serious" westerns, "superior" westerns, they point to Ford—they say it was *Stagecoach* and the rest of Ford's big-budget cowboy pictures that opened up the cowboy story from what it was. But if you ask me, this mostly means, even now, better filmmaking, a bigger budget, more realistic violence—but the same old stories. It's always been rare for any western, even the "superior" ones, to spend more than a minute or two counting the cost of what it means to be a hero.

I didn't know enough back then to make that point, I just knew there were certain things you could count on in cowboy pictures: chases, fights, shootouts, an Indian raid, a hero who can't marry the girl or ride out of town until he does away with the bad guys and the savage Apaches. And *Stagecoach* covered them all. Well, it was a big-budget picture from United Artists, so I had come into it expecting more than just more of the same. I liked the picture, but I didn't see much that was new except the location over there in Monument Valley and Yakima Canutt pulling off that crazy stunt—tumbling off the stagecoach right between the galloping horses and getting dragged back under the coach.

When I told Lily I hadn't seen anything new in Ford's picture, we got into an argument about it. Or not an argument so much as Lily sounding off about what she thought I had missed—her lecture full of hundred-dollar words like "archetypes" and "ethos" and "redemption."

I can look back now and know that we were both trying to get some traction on what had happened that week, the things we weren't talking about. And at that point Lily and I weren't getting along anyway. I had been showing up late, looking hung over and bloodshot, not every Sunday but often enough for her to notice. Sometimes when I did finally show up at the Studio Club, Lily wasn't waiting for me. The girl at the reception desk would hand over a note she'd left for me—*Avalon,* maybe, or *Bagdad,* just the one scribbled word, and I'd head for that theater, come in after the movie had started, and sit down next to her in the dark. She never acted like she was mad, she'd just pass me the sack of popcorn without taking her eyes off the screen, but afterward, walking back to her dormitory, she wouldn't say much. She'd look in shop windows and act like she only halfway heard me when I said anything. Or she'd invite my opinion about Roosevelt's politics, or Hitler, Gandhi, whatever was in the news that day, and then dispute every opinion I had.

I had been spending Saturday nights with girls who mostly made me feel like a top hand, so on Sundays I was beginning to be tired of Lily knowing more than I did about everything. And Lily, by then, had begun to think I might be too narrow-gauged to bother with. It's hard to know what else was going on, but one thing I know is that people are never as coherent and integrated as the characters in movies.

I told her that if Ford wanted to break new ground he should have had somebody like Clark Gable or Errol Flynn—an A-list movie star—play the part of the Ringo Kid, not John Wayne, who was nothing but a second-rate cowboy actor who'd been in a bunch of Poverty Row shoot-'em-ups—I had wrangled horses for one of his movies while I was still working for Harold.

She frowned and said, "I think he put Wayne in it because he's making a comment on western stereotypes. I think it makes the Kid ironic."

Sometimes when she talked over my head I didn't mind it—she could make it sound like she was just thinking out loud, not expecting any kind of answer from me. But this rubbed me the wrong way. I didn't have any real ammunition to fight her with, but I said, "I think he put Wayne in it because he works cheap."

Lily gave me a look I was used to by now, her brows knitting together in an unbroken line. "That's a stupid thing to say." Definite and pointed.

My face grew hot. We walked the rest of the way back to the Studio Club without speaking. At the steps of her building she looked over at me and said, "I better not spend money on a movie next week unless I find another job."

I could have said something about getting together to play cards. What I said was, "I was thinking I might go down to the horse races at Del Mar with some friends of True's on Sunday."

She just nodded and went on inside.

A couple of weeks later she called me at True's. It had been a slow time for me—no work at all, too much dull and damaging time on my hands. And the funeral for Steve Deets that I'd skipped out on. I thought Lily had called to ask me to a movie, and I know I would have said yes. But she had called to tell me she'd landed work as a staff writer at RKO. I could hear in her voice how happy she was, needing to tell somebody who would know this was big news, a big step up.

She said Bob Hewitt's uncle had put in a call to a friend at RKO, and a copy of *Death Rides the Sky* had made it up the chain in the Story Department over there. Phil Auerbach, the story editor, had liked the script, she said, but he thought it was "a little too soft around the edges." And he had put her to work with a writer named Dorothy Crowther, who was known around the studio as "Doc" for her hard-boiled style.

"Remember that movie *Rendezvous?* We saw it a couple of months ago. Dorothy wrote it. She's good."

I said, "That's pretty great. I guess you're major league now. Your story's not too soft, though. Don't let her change it too much."

"Well, thanks. But she's good, I can learn from her."

"Just don't let her change your story too much."

"No. I won't."

We were both being too polite, but I guess neither of us could figure out how to get out of it. We didn't talk long. She said she was working on a new screenplay, going without sleep on the weekends, writing under a blanket at night with a flashlight. This didn't leave much of an opening for us to get back to seeing movies on Sunday, so I didn't bring it up. Those were the restless twitches of my mind at the time.

I want to say just a little more about Dorothy Crowther. I left

Hollywood a few weeks later, so most of what I know about her I heard from Lily in the years afterward, but I can tell you she was a striking brunette who looked like she belonged in a magazine advertisement for mink coats. But in some ways she made me think of my sister—the kind of woman Mary Claudine might have been if she'd lived. Dorothy had grown up a tomboy, running up and down the beach, climbing trees, battling with her brothers. She had read everything when she was a kid, but she especially devoured Edgar Rice Burroughs and Jack London, had loved *Robinson Crusoe* and *Smoky the Cowhorse.* When she started writing at age twelve or thirteen, she wrote fantastic science-fiction tales, crime fiction, adventure stories. Her heroines were always cynical and wisecracking, and her stories were shot through with danger and villainy. Conventional heroines and domestic stories bored her.

At RKO, Dorothy had been the only woman in a field of men. She wanted to be thought of as one of the boys, but she was a beauty, so she had to work pretty hard at it: she learned to swear a blue streak, play craps, and sneer at other women, and she'd developed an archive of raunchy jokes. She and Lily figured Phil Auerbach had put them together because they were the only two women in the writers' building, and Doc worried that being thrown together with another woman might cause the men writers to go back to thinking of her as a "girl." But they weren't pushed out of the men's clubhouse for long—Lily was used to being taken for one of the boys; she'd never had to work at it.

They never did get *Death Rides the Sky* onto the floor, but they went on writing together intermittently for years—they wrote *The Huntington Affair* and *The Dry Years* as a team. Crime noir is what they were known for.

Sometime in the 1960s, when feminism was making its comeback, Lily wrote a scathing piece about Hollywood culture in the forties and fifties, the way women were held back, treated lightly— which as far as I can see hasn't changed a lot in the years since. But she took a harsh view, too, of what she and Doc had to do to succeed in the movie business: "writing like men, writing for men," is how she put it, then dolling themselves up in jewelry and lipstick for magazine interviews, pieces that always ran under a patronizing banner like "The Beguiling Script Girls of RKO."

It was while she and Doc were working together, watching their scripts rewritten beyond recognition, mangled by poor directors or self-important stars, that Lily went to a few Communist Party meetings. The irony, given that those meetings got her blacklisted for ten years, is that even there she found patriarchy the governing principle.

Lily and Doc were friends for twenty-five years, right up until the end of Dorothy's life. And early on, after Lily and Bob Hewitt stopped seeing each other, she and Doc had a quiet affair that lasted a few months. Lily has written about it, so I won't say much more except that Lily was in the middle of her second divorce when Dorothy died, and the letter she wrote me afterward was shot through with self-loathing, heartbreak, regret.

She and Mike Beahrs were married for nearly ten years, and they might have made it all the way except Mike died of lymphoma right around the time Lily was testifying before the HUAC. She was married twice more after that, but she may have loved Doc more than any of the men. It was just a different world back then, and even someone like Lily, someone who was always swimming against the tide, had to find her own way to live in it.

The last picture Lily made before her decade on the Hollywood blacklist was *The Golden West*. By then she had begun to look at the western as our great American lie, and *The Golden West* had more to do with postwar repression and paranoia and the dark side of the cowboy mythology than with anything in a John Ford film. It took aim squarely at the cowboy's bigotry, his fear of uppity women, swarthy foreigners, and government conspiracies, as well as the role our cowboy heroes have always played in the American fascination with violence. Solving every problem with his gun. Lily and Mike Beahrs financed the picture themselves—no studio would have touched it.

She asked me to the New York premiere, but Simone was seven

months pregnant with our daughter, so a six-hour plane ride wasn't in the cards, and I wound up taking my mother.

My mother had begun to take college courses through the public library and had joined the Sierra Club and the Audubon Society. She and my father didn't follow politics, or they claimed not to, so I wasn't sure if she would see what Lily's film was getting at. But after the screening, my mother said to her, "Senator McCarthy ought to see your picture. It might do him some good."

Lily laughed. She had always liked my mother. "Well, this picture will either do him some good or land me in jail."

I had a teacher once who liked to tell us to grab our courage with both hands. At the time I thought this meant we shouldn't cry when we were hurt. Cowboys never cried is what I thought she meant. But I think she must have meant Lily. Someone like Lily. Grabbing courage with both hands.

29

A COUPLE OF WEEKS after Steve's wreck I got hired for a Civil War movie they were calling *The Battle at Valverde Ford*. The director was Albert Jamerman, who, like De Mille, had made a name for himself directing big-budget epics. He had hired an action director named Ute Renner, who had ramrodded war movies for a few major studios, movies with big infantry battle scenes. But Renner didn't know much about horses, which is how he came to hire Cab O'Brien to coordinate the cavalry charges, and that's how I came onto it.

I can see, looking back, that Steve's wreck out at Westerlund was the beginning of the end of my Hollywood days. But when I got called for *Valverde* I thought I had stepped up a notch. This was an RKO picture, my first for a major studio, and it was my first location shoot, a month in Arizona; they were putting up the crew in motels, feeding us three meals a day. At least a hundred riders had been hired in Los Angeles, and we heard they were hiring hundreds of local extras—it was a pretty big picture, even for RKO.

The studio had arranged to drive all of us from LA to the locations around Flagstaff and Sedona—five hundred miles—in a caravan of buses driving straight through, day and night. But Dave

Keaton had his old Franklin sedan, so five of us crammed into it and took two long days for the trip.

It was the first time I'd been out of the city since I'd stepped off the Greyhound bus back in September. I wouldn't say that I had forgotten what the real West could look like, but for months I'd been making movies on patches of ground fitted up with fake sagebrush and plaster rocks, so maybe I was a little more awake to the view outside the car than I otherwise would have been.

The first part of that drive was just orchards and irrigated farms, then parks and hills dotted with live oaks, but gradually we came into country that looked a lot like places I knew around Harney County and Lake County—dry lakebeds, blackish crackling malpais, miles of flat grassland, sand, and sagebrush. We spent the night at a tourist court in Needles, then crossed over the Colorado River and drove back roads up into stands of pine and aspen around Brannigan Park, country that made me think about the Ochocos. That's where my mind went on much of that trip—to Echol Creek, for the first time in god knows how long.

And then we got into those copper- and sand-colored monoliths and buttes around Sedona. Parts of Arizona had been showing up in cowboy pictures since the twenties, so that country was weirdly familiar to me, but it was hard to let go of the feeling that it was a big plaster-of-Paris backdrop for a movie. Years later, when I lived in Flagstaff, it seemed to me that the San Francisco Peaks, Oak Creek Canyon, Red Rocks, exposed something false about the movies; but the first time I saw that area, it was the land itself that felt make-believe.

They parceled us all out to lodging houses around Sedona and Flagstaff. I was put up at the Wagon Wheel, a rundown auto court right on Route 66, along with twelve or fourteen other guys. I roomed with Ralph Foster, who had been on that Wild Bill Elliott picture when I was getting started as a rider, and he'd been over at Westerlund with me when Steve got hurt. I hadn't seen Ralph since Steve died, and all that first night at the Wagon Wheel I kept waiting for him to bring it up or thinking that I would. We were in bed with the lights clicked off before I said, "Too bad about Deets."

He just said, "Yeah." And that was all either of us said about it.

There's a joke I've heard more than once—well, I guess it's a joke—about marines getting ready to make a beachhead landing and the lieutenant telling them, "Nine out of ten of you fellows will be shot to hell before the day is over," and every one of them looking around at the others, thinking, "Those poor sons of bitches." That was me—hell, that was every stunt rider I met while I worked in Hollywood. But Steve had known he was done for—I had seen it in his face. He was forty years old and busted up for good. I had never seen a man look that scared, and I guess that might have been what Ralph and I didn't want to talk about.

Valverde, far from the main theater of the Civil War, was a little-known battle, but it was the only time in that war when a lancer company mounted a charge—a hundred men galloping on horseback, their nine-foot lances fluttering with little swallowtail flags. And Kit Carson had commanded the 1st New Mexico Volunteers in that fight, so probably somebody at RKO thought Carson would give their war movie a cowboy flair.

For the climactic cavalry battle at Valverde Ford, Oak Creek was a stand-in for the Rio Grande; they had found a location with low banks where the creek spread out shallow and so clear you could see the hard sandstone bottom. For shooting the big encampments and infantry skirmishes and the lancer charge, they had leased a private ranch in the valley east of Sedona, a thousand acres of pastureland with scattered oak trees, eroded rock formations streaked with bands of red and ocher and black earth, and creeks edged with willow brush. Country I'd seen in a dozen movies. Some of it a lot like country I'd lived in.

They picked us up at five every morning, and before sunrise we were eating breakfast under canvas awnings in a dry grass field. And then we put on our hot wool cavalry uniforms and spent a lot of time waiting around. This wasn't the kind of fast riding and hard falling I was used to on the two-gun cowboy movies. We had some big scenes to shoot, but it took days to get those set up. In the meantime they filmed us plodding along in formation at several different places on the ranch and in the canyon, with long shots of us sitting on our ponies, and then for three or four days we shot close-in scenes, swinging sabers and rifle butts on horseback and spurting squibs of blood. None of it was hard work, but the days were long, twelve or fifteen hours.

I was used to riding in a posse or a bunkhouse crew, maybe a cavalry patrol, just ten or twenty riders at most. For the lancer scene in *Valverde* there were more than a hundred of us, a Rebel troop charging a line of Colorado infantrymen. We'd be galloping in a long battle line, charging across the field with leveled lances—nine feet of wood tipped with twelve-inch metal blades. They were props, the edges and tips not really sharp, but sharp enough to kill you if you accidently ran into the business end, so we spent a lot of our time the second week of the shoot just rehearsing the charge, getting used to riding at a gallop with the heavy lances couched.

The director, Jamerman, had left Renner in charge of the action scenes, and Renner had left the planning and rehearsal of the lancer scene to Cab, but the day before we shot the scene, Jamerman showed up at the location, evidently just to let us know that this was his picture—that everybody, even Cab, was working for him. Cab had already gone over with us more than once how the scene was supposed to go, but he stood back and let Jamerman act the big shot, the director lifted above us in the bucket of a crane so he could see and be seen, shouting down through a megaphone to make himself heard.

We were to ride like hell, he said, across a field rigged with tripwires, because this would give him the look he wanted: men and horses falling randomly, our charge broken by withering rifle fire before we got close enough to use our lances. And then he wanted us to loosely regroup for a second failed charge before staging a wild, panicky retreat. The movie's star was Alan Greer, playing General Henry

Sibley. Jamerman smiled slightly and made a loose salute in Greer's direction when he said Sibley would lead the charge. And when the advance was broken, Sibley would lean out of the saddle to pick up a fallen battle flag and rally the men for that second charge.

What I heard from Lily later on was that the real General Sibley was drunk for most of the two-day Valverde battle, hauled everywhere in an army ambulance because he couldn't stay on his horse, and in any case he wasn't a lancer. But Alan Greer was one of RKO's big stars, and the movie had been written with him in mind.

Greer was the real thing. He had grown up on a ranch and then worked for a wild west show before coming to Hollywood, so he did his own falls and jumps, his own mounts and dismounts. Rocking Chair, the big bay horse he always rode in the movies, belonged to him, not to any barn or studio. Greer had trained the horse to untie ropes and unlatch gates and limp along like he was sore-footed if the plot called for it.

Working with the second unit, you don't usually see much of the principals, but Greer never used a stunt double, so on this movie we'd seen quite a bit of him. He'd been in all the action scenes we had shot, and he'd been out with us the day before to rehearse the charge, not riding with a lance but brandishing a gleaming officer's saber.

Jamerman called down to Cab, "Sibley's gotta stay in the saddle, I don't want his horse going down. And I sure as hell don't want my star to wind up in the hospital. You got that figured out?"

"Yes sir. We laid out a clear path for him through the wires."

"I guess you've already been over that with Alan?"

Cab was standing with his hands in his jeans pockets, as meek as I'd ever seen him. "Yes sir, we talked it over, and we walked it and rode it both." He looked over at Greer, and Greer mimicked Jamerman's loose salute.

Jamerman turned back to the rest of us and brought up the megaphone. "So I guess now you men know your job! Which is to charge like hell and die bravely!" There was a slight delay and echo as his words made it to the back of our crowd, and he waited, smiling, as if he thought we might give him a rousing cheer. A stuntman had been killed making *Charge of the Light Brigade,* when he was thrown off his horse and landed on his own lance—everybody knew about it. Cab hadn't brought it up, and it wasn't anything we practiced, but word had gone around to all of us: drop the damn lance flat on the ground if your horse trips on one of the wires. Try not to skewer yourself or somebody else.

So the silence went on for half a minute or so. Finally somebody called out, "You bet," and a few others joined in, and Jamerman nodded and smiled, completely satisfied.

I didn't think I was nervous, but I woke up early on the morning of the filming—it was still dark, but I could feel the stars turning toward morning. I washed my face and got dressed and went outside, sat on a bench, and just for something to do I took out some paper and sketched the row of cars parked in front of the motor court. The first time I'd drawn anything in weeks. Finally the men in the other rooms started to stir and wake—I could hear their voices and coughs—and after a while a bus picked us up.

The light had brightened by the time we got to the field, and then the sun broke suddenly in a red line along the low range of hills in the east. It was already warm, would be hot later, so after we had suited up in our lancer costumes we found what shade we could at the edges of the battlefield and waited to be told when it was time to do some riding. A few men got up card games, but I lay down on the dry grass, pulled down my hat, and tried to sleep.

Cab and Renner and Jamerman were still parleying about how the charge would start and end and how long it would run. They were walking over the field mapping out details of the action, talking things over with the cinematographer—angles and focus for the three cameras. I thought the tripwires had been rigged the day before, but there were grips out on the field rigging more of them.

Wranglers had brought in a hundred horses under saddle, crowded together inside a rope pen, but the one handling Rocking Chair kept him under a shade cloth away from the others, and every so often he walked the horse out and back so he'd stay limbered up while he was waiting for the action to start. Alan Greer showed up early with the rest of us, but nobody mistook him for an extra. An assistant brought over a canvas chair with his name stenciled on it, and he sat there reading a script. After a while he put down the pages, dropped his chin on his chest, and took a nap.

It was noon before we got word they were ready to shoot the scene. The sun by then was hot, the sky pale with dust. The mountains to the west seemed almost white in the dazzling sunlight. We sorted out the horses and got mounted up, which took a while, and then a bunch of prop men went around handing up the lances. I was riding a tall, big-headed chestnut that day. He was nervous, skipping his feet, flicking his ears back, rolling the bit in his mouth—he didn't like the small banners on the tips of the lances or the fluttering battle flags. I rode him in circles to quiet him down.

Jamerman was watching from a wooden blind built around one of the cameras, but the action scenes were Renner's responsibility, and he was letting Cab call the shots that day. We drew up in our battle line, and Cab, from the bucket of a crane lifted above the field, shouted over our heads his idea of a pep talk: "Y'all better make it look fucking good."

I wasn't the only one on a nervous horse. The line broke again and again as horses danced out and had to be reined back in. I don't know what sort of moment Cab was looking for, but it was a long couple of minutes before I heard him shout the warning call. A puff of wind moved across the silence afterward, bending the flags, lifting a fine mist of dust along the battleground. Finally the whistle blew for the take. Alan Greer trotted his horse a few steps forward of the line. The chestnut, jittery, wanted to follow him, but I touched his neck, touched the reins, told him quietly, "Wait, wait, not yet." I didn't know his name or if he had one.

As Greer lifted his saber, Rocking Chair whirled in a neat pirouette. "Ride like hell, boys!" he shouted, and we roared back our cheer, leveled our lances, and the horses all jumped out at once.

By about the third stride the chestnut was wide open, and I could feel the power he had, the gather and reach of his springing legs. I tried to watch the ground as it streamed by, thinking to catch a glimpse of a tripwire before we were right on top of it, but my eyes blurred in the wind, and the grass in the field was tall under a veil of dust, and then horses started falling around me, horses and men both, and it seemed to me that the whole charge just collapsed in a matter of moments.

A dark shape fell in our way, and the chestnut reared, swerving away from it. I leaned over his neck, and when he jerked his head he struck my cheekbone a hard blow. I think that might have been when I let go of the lance, but anyway it was gone. Alongside me a horse lunged suddenly to its feet, one of its hind legs dangling broken, and the chestnut sprang away from him, a sideways lunge, and then his hooves scrabbled, kicking a mass on the ground, a man on the ground, the thick sound of a hoof striking bone. My eyes burned. A hot flare of wind lifted the chaff of dry grass and dust, a dry fog that hid the field. Shapes rose up through the yellow cloud or fell through it, and I could hear men calling out and horses squealing their pain. The hack of my own breath was loud in my head, but I could still hear the thud of bodies striking the hard, dry ground. The chestnut ran, and I let him run. We were under the oaks at the other side of the field before I asked him to stop. I got down and stood, shaky, with my hands on the pommel. I could hear the horse's winded breath, the labored rise and fall of his panic.

Other men and horses had made it down into the hot shade with us. I turned and looked back at the battlefield, at the injured horses running loose across the field, the men on the ground, the litter of fallen lances, the dead horses heaps of darkness against the dust and the yellow grass. I looked, but all these things were at a remove. I saw Greer standing in the middle of the shambles, holding his horse by the reins. The horse's head was very high, jerking up and down, his nostrils flaring, the ears pointing and swiveling. Crewmen were streaming out onto the field, and after a moment Greer led his horse through them toward the top edge of the field, where we had formed up our line just minutes earlier. A wrangler stepped up and took the horse from him, and Greer walked on past him, stopping briefly to speak to Cab, who was just stepping off the bucket of the crane. And then he walked on out of sight.

A horse plunged loose through the shade under the oak trees where I was standing, ran so close past me that the dirt he kicked up peppered me in a dry hail. The chestnut half reared in alarm, and when the reins slipped out of my hand he took off running with the other horse. I didn't try to go after him. When I heard a loud crack out on the field, I knew what it was and I came back as if from a journey. I walked out onto the grass to see who was hurt, see who I could help. Around me, three or four men, wranglers, I think, were walking from horse to horse, and every time a gun popped I couldn't keep my shoulders from jerking. Horses were screaming, men moaning. A wind came up, pelting grit and chaff, blowing across the valley from the sandstone bluffs to the west.

30

SO MANY HORSES were brought down in that Valverde battle scene that I'm surprised no men died. Plenty were hurt—stabbed or sliced with lances, thrown, trampled. There were a lot of broken bones. Dave Keaton broke his leg in a bad way. I don't know how many horses died—died outright or were shot afterward. Twenty-five, I heard, or thirty, forty.

I heard later that Jamerman was satisfied with the footage. It hadn't gone as he'd planned—there hadn't been a second charge—but the wreckage of horses and men gave him a battle scene that was more dramatic than the one he had been carrying around in his head. I heard he walked over to Cab afterward and shook his hand.

This was Saturday, at the end of a long week of long days, and we weren't shooting film on Sunday, so even if horses hadn't died that day, even if men hadn't been hauled off to the hospital, I imagine we'd have wanted to find a bar that stayed open late. As it was, we went at it with pretty serious intention. The dozen of us staying at the Wagon Wheel walked down the sidewalk half a mile or so and turned in at the first bar we came to.

There were several local fellows in that bar, men who worked for the railroad, I think. At some point they were laughing about something that could have been a slur against movie cowboys or could have had nothing to do with any of us. I went over there and took a swing at one of them. I was hoping for a brawl, but my swing went wide, and then Ralph Foster, who wasn't quite as drunk as I was, stepped in front of me, put his hand on my chest, and shoved. I went down on my butt, and I was too drunk to get to my feet. Ralph spoke a few friendly words to the locals and wandered off with them to a table in the corner. Nobody helped me up. I went on lying there with men stepping around me like I was an overturned chair. When I finally got back on my feet, Carl Frisson came over and dabbed at me with a bar towel—I had dropped my drink when Ralph pushed me, and the spill was all over my shirt front and my chin. He said, "Fool, you got to remember to set your drink down before you start a fight."

He then set his drink down and walked over to the table in the corner and punched one of the locals in the face. Blood spurted from the man's cheek, and when the rest of them registered what had happened they climbed over the table onto Carl. Ralph Foster stood up too, took a moment to make up his mind which side he was on, then randomly thumped one of the railroad men on the back of his head.

There was a big bouncer working that night, or maybe he was the bar owner, and he might have been the one who broke my nose. My nose had been broken once before, in another bar fight. The barroom brawl is a movie cliché, and this is probably the time to tell you I had been living up to that particular part of the cowboy stereotype for a while.

In the movies, men get punched in the face and don't even wind up bruised, but I can tell you a broken nose hurts so much it will just about make you weep. I was bleeding all over the front of my shirt and barely able to see to walk, but when they booted us out of that bar and the other men went looking for another bar to inhabit, I went along, and we only came weaving back down the sidewalk to the Wagon Wheel as the early risers were stepping out of their houses to go to Sunday-morning church service. I made it all the way back without puking or falling down. I drew the shades and slept all day. Ralph always snored like a bugling elk, and I'd been having trouble sleeping through his racket, but that was one time I didn't hear it. I sipped ginger ale for supper and went to bed again.

Monday morning I wasn't the only one who turned up for work bleary and with a marked face, but Cab looked us all over without saying a thing about it. The work that day, and the rest of the week, had us riding hard and taking falls—it was the cavalry battle at the ford—so he pushed us through some long days, and maybe that was how he made his point.

Carl Frisson had driven Dave Keaton back to LA in the Franklin after he broke his leg, so I rode the crew bus back to town at the end of that shoot. Leaning on the window, looking out at those weird streaked monoliths and sandstone bluffs, what came into my mind was Glass Buttes up in Lake County, the outcroppings of volcanic glass half a day's ride to the west of our ranch.

Mary Claudine and I had gone to Glass Buttes overnight on horseback a couple of times to collect obsidian arrowheads when we were kids. Sedona was a thousand miles from Glass Buttes, and those rock-hunting trips had been years earlier, but memory is a disjointed thing, and from thinking about Mary Claudine I was thrown back suddenly to the Christmas dance I'd gone to in Foy a few weeks after we gave up the search for her. I wasn't drinking back then, I didn't even like the taste of it, but somebody had brought whiskey and stashed it under the edge of the dance hall porch. That night I got pretty drunk for the first time in my life and got into a fight with a man I'd never seen before, an unshaven fellow about forty, wearing baggy pants and a soiled shirt. There were lots of itinerants, bums, and out-of-work cowhands passing through on the cross-state highway in those years, and one of the ideas I had been entertaining for a while was that one of those men might have grabbed my sister. I didn't think about why somebody like that would be traipsing around in the canyons above the ranch, miles from any road. Or the odds of his coming upon a girl out there. I was looking for somebody to blame and some reason for what happened other than a meaningless accident, and what I thought was this: if she'd been taken by somebody—a man looking for a girl to rape—he might still have her and she might still be found alive.

The man I picked a fight with was not as drunk as I was, and he had twenty or thirty pounds on me. I came away with a chipped tooth and a broken nose.

It was right after that Christmas party that hunters happened to come upon Mary Claudine's body. My face was still swollen, still purple with bruise, the day we buried her bones.

31

WHEN I GOT BACK TO TRUE'S HOUSE on Saturday night, he was dressing to go out. I took off my boots and lay down on the sofa in my clothes. From the bedroom he called to me, "Some of us are going out to the beach. I'll wait if you want to get cleaned up first. Lorraine might be there."

I said, "I'm pretty done in."

I went on lying there after he drove off. I could hear some kids in the yard next door playing cowboys and Indians, shooting cap pistols and whinnying like horses.

When it started to get dark in the house, I sat up and turned on a lamp and phoned the Studio Club. They called Lily to the phone, and when she said hello I said, "You want to see *Dodge City* tomorrow?"

I hadn't seen her in about a month, hadn't told her I was leaving town to make a movie in Arizona, hadn't talked to her at all since she told me on the telephone about starting work at RKO.

She was silent a moment. "All right. It's playing at the Music Box."

So I met her at the Music Box and we saw *Dodge City*. We didn't talk much. Lily didn't want to stay for the second feature—it was a silly comedy with Louis Jossup—so we went out to a spaghetti joint and ordered some supper. I still had lurid yellow bruises from the bar fight and a swollen lump where my nose was broken. She waited until we were in the cafe before she said, "Did you get in a fight?"

I said, "I fell off a bar stool."

"That's stupid," she said, and I knew she meant the fight, not the joke.

We ate our noodles in silence. Finally she asked if I'd been working much, and I told her I'd been in Arizona making a picture. When I told her it was an RKO movie, she guessed right away which one it was. "Dorothy worked on part of it, the dialogue where Kit Carson and Canby are arguing about the retreat." I didn't know that part of the story, but then she said, "And she wrote the scene where the mules are blown up."

I said, "I watched them film it."

"Did you? How did they do it? Do you think it'll look real?"

In the scene Union soldiers were supposed to fit up a pair of mules with fused barrels of gunpowder and send them over to the Rebel lines to blow up the picket posts. We had been waiting around a lot that day, standing in the shade about a hundred yards from where they were setting up the scene with the mules, so we watched for quite a while. On a big picture like this one, it could take a couple of hours to set up and film three or four shots that would run less than a minute in the final edit.

We had always kept mules on our place to do the heavy hauling and pull a wagon. My mother said they had less brains than a horse, but I think this was out of loyalty to horses and not from any evidence; I know she respected Mike and Prince, who would do just about anything we asked them to do. The mules they were using for the movie were smaller, but one of them was almost oxblood in his coloring, like Mike—not a color that shows up too often in mules. It gave me a start when I saw him, that half-second when you think a stranger is somebody you know.

In the movies I'd worked in, the red sticks of dynamite were always phony, and the flash-bang, triggered by somebody off camera, was a pine mortar buried in the ground, packed with black powder and loose fuller's earth, the lampblack ignited with gasoline to make black smoke. It would send up a nice cloud of flame and dust without doing any damage. Watching all the preparation for the shots, I had been thinking the barrels of gunpowder loaded on the mules were phony, like the sticks of dynamite. I figured that a powder monkey would rig up mortars on the ground, and then the film would be edited so it looked like the mules had been blown up in the explosion. They were setting up for the last shot before I came awake to the fact that they weren't burying the mortars in the ground but loading them into the barrels on the mules.

These were big mortars and maybe wrapped too tight. I had helped my dad blow up stumps, so I knew what a real explosion looked like, and when those blasts went off, one after the other, geysers of flame and smoke went thirty or forty feet in the air. We weren't anywhere close to the setup, but the booming thunderclap of sound just about deafened us. Shapes, pieces of shapes, landed, smoking, smelling of gunpowder and burnt hair. Through the smoke, I could see one of the mules lying with its side torn open, working its legs mechanically in a spreading pool of blood.

Wranglers had strung up a temporary rope corral close by to hold our saddled horses while we waited to be called, and another fifty or sixty horses were spread out on pasture behind us. The explosions stampeded all the horses, and we spent the rest of that day rounding them up from the far corners of the ranch. We lost the next day too, while people in the costume crew cleaned the shrapnel—the mules' flesh and blood and slivers of bone—from our cavalry uniforms.

I said to Lily, "They blew up the mules."

She looked at me.

"They loaded some big mortars on two mules and lit the fuses and blew them up. I was picking bits of mule out of my hair for a couple of days." I wasn't sure why, but I meant to shock her, horrify

295

her. I said, "There's other ways they could have filmed it, they didn't have to kill the mules." And I know she heard something in it, something like blame.

After a moment she said, "Dorothy told me she didn't make it up, it really happened. At Valverde, I mean. It really happened in the war." And then after another short silence, "You don't have to blame Dorothy for it."

I should have said no, I didn't blame Dorothy. What I said was, "Maybe I'll blame Kit Carson for thinking it up," as if I was making a joke.

There was a prolonged silence. Then she said, "Are you mad at me for some reason?"

"No."

She watched me, then said, "Well, you're mad about something."

I was well acquainted with that tone of voice from her. "You don't know what I'm feeling."

She looked away. "Well, you are being mean, so I think you're mad at me." I know now her own father had been one to go mean and throw blame around, which she had learned was a signal of trouble to come: heavy drinking, storms of shouting. The truth is, she had been watching me for weeks—ever since I started turning up on Sunday bleary and bloodshot—waiting for an eruption.

I swept up some spilled salt into a little drift and then brushed it onto the floor. "It doesn't have to do with you," I said.

I had come back from Arizona with something shaken loose, but I wasn't sure I could say what that was. In our family and in all the families we knew, people steered clear of anything having a whiff of sentiment. Deep feelings were held close, unspoken. In some way this had to do with never crying when you were hurt. Lily always expressed whatever was on her mind—at least this is what I thought— and she could be impatient with me for holding back. Of course, I didn't know all that she was holding back.

But all at once I was filled with the need to tell her about the wreck of horses and men, and my part in it. I wanted to tell her about how I had been having trouble sleeping. Well, I had been having trouble sleeping for a long time, but that last week in Arizona, after the lancer charge, I lay in bed every night seeing, over and over, horses and men falling through a veil of dust and shattered grass, turning over in my head my hatred of Cab, and then in the long hours of darkness coming around slowly to knowing I'd been looking for something like this to happen, a big fall—maybe even hoping for it. And knowing if I'd been hurt or killed I would deserve what I'd been given. A settling of accounts for getting my sister killed.

But I didn't know how to start saying any of this to Lily. I needed her to ask me, and she didn't know the right thing to ask.

After a minute she asked me what I thought of the movie. I had to think a bit to realize she was talking about *Dodge City*. I said Errol Flynn was an Englishman and I didn't think he should be playing a western sheriff. He didn't have the right look for it, I told her.

"Well, he's Australian," Lily said, as if that made a difference. And then she wanted to know what I thought a western sheriff should look like, and we might have gotten into a quarrel about it except I didn't care enough to argue.

When I walked her back to the Studio Club, I didn't offer to come in and play cards, but I said, "Do you want to see the Sherlock Holmes movie?"

She studied me. "If you do."

So we went back to seeing movies on Sunday. The night we saw Sherlock Holmes we skipped the second feature, a singing-cowboy picture neither of us was interested in, went back to her dormitory, and played a few hands of pinochle. She shuffled and dealt, but then she laid her cards down and took off her glasses to polish them with the hem of her sweater. While she was looking down at her fingers working on the glasses she said, "I don't know why you didn't tell me what happened over there in Arizona. Everybody at RKO is talking about it."

I was caught off-guard, but I knew she meant the big cavalry charge, men hurt, horses killed. "Dave Keaton broke his leg, a couple of other fellows got hurt. Guys get hurt all the time. Horses too. I didn't think you'd want to hear about it."

She was silent for a good while, and then she put on her glasses and picked up her cards. "Jamerman is a son of a bitch, everyone at RKO knows it."

It was the first swearword I had ever heard from Lily, although that didn't register at the time. I said, "Well, it was Cab who set up the tripwires, so they're all sons of bitches, aren't they?"

She played a card. "They are," she said matter-of-factly. I hadn't heard about Lampman yet, or I might have understood why she suddenly held a dim view of the movie business and just about everybody in it.

We played a little while in silence, and then she said, "I heard Jamerman wanted to outdo De Mille. He was bragging that he killed more horses in his movie than De Mille killed in *Charge of the Light Brigade*."

I didn't know how many horses had been killed in the De Mille picture, but I said, "He might have. I saw maybe twenty-five or thirty go down."

I didn't tell her everything, but as we went on playing cards she pulled out of me a few more things I had seen: horses killed outright, horses crippled and shot, men who'd been hurt. It took a while to get the words out, but I told her I was pretty sure the chestnut horse I was riding had kicked one of the men lying on the ground.

I thought she might tell me it wasn't my fault or something else completely pointless. What she said after a long silence was "I sprained my ankle once, but I haven't ever been really hurt. Have you, Bud?"

Riding for the movies was a good way to get yourself wrecked or killed in those days, and looking back, I wonder why I didn't get hurt sooner than I did, doing all those stunts without any padding or much coaching. I was young and pliable, I guess, or just lucky. Lily could look at me and know I'd had my nose broken, but she also knew I'd been riding for the movies for a few months without once being hauled off to the hospital.

I guess I knew she was asking about something else.

I said, "I've been hurt a few times."

I might have let it stay there, but she kept looking at me, waiting for more, and silence can prod you into saying something you don't plan to say. "You can't hardly work around cows and horses without getting hurt. Everybody in my family's been hurt one time or another." Then, I don't know why, I said, "My sister got killed just riding for cows. She got thrown from her horse and the horse stepped on her."

Lily made a small sound, a slight intake of breath. I wanted her to know about Mary Claudine, but I sure didn't want any sympathy from her, didn't want her to pump me for the whole story—not that night, anyway—so I played a trump card and gathered in the trick, put down my next card, and gestured with my chin that it was her play. She studied me. She knew what I was doing, and I guess she was making up her mind if she'd let me get away with it. Finally she looked down at her cards and played one, and we went on with the game. The only other thing she said, after a long, long silence, was "I hope you don't get killed in one of their stupid movies, Bud."

I kept my eyes on the cards in front of me. "I've been killed a bunch of times already, so I'm starting to get the hang of it."

She threw me a look. "Ha ha. Funny boy."

32

AFTER WHAT HAPPENED IN ARIZONA, I started asking who the ramrod was every time Central Casting called about a picture, and I steered away from anything Cab O'Brien was running. This was a stupid thing to do: plenty of other action directors were just as cold-blooded as Cab, and you couldn't hardly ride in a cowboy picture without seeing men hauled off to the hospital and horses thrown, tripped, ridden through saloon windows. So I can't tell you why I was so dead set on not working for Cab, but I guess it's not hard to come up with theories.

Things went along okay for a while. I rode in a picture with Hoot Gibson, and I had a couple of lines in one of Tim McCoy's hayburners. Then there was a two-week stretch at the end of August when the phone didn't ring, and I got down to hard bread and a couple of thin dimes. I called Central Casting, and late in the day they called back with two days of work on an oater called *Mojave War Drums*. They were shooting at The Canyon. I didn't ask who the ramrod was, but I knew it might be Cab. He ran a lot of pictures at The Canyon.

I rode a bus out there, and they were already shooting film when I

got on the set. The picture was half done but running behind schedule—the horse they had been using as a double for the star horse had
come up lame, and it had taken a while to find another lookalike for
a tricky river crossing. They had finally put that scene to bed, but Cab
was in a foul mood, in a hurry to finish the movie on time. A man
riding a horse fall had been hurt the day before, which was the reason
I'd been called. Cab shouted at me, "Where the fuck have you been?
Get dressed and get in here, fucking pronto."

They put me in a black wig and greasepaint, playing an Apache
Indian, and the wrangler gave me a long-necked pinto horse he said
was high-strung. I had come to know that "high-strung" in a picture
horse meant he'd been hurt more than once and was naturally worried he might be hurt again. The horse was rigged up in the usual
"Indian" fashion, with a blanket thrown over the saddle, and if I'd had
time I would have pulled off the saddle and ridden him bareback,
which might have saved me a little bit later on. But Cab was roaring
about delays, so I toed the stirrup and trotted out to where two other
Indians were waiting. One was Lon Epps, and the other was a man
named Pat McDermott, whom I'd met once or twice. Lon wiggled
his eyebrows like Groucho. "Hey, kid. Ain't we got fun." He spoke
low, barely moving his mouth, while Cab was shouting his directions.

The Canyon was pretty small for a movie ranch, just twenty acres
and a couple of tame, chaparral-covered hills; if you were to guess
where I'd wind up busting a gut, it wouldn't be The Canyon. But one
thing I learned that year is that men and horses could sometimes
walk away from the most appalling-looking wrecks, could walk away
without a scratch, or a man could step off the saddle wrong and break
his damn head. There is just no way to make sense of it.

Cab wanted us to ride single file across the face of one of those
hills, following a beaten trail with the shoulder of the hill on our
left. And since this was Cab, he wanted us racing along at top speed.
It wasn't anything out of the usual. I had been riding the same way
when I was twelve years old and chasing cows. I was in the middle,
Pat was up front, Lon brought up the tail. The pinto was anxious

about getting to the other side, so he was moving at a very fast clip, swiveling his ears from side to side, alert for anything that might hurt him, and my eyes were slitted against the dust that Pat raised ahead of me. And then something started rocks rolling from above us—some creature scrambling to get away from us, maybe—and in the instant between the veer and the snort of my horse I saw what was coming, but it was too late. The pinto whirled and reared up, pawing the steep slope, and I pulled my hand back and the horse came too high—I saw it was too high. I slipped off his tail end, my right hand still clenching the reins, which might be why the horse came above me, looming dark. I landed on my feet and tried to throw myself to the side, but I lost my footing on the slope. The ground or the horse rose up and hit me—a white flash behind my eyes—and then we were both sliding downhill, a long slide it seemed at the time, but maybe not more than thirty or forty feet before I hit a bit of flat shelf and the horse rolled over me—incredible red-hot wires of pain flashing through my hips and my legs. The pinto kept going all the way down the hill and came to his feet at the bottom without a goddamn mark on him.

I couldn't move but I did, scraping my heels and my hands in the gravel, because the pain was more than I thought I could stand, and I had to writhe around like a crab to stand it. I was on the border of being sick. The wires in my pelvis twisted and pulled, scraping through my bones. I held on, grinding into the gray, almost gone but then coming back with Lon's face leaning over me, his hand gripping my wrist. I caught a breath and another. I was trembling cold, my heart racing high and desperate.

Lon said, "Lie still, kid, be quiet."

I heard other voices. I couldn't see well. A shout came from below, and Lon shouted down, and I saw through a watery haze the legs of men and then faces closing around me. I was working hard to hold back the sounds that were trying to come out of my throat. There was talking, but I couldn't focus on it. Then Lon's voice by my ear, "We got to move you off this here hill."

I think I tried to say no, don't move me, don't touch me, but I'm not sure any words actually came out except "No."

"We got to, kid, just don't try to do anything for yourself. Let us carry you. We're gonna lift you onto this board now, easy does it."

They lifted me. The wires flashed, a white melting heat, and I went flat out for a while.

Then I heard Lon say into my ear, "We got you, kid," and I was sweating cold, and I heard the men grunt as they carried the board with me on it, lurching. I was almost level with their belts as we went crosswise down the hill, jerking and swaying. I slipped in and out of someplace gray. We went under some dry trees, and they set the board down on a table. I was cold, my teeth chattering. Somebody brought a blanket and put it over me. Lon brought my hat and set it down on the table where I could reach it with my hand.

It was a while before the ambulance showed up. I heard Cab shouting, and then Lon said, "Sorry, kid," and all the men went back to work and left me alone. I lay still, swallowing down nausea. I was in a shaking, icy fever of weakness and hurt. Broken open like a wishbone, dragged a hundred miles by a wild horse, that's what it felt like. And I was in a lonely place, caught between rage at the fucking horse and rage at my hand yanking back on the reins, bringing him over, goddamn it, right onto me. Racked by knowing that this was the pain Mary Claudine had borne in the hours after Goldy rolled onto her and wrecked her small body.

At the hospital they asked me who was my closest relation, who they should call. They meant who would pick me up when I was turned out of the place, or maybe who would pay the bill, but I thought they meant who to call in case I died, and after I rummaged through the reasons for calling or not calling my folks, I told them Lily Shaw.

33

I HAVE SAID this wouldn't be the whole story of my life, that I would stick to that year I worked in Hollywood, riding for the movies. But before we get to the end of it, I want to say a few things about the years that followed.

I met my wife in the summer of 1947, standing in line at the Vanport Extension Center, one of those adjunct colleges put together quickly to handle all the veterans wanting to take advantage of the GI Bill. I had mustered out of the army a year earlier and gone home to work for my folks, who were living in Mason Valley, Nevada, by then. They had scraped together the money for a little place of their own, a scant half-section. It was mostly flat and arid, but the drought that had held on through most of the thirties had finally abated, and the Mason Valley property had the Walker River running through it and a good deep well for irrigation. So they could make a meager living raising horses and mules and growing hay they sold to Nevada Fish and Game for overwintering mule deer and elk on a couple of nearby refuges.

I had been away from ranching for almost three years, was mostly glad to get back to it, and probably thought I'd stick with it for the rest of my life. It was my mother who pushed me to sign up for college; if the government wanted to pay all the soldiers to go back to school, she felt I should take them up on it.

If it were up to me, I would have gone into an agricultural program, but all the Nevada colleges were full up with returned soldiers. Vanport, up in Oregon and the nearest place with any room, was strictly a city college, with no ag programs. In any case, my mother was adamant that I get a general education; I already knew everything I needed to know about ranching, she said, and I should learn what else was out there in the world. There may have been more to it than that. During the two years I was in the army, she and my father had spent every evening listening to the war news on the radio and poring over my letters trying to figure out where I was and whether the battles being fought might involve me. And I wasn't in great shape when I came back to them—I was still leaning on a cane when I mustered out. It hadn't been that many years since I had returned home from California with a broken pelvis, and I guess, along with her other reasons, my mother didn't want to see me hobbling around like a cripple anymore. Ranching was all right for her and my father—they had both been laid up in plaster a few times—but I believe she had in mind that her only living child should take up some kind of work that didn't regularly involve accident and injury.

I stood in a long line to register for classes, and when I got to the head of it a woman pushed papers in front of me and pointed to the few classes that were still open for enrollment: Art History, Principles of Archaeology, Introduction to English Poetry. Nothing, as I remember, that related to real work, work you could earn a living at. I went ahead and signed up for all three, which I think surprised the woman sitting behind the desk. She looked up at me for the first time.

I was wearing my flat-crowned hat, a neckerchief knotted at the side, and a sheepskin vest; my toothbrush mustache hadn't grown all the way in yet from army smooth, but I'd made a start at it. I could see that she'd expected another soldier still wearing his uniform, as a lot of them were, and here I was in another sort of uniform altogether. But then she said, "Are you Basque?" so I was the one surprised. And, frankly, that was the first time I really looked at her. She had dark hair and a small cleft in her chin. I thought she looked about seventeen, but in fact she was twenty-four.

"No, ma'am, but I grew up around some who were, and our family took up the buckaroo tradition."

"My father's family was Basque way back, or some of them. I had an uncle who ran sheep, and he dressed like that." She indicated my whole self standing there in front of her.

When she handed me the paperwork for the classes, she said, "Art History is mine," and I thought she meant we would both be students in the class, but when I walked into the room the first time, she was up at the chalkboard writing her name: "Miss De Beau Soleil."

About a year later, when the Vanport college was flooded out, we decided to get married and move down to Flagstaff, where Simone had an offer to teach. By then she and Lily Shaw together had begun to persuade me that I could be an artist, and when I finished my degree we moved to Missouri so I could study with Tom Benton at the Kansas City Art Institute. Simone went on teaching, which she loved, shouldering the financial burden of our household while I went on studying and painting, which for an artist is the most fundamental and valuable kind of affirmation. I was the cook, and I kept the house; it was more or less the same arrangement my dad had made with my mother.

But I wanted to make a living at painting if I could, and I half expected to wind up selling to tourists in the Taos galleries and maybe doing some greeting-card art for Leanin' Tree; but while I was still at the Art Institute I got a commission for a pair of frescoes for the Nevada state capitol. And though I haven't run in the gallery scene very much, I have not often lacked for work in the years since.

We moved to Nevada while I was working on the frescoes, partly to be closer to my parents, and then Simone went back to school herself and became an art therapist, which was a brand-new field at the time. By then we had Jim and Lora, and when Simone brought home a six-year-old girl who didn't have a family, Pilar was our third.

In my public art I always seem to be looking at the hard knot that is our myth of the cowboy West: the violence on the movie screen and behind it and the way the humanity has been hollowed out of our movie heroes and villains, the poverty, isolation, and precariousness of ranch work, the dignity and joy of it, and the necessary cruelty. At the start I thought that if I could get everything right, people would see where the cowboy stories went wrong, what we have missed or lost, and they might see that the cowboy life doesn't have to be so goddamn brave and bloody and lonesome as the movies make it out to be. But I have learned over the years that all I can do is reach for something difficult—try to get the colors right and the negative space, the angle of the light. And if a few people can see it, that has to be enough.

I didn't come to this understanding on my own. I learned it, over the years, from Lily Shaw.

34

IT WAS LILY who finally got in touch with my folks. She went to True's house and searched through my belongings and found the telephone number I had written down the last time I talked to them, when they said they were moving to a place in Bear Valley. My dad answered the phone when Lily called. He would start out the next morning, he said, and drive down to get me. I don't know where he would have found the money for gas, and anyway they were still driving the old truck with a homemade box that my mother had cobbled together from a car chassis and spare parts when I was a kid. It's doubtful that truck would have made it all the way to Los Angeles, eight hundred miles or better from where they were living, and eight hundred back. But Lily told my dad that she and True had already figured out another arrangement, a friend of True's who was towing a livestock trailer from Los Angeles to Red Bluff, delivering a pair of horses up there. So that's what happened. This fellow, Gil Newhart, drove me north in the cab of his truck and handed me off to my dad, who drove a hundred and fifty miles down from Bear Valley, which was just about as much distance as the old truck could manage.

· · ·

Gil was hauling a couple of thoroughbred horses that a wealthy rancher had bought. I've heard about men transporting horses hundreds of miles without stopping a single time, but a lot of horses can't urinate in a moving trailer, and Gil was mindful of the value of those horses, so he stopped every three or four hours, took them out, walked them around so they could stretch and void. Then he watered them, forked some hay into the net, shoveled out the trailer, and loaded them back in — an hour or better each time. Sometimes when he stopped at a filling station the truck would vapor-lock and we'd have to sit there and wait for the engine to settle down before he could get it to start. With all that stop and go, and more than six hundred miles to cover, it took the greater part of three days getting up the road to Red Bluff.

If I didn't stand up and move around every little while myself, I'd freeze in one position, and when I finally did move, the pain would be just about enough to make me cry, so every time Gil stopped to take care of the horses I'd try to get up and walk around some. My crutches were in the truck bed, where I couldn't reach them by myself. Anyway, I couldn't stand up or sit down without help. If I wanted to move my left leg, I had to reach down and lift it with my hands. I had a jar to piss in, but if I had to take a crap, I needed somebody to pull down my damn pants while I held myself up on the two crutches, careful not to put any weight at all on that left leg. When we stopped at roadside diners, it was always a big production getting me out of the truck and hobbling across the parking lot to the cafe.

Gil hadn't planned on any of this. He gave me a hand when I asked for it, but I usually had to ask, and he didn't speak to me beyond the necessary. He was heavy-jowled, powerfully built, with a sightless glass eye — True said he'd been with Pershing's expedition against Pancho Villa. If he'd been an actor, they'd have cast him as the cigar-chewing mobster. But I didn't blame Gil. He was probably a decent enough guy. It was just that True had talked him into giving me a ride and, I think, must have paid him a few dollars, without warning him how stove up I was. So I didn't blame him. I wasn't happy about any of it either.

We took the same highway going north as the bus had taken coming down. But what I noticed on the northbound ride sure wasn't avenues of eucalyptus trees or mountains like ice cream cones or rafts of birds settling down on sloughs and rice fields. What I saw were the migrant labor camps and wrecking yards filled with scrapped farm machinery and crop-duster planes flying just a couple of yards off the ground, laying down a wet blanket of poison. In one town we passed through, dead Christmas trees were tied to all the street lamps, their shed orange needles in ragged circles on the pavement underneath each one. At a labor camp outside Lodi, a woman stood in front of one of the tents watching the traffic go by, her face all black and blue and a little child in a dirty smock hanging behind her skirts. The oak hills we drove through were dry and brown in the heat of day but at sunset turned the color of a livid bruise.

Both nights we pulled off the highway after dark, and Gil staked out the horses on a strip of grass alongside the road. He slept in the bed of the truck on top of the loose hay while I tried to sleep on the cab seat. In those first weeks after the accident I was in so much pain that no position was comfortable. The only way I could sleep at all was flat on my back, but I was too tall to stretch out on the seat, so I had to prop myself against the door with my legs out in front of me and Lily's pillow shoved behind my neck and shoulders. If I popped a few aspirin I could sometimes manage to doze off for a few minutes. Gil never asked me what I wanted, and when he took the truck bed for himself I didn't feel I could say anything. And anyway, I might not have been able to climb up into it.

The second night, while I was lying there half asleep, Mary Claudine lay down alongside me and slipped one arm under my back and the other across my hips. It had been a warm day, we had driven with both windows rolled down for the moving air, but by now it was cold in the cab of the truck. The light from a thin wedge of moon threw a yellow blanket across my shoulders, but the warmth I felt was my sister lying against me. She was only ten years old and small for her age, but she was holding me in her arms like I was the child, and this seemed to take off some of my pain. I said, "Thanks, Emsy." She was named for our dad's mother, and in our family we always called her by her whole name. It was her school friends who had called her Emsy, so I don't know why I said it like that.

"Bud, tell me about Hollywood." She spoke drowsily, almost a whisper.

I didn't want to tell her about all the dead and maimed horses or about Steve Deets, none of that. I said, "I met Gene Autry the other day." She liked the singing cowboys more than I did.

"Did you see Champion? Is he pretty?"

"Sure. He's darker than I thought he'd be, he's a really dark sorrel. They put some kind of white powder on his socks and his blaze to make the white stand out, but even if they didn't, those white socks sure are bright against his color."

She hummed a little bit of an Autry song, the one about riding through a canyon, watching the sun go down.

"Where did you hear that, Mary Claudine?" I was pretty sure she hadn't lived long enough to see the picture that song had been in.

She didn't answer me, but went on humming. I couldn't remember all the words, but I tried to sing the chorus with her. And then something came over me, a wave of melancholy. A lot of those cowboy songs have got such sadness in them. I wasn't really crying, but tears leaked out and ran down the side of my jaw.

She said, "It's all right, Bud," and stroked my head like you'd pet a dog or a horse.

I wanted to tell her something else, something about Hollywood, but every thought that came into my mind was sad or terrible.

I said finally, "Emsy, what happened to you?"

She knew what I meant. "It wasn't Goldy's fault. You shouldn't feel bad. It wasn't anybody's fault, Bud."

"Well, what happened?"

We weren't a churchy family, but Mary Claudine had always been interested in God, and she asked questions my parents had trouble finding answers for. A neighbor on one of the homestead farms to the south of us was killed when his tractor went over on him, and one of Arlo Gantz's granddaughters was born blue and died before she'd lived a week in this world. Mary Claudine wanted to know why God let those things happen. Why didn't God make sure all the calves were born the right way? Why didn't God put the baby bird back in the nest when it fell out? My parents' answers didn't satisfy her. Mary Claudine never said she blamed God, but she was always unhappy about the unanswered questions. Now, though, she sounded untroubled about her own death.

She sighed. "I couldn't find the Rim Creek bench, so I just rode around a long time looking for cows. Goldy fell going down the side of a steep hill, and she threw me up against the bank, and when she got to her feet she stepped on my chest and then her hoof hit my head."

"You said it wasn't Goldy's fault."

"I was trying to turn back a cow, and I rode down the ravine too fast. It was awful steep. Goldy did what I told her."

I had been in enough wrecks to know what Mary Claudine meant. Hell, I was lying there with a broken pelvis because a horse did what I told him.

"I wish we could have found you sooner."

"It was all right, Bud. Goldy waited with me. She was worried and she didn't know what else to do, so she just stood over me for the longest time."

I didn't ask her if she suffered at all. I was afraid to hear the answer.

Then she began humming again, her voice very soft, a song I had heard Ken Maynard sing in a movie I'd worked on. "He does all his own riding and falling," I told her, and she didn't ask me who I meant, she just said, "Does he?" and then went on with the song.

I thought about telling her I had met Tim McCoy—I had always liked his movies better than Autry's or Maynard's—but after a while I drifted off to sleep.

I don't want you to think this was my sister's ghost—I'm not somebody who puts much stock in ghosts. I'd been feverish off and on, and hazy from pain and needing to sleep, and I imagine that's all it was.

Maybe a year later I told my folks about it. This came up because my mother one morning at breakfast told us a dream she had had the night before, a sweet little dream of Mary Claudine, who had found a baby porcupine caught in a sticker bush. She didn't have anything else handy, so she took off her underpants, gathered the porcupine into them, and carried it home that way. Which was exactly what my sister would have done.

It was the first time my mother had volunteered anything like that, and there was something about the dream, or my mother's telling it to my dad and me, that opened a door. I told them everything Mary Claudine had said to me that time when I was hurting and half asleep in the cab of Gil Newhart's truck. When I got to the part about Goldy, about the horse standing over her, my mother took in a loud breath, which I knew was to stop herself from crying, and she said, "I always wanted to blame Goldy."

This brought me up short. In the first few weeks after Mary Claudine went missing, I had spent a lot of time blaming myself for sending her after those cattle alone, and I guess thinking my parents blamed me too. But after she was found and we heard what damage had been done to her—where the horse had stove in her ribs and clipped her head—I shifted the blame to Goldy. I hadn't ever told my parents how I felt, how I used to think about walking out to Goldy in the pasture and just shooting her right through the eye. My mother had sold that horse soon after we buried my sister, and I had always thought it was to rid herself of a sad reminder. It was a shock to learn that her feelings toward Goldy hadn't been far off from mine.

My dad, as if this was an old argument, said quietly, "You know that horse was always good with the kids, a safe horse," and my mother quickly said, "I know it. I know she was. But I wanted to blame her." And she looked around the room, blinking to keep herself from tears.

35

AROUND DUSK ON THE THIRD DAY, we rolled through Red Bluff and out a dirt lane to the ranch where Gil was to deliver the horses. My dad was already there. His truck, parked under a big old cottonwood, was nearly white under a blanket of shed fleece off that tree, so I guess he'd been there a while. This was a fancy big place with a lot of buildings and corrals and board fences, the ranch house bricked and everything else whitewashed or painted barn red, but at the moment my dad was the only person in sight. He was sitting on a flat stump they used for splitting wood, and he was looking off toward a big Hereford bull grazing in a field by the road. When we came up the lane, raising a boiling tail of dust, he stood up and squinted until we got near enough he could maybe make out that it was me. Then he put his hands in his pockets and turned and looked at the bull one more time, and after a minute he looked back toward Gil's truck and walked out to meet us.

He went around to the driver's side first and shook hands with Gil and thanked him for bringing me, and then he came around to me and opened the door and leaned down to look in. That dirt road coming into the ranch had been rough on me, and I imagine I looked pretty sick. He said, "Buddy, did you find a way to get out of work for a while?" which was the joking thing we said in our family whenever one of us was laid up.

I hadn't seen him in over a year. "I can still cook," I said, which was the other half of the joke, but I had to pull in my mouth and tighten it to get the words out without crying like a damn kid.

He nodded, frowning, as if what he was about to say was a flat fact and a relief to him. "Well, good, I guess we don't have to take you out and shoot you then."

We started north just as the sun went down, and we drove through the night. The truck didn't have glass windows you could roll up, and there wasn't a heater. You could feel some heat coming off the engine, drifting into the cab through the floorboards and through gaps in the dashboard. Whenever the road dipped into hollows where cold air had settled, a chill would come inside that same way. In the darkness I couldn't see the country we were going through. The truck blew oil, but even so, I got a whiff of clover or pine or cow shit every so often, and I could guess what was out there in the dark. There wasn't much traffic, but we weren't the only rig on the road. Where the pavement was flat you would see the headlights of an oncoming car a mile or more away, growing from pinpricks. In hilly country you'd see the faint wash of light silhouetting the crown of the hill just before a rig topped over and rolled down toward you. Those headlights were always blinding after the long stretches of darkness, and my dad would slow way down until they passed us by. When the headlights swept through the cab I could see his face, skull-like, hollowed out by shadows.

The truck liked to boil over on the steep grades, so we climbed slowly and then picked up speed on the downhill. Our tires on the road made a low rumble, like surf, or like wind pouring through a canyon. Most of the time that was the only sound, that and the tappets rattling a little bit. I didn't sleep, but I drifted in and out.

"Dolly died this past summer," Dad said. He spoke so softly I wasn't sure he had spoken at all. It seemed possible I had only imagined the words, or they'd simply floated from his mind into mine. I opened my eyes. There weren't any dash lights in the truck and I could barely make out the shape of him, black against the black night. When he spoke again after a long silence, it seemed that the words didn't come from him, that they must have come drifting up from the floorboards like the cold air or the heat off the motor. "She was old. Your mother had her for twenty-five years and she wasn't young when your mother got her."

I had learned to ride on Dolly. My mother set me on her broad back when I was two years old, handed me the reins, and walked away to let the horse school me. I couldn't remember any time when that horse had behaved badly. She'd been retired to pasture years earlier, and the last time I saw her, which would have been a few months before I went down to California, she was looking pretty sad. Flies clustered on her back out of reach of her tail, which was nothing but wispy remnants by then. Her old burn scars had formed a ridge of hard horn on her poll. She walked around stiffly on her ancient limbs, and she'd gone mostly blind. That last time I was home I had heard my parents talking, their voices whispering late at night, Mom saying that Dolly still knew her way around the pasture, even sightless; that there were always other horses with her, keeping her company. Shady, one of the mules, often stood near her and lashed his tail against the tormenting flies. And Dolly still enjoyed having my mother work over her shoulders lightly with the knuckles of her hands, a gentle massage that made her eyes glaze over, caused her to lick her lips and stretch her neck out with a soft groan of pleasure. "She'll tell me when she's ready to go," my mother had said, and after a silence my father had answered, his words too low for me to make out. If it had been any other horse, I think my mother would have put her down, and at the time I was strongly of that opinion. But a few years later I had grown up enough to understand: she couldn't have borne the idea of it so soon after losing Mary Claudine.

My mother had written me three or four letters in recent months, and I had talked to both of my folks on the telephone a couple of times that summer. Neither had said anything about Dolly. Then again, I hadn't asked. Now I said to my dad, "Did one of you have to put her down?" What had come into my mind was the men on the *Valverde* set walking back and forth across that field, shooting the injured horses one after the other.

The answer was so long coming, I almost wondered if I had failed to speak out loud. But I think my dad was just off somewhere in his head and it took him a while to come back inside the truck and to hear me. "No. No, we didn't. Your mom had been making it a practice to go out to the pasture every morning to check on her, and one morning she went out and Dolly was just lying on the ground. She'd passed in the night. I don't think she suffered. Your mother wouldn't have wanted her to suffer." After a minute or so he said, "Things just happen and it's nobody's fault." After another pause, he said, "You ranch long enough, you make peace with what you can't help."

He went silent again. The headlights threw out two dim overlapping puddles of light that ran ahead of us, rippling over the pavement like water. Otherwise, the world inside and outside the truck was featureless darkness. The sky was so big that sometimes when we crested a hill it seemed as if we were driving right up into it, lifting slowly into the stars like a dirigible. I wonder if dying might feel like that, like letting go of the earth's hold, just floating out into black nothingness.

I don't know how much time passed. In the silence, I fell into thinking I was alone, leaning back between the thwarts of an oarless boat, rocking on the swells. What took me out of it was a rough bumping that sent a bolt of pain through my groin. It took me a few seconds to come completely awake — I thought at first it was the boat breaking up against shore rocks — and by then my dad had steered off the road and come to a stop. He shut off the motor and the headlights, and for a minute or two we both went on sitting there, because in the sudden complete darkness you couldn't see a damn thing. Black as the inside of a cow is what we used to say. When my eyes got used to it, I could make out the dark shapes of hills all around us, and a few black topknots of trees, and I thought I recognized that rolling country between Weed and Klamath Falls, the borderland between Oregon and California. I couldn't see any moon, just a smoky swath of stars. It occurred to me that if there had been a moon we might have been able to see Shasta, and although I didn't know for sure where we were, I imagined I could feel the physical presence of the mountain, its huge black bulk pushing up against the stars somewhere off to the east or south of us.

When Dad had his night eyes back, he looked over at me and said, "I had two blowouts coming down. This one better be a puncture, because there's no more tubes in the back."

We usually ran bruised or recapped tires on the truck, and on rough ranch roads you could count on blowouts and leaks at regular intervals, so we always carried a couple of extra inner tubes in the back, as well as a bunch of patch kits and a hand pump. If this was another blowout, we'd be stranded by the side of the road until somebody happened along with a spare tube, or maybe I'd be waiting alone while my dad walked or hitched a ride to the nearest garage. If this was the road between Weed and Klamath Falls, we were likely twenty miles from any service station, and there wouldn't be anybody to open up the shop and sell us a tube at this time of night.

When he got out to see about the tire, Dad said, "You just sit still," but I had been sitting still for more hours than was good for me, and I needed to move my legs a bit.

I said, "I should stand up a while. I get pretty stiff if I sit for too long."

He hesitated. "You need my help?" At the Red Bluff ranch we had both been self-conscious. It somehow felt worse needing my dad's help than needing Gil's, so I had kept myself from asking him, and he had stood back, watching Gil do all the helping. We were still self-conscious, but I said, "Yeah, I could use a hand getting out of the truck."

When he came around to my door he said, "You've got to tell me what to take hold of, so I don't hurt you worse."

319

There was no way for me to stand up without it hurting like hell, but I didn't say so. I just held out an arm and said, "Take hold of me and pull, and then when I'm standing reach me those crutches out of the back." After he had stood me up and handed over the crutches, he didn't move off right away. I guess he was listening, waiting for me to get my breath back. In the darkness I couldn't really see his face. His hair looked almost white. He was fifty-two years old and he'd been going gray for years. I said, "I just need to hobble around for a bit to loosen myself up," and took a step away from him. Finally he turned from me and dug a flashlight out of the box and squatted down by the flat tire. I shuffled off a few feet, dragging my left leg, and I managed to pry open the buttons on my jeans so I could piss into the roadside weeds.

By the time I turned back around, he had pulled his tools and a patch kit out of the truck and was bracing the back wheels with a couple of big rocks. "If there's one nail on the road, this truck will find it," he said, but I knew he was relieved—we both were—that it wasn't another blowout.

While I crutched back and forth along the edge of the road, he jacked up the truck, pulled off the wheel, and began prying the tire away from the rim with the spoon end of the tire iron. He had propped the flashlight against a rock while he was doing the take-off, but once he had the tube out of the limp rubber casing he sat on the ground and held the flashlight in one hand while he fumbled the tube around in his other hand to find the puncture.

"I can hold the light," I said. It was pretty much all I could do to help.

He handed up the light, and I shined it down onto his hands as he turned the tube around slowly. When he found the hole, he squirted some cleaning fluid on a rag, wiped a clean spot on the tube, roughed it up with emery paper, and cleaned it again. He cut a piece of patch with his pocket knife, and after he cemented the patch to the tube he sat there holding it stretched down tight against his knee until it dried. When he stuffed the tube back into the tire, he was careful to

320

line it up so the stem fit squarely through the grommet hole in the tire—if it pinched or twisted, we'd be broke down by the side of the road again before very many miles.

With the tire back on the wheel and the wheel back on the truck, he pulled out the hand pump. He had been quick up to now—he'd had plenty of experience—but pumping air into a flat tire could take twenty minutes of hard work. If I hadn't been on crutches, we would have spelled each other. He did thirty or forty quick pumps in a row, then straightened up and shook out his arms before going at it again. After a while the spells of pumping got shorter and slower and the breaks came closer together. I was ashamed to stand there watching him, no help at all—he didn't even need the flashlight for this part of it. In truth, I was worn out from just dragging my legs a dozen steps each way along the road. I couldn't even sit back down in the truck without his help, that's how useless I was, so I had to lean my weight against the truck sideboards and wait for him to finish.

When he thought the tire had enough air, he cranked down the jack most of the way but waited a minute to make sure the tire would hold before letting it down completely. Then he stood up and bent over to loosen a kink in his lower back. When he straightened again, he said, "I hope that's the last one until we're home."

"How far, do you think?"

"Oh, another couple of hours." He looked in my direction. "How you doing?"

Just watching him stretch out his sore back had been enough to give me a reflexive spasm of pain. "I'm all right."

"It's not your leg that's broke, is that right? It's your hip? I was expecting to see you in heavy plaster."

"I don't know if they'd call it my hip. They said I cracked my pelvis in three places. There's nothing they do for it except tell you to keep your weight off as much as you can and wait for the bones to join back up."

"Well, that don't sound comfortable."

"No. Not as much as you'd think."

He might have smiled. I could see a movement somewhere around his mouth, his chin. "I s'pose not."

He helped me sit back down in the truck, but then he walked to the front and lifted the hood, unscrewed the radiator cap, and shined the flashlight down the neck to see if we were running low on water; then he ran the dipstick in and out to make sure we had enough oil. My mother was the mechanic, and these were about the only two things—plus fixing a flat tire—my dad knew how to do on his own. I had heard the brakes squeal against metal when we stopped, but that was something that could wait for my mother to work on.

While he was up front checking fluids, I swallowed a handful of aspirin. Moving around was always painful, but so was sitting until I got kind of settled. When he fired up the engine and we started off again, I looked ahead at the road passing under the dim headlights, and I tried to keep from breathing louder than normal.

"Do you think you'll stay home now, Bud?"

These words came after a long period of silence. I knew what he meant: When your bones mend, are you leaving again? But there didn't seem to be any judgment in the question, or expectation.

I didn't have an answer, and in the darkness it was easy to just float on a raft of silence. The stars were so bright they seemed almost close enough to touch, and the Milky Way cut a broad bright swath through the blackness. I thought about looking for Scorpius, but it was behind us and would have been half below the horizon anyway.

A long while went by before he said anything else, and it wasn't anything I expected. "Are they hard on the horses, down there in Hollywood? It always looks to me like they're being rode too hard, and then jumped off cliffs and whatnot."

When I was a kid I never paid much attention to the way horses were used in the movies, which baffles me now when I think about it. I had grown up in a life with horses, in a family where horses were treated with particular consideration. I had seen them badly used a few times by neighbors and ignorant cowhands, and I'd seen

rodeo stock sometimes poorly handled, but for the most part ranchers treated horses as necessary and useful tools. They might be broken out pretty roughly, but after that they were usually treated well. I
hardly ever saw outright cruelty. In the movies, though, you couldn't
watch a cowboy picture without seeing horses used in terrible ways,
whipped and spurred by stage drivers, by posses and outlaw bands,
ridden hard up and down steep ravines, through flooding rivers,
into deserts or snowstorms without water or food or shelter. They
were always being jumped through plate-glass windows or trapped
in burning barns, caught in the middle of gunfights, and shot at,
wounded, killed, by just about everybody in the picture—good guys,
bad guys, cavalry, Indians. Ridden hell-for-leather until they staggered and dropped dead on the ground. I don't know why that didn't
strike me as wrong at the time—why I didn't pay more attention to
the mistreatment of horses in the movies I saw as a kid. When I was
young, the thing I remember being fixed on was a kind of frustration
that the horses I rode could never get up as much hellbent speed as
the horses I saw in the movies. When I went to Hollywood, one of
my first disappointments was learning how they undercranked the
camera to make the action race along.

"Yeah, they're hell on horses," I said to my dad.

I wasn't sure what had brought this matter into his mind, but now
it was in mine. I told him, "When I first got down there, I worked for
a fellow who treated his animals right. And the star horses, they get
pretty good treatment. But I saw a lot of horses run into the ground."

After a silence he said, "Well, that's what I thought."

I wasn't sure I wanted to get into the rest of it, but sometimes,
once you're started, you just go on and say what's in your head. "I rode
in a movie a while ago where they tripped a lot of horses in this one
big scene. They had a hundred of us galloping flat out, and when the
horses hit the tripwires, they had their legs yanked out from under
them. Some that weren't tripped got all tangled up with the ones that
were. A bunch of horses died. Died on the spot or wound up with

legs broke, broken backs, they had to be put down. It was—" I was going to say *a fucked-up mess,* but that felt suddenly like I'd be bringing Cab O'Brien home with me, so I worked my mouth and finally said, "It was a hell of a thing."

My dad glanced over at me. "That wasn't when you got hurt?"

"No, I was on a horse that time that kept his feet. But they hauled some riders to the hospital. A guy I knew got pretty busted up. If I'd had any sense I would've quit the movie business right then. I guess if I'd quit, I wouldn't be sitting here."

I heard how this must have sounded to him: that I wouldn't have come back home except I was hurt. I hadn't meant to say it like that, but there didn't seem to be a way to unsay it, and anyway it might have been true.

For quite a while he didn't speak, and then he said, "I didn't tell your mother you were hurt. I told her you didn't have the money for a bus ticket and you were asking for a ride home. I didn't want her worrying."

This shamed me in some way I couldn't have articulated. I hadn't really expected both of them to make the trip to pick me up, but at the Red Bluff ranch, when I had realized it was just my dad—that my mother hadn't come—I had given in to a moment of self-pity.

I said, "I told Lily not to call you," as if I was blaming her for making the call or him for answering.

He looked over at me. The night had begun to thin, and his features were a dim map, a map I could almost read. "You were hurt bad, and when you got kicked out of the hospital you needed a place to heal up, that's what the girl said. But you'd rather sleep on the damn sidewalk than come back home, is that it?"

I hadn't expected him to snap back at me, and anyway I wouldn't have been able to put into words what I was feeling. What came out was a muttered, stupid complaint. "We don't have a damn home anymore."

He flung his answer back, quick and angry as a slap. "You blame me for losing the ranch, go ahead, but Echol Creek is just a goddamn place, that's all it is, and your home is with your mother." He gripped the wheel with both hands and looked straight up the road.

My dad had a temper, and when I was a little kid it used to scare me when he flared up, even when his anger wasn't aimed at me. A lot of men in those days thought they weren't doing their job right unless their children were afraid of them, and some of them took it farther than that. I had gone to school with a boy—was his name Bradley?—whose father beat him halfway to death once. He missed three or four months of school, recovering from losing the sight in his left eye. And I'd had plenty of teachers who believed a wooden stick across the back of your hand or your buttocks was the right way to get your attention. Well, that wasn't my dad. He was patient with his animals and his wife, and mostly patient with his kids. His anger was generally aimed at inanimate objects—a cinch breaking at the wrong time, a frozen pump, a hammer if it happened to land on his thumb. He had hit me a few times—his bare hand, mostly, or a doubled-up belt across my backside—not usually for disobedience but for some idiotic stunt that could have landed me or somebody else in the hospital. All my life, whenever I remember one of those times, heat climbs up into my neck and my face—ashamed of myself, mostly, and ashamed on my father's behalf.

I had never once thought to blame him for losing the Echol place—I was astonished he would think so. I turned and looked out the side window. I wasn't anywhere near crying—I wasn't a kid any-more—but I had to work to get any breath past the hard mass in the center of my chest. If he heard me trying to breathe, he didn't let on.

We rode a long while in silence. In the gradual light I could just make out the dark, straight shapes of trees alongside the road, big old ponderosa pines like the ones I had grown up with. The road had been climbing for miles. We were in the Siskiyous, I figured.

When enough time had gone by, he said, "Do you need to stand up and move around again? It'll be another forty minutes, I guess."

I had begun to ache from sitting still, but I said, "No. I'm okay." Then I said, "I'd just as soon get home," which was as close as I could come to saying what was stuck in my throat.

After another while passed, he said, "Who's that girl Lily, the one that called me? Is she an actress?"

"No. She's a writer." I wasn't sure what else to say about her. "We met on the bus going down."

He nodded as if he already knew it. "She said you've been going to the pictures on your day off." Then he looked over at me. "Is she somebody we ought to start getting used to?"

At the time I didn't know whether I'd ever see Lily again or keep in touch with her, but I knew this wasn't what my dad was asking. "No, I guess not. We're just friends."

"Well, that's how it starts sometimes."

My dad had a romantic streak in him—both my parents ran that way—and I realized I shouldn't have left any guesswork in my answer. "Lily doesn't plan to get married. She just wants to write for the movies."

He smiled slightly. "Well, your mother just wanted to punch cows and break horses." I understood what he meant: that my mother hadn't planned to marry either.

He hadn't really been saying my situation was like his, but I wanted to be clear, so I said, "Lily's pretty set on making pictures and being famous. And I'm all done with Hollywood, so I don't imagine I'll see her again."

He kept his attention on the road. The sun wasn't up yet, but the sky was pearling and we could see a long way ahead now, the pavement curving through shadowless grassy hills, smudged here and there with dark clumps of pine. "So you're not going back down there?"

"No." I didn't feel like saying any more about it, and he didn't ask.

After a while he turned the truck off the highway onto some branching back roads and finally drove under a ranch gate painted white with carved-out letters on the overhead arch: Rocker Z. The ranch lane was dirt but graded smooth, and the first quarter mile was neatly lined with rock fence on both sides. The lane wound back into the hills a couple of miles. Every time we came to a livestock fence, my dad had to climb out and open the gate, get in the truck again and drive us through, then get back out to close the gate, while I sat there like a worthless lump.

We were heading more or less east, and when the leading edge of sun broke over the low range of hills, the sudden slash of light dazzled us both, red like the blood of battle, outlining the dark crowns. My dad slowed the rig and leaned forward, squinting to make out the curves in the road. Long black shapes stretched out behind every rock and blade of grass. Cattle and horses on the hillsides were flattened silhouettes, their bodies all of a piece with their elongated, distorted shadows.

The Rocker Z home place lay in a treeless bowl, a sprawling white house in need of a coat of paint, a windmill, a tall paintless barn, and a couple of corrals leaning slightly on rotting timber uprights. It wasn't much like Echol Creek, but there is a certain sameness to such places. I felt a sudden tight ache under my sternum.

My mother must have heard the truck from a long way off, or maybe the dog had barked a warning. She was already on the porch when we came over the last rise, though I didn't realize it at first: she was nothing but a dark shape in the darker space under the porch roof. Then she stepped into the sunlight at the edge of the porch, and her shadow went out long across the yard. She was gripping the upright porch rail with one hand, her other hand holding Mary Claudine's dog by the loose skin of his neck, and then she sat down on the porch steps as if her legs had given way, and she pulled the dog against her chest. He squirmed and squirmed to get loose, and finally, when we came to a stop in the yard, she let him go, and he came across to meet us, barking and waving his flag of a tail.

ACKNOWLEDGMENTS

FOR TAKING THE TIME TO READ THIS BOOK in early drafts, and for their smart and useful criticism, I am very much indebted to Tony Wolk, John and Kim Transier, Ursula and Charles Le Guin, Barbara J. Scot, and especially Bette Lynch Husted, who read the entire book more than once, brought me out of blue funks more than once, caught many stupid mistakes, and just generally cheered me on to the finish line.

For insight into movie stunt riding and wrangling I'm grateful to Martha Cantarini, Liz Dixon, and Thomas Bentley. They are all too young to have ridden in the films of the 1930s, but their knowledge of the movie business and the life of a stunt rider was nevertheless invaluable; Martha Cantarini's memoir *Fall Girl* was a particularly useful resource.

For details of how it was in the 1930s, I relied a good deal on Diana Serra Cary's memoir *The Hollywood Posse: The Story of a Gallant Band of Horsemen Who Made Movie History,* and Yakima Canutt's auto-biography, *Stunt Man.* For anyone interested in behind-the-scenes photographs and stories of the 1940s B westerns and 1950s television westerns, I recommend *And . . . Action!* by Stephen Lodge.

Thanks to Gretchen Corbett for her helpful knowledge of moviemaking and the language of moviemaking; and to John Zagelow for his knowledge of old trucks and tube tires.

I'm grateful as always to my marvelous, and marvelously patient, editor, Susan Canavan, and everyone at Houghton Mifflin Harcourt for their support of this novel.

Over the five years I worked on this book, Wendy Weil was the particular reader I kept always in my mind. She died before reading it. This book is, above all, for her.